To Ash and Dust

The Deliverance Trilogy: Book Two

H. L. Walsh

H. L. Walsh Books

Kansas City, Missouri

List of books by H. L. Walsh

The Deliverance Trilogy

ANGEL
EMRALD BASIN
PANTOR RIVER
FAIRDENN
LANIFAIR HARBOR
THE DIVIDE
LINDOW
NEWTAUGHT
SHADOW LAIR
THE DIVIDE
SWAMP
GREAT OCEAN
YARGATE PORT
TWISTED DESERT
DEADPOST
CAISTER

UNRELENTING MOUNTAINS
BRIGHTWOOD
WHITESHADE
PANGOR RIVER
ANGEL TERRITORY
UNEXPLORED REGION
ANGELCROSS
THE DIVIDE
THE DIVIDE
RARGOD
RAGEWOOD FOREST
DEMON TERRITORY
RAGEWOOD
DEMON COMPOUND

Chapter 1

Kragen stole through the shadows. The rest of the town slept, blissfully ignorant they had seen their last sunset. Kragen had infiltrated Whiteshade under the guise of a former guard of Newaught, now a refugee. He even managed to work his way into a group of refugees from the actual town he claimed to be from. Most of the town had evacuated, making it all the easier to gain the people's trust. Simply put, they didn't have enough guards to defend the people who hadn't fled to the Angel Army's camp, they had trusted him quickly.

Too quickly.

Tonight was the night that he would finally be able to shed his disguise and kill these people. Their kindness and generosity disgusted him. These people didn't understand that the only way to get ahead in life was to take what you wanted, even if it cost others dearly. They assumed that their kindness would save them, but they were sorely wrong. To make things worse, they refused to believe angels and demons never left and the war hadn't started again.

Simpletons, he scoffed at their ignorance.

Kragen had been trained for years by a particularly nasty demon. This demon knew no mercy, and for each failure that Kragen had made, he had taken his due in unspeakable terrors. Never Kragen's hands or fingers, as he had with some of the other, lesser servants. No, the Demon had taken his revenge in terrors that would never leave visible scars. Now, Kragen was one of the best spies in the Demon Army and most proficient with the devices that the demon had invented. They called them explosives. Kragen called them Hellfire Machines. He had to sneak the pieces of those infernal devices into the city and created each one once inside. They could be made to size, and sometimes Kragen bought the ingredients needed from the very people he would use them on. Once the powders inside were mixed correctly, they would make a large, fiery explosion that could collapse a single building or whole sections of a city wall. The power that Kragen wielded gave him an indescribable rush.

This city's wall wasn't even made of stone. He had only planted three devices: two on the side that the army would infiltrate, and one as a distraction on the other side of the city. The one on its own was hidden next to the main barracks and would also serve to kill most of the remaining guards. All three devices would set what was left of the wall on fire and burn it to the ground. They wouldn't even have much of a fight. The Demon would be disappointed. He enjoyed killing.

Kragen received the signal that the army would move against the city that night and was off to set the first device. He had signaled back he was still alive and that the walls would be down. He arrived at the first device and lit the fuse with a flick of his flint and steel. He turned and ran right into the Captain of the Guard.

"Sir, I found something I think you need to see," Kragen said, the lie automatically springing to his lips.

"Save it," the Capitan's sword was already drawn.

"So be it."

A few short minutes later, Kragen was running through the city at full speed. It wouldn't be long, and either the Captain's body would be found, or the explosive would detonate. He hadn't pulled his sword to fight the Captain. He simply pulled his firearm and shot the man. He was given the firearm as a reward for assassinating the leader of the Dark Hollow, a group of assassins in Newaught. He kept the thing loaded and on his person for a situation just like this. The crack of the shot would draw attention but so would a drawn-out fight, and there was no guarantee he would have won. The warning bells rang only seconds before the explosion shook the ground.

The explosion silenced the bells, no doubt collapsing the tower attached to the barracks. Kragen was able to cover a lot of ground quickly with his six-foot-four-inch frame and the conditioning he received. Soon the other two devices would detonate as well, and he would be off on his next assignment.

Malach Tresch rode alongside his mentor, Elzrod, a Blade-Bearer, who was more than two thousand years old. With them was a group of human refugees and several angels. Some of them rode horses but most walked. They were all headed toward what they prayed would be safety. Surprisingly enough, the group would be traveling close to his home town. The Demon Army had seized control of Newaught, the only neutral town, just days before. Now the army of the angels was gathering all of its people to one location; they were readying themselves for war.

From the reports, the Demon Army was nowhere near ready to send their forces in all-out war. Although the demons weren't ready, they had been working to stop people in Angel Territory from journeying to Fairdenn, the gathering place. They sent small patrols on the main roads to capture or slaughter the refugees and would-be soldiers. Malach and Elzrod had been in constant motion, gathering any they came across into their group in the hopes of gaining strength through numbers to discourage the patrols.

Daziar, Malach's best friend was riding next to him on his left. His hulking friend was almost as tall as he was and about twice Malach's size. Despite their difference in size, Malach was still stronger than his friend, due to the fact Malach's father was an angel. Malach's parents had been taken by demons, and Daziar and his family had taken him in. They took care of him for most of his youth. In all the ways that counted, Daziar was Malach's brother, and he loved him like one. They had been through a lot together, and it seemed like they would be going through a lot more in the days to come or die violently.

Only a few days prior, Malach had stood on the walls of Newaught as the demons revealed their new weapon. With a deafening boom from a device, later he would learn it was called a cannon, a whole section of the city wall had fallen. The demon in charge had called for the city leaders to turn Malach and his friends over to them, in retribution for the death of two demons, one at the maw of a large monster and one at the hands of Malach himself.

Malach and Amara had been standing on the wall on guard duty. Amara, a former thief, who, at one point, was a member of the notorious Shadows, had warned Malach of an assassination attempt and saved Daziar's life in the process. She had even gone as far as attacking one of the assassins herself. She had almost been put to death for the help she gave them, but Malach and Elzrod had gotten her off with a minor sentence. She was small, with a slight build, a bit of a spitfire, who had grown up on the streets of Caister, a city in the Demon Territory.

Amara had been just about to tell him something when they spied the enemy troops. Five demons marched at the front, and they had brought the cannons. A cannon used fire to propel a metal ball through the air faster than an arrow loosed from a bowstring. At least, that's how it was explained to Malach. He still didn't quite understand how they worked. However, the new weapon and the fact that several city officials were already allied with the demons, allowed the demons to take the city. They had asked for Malach and his friends to be turned over. Malach thought back to what happened that day.

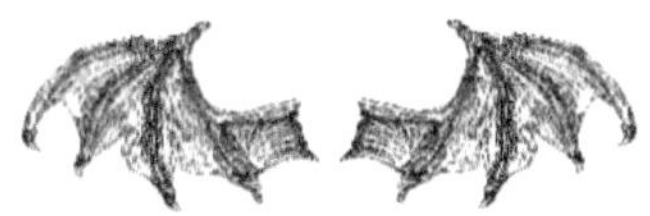

The demon flew up until he was level with the wall but just out of bow range and bellowed, "bring me the men responsible for my brothers' deaths, and we will destroy your city last!"

Cathetel and Camael, the two angels who helped Malach save his father, came up on the wall at that moment. "Malach you must leave with us now. You will not be safe much longer." Cathetel physically guided Malach away from the wall's edge.

Malach spotted guards already moving their way as they descended the stairs.

"City officials have already put out a warrant for your arrest and any seen with you," Camael replied. "We need to leave the city before they close the gates, if they haven't already."

"What about Honora, Daz, Elzrod, and my father?" Malach asked.

"They are meeting us with the horses at Angel Gate." Cathetel turned down an alleyway off the main street.

It didn't take them long to get to the gate, but what they found there wasn't what they hoped for. A dozen guards stood at the gate, some in Newaught uniforms, and others in the uniform of the Demon Army. The gates were firmly closed.

They spotted Honora waving them over in another alley and worked their way around to her.

Honora had grown up in the same town as Malach and Daziar, and the three of them had become good friends. She had a deep love for horses, and though she was not much of a fighter, she could hold her own. She even surprised Malach from time to time when they used to spar. They all made the journey to Newaught only a few months prior to the demon attack. She had been the one who procured the horses for them to escape the city. Along the way, she helped with all the wounded refugees, and she was becoming a skilled healer, out of necessity.

"Ariel, Daziar, and Elzrod are waiting a little farther in the back alleys," Honora explained as they walked up to her. "They closed the gate before we arrived."

They followed Honora to the others where they were waiting with the horses Honora had procured for them.

"Then we will need another way out," Malach stated the obvious as they approached.

"We could go through the Shadows' lair." Amara offered.

Everyone looked at her.

"What?" She shrugged.

"Why didn't you say that in the first place?" Daziar asked.

"Because I didn't think of it."

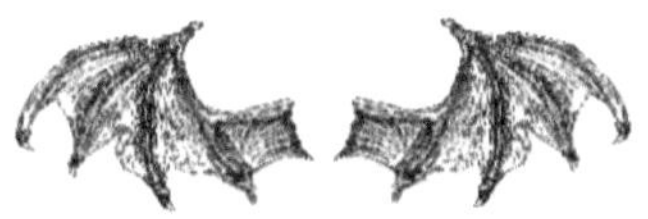

And that's what they did. Amara had to do a little negotiating, but she had saved the Master's life at one point and called in her favor. Daziar was able to see the Shadows' lair, witnessing their operation for himself. It was everything he had ever dreamed of. The only thing that would have made it better for him would have been to come down with a full battalion of guards to get the credit for finding them. As it was, the Shadows were helping them now, and Malach, for one, was thankful no one had been able to catch them thus far.

They hadn't met anyone but the Master and one of the thieves who had taken the horses out of the city for them. Malach couldn't recall his name now. They had traveled across a huge chasm in a massive underground cavern. Ornate pillars held up the ceiling and walls, keeping it from caving in on their heads. Malach had peered into the darkness, unable to shake the feeling someone or something was watching him go by, silently waiting in the depths for a chance to drag him down and destroy him. He had mentioned it to Elzrod, who had told him it was his mind playing tricks on him. They had made it out of those tunnels without incident, meeting the thief with their horses, and headed toward safety.

Malach spotted the three angels a little removed from their group. Cathetel and Camael were walking with his father, Ariel, well ahead of the rest of them. Malach first met the two angels in Newaught, and they appeared normal and mundane. They had been traveling in disguise so as not to draw attention to themselves. Now, however, they didn't hide their majestic wings, nor camouflage their extraordinary silver and gold armor under rags and dirt. They were an impressive and awe-inspiring sight to behold.

Malach's father also wore a set of armor, much like the other two angels. The only difference was his armor was totally black, and no color or shine showed. Malach imagined his father would disappear in the darkness. His father was also missing his wings. The demons had cut them off when he was captured, and Malach was told he would never regain them. However, Ariel wore his armor with all the pride the other two angels did and seemed to have come to terms with the loss. Their wings folded in a gesture of respect, the other angels walked along beside him. Malach studied their wings. They didn't look anything like he had always imagined angel wings looking. They weren't white, feathery, and majestic, but each feather was a flat, metallic shaft. Malach didn't understand how they could fly on wings of metal, but he had witnessed them do it.

"How far is it to Brightwood?" Honora walked up to Malach and Elzrod.

"About a week's ride at a good pace," Elzrod replied.

"But it depends on the passes and hard they will be to travel," Malach put in.

"Yes, and two days after that we will reach the Angel Army stronghold."

"What did the last rider have to say?" Honora had been off helping one of the refugees and missed the latest news.

"The army has sent riders to every city in Angel Territory, letting people know to retreat to Fairdenn." Elzrod pointed to the left in the general direction of Fairdenn. "But we also received word from a passing angel about a day ago who told us many had already arrived at Fairdenn from many cities. They are calling each town to arms or safety and most people have responded to the call; however, there are still people in each town holding out. Which is why they are sending more riders out."

Malach understood why people were reluctant to leave. It would be hard for them to leave their homes simply because someone told them to, especially if they hadn't seen proof of what was happening. He turned to Elzrod. "That last rider was headed toward Fairdenn, right?"

"Yes. He had just delivered his message to Lindow. However, he had no information on enemy movements. He was going through Whiteshade and then back to Fairdenn to report in."

Winter was far from safe in the mountains. There were many places that had several feet of snow laying heavily on the roads. They left the city too quickly to procure the proper gear and were forced to slog through the snow. There were a few people who had joined their party along the way who had large snowshoes. The snowshoes packed down the snow, allowing the lighter women and children walk on top of the snow without plunging deep into it.

Malach and the other men weren't so lucky. When it got deep, they took turns walking in the lead pushing through the snow. Sometimes sinking up to their hips in the cold, wet stuff. Once the man in the lead slowed, he would fall back and allow the next man to take his position. Unfortunately, it had added more than a week to their travels. They were almost out of food, and if not for Malach's skilled hunting, along with a few others in the group, they would have already run out of provisions.

At the moment, the snow in the valley was shallow enough that they were able to ride the horses. Malach glanced down at Skie who plodded along between Malach and Elzrod's horses. The big she-wolf was almost half the size of Malach's horse. He rescued her from one of his traps she sprung when he was young, and he nursed her back to health. She, in turn, saved his life a couple of years later, and they had been inseparable companions ever since. She approved of most of the people Malach had surrounded himself with lately, although she didn't take a liking to just anyone. She was not his wolf, however, and he could not command her any more than he could command any one of his friends. She chose to follow him and never hurt anyone who didn't ask for it first.

The only other entities in their group were the five sentient Angel Blades. Each of the blades had their own personalities, feelings, and thoughts. Malach didn't know the names of Cathetel's and Camael's blades, and they had kept to themselves. Reckoning was the blade that hung at his side. It used to belong to his father but was held by a demon for two hundred years. Malach had taken Reckoning back from the demon, and Ariel decided Malach should continue to wield the Angel Blade. They had rescued another blade, Fury, from the demons, but he was a touch insane from the horrors he had witnessed. Ariel had taken him and was working with him to set its mind right. Fury improved in leaps and bounds in a short couple of weeks. He was still a little weird about certain things and would absolutely lose it if he saw a demon or an image of a demon, but he was recovering as well as could be expected. Hopefully, he would fully recover with time.

When Reckoning had first communicated to Malach in his dreams, the Blade looked skinny and malnourished, not to mention he had scars and open wounds on his body. Now, however, all his wounds had healed, and he appeared to be at a healthy weight. Elzrod said that this was because the demon had starved him of good and abused him with evil. Fury had been the same way, only much worse, since he had been held by a demon for much longer. Storm, on the other hand, had few to no scars that Malach could see and was fit and trim. She was Elzrod's blade, but in the mental world, she took the form of a beautiful young woman, whereas Reckoning and Fury took the forms of young men. She was graceful and alluring when she fought, and Malach had to be careful to master his feelings or he would find her sword through his chest when he fought her.

In the mental world, people could die over and over again without any ill effects. However, it was a little disconcerting to watch a sword plunge through a person's chest or watch their body fall to its knees with their head freshly decapitated. Malach worked hard to minimize how many times that happened.

Malach caught sight of movement ahead of them, snapping out of his thoughts. Something was coming down the road toward them. He couldn't tell what it was yet, but it was bigger than a man. He squinted to try and bring the figure into focus. It was then that he spotted the wings unfurling from its back. The bat-like wings stretched until they were almost twice the demon's height in length. It flapped its wings once and took off, but it wasn't headed their direction. Instead, it banked left and flew east before turning south toward Demon Territory. The two angels spread their wings and took chase. It wasn't long before they were lost to the sight of the group. Malach turned his head to see Elzrod's reaction, but his eyes were glazed over and he was staring at nothing.

Reckoning what's going on with Elzrod? Malach asked the sword.

He is looking through the eyes of one of the angels to watch in case the demon swings back around to attack, Reckoning responded.

Can I do that? Malach asked, eyes widening.

If you were in range, Reckoning told him. *But since you are only part angel and not a Blade-Bearer blessed by God, like Elzrod, your range is too short to be of much use.*

Oh, Malach replied, and he slumped in his saddle, deflated.

"The demon is outpacing Cathetel and Camael," Elzrod reported. "They are giving up the chase and coming back."

"Why didn't that demon attack us?" Amara asked, a puzzled look on her face.

Elzrod turned around in his saddle to face her. "Most likely he was a scout, and we were too well armed. He was probably hoping to pass by us on the road, thinking we were everyday travelers. Once he realized there were three angels with us, he fled."

"That makes sense," Daziar said, nodding thoughtfully. "I bet they have many spies in Angel Territory now. They'll be searching for information on how strong the Angel Army is and where it is amassing."

"Yes," Elzrod agreed. "Although most of those spies will be human, not demon."

"Then how will we ever know who to trust?" Honora asked. Her eyes flitted around at some of the refugees as if any one of them might be a spy.

"You won't, but you will be searched from head to toe when you arrive at the war camp," Cathetel told them as the two angels alighted softly, the snow making a slight crunching noise.

"And you will be asked questions about your past to try and weed out any potential spies," Camael added.

"What?" Honora sat up straight in her saddle. "No one is going to search me like that!"

"Then you won't be able to enter the main war camp," Cathetel stated simply. "Only the outer area where the main group of refugees will reside."

"Don't worry Honora," Camael consoled her. "The angels who do the inspections are very discrete."

"I still don't like it," Honora told him.

"You have a bit longer to think about it. Right now, we are coming up on the town of Whiteshade," Elzrod told them. "We should be seeing it anytime now."

Malach remembered the town. They had passed through it on their journey to Newaught a couple of months ago. It was a larger town than Brightwood, and they even had a division of guards that patrolled the main roads for any would-be highwaymen. They should have come across one of those patrols by now.

They turned the bend on the road and in front of them was the town. What they saw wasn't the gate and wooden walls, but rather the remains of a burned-out city. The walls were gutted and burned to the ground, as well as anything made from wood. Fires continued to burn where there was tinder remaining. The sight stopped most of the group in their tracks. The three angels rushed forward, covering the distance to the city quickly, wary of any enemies who might still be around. Malach and Elzrod quickly followed suit. Daziar was next to snap out of his stupor. Not long after, everyone was out looking for survivors, combing the debris for anyone who might need help.

They systematically picked their way across the town, finding many bodies until finally, Daziar found the first survivor. It was an elderly man who had been bedridden before the attack. The house had collapsed around him, but some of the rubble had held up the wall he was lying next to. The demons must have passed him over. Daziar called for help, and they dug the man out. They freed him, dragging his unconscious body away from the crumbling buildings where he would be safe. They called for Honora leaving him in her care and continued searching for more survivors.

The sun was going down by the time they finished searching the town. They had found two children and one middle-aged man, who had been pinned under another fallen building. His leg was badly broken, and he too was unconscious from dehydration. Malach shuddered as he watched Honora and Ariel set and splint his leg. They built two makeshift sleds from some of the debris and hooked them up behind two of the horses, laying the two men on them.

Surprisingly, they didn't find a lot of bodies in their search, certainly not enough for a whole town. Malach hoped the rest of the townspeople had already left for the army camp and these were the people left over. Although, he was more worried about the implications of this attack. If the demon had made it this far and razed a town, even a mostly deserted one, that meant they were much closer to attacking the main army than anyone had realized.

The group left the town and camped just out of sight of it. No one wanted to camp, staring at the destroyed town, much less in the town. The two children that they found among the ruins wouldn't talk to anyone. Whatever horrible things they had witnessed struck them mute. Honora was taking care of them, and they appeared to be comfortable, but neither of them smiled, much less laughed. In fact, Malach hadn't seen them do anything that normal children would do. Would they ever be normal? Malach forced himself to tear his gaze away.

Elzrod, Daziar, Amara, and the three angels were all huddled around one of the campfires, and Malach walked over to join them. They had pulled over logs from the surrounding forest to sit on, trying to stay warm in the rapidly cooling night. Malach picked a spot next to Amara. His choice in seating forced Daziar to scoot over to give Malach room on the log.

"Sorry," Malach apologized, giving Daziar a weak smile.

"Are you?" Daziar asked, grinning at Malach.

Daziar always gave him a hard time about every girl Malach became close with. Granted the list only included Honora and Amara, but they were the only two girls Malach really knew.

Malach rolled his eyes at Daziar, and Amara turned to look at the two boys.

"Huh?" Amara asked. "What did you say?"

"Nothing," Malach answered before Daziar could embarrass him.

"Well, be quiet then. We're talking about the town and what to do," she answered, annoyance evident in her voice.

"Sorry," Malach replied and turned his attention toward Elzrod, who was still talking.

"Yeah, Malach. Quiet!" Daziar reprimanded.

Malach shot him a dirty look.

"If Whiteshade has fallen, then it could mean that there is a faction of the Demon Army ahead of us. This also could mean that they know where the Angel Army is being amassed," Elzrod explained. "Although, it's more likely they don't know, and they'll be headed to Fairdenn, where we've told all refugees to go. We need to send scouts out to discover which way this contingency has gone. Once we know where they are, we need to take them out before they can harm anyone or relay any information back to the main army."

"I can go," Daziar volunteered. "I'll ride toward Brightwood, and if I find them, I can send word back."

"As much as I appreciate your bravery and eagerness, I think it would be best if Cathetel and Camael flew out." Elzrod reasoned. "They can relay information back without having to fly back to us, and they can quickly warn the towns in the path of this army."

"Fair point," Daziar sighed.

"From the look of some of the fires that are still burning in town, the army shouldn't be more than a day or two ahead of us," Cathetel pointed out. "Camael and I should be able to catch up to them much faster than they can march and report back where they have gone."

"What are we going to do when we find this contingency?" Malach asked. "I mean, if they are big enough to destroy a whole town, then they are too big for our little party to fight."

"Malach, you would be wise not to underestimate the power of three angels and two Blade-Bearers," Ariel told him.

Malach's chest swelled with pride at his father's implication that he was a true Blade-Bearer.

"Right," Elzrod agreed, "but it will depend on how many demons are with this group. We will have to wait and see the strength of our enemy before we know what action we will take. We may simply warn the towns in their path, then go around them, or we may be able to defeat them with the help of either Fairdenn or Brightwood."

"What do we do until the angels report back?" Amara asked, unable to sit still on her log.

"Unless we find an abundance of food and supplies, we won't be able to stay for more than a couple days before we have to move on," Ariel warned.

"While we wait, we might go back to Whiteshade," Daziar suggested. "I know we found some supplies while we were looking for the survivors, but maybe we can go back through it and find more."

"That's a good idea, Daz," Malach agreed.

"That sounds like a well thought out plan," Ariel replied. "Daziar, you will be in charge of the search, while Malach takes a group to continue hunting for game."

"Then it's settled," Elzrod leaning back and got to his feet. "Now we need to get our rest. It's been a long day today and will be a long one tomorrow."

The group broke up, each person laying out their sleeping mats around the fires and bundling up in whatever coverings they had. Some of them had heavier furs, but for the most part, they had distributed everything that they had as evenly as possible. Malach and Ariel would take first watch, moving toward the edge of camp.

"Malach," Ariel started to say something but let his voice trail off.

"Yes?" Malach prompted.

"You've grown into a man while your mother and I have been away." He said looking off into the darkness. "From the things that Elzrod has told me you are, in a lot of ways, wiser than your years. I just wanted to say I'm proud of you, and your mother would be too."

"Don't lie to me," Malach replied, surprised at the anger boiling inside of him. "I know you didn't want me to become a Blade-Bearer. I know you wanted to keep all your old life from me. I never knew you were an angel. I never knew any of this. You and Mom could have prepared me much better if you had just told me something."

"Malach, what I told you is the truth." His father's brow knitted together, pain evident in his expression. "I am proud of you. Yes, I would have chosen another path for you if I had had the choice, and as for telling you about this life, you were twelve. If I told you then, it wouldn't have made much sense to you. Your mother and I planned on telling you when you turned twenty-one. We assumed we would have much more time with you. I'm so sorry that we didn't get to see you grow up and help you along the way."

"I spent most of my life thinking I was a demon, hiding who I was from everyone," Malach snapped. Maybe he was being unfair, but if he had only known what he was and who his parents were, maybe his life would have been different.

"Malach, all I can say now is I'm sorry, and I can work to make it up to you," Ariel told him. "I haven't forgotten about your mother. I know she is still alive, and I promise as soon as we get these refugees safely to the Angel Army, we will go find her together."

"Fine," Malach replied, "but don't expect a father of the year award."

"I understand," Ariel replied, his head drooping. "Malach, I wish I could go back in time and do things over, do things differently. I wish I could be there to see you turn twenty-one, be there to see you graduate from training, and everything else we missed along the way, but we didn't have any choice. The demons took us, and for the time we missed, we instead received torture and pain. It wasn't easy for us either, you know."

"I know," Malach replied, but his anger hadn't fully dissipated. "But if you had just told me-"

"You were a child," Ariel threw his arms up in exasperation. "Let's say, for a moment, that I had told you, and, while we're at it, that you understood everything I told you. What could you have done?"

Malach crossed his arms. His father was right, in some capacity, but he was right too, and his father needed to see that. "But if you had told me, I could have held my head high, knowing that I was an angel. Instead, I was an outcast, a hermit, living alone, skulking in the shadows."

"You're right, Malach, I'm sorry" Ariel sighed and visibly deflated. "I can't change what has happened, but now we have a second chance. We just have to get your mother back."

Malach forced himself to calm, wanting to shout a bit longer at his father but knowing it wouldn't do anyone any good. His father and mother hadn't meant to abandon him. They had been forced to.

Skie plodded out of the darkness in front of them, and Ariel jumped, pulling Fury partially out of his sheath before realizing it was her. "Lord in Heaven," Ariel breathed heavily. "That beast makes me jump every time."

Malach chuckled. "She has that effect on a lot of people."

"You know, your mother always had a way with animals," Ariel said, seeming lost in a memory. "She would always befriend any animal she met. You get that from her."

Skie laid down next to Malach, licking her chops as if she had just finished eating. "I remember Mom would never kill anything, even if it was for dinner, so you or I always had to do that and prepare it. Then she would cook it."

Ariel chuckled at the fond memories. "No, she wouldn't. She sometimes hated that I would go hunting. You know, I was never allowed to kill anything 'cute' when she was around."

They sat next to each other for the rest of their watch, reminiscing about their old life. Malach told his father stories of the years he had missed. Ariel told him a few stories of his life before the valley, when his mother was with Ariel in the war. Although Malach knew he wasn't telling him the full story, leaving the worst parts out.

Malach finally laid down on his mat at the end of their watch. He was happy. He was genuinely happy. His father was back, and they were on their way toward making amends. He gazed across the fire to where Amara was curled up. One of her furs had been partially blown off her shoulder, and she was shivering. It was a wonder she hadn't woken up. He got up, walked over to her, and pulled the fur covering back up onto her shoulder, tucking it in around her. She stopped shivering only a few moments later, and he laid down again. This time, he drifted quickly off to sleep.

Chapter 2

The next day, the two angels left before the sun and crested the horizon. Malach, Amara, and Skie went hunting, and Daziar put together a small group of people and went into the city, as planned. The three hunters returned that evening to find the angels had reported back. They had not found the contingency of troops but were going to continue forward. Daziar's group had found a few items in the ruined town, and even though those hunting had brought back a small assortment of game, the group had used almost as many supplies as they had gained.

The next day didn't prove to be much better, although Malach was able to bring down a small doe. Daziar's group found even fewer supplies than they did the day before. Elzrod decided no one should leave the camp the next day, since they would most likely be forced to leave by midday, due to the lack of food. The two angels again reported nothing of interest. Although, Cathetel, who had headed toward Fairdenn, had seen smoke in the distance before he stopped for the night. He admitted to Elzrod and Ariel that it could have been smoke from the city itself that he had seen. However, he didn't believe he had flown far enough to see that yet.

They went to sleep wondering what the next day would bring. If they didn't hear anything back from the angels by midday, the group would continue heading toward Brightwood and then onto the Angel Army. If they did hear back, they would have to decide what to do after they knew how large the demon contingency was.

Malach watched Daziar head toward the medical tent, no doubt to spend his day with Honora. He chuckled to himself. Honora would put Daziar to work instead of letting him sit around. He would be almost as tired by the end of the day as he had been scouring the town for supplies. What he didn't expect was the two of them to walk up the fire he was sitting at less than an hour later.

"Malach," Honora said in her you're-in-trouble voice, "can we have a word?"

"Umm, sure," Malach said, a little nervous about what she wanted to talk about.

Daziar didn't say anything. He just studied his feet, not making eye contact with Malach.

Malach got up and Honora lead the two boys out of earshot of the camp. Malach looked at Daziar as they walked and arched an eyebrow, silently asking what they were in trouble for.

Daziar just inclined his head toward Honora as if to say, *you'll have to hear it from her.*

Honora turned around finally and placed her hands on her hips, glaring at Malach. Daziar moved to stand beside her.

Malach narrowed his eyes at his friend, and Daziar shrugged. Malach couldn't judge him too harshly. Most people would rather stand on Honora's side than face her wrath. Malach didn't think he was going to be able to get out of it this time though.

"So," Malach decided to just get it over with, "what did you want to talk to me about?"

"This girl you are smitten with," Honora pointed an accusatory finger at him, nearly poking him in the chest with it.

"I'm not smitten with her," Malach held up his hands in defense and took a step backward.

"Oh, yeah? How long have you known her?" Honora asked.

"I don't know," Malach started, realizing that wasn't a very strong argument. "Maybe two months." He knew it probably hadn't been that long, but it sounded better if he rounded up.

"And in that time, you have given her your total trust and shared your whole life story," Honora stated, still jabbing her finger his direction. "You barely know her!"

"I disagree," Malach replied. "She helped save my father."

Honora looked at Daziar for help. He however had lost interest in the conversation and was staring at something off in the trees, daydreaming. She elbowed him in the side.

"Oomph! Whatever she said, she's right," Daziar said quickly, but it only earned him another elbow to the ribs.

"I was saying that Malach was trusting Amara too quickly," Honora reiterated, glaring at him with her hands on her hips. "You agree, right?"

"Uh, yeah," Daziar said and looked at Malach. "Maybe you ought to slow down a bit. For all you know, she could be a spy."

"Really?" Malach cocked an eyebrow at them incredulously.

"I mean, it's possible," Daziar mumbled and looked at his feet again.

"So could Reckoning," Malach replied. "Should I mistrust him now?"

Please don't bring me into this, Reckoning implored.

"That's not what we are saying, and you know it," Honora snapped, putting her hands on her hips again.

"This is because I told her she could stay with you without asking you, isn't it?" Malach accused.

"No," Honora growled at him. "This is because we care about you and don't want you to get hurt. Although, you will pay for that someday."

"Sorry I asked," Malach sighed. "Fine, I will be more careful, but I'm not going to treat her like she could be a spy."

"Fine," Honora replied, not sounding satisfied at all. "But if she betrays us all, I get to say, 'I told you so.'"

Malach rolled his eyes at her and walked away. He heard Daziar and Honora talking behind him as he did.

"Are you jealous?" Daziar asked, the idea seeming to dawn on him.

"No!" Honora said, too quickly for anyone to have believed her.

Malach chanced a glance back and saw Honora storming away from Daziar back toward the medical tent. Daziar smiled to himself, and then noticed that Malach was watching him. He walked over to Malach.

"You're not afraid she's going to hate you for that?" Malach asked.

"She'll get over it. I don't think she'll ever want to court me anyway."

Malach nodded slowly. "Between you and me, do you think I'm trusting Amara too quickly?"

"I think you're trusting her faster than you've trusted anyone in your entire life," Daziar replied. "I think you need to take stock of why that is. I trust you to come to the correct conclusion."

Daziar walked away from Malach and back toward camp. It was getting close to midday, and people were beginning to pack up in preparation to start moving again. Malach waited for a few moments thinking about what Daziar had said and the apparent wisdom in the words. When had Daziar become so wise?

He walked back to camp and started to pack his bedding and supplies. Amara caught his eye and smiled at him. She was so beautiful when she smiled. He smiled back but went back to work. He had too much on his mind concerning the young woman to talk with her right now.

He finished packing and wandered over to where Elzrod was sitting, warming himself by a fire.

"Malach," Elzrod greeted him.

"Elzrod." Malach nodded in return.

"I'm glad you are here. We haven't had much time to talk since Newaught."

"What would you like to talk about?"

"Since we've been training, we haven't had much time to focus on multiple opponents," his mentor explained. "We are likely to encounter these situations soon, and war is messy."

Malach nodded again to acknowledge his mentor's words.

"War waits for no one to be ready, and the enemy won't hesitate. . ." Elzrod's voice trailed off, and his eyes glazed over for a few seconds.

He's receiving a message from one of the angels, Reckoning informed him.

"Cathetel has found the contingency," Elzrod spoke softly and in a monotone, as if he wasn't fully aware he was talking. "He believes it is in our ability to defeat them with only minor losses."

"Good!" Malach replied, clenching his fist in eagerness. He was tired of waiting around.

"Your father is contacting Camael now," Elzrod continued, as if he hadn't heard Malach. "Cathetel will continue forward to warn Fairdenn as planned."

"How large is the enemy force?" Malach asked.

"That's the surprising thing," Elzrod said. "There aren't even enough troops to have taken Whiteshade, if they had put up any fight at all. They would have had the wall to hide behind and enough arrows to drive them off. Cathetel counted around fifty troops and only one demon."

"How did they take the town then?"

"Hopefully we can find that out when we catch up to them," Elzrod replied. "Fairdenn is fortified much more than Whiteshade was. There are about five hundred troops and two angels stationed there for its defense. They would be foolish to attack the city with that small of a force."

"Then why don't we let them attack the city and let Fairdenn take care of them?" Malach asked. It wasn't that he didn't want to help, but if they could take care of the enemy why would Malach and his group risk their lives outside the wall? They had a perfectly good wall to hide behind.

"The demon wouldn't attack unless he knew he could win somehow," Elzrod explained. "Which means that they probably have something else planned."

Elzrod stood up and started calling out orders. Men hopped up and ran to do what Elzrod commanded.

"What is our plan?" Malach asked, following his mentor through the camp.

"To disrupt whatever the enemy plans by any means necessary," Elzrod replied.

Malach whistled for Skie as he hoisted his pack over his shoulder. He grabbed the reins of his horse and moved with the rest of the group down the road that led to Fairdenn. It would take them a total of five days to travel to the city. On day two, Camael caught up with them, but by day three, they hadn't heard anything from Cathetel, despite several attempts to reach him.

Camael served as an advanced scout, and on day four, spotted the enemy camp. The night before their final march, they made preparations to leave those unfit to fight behind. They would come back to get them once they knew it was safe.

Malach couldn't sleep. He spent most of the night walking around the camp, hoping to tire himself out enough to drift off. However, the nervous energy that came on the eve of battle wouldn't allow him to do that. Amara came up beside him while he stared down the road. They hadn't seen any sign of the enemy, but they had seen smoke rising from the city's direction. However, in the heart of winter, there would be many fires keeping the people warm.

"What are you thinking?" Amara asked.

"Not much." Malach shrugged. "Just wondering what we will find at Fairdenn."

"Yeah, me too," she admitted. "Why do you think Cathetel hasn't responded to Camael and Elzrod?"

"I don't know what to think," Malach responded. "Even if he was busy fighting, you would think he would be able to think a quick response. It's not even like he would have to say much."

"Yeah," Amara said quietly. "Do you think he's dead?"

"No," Malach replied. "They would have felt that. When an angel or demon dies, it sends out a kind of ripple that all other angels and demons can feel. I can't feel them, but Elzrod, Camael, and my father can, and they haven't felt one yet. Whatever is happening at Fairdenn, no angels or demons have died yet."

"Huh," Amara huffed. "I guess we will just have to wait and find out what's happening tomorrow."

"You're not staying with the women, are you?" Malach asked, already knowing the answer.

"And let you and Daz take all the glory?" she asked, laughing. "Absolutely not. Besides, if you need anyone to sneak in or out of someplace, you will need me."

"Right," Malach said, wishing she was staying behind. Not because he didn't want her there, but because he didn't want her in harm's way.

"Is Honora staying?" Amara asked.

"Honora is staying to help with the children and wounded," Malach answered. "She doesn't like fighting. And she is probably better off here anyway."

"Really?" Amara asked. "She seems capable of handling herself."

"Don't get me wrong," Malach said, holding up a hand, "she can hold her own in a fight, but she has never killed anyone before. If push came to shove, I think she would be able to take a life, but I don't think she wants to be put in that situation. I know the angels have been showing her a bit of healing on this trip, too. With them leaving tomorrow, she will be the best healer around, and we still have a few wounded to take care of."

"I understand," Amara replied. "If she is reluctant to take a life, she would just be a liability anyway. She has other talents that she has chosen to pursue."

"How about you?" Malach asked. "Are you ready for an all-out battle, if it comes to that?"

"I don't know," she told him. "I've killed before, but it was one-on-one, and it was self-defense. I'm not sure if I'm ready or not."

"Well, if you find you are not ready, there is no shame in staying behind," Malach said. "As you have pointed out, someone who isn't ready would just be a liability."

"You think you are ready then?" she asked, looking at his face to judge his reaction.

"I believe I am," he replied, his black eyes growing hard. "I've had to kill many times before and Elzrod has helped me train for larger-scale battles in the last few days, though I've never been in one. I think I will be alright though. You just never know. One mistake can end your life."

"Yeah." Her eyes fell to the ground.

They both fell silent for a while. The silence wasn't awkward and both left each other to their own thoughts. Malach looked down the road and saw a faint flicker of light for just a moment, then it was gone.

"Did you see that?" Malach asked in a hushed tone, wondering if his eyes were playing tricks on him.

"I think so," Amara replied, leaning forward to peer into the gloom. "I thought I saw a light."

"That's what I saw," Malach confirmed. "I couldn't make out what it was though."

Reckoning? Malach contacted his blade. *Any idea what that was?*

It looked like someone trying to cover a lantern to me, Reckoning replied. *We should let Elzrod know.*

Do that and let him know Amara and I are going to check it out, Malach responded, then said out loud. "Elzrod will know what's going on shortly. Let's go check it out. You take the left side of the path and I'll take the right. Don't reveal yourself until I tell you."

Amara nodded and melted into the shadows.

Malach admired the way she could disappear so effortlessly. He moved to his side of the path and made his way down it, Skie stalking right behind him. He knew that Amara would be watching his progress and mirroring it. He was not as good as she was when it came to sneaking through the shadows, but he could still do a decent job of it.

He caught sight of another quick flicker of light on the path. It was closer this time, and he could make out the silhouette of a figure when the light illuminated it for that split second. The silhouette appeared larger than a human, but that could be the angle of the light. The figure was on the edge of the path, on the side Malach was moving along. It gave no indication that it knew Malach nor Amara was there.

Malach signaled Amara to wait where she was and stopped his forward momentum as well. He squatted down, pulling Reckoning from his sheath. He left the blade in the form of a knife.

The weapon of an assassin.

Don't kill the man, Malach, Elzrod's voice sounded in Malach's head, making him start slightly. He still hadn't gotten used to the mental communication. He didn't think his slight movement had given him away. The silhouette came closer, and Malach was aware it was too small to be an angel or a demon.

I won't kill him, Malach promised. He didn't know if Elzrod was close enough to hear his response, since his range was much less than the other Blade-Bearers.

The silhouette got closer. It was almost between Malach and Amara. It was a young man, not much older than himself. He was carrying a lantern, as Reckoning had predicted. It was shuttered, but as Malach peered out from the bushes the young man lifted the shutter for just a moment to let the light fall on a shadow that was in the path. He was using it to see if the shadows were anything that would harm him. Malach ducked behind a tree so the light wouldn't reveal him, then let the man pass. Malach walked out onto the path behind the young man, as silent as the night. He covered the distance between him and the young man quickly. At the last moment, he wrapped an arm around the man and pressed Reckoning up to his throat.

"Don't move." Malach breathed and Skie growled for emphasis.

The young man whimpered and dropped the lantern. It clattered to the ground, the shutter falling out of place illuminating his face.

"Auron?" Malach asked and spun him around still holding the knife up. "What are you doing here?"

It was Auron, the young man Daziar, Malach, and Honora had met in Newaught their second night there. Auron and his wife Prinna had brought them food and wood to burn in case they didn't have any their first nights in the new city. They had stayed and talked with Malach, sharing the meal they had brought. Malach had never seen the couple again after that. He never expected to see either of them again after their flight from Newaught.

"Malach?" Auron asked, visibly relaxing at the sight of his old neighbor. "Thank the heavens. And you still have Skie with you I see."

Skie growled again which puzzled Malach. Normally she was a great judge of character, and she had liked Auron in Newaught. He turned toward Auron, skeptical of his intentions.

"Auron, this is important," Malach said, eyes narrowing. "Why are you here?"

"I was told a group would be out here seeking to gain entrance to the city. I was sent here to guide them." Auron replied, his hands were still raised showing he had no weapons.

"Then you are on the angel's side?" Malach questioned.

"Yes, of course," Auron answered slowly lowering his hands. "I thought I was a dead man when you put your knife to my throat. I thought the Demon Army had found me, and I would fail my mission. Are you with the group out here?"

"Yes," Malach motioned for Amara to come out of hiding and removed Reckoning from Auron's throat. "We escaped from Newaught when the demons attacked and have been working our way toward the Angel Army's camp. We came across Whiteshade and knew something was wrong. Auron, this is Amara, a friend of mine."

"Pleased to meet you," Auron replied, holding out his hand to Amara.

"Amara, this was my neighbor in Newaught," Malach told her as she walked up.

She nodded toward Auron in greeting but did not take his hand. The three of them started walking back toward camp. Malach picked up the lantern as they went. Elzrod came out to meet them extending a hand to Auron. "Reckoning told me what was going on. Auron, it is good that you have come."

Before Elzrod clasped Auron's hand Skie growled a warning growl a third time.

Malach started to shush her but Elzrod acted quicker. He pulled Auron in by his hand and lifted his sleeve up past his elbow roughly. On Auron's forearm was a symbol, branded into his skin, which had only partially healed. Elzrod pulled Storm from her sheath and stuck the point under Auron's chin. Amara and Malach stood there for a second, caught off guard at the sudden change from friend to foe.

"He has the brand of the enemy," Elzrod growled.

"Auron, you lied to me," Malach said, shocked his once-friend would be allied with the demons. "Why?"

"They have Prinna, Malach," he implored, both hands outstretched, palms up. "I didn't have a choice."

"Then you are our prisoner," Elzrod told him. "And you still don't have a choice."

"If I don't return with your group, then her life will be forfeit," Auron told them.

"How do we know we can trust you?" Malach pointing an accusatory finger at him. "You haven't been honest with me since you got here."

"I'm sorry, Malach," Auron apologized. "I don't know how I can convince you that I'm telling the truth now. I can tell you that the contingency I am with is waiting for a much larger company to arrive on the other road from Lanifair. They will be coming with a large enough force to take the city, and they have some plan in place for the city walls. They will be here tomorrow evening and are planning on starting their attack sometime during the night."

Skie seemed satisfied with his response and sat down, the hair on her back starting to lower. Malach could swear she had a smug look on her face as she stared at him, as if to tell him, *I tried to tell you he was lying, but now he's not.*

"That makes sense," Elzrod said, lowering Storm slightly. "We were wondering why such a small group would attack the city, but now we know for sure there is a larger force on the way."

Elzrod, Malach called mentally.

Yes, Malach? he replied

I think we can trust him.

I agree. He might be telling us the truth. What do you have in mind? Elzrod asked.

Let him take us to the demon camp, Malach proposed.

That just might work, Elzrod replied, catching onto Malach's plan.

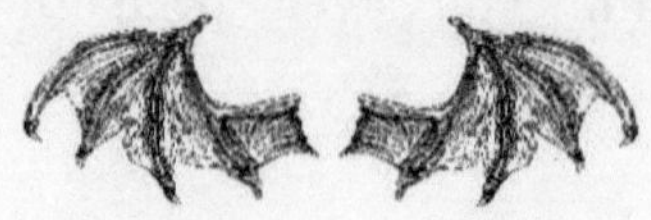

Malach and Skie, along with Amara, Daziar, and about half of the men who could fight, walked with Auron toward the enemy camp. Almost all the men were disguised as refugees. Some walked with limps, others hunched so far over that they looked like they might fall if the wind blew in the wrong direction. Elzrod, Camael, Ariel, and the rest of the men stuck to the shadows off the main trail. They planned to turn the ruse around on the demon and his men. If they could take the demon by surprise and kill him, Camael was confident that they could take the humans that were with them.

Auron informed them that there were only forty men with the demon. Elzrod counted sixteen among their number that could fight, excluding Camael, Ariel, and himself. It would all come down to how quickly they could kill the demon. As they approached, one of the men from the demon camp came out to greet them. He wore a fake smile that was overly large but didn't touch his eyes.

"Welcome, weary refugees and warriors alike." He bowed low. Even his voice sounded strained, as if he didn't have much practice being happy. "It is not far now to the city. Please follow me, and we will get you bed down for the night."

They followed the man into the camp, and he kept glancing warily back at Skie. The camp was made to look like it was deserted. The enemy troops peeking from just inside the tents. If Malach didn't know that they were there he would have assumed the camp was empty. The men were hiding, presumably waiting for the right time to spring their trap. They were going to have to wait for the trap to be sprung before they could act, which meant playing a part. Only Amara, Daziar, and himself were visibly armed. They would most likely be made, or at the least asked, to give those weapons up. Reckoning was safely tucked away in his boot until Elzrod sprung their trap.

Their group arrived at the center of the camp. This is when the enemy would reveal themselves. The trick would be for the three of them to put up a good enough front that it didn't appear as if they were giving up too easily but not enough to get them killed. A few men who were sitting around a fire stood, and none of them looked inviting.

"Please," the man who was leading them said. "Let my men relieve your burdens. We would be happy to take your pack and weapons to a tent that will be set up for you."

"If it's all the same, we would rather keep our weapons with us." Daziar put a hand casually on the pommel of his sword.

The man sighed as if disappointed in them. "Very well, we do this the hard way then."

Just as Malach predicted, the demon ducked out of the tent directly in front of them and stood to his full, extremely intimidating, height. Malach, Amara, and Daziar all pulled their weapons. Enemy troops took their cue from the demon and emerged from their tents, surrounding the small group. Malach had to work at not smiling. Auron moved out of the group and got behind the line of soldiers.

"Auron!" Malach feigned surprise. "You betrayed us?"

Even Skie got into her role. She growled menacingly at the men who were closest to her, causing them to back up a few steps

"Yes, he did," the demon responded. "Malach Tresch, I didn't know we would be capturing you tonight."

"How do you know my name?" Malach asked, his brow furrowing in real confusion.

"There are orders to take you alive," the demon told him. "I'm told you will be one of the deciding factors of this war. Although, looking at how puny you are, I have no idea why they would think that."

"I'm not sure whether I should be flattered or insulted," Malach growled, he lowered his weapon and motioned for Amara and Daziar to do the same.

Three of the enemy troops came forward and collected their weapons. Malach let them take the sword from him. He had to wave Skie off as she snapped at the man taking his weapon. Now they just had to stall until Elzrod and the rest of the men were in place.

"You know, I met your mother and father." The demon paced back and forth in front of them, sneering. "I even got to help clip your father's wings."

Malach ground his teeth together. He would enjoy cutting this demon down.

"Where is your father, anyway?" The demon asked stopping to look at Malach. "Did he leave you already? He probably got orders from his God and ran off like the obedient dog he is."

Malach was going to kill this demon personally.

"And now that we have you, we can kill your mother," the demon continued.

"What?" Malach was shocked, this was not going as planned.

"The only reason we were keeping her alive is to use her against you," the demon told him.

"I'll kill you!" Malach yelled, anger boiling up in his gut.

"If it helps, I'll take you to Serilda to be reunited with her and then kill her in front of you," the demon laughed manically.

Malach, don't! Reckoning warned, but it was too late.

Malach pulled Reckoning out of his boot. He changed Reckoning into his double-bladed pole weapon and charged. The demon was taken off guard and was slow to draw his own weapon. Malach took the opportunity to draw first blood, taking off the demon's sword hand as it reached for its sword. Malach spun away as the demon reeled back, bellowing from the pain.

Two men were bearing down on Malach their swords already drawn. He ducked one swing aimed at his neck and blocked the other sword meant to cut through his knees. Malach used his weapon to steady himself as he sent a kick into the man who had attacked high. He pushed the sword of the second man away, spinning his weapon once and ending the man with a thrust from the other end of his weapon. The first man had recovered and was coming at him again. A knife seemed to sprout out of the man's neck, and he fell. Malach looked to where the knife had come from and found Amara. She had thrown one of her knives to save him.

"Malach!" she shouted pointing with her now free hand. "Watch out!"

Malach turned.

The demon had managed to draw his sword with his remaining hand and was walking toward him.

"I'm going to enjoy killing you," the demon taunted. "To Heaven with my orders. You will die today."

"Come and get it then!" Malach shouted in defiance.

Skie hit the demon broadside, knocking him off balance. She bit down on his arm holding the sword with her powerful jaws. However, she couldn't hold on long enough for Malach to take advantage of the distraction and was flung away from the demon. She landed on her feet, but her momentum caused her to roll when she hit the ground. She looked dazed.

Malach readied himself as the demon advanced. He ducked a swing from the demon's sword and dodged to the side as it was followed with what would have been a devastating kick. The demon's back was turned for just a second as its momentum turned it around. Malach rushed forward and stabbed one of the ends of his weapon into the back of its knee. It bellowed again, kicking out with the other leg in response. The kick caught Malach across his chest and sent him flying. Luckily, the kick didn't have the demon's full power behind it, or it would have broken bones. As it was, the air was knocked out of Malach. He landed on a tent and it collapsed in a heap.

Malach struggled to untangle himself from the material as the demon advanced on him slowly. He couldn't get out of the mess of tent that entangled him. The demon sneered at him and raised his sword for the finishing blow.

Ariel tackled the demon with the full power of an angel. They hit the ground hard enough for Malach to feel the ground shake beneath him. Ariel used the momentum of the landing to roll and vault to his feet. He unsheathed Fury, righteous fire igniting along the length of the blade. This was the first time Malach had seen an angel fight with an Angel Blade, and it was breathtaking. The demon stood and matched Ariel's flame with his own, igniting his blade with dark Hellfire. The two titans clashed, shockwaves emanating from each blow.

Daziar reached Malach and helped him out of the mess of the tent where he was entangled. Malach had to stop watching his father and the demon fight, since he was now forced to fight the human troops with Daziar. They fell into a familiar cadence, each attacking and defending, complimenting the others moves with practiced ease. They cut down any enemy that came within reach until the troops didn't attack as readily, wary of the two young men. Each wanting to kill them, but not wanting to get killed in the process.

There was a break in the attacks and Malach took the chance to look around. He found Elzrod and Camael had come to Ariel's aid. They had the demon disarmed and on his knees. He watched as his father beheaded the defenseless demon. Many of the human enemies saw the same thing and lowered their weapons raising their hands in surrender as the Blade-Bearer and two angels turned to finish the fight. The rest of the enemy quickly followed suit, and the battle ended almost as quickly as it had begun.

Malach sighed and sat down. Nothing tired a person out faster than a fight, and Malach was already tired from traveling all day. He was glad this was over. It was time for some much-needed rest. Skie came trotting up to him, her snout covered in gore.

"Malach!" Elzrod called. "Come quickly, our job is not yet finished."

Malach sighed again and used Reckoning to get back to his feet. "What is it now, Elzrod?"

"Communication between us and Cathetel has been restored," Ariel told Malach. "Somehow the demon was blocking our communications, but killing him has allowed us to talk once more."

"Great," Daziar said unimpressed, trailing Malach. "We can get an update and go to sleep."

"He has already given us an update, but that's not the problem. We need to get to the city quickly," Elzrod said, urgency still evident in his voice.

"What's happening?" Malach asked.

"When we killed the demon, its blade reached out to us, telling us the enemy's plan," Elzrod said. "We now know how such a small group was able to take a much larger city."

"Come. Leave the prisoners to the men and follow us," Camael said. "We will explain on the way. There is no time to lose."

Malach, Daziar, and Amara all followed the angels and Blade-Bearer. The blade that had been wielded by the demon had told them that the enemy had another new weapon that had not been revealed yet. The demons called it an explosive. They had an inside man infiltrate the city they were going to attack and lay several of these devices at key points in the city and wait until the main force was ready to strike. Once they were in position, this inside man would set the devices off, destroying all these points. Then the army would simply walk in and finish off any survivors, burning and pillaging as they went.

The second force of the Demon Army was only a day or two away from the city, according to Auron, so they didn't have much time to find this inside man and the devices before it was too late. They arrived at city gates only a few hours later and were ushered in quickly. The gates barely opened enough for them to slip in one at a time. There were already healers and extra troops at the gates in preparation for the prisoners and wounded.

They were taken to one of the biggest buildings in the city. It was three stories high, which was big for any city in Angel Territory. They were taken to the top floor, where Cathetel was in conference with two other angels.

Malach had been told about the setup here in Fairdenn by Elzrod on the way to the city. Two angels, Barachiel and Eloa, were stationed at the city to oversee the vetting and take recruits. Eloa was the first female angel Malach had heard about. Once there was a large enough group of recruits and refugees, Ananiel, a third angel, would take them to the stronghold north of Brightwood. The three angels were standing in the middle of the room pouring over a map of the city laid out on the table. None of them even batted an eye at Skie as she walked in the room behind Malach. He guessed they weren't worried about a large wolf covered in ichor.

Cathetel turned to them as they approached the angels. "We have people searching for the explosives. They have found two of the devices already. Although, no word on the traitor yet."

"What do these devices even do?" Daziar asked. "I mean, what's the big deal?"

Cathetel turned toward him as if he hadn't seen him until he spoke. "Do you remember the cannons at Newaught?"

"Yeah, how could I forget those?" Daziar replied.

"Think of the damage they caused, then think of these explosives as being three times more destructive," Cathetel said, turning back to the map.

"And they are inside the wall, so the wall won't be the only thing that is damaged." Amara pointed out.

"Good point!" Ariel praised. Malach got the feeling that Ariel liked Amara in a fatherly way.

"What about the traitor?" Elzrod asked.

"We are detaining anyone who has not been vetted by the Angel Army already," Eloa informed them. "We started as soon as we got word that he or she was among us. However, we haven't told them why we are detaining them yet. We don't want to cause widespread panic, nor do we want to tip our hand to the traitor that we know about them."

"So what do you want us to do?" Amara asked.

Cathetel pointed at the map on the table. "I have a group here and here moving down the wall in opposite directions. Malach, you take Amara and Daziar and start your search here, moving counterclockwise around the wall. Elzrod, you take Ariel and start at the same point, going clockwise. Keep your eyes open for anything, we found one device buried in the ground so they could be anywhere."

"Yes, sir." the three young adults saluted as they had in the guard at Newaught.

Chapter 3

Honora had stayed behind with the rest of the refugees when Malach and the rest had headed off to defeat the demon contingency. The man with the broken leg they had pulled from the wreckage of Whiteshade stirred as she was helping a woman who had sprained an ankle. She finished quickly and moved to his side.

He had survived, despite his dehydration, and he was waking up. She suspected that he would make a full recovery. She helped the man sit up and held a cup to his lips. He sipped at first but soon tipped her hand and gulped greedily. She had to pull the cup away from him to stop him. Once he had quenched his thirst, he asked a lot of questions about where he was and what had happened. Honora answered them to the best of her knowledge and then asked for his story.

"I was one of the few guards that didn't leave when the news of the Angel Army amassing reached Whiteshade," he told her. "I couldn't leave the people I vowed to protect."

"I understand. What do you remember about the destruction of Whiteshade?" she asked him.

He contemplated her question. "I don't remember much. I heard a loud crack, like when a tree splits when you are cutting it or like a clap of thunder. But it originated from inside the walls. I came rushing out of the barracks with the rest of the men who weren't on guard that night and found our Captain lying on the ground, dying of a wound that wasn't made by a sword. None of us could identify the weapon that had been used, but it didn't matter. One of us sounded the alarm, but it was too late. I don't remember much after that except the barracks and bell tower collapsing. That is most likely where you found me."

"Very likely," Honora replied. "It sounds like the demons are using a new weapon. I need to get this information to the angels."

Honora stood to leave but the man caught her wrist. "There's another thing. Before the captain died, he told me that it was a guard that betrayed and killed him. He must be the reason that the Demon Army was able to destroy the city so easily. The only guard that I would think would have betrayed us was one who had come to us from Newaught. If they are moving to the next city, they will most likely use that same tactic. You need to warn them."

Honora nodded. She found one of the women to look after the man, then found her horse, Celwyn, and galloped out toward Fairdenn with the description of a traitor. She just hoped she wasn't too late.

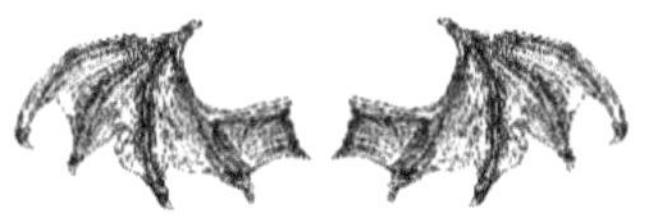

Malach, Amara, Daziar, Elzrod, and Ariel followed the guide as he traversed the city to the part of the wall that Cathetel had shown them on the map. The three young adults wished Elzrod and Ariel good luck and started moving down the wall. They were looking for anything out of place or any good spots to hide one of the explosive devices. It was slow going. Daziar, of course, made a game out of it. He bet Malach that he could find more of the devices than either him or Amara. Malach played along to keep his friend happy, while Amara rolled her eyes at them both.

They arrived at a barracks only a few hundred yards from where they had first started. It had been built onto the wall for the guards who were assigned wall duty. Malach started to walk past it. He assumed there wouldn't be any reason to search in there, since civilians wouldn't have access to it.

"Hey, aren't we going to check in here?" Amara asked.

Malach turned around to see she had stopped. "I didn't think it was necessary."

"I think we need to search it to rule it out." Amara pressed. "If there is nothing in there, then we only lose a few minutes searching."

Daziar moved quickly to Amara's side. "Yeah, Malach. I think we should too."

Malach gave his traitorous friend a withering look. "How quickly you turn on me," he muttered.

He walked back to them anyway not wanting to turn it into an argument. Malach opened the door to the barracks. They were accosted by one of the worst smells they had ever smelled.

"Ugh!" Daziar pulled his shirt up over his mouth and nose. "Don't they ever clean this?"

"This smells awful, and I grew up in a sewer." Amara pinched her nose as well.

"Even a barracks housing twice as many guards in Newaught wasn't this bad." Malach agreed, assuming the same posture as Daziar.

"We better check it though," Amara said and walked in. "Anyone else might have thought the same thing and left before fully searching it."

They suffered through the smell, though in Daziar's case, not in silence. They sifted through the beds and chests that housed the guards' uniforms while Daziar kept up a constant complaint. They were almost finished with the main room when Malach stumbled onto a second room and the source of the smell.

"Ugh!" Malach groaned. "They have those indoor outhouses like in Newaught except every one of them is clogged and full!"

Daziar and Amara didn't follow him in to see for themselves. Instead, he could hear them rifling through the guards' uniforms a second time. He presumed they did that so they wouldn't have to help him, and he decided he was on his own.

He walked down the row of receptacles until he noticed a box at the back of the room half hidden by one of the receptacles. He walked up to it and studied it. It was too new and too out of place for it to be a part of the original construction. There was a piece of oil-soaked rope sticking out of the box.

"I found one! Daziar, come give me a hand with it!

Malach didn't hear anything from his companions, so he moved to the door to the main room peering around the corner.

Amara and Daziar looked at each other, neither wanting to be the one that had to go.

"Don't look at me," she said, holding up her hands. "You are much stronger than I am, and he called your name."

"Fine," Daziar sighed, "but you owe me."

"You both owe me for lollygagging and making me do the dirty work," Malach called, ducking back through the door as he did. "Now get your lazy backside in here, Daz!"

Daziar entered the room and made a gagging noise. He walked, a little unsteadily, down to Malach at the far end of the room. He helped Malach pull the device out from behind the last receptacle and carry it out into the main room.

The device was large and heavy. It was a large wooden crate, but the cracks between the boards had been sealed with some kind of tar. It was heavy enough that both Malach and Daziar were needed to carry it. He didn't know how many of them could be hidden around the city simply because they would be too hard to hide. How did the enemy spy carry this to the barracks by himself and without being spotted? They set the crate down in front of Amara.

"Ugh," Amara said, pinching her nose. "This smells like it was *in* one of those receptacles instead of beside it."

"You found one!" a surprised voice said from behind them.

The three whirled to find the source of the voice. Malach drew Reckoning from the holder on his back. Daziar and Amara did the same with their weapons, flanking Malach.

A guard was standing in the door with his weapon drawn but lowered to his side. He was an extremely tall man, rivaling Malach's height of six feet, five inches. He held a hand and a half sword, which was as long as Amara was tall. He sheathed his sword and Malach relaxed a little, putting Reckoning away.

"Yes, we did." Malach was still wary of the guard. The guardhouse had not been lived in for a while, or at least not taken care of. What was a guard doing here now? Just when they had found a device too.

"I can take it back to the angels for you, if you three want to keep looking." The guard took a step forward.

Skie growled a low warning growl.

Malach glanced at her then quickly turned back to the guard, narrowing his eyes. "I think we will take it ourselves, besides it too heavy for one man."

"Have it your way." The guard shrugged as if he didn't care and turned to walk away.

"Wait," Malach commanded. "What were you doing here anyway?"

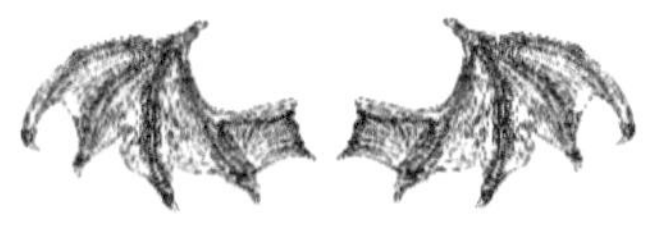

Honora made it to the city stopping only long enough to convince the guards to let her in. She found out from them where the angels were at and she headed straight for the building. Lucky for her, there were very few people in the streets to get in her way and she was able to go straight to the building she had been directed to. She hopped off Celwyn and ran inside. Taking the stairs two at a time, she turned the corner, holding onto the banister. She stopped in her tracks as all the eyes in the room fell on her.

Three angels and two other important looking men turned her direction. Maybe she should have knocked. Her nerves failed her and so did her voice.

"Is there something so important that you needed to barge in, Honora?" Camael asked, gesturing with his hand that she should say something.

"Uh, yes," she answered, trying to clear her mind.

"Would you mind enlightening us as to what that is?" Cathetel leaned on the table with both hands, clearly frustrated with her.

"Oh, yeah," she said, fully snapping out of her stupor. She related to them what the man from Whiteshade had told her. When she had finished, the other two men started conversing with each other in hushed tones.

"You think the spy is posing as a guard here, too?" Camael asked, furrowing his brow.

"It would make sense," Cathetel answered for her. "He wasn't caught last time, so why change his tactics?"

"There was a guard who came to us a week ago, saying he was a refugee of Newaught," one of the two men spoke up; however, he was hanging his head and wouldn't meet any of the angels' eyes. "He came from that direction, but he got here right after word of Newaught's downfall reached us. We thought it was a little soon to be receiving refugees but didn't think much of it."

"Where is this man now, and why didn't you tell me?" the third angel, Honora hadn't caught his name, asked.

"He should be on duty on the wall tonight," the second of the two men replied, assuming the same postures as the first man. Honora thought he might be the Captain of the Guard in this town.

"Was he vetted?" Cathetel growled, advancing on the men, sounding like he already suspected the answer.

The two men looked at each other like two children caught doing something that their parents told them not to do.

"You sent a man out and you didn't vet him?" the third angel roared. "Do you understand the ramifications of your actions?"

"We will deal with this oversight later. Right now, we need to find this spy and stop him before he sets off one of these devices," Camael said, rubbing his eyes with one hand. "If even one of those things goes off in the wrong place, it could render our wall useless and ruin our chances of victory."

A peal of thunder shook the building.

"I don't remember any storm clouds when I was riding in." Honora moved to the window. She could see the moon shining with very few clouds in the sky.

"I don't think that was thunder." Cathetel glanced up from the two men suddenly. "The noise came from the direction we sent Daziar, Amara, and Malach."

The group sprang into action suddenly. Everyone ran down the stairs and outside. As soon as each angel cleared the threshold of the building, they took flight. Honora and the two men followed as quickly as they could but lost track of the three angels. She hoped her friends were safe.

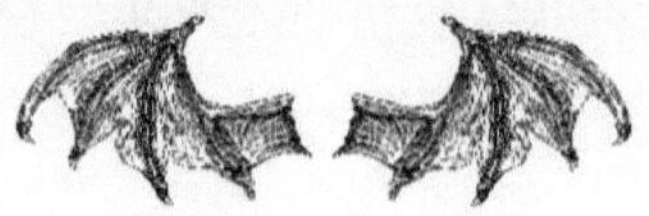

The man turned to Malach. "I was on wall duty and saw you and your companions enter the barracks. I came to investigate and realized you found a device that the spy had set."

"How did you know about the device?" Amara narrowed her eyes. "That information hasn't been spread past the angels and those chosen to search."

"Well, uh, as I said, I was on duty looking for the devices." The guard was floundering, and no one believed him. "I was sent by the angels to search."

Malach, Reckoning said with some urgency, *this man is a Nephilim!*

A what? Malach asked.

A descendant of a demon, Reckoning replied. *He must be the spy we are looking for.*

I understand, Malach replied. *And I agree with you and Skie, but just so we're clear, I'm technically a nephilim, which means not all of them are evil.*

Yes, I know, but he has a firearm in his belt, Reckoning warned.

The man reached down to his belt where the handle of a firearm was protruding.

"Down!" Malach shouted as the man pulled out the firearm and aimed it at them.

Malach pushed Amara to one side and Daziar jumped the other way. The man followed Daziar with the gun, waiting for him to come to a stop to get a clear shot. He might have succeeded except for Amara's knife, which seemed to sprout out of his shoulder. He jerked with the pain and impact of the weapon and his shot went wide.

I told you so, Reckoning gloated.

Not now, Malach retorted sourly, pushing himself to his feet.

The man snarled when he saw Malach and reached with his good hand for a second handle on his belt. Malach vaulted over the bed he was behind and rushed the man. He tackled him about the time he got the firearm up. The impacted dislodged the firearm from his hand and it skittered away out of the reach of the man.

The man punched Malach in the face, pushing him off. He didn't go for the firearm, however, but instead ran for one of the lit torches on the wall. Skie attacked, latching onto the man's calf as he ran. The man let out a pained yell, but to his credit, he kept his footing and lashed out with his free leg, kicking Skie in the head. She let go, dazed from the impact, and the man reached the torch, pulling it from the sconce. Malach realized he was heading for the device to set it off.

Daziar and Amara were finally gaining their feet and though they weren't directly between the man and the device they were much closer than Malach was.

"Daz, stop him!" Malach pointing at the man.

Daziar placed himself in the man's way, drawing his sword as he did. The man didn't stop but barreled into Daziar, taking Daziar's thrust directly in his gut. The impact pushed Daziar out of the way and the man twisted, pulling Daziar's sword from his grasp. With the sword still embedded in the nephilim's stomach, he stumbled forward. A second of Amara's throwing knives hit the man in his neck. He lurched to the side but didn't fall. He took the last couple of steps to the device and lit the fuse.

"Run!" Malach didn't wait to see if the others heeded his warning but took off toward the door.

Amara was directly on his heels. He thought she might have started running before he said anything, He didn't blame her. Skie made it through the door ahead of the two of them. Malach stopped just before the door and ushered Amara through. He glanced back and spotted Daziar, halfway to the door, his bulk slowing him down. He must have twisted or sprained his ankle too. He was limping on his left a leg a little. As Malach watched, the sparks from the fuse disappeared inside the device and his heart sank, there was no time left to go back for Daziar. It was over. He turned once again and ran through the door. He heard Daziar's shuffling footsteps reach the door only moments after, and he was reassured his friend would make it out. Daz's injury must not have been as severe as he thought. They were going to—

The world erupted in fire.

The explosion lifted Malach from his feet. The heat seared the skin on his exposed neck, leaving it raw and tender. He hit the ground a moment later, a good twenty or so feet beyond where he had left the ground. He rolled onto his back soothing the burns with the snow on the ground. He looked back at where the building used to be but was forced to cover his head as some of the rubble came raining down on him.

When it stopped raining debris, he looked up again. Amara was just getting up on his right. She looked a little shook up but didn't seem hurt. He searched for Daziar, praying his friend had made it out before the device blew up. He spotted a mass of furs moving a little to his left, closer to the building. Malach got up on shaky legs and walked toward the lump. He knelt next to it and turned it over. It was Daziar. Skie came up to them and licked Daziar's face.

"Huh? What happened?" Daziar's voice was muffled, and Malach became aware of a ringing in his own ears.

"You decided that staying closer to the explosive would give you a longer flight time," Malach said smiling. "I believe you're alright, except for a few burns."

Daziar did have a couple of burns on the parts of skin that had been exposed and some of his hair on his head had been burned away. Although, for the most part, the heavy furs that he wore to keep him warm took the brunt of the explosion. He would have to replace those, though. A slight whistling sound made Malach look up. He sidestepped as one more piece of debris hurtled toward his face. Daziar's sword, blackened from the explosion, landed point down between Daziar and Malach.

"Phew," Daziar sighed. "That was close."

"Malach!" Amara called, worry in her voice.

"Don't tell me that rat survived the explosion," Daziar moaned as they both looked at Amara.

She was pointing at where the building had been. The explosion didn't simply take out the building but had also taken a large chunk of the wall. Surprisingly enough, the top of the wall was still mostly intact, but there was a large hole where the explosion had pushed out the stone. He could see the forest surrounding the city. Cathetel, Camael, and Barachiel landed in front of them, facing the opening in the wall.

"This is not good," Cathetel said and turned to the three. "How could you allow this to happen?"

"Yeah, we're fine. Thanks for asking," Daziar remarked as Malach helped him to his feet.

Cathetel fumed, but Camael put a hand on his shoulder to calm him. The seething angel shrugged off his brother's hand, turned, and walked away from the group. Camael watched him go and turned back to them, his face a picture of tranquil determination.

"What happened?" Camael asked, crossing his arms in front of him like a teacher disappointed with his pupils.

Malach recounted how the group had found one of the devices but then had to fight the spy for it. He told him how they had tried to stop the man from setting it off, but in the end, had failed. He hung his head, knowing they should have done better.

"You did your best, Malach," Camael told him. "Don't dwell too long on what could have been. We need to figure out a way to mitigate the damage, or this could be this city's undoing."

Honora and two men came running up.

"Thank God you are alright," Honora said seeing her friends in one piece.

"Daziar could use a little patching up," Malach said without preamble. "He has some pretty bad burns."

"My sword," Daziar said despondently, reaching for it.

"Don't worry," Honora soothed. "It will clean up. I'm more worried about the burns you sustained."

"But the crossguard is bent and the leather on the pommel has been burned away," Daziar complained.

"Yes, but your neck is red as a tomato and you're starting to blister," Honora informed the distraught Daziar.

Malach left Daziar in Honora's hands. He knew his friend would eventually see reason, and then they would repair his sword later. He needed to help the angels plan for the quick repair of the city wall. The crater in the wall that had been created by the blast would be the city's downfall if it wasn't properly repaired and defended.

Malach walked up to the angels. They were deep in conversation, and he didn't want to interrupt.

". . .we need to evacuate the city and fall back to the main camp." Cathetel was saying.

"We need to talk about the fact that the spy was a nephilim," Malach told them.

Cathetel waved his hand dismissively. "The demons have procreated with humans since the beginning of the war."

"Yes, but this one made it past our defenses," Ariel pointed out. "Usually we have been able to sense them if they have gotten close and deduce if they were a threat. However, I didn't sense anything when entering the city, nor any time after that."

"Perhaps you have become lax in your attention to detail during your time with your human harlot," Barachiel spat.

Malach gritted his teeth and swung Reckoning's blade, stopping it a faction of an inch from Barachiel's throat. "You will take that back or you will lose your head."

"You think the bastard child of an unholy union could take my head?" Barachiel didn't move an inch, but something about his calm demeanor made Malach doubt he could harm the angel.

"Enough," Ariel commanded. "Malach, put your weapon down. And Barachiel, no matter our differences, we need to work together to stop the Demon Army."

Despite Ariel's words, Malach still held Reckoning in place.

Malach, as much as I agree that Barachiel should be punished for his callous words, your father is correct. We need to work together, Reckoning reasoned.

Malach ground his teeth together and growled. He fought his instincts and let his weapon drop.

"Now that everyone knows their place-"

Barachiel was interrupted by Malach's fist colliding with his jaw. He stumbled away, managing to stay on his feet, and turned just in time to catch Malach's boot. Blood spewed from his broken nose.

Ariel grabbed Malach and hauled him off the angel. "Son, he's not worth it, and he's not our problem right now."

Barachiel righted himself, holding his nose.

Camael was there to stop him from lunging at Malach.

"Keep your mutt under control," Barachiel yelled angrily at Ariel.

"Enough," Eloa shouted from above the group. She landed between the two combatants. "Barachiel, you are needed back at command. Just as we were told, there is a large enemy force coming toward us, and you are needed to organize the troops and inform them of what's happening."

"With the damage to the wall, against a much larger force, I don't believe defense is feasible," Cathetel reiterated.

"But what about any refugees or recruits that haven't made it to the city yet?" Ariel asked. "If we abandon the city now, they will be caught and most likely killed when they arrive."

"We will send out messengers to tell people of the change," Camael moved to his brother's side.

"I think we ought to try and defend the city." Elzrod agreed with Ariel. "We don't know when the other demon contingency will arrive, and we don't know their strength. I think we might just have enough time to patch this wall well enough to defend the city."

"We barely have any troops." Barachiel shook his head. "If the wall falls, the city falls. We might lose more people that we stand to gain from refugees and recruits."

"Why don't we evacuate those who can't fight?" Malach spoke up.

Barachiel glared at him as if he wanted to spit some scathing remark, but he held his tongue.

"Please, son," Ariel said with a pointed glance at Barachiel, "finish your thought. You are as much a part of this as the rest of us."

"Well, I thought that we might evacuate anyone who couldn't fight," Malach repeated. "They could wait a few miles northeast of the city, which would put them in the forest and out of harm's way. Then, if we did have to retreat and give up the city, we wouldn't have to worry about the refugees."

"Where would we send them to?" Cathetel asked. "Most of the people that are here haven't been vetted. I don't think we should rule out the possibility of more than one spy amongst our ranks."

"Then we go to Brightwood. It wouldn't be too much farther to send them to the main camp once they are vetted," Malach replied, "and we can still send out messengers if we are forced to retreat."

"Sounds like a well thought out plan," Eloa said, nodding thoughtfully.

In the end, all but Cathetel and Barachiel agreed with the plan. Malach suspected that Barachiel didn't agree just to spite him and Ariel, but he couldn't prove it. They would fortify the wall as best they could in the time they had. The hole was not visible from the main road, where Eloa told them the Demon Army was advancing. It was possible they could get by for a while without the enemy knowing about it. They set to work anyone they could spare to repair that part of the wall.

The search teams found three more of the large explosive devices hidden in various buildings next to the wall. That brought them to a total of five devices: four they controlled and one that had detonated. They also found one set of smaller explosive devices that had been set into the wall. It would have gone unnoticed, except for the series of fuses that connected them. All a person had to do was set the fuse, and it would detonate the devices from top to bottom, destroying that section of the wall. Malach thought it might have worked better than the larger explosive devices.

Daziar had the idea to bury them a little way out from the gate. They should be able to set them off with flaming arrows, turning the enemy's devices against them. He was charged with taking a team out to do just that. By the end of that day, most of the small group that had come with Malach hadn't slept but they were most of the way through the repairs to the wall and much better prepared for the Demon Army.

They sent out a rider to get the people who had been left behind on the road. They arrived just after dark and many of the men left for time to reunite with their loved ones or to give the bad news of a death to others. There were a lot of tears either way. Malach slipped away from the group and found his way to the barracks. Inside, he stripped off his furs and the few pieces of leather armor given to him by the guard. He didn't know how the room was heated, but he was grateful for it. An empty bunk waited for him and he flopped down on it, every muscle in his body screaming for rest. He was asleep within seconds.

Chapter 4

Malach awoke to Reckoning mentally yelling at him. *What's wrong?*

The enemy is at our gates! Urgency was evident in his voice. *They have arrived earlier than planned and you are needed.*

How long have I been asleep? He asked groggily, pulling on his pants.

A few hours, Reckoning replied. *Daziar will not be able to join you for this battle. His burns were worse than we had previously thought. Honora is looking after him, but they are already evacuating with the rest of the refugees.*

I understand. Malach finished pulling on his clothes and proceeded to strap on his equipment. He snatched up his bow and clipped his quiver of arrows to his belt. He would be one of the archers to light the explosives that they had buried, provided the enemy hadn't found them.

He hustled out of the barrack, Skie hard on his heels, as always, and joined a few of the men who were headed to the wall. No one spoke. He could tell they were all nervous, and he was too. None of them had ever been in a full-on battle. Even the fight on their way to the city was only a small skirmish. This would be, hopefully, several days of war, unless the Demon Army found the destroyed portion wall. Then it would be over quickly.

Malach took the stairs to the top of the wall two at a time. When he made it up and looked out, his breath caught in his throat. His eyes were drawn to the five demons who were commanding the troops. Four of them were either standing or flying well behind the front lines, but one stood in front of the army. He was several paces ahead of the front line, although many paces outside of bow range. With them were a few thousand troops.

Malach knew that, including the small band they had brought to the city, they numbered about eight hundred. If this army found the break in their wall, there was no doubt in Malach's mind that the demons would win this battle. The only way that they had a chance was to pepper the enemy from the relative safety of the walls.

Malach found the angels, and he moved through the troops toward them, taking his place beside Elzrod. Amara was already there with her bow, quiver, and a full complement of throwing and fighting knives. They would try and keep all of the attention on the main gate. They had set up their archers to push any troops on the edge of the main force back toward the gate, and they had men stationed at the breach in the wall to watch for any scouts and kill them before they could report back.

The demon in front of the mainline walked forward even farther. It felt like an eternity, watching the huge demon's slow steps. It was an impressive and intimidating sight. It walked almost all the way up to the wall, and it was all that Malach could do not to laugh as the demon took his final step, placing his right foot almost directly on the top of one of the explosives they had buried. The arrogance of the demon would soon be its downfall. Malach pulled one of the specially prepared arrows out of a quiver that was set up on the wall and readied it to be ignited and fired.

"Surrender and we will show mercy to the humans!" The demon bellowed.

"We will never bow to you, Hellspawn!" Barachiel shouted back, drawing the demon's attention to him.

The troops supported his sentiment with a war shout, and Malach took his chance to light the arrow and let it fly.

The demon calmly stepped back allowing the arrow to hit the ground just short of him. "If that is the best your archers can do, then you are more foolish than I thought."

Malach held his breath as the lit fuse slowly was eaten away and disappeared into the ground.

"You and all in this city will die at the hands of the Army of Satan!" the demon called again.

Malach waited for the imminent explosion. None was forthcoming and he wondered if something had gone wrong.

"We will kill your men, take your children, and exploit your wom-"

BOOM!

The demon, more accurately, half of the demon, went flying. Not by its own power, for only one wing was still intact, but propelled by the force of the explosion. What was left of the demon rained down on the earth between the army and the wall of the city.

No one moved.

There was absolute silence as both sides were shocked by the sudden violence and noise. The silence lasted only a few moments, however, before the four remaining demons started shouting for vengeance and propelled the army forward. The collective war cry made the hairs on Malach's arms and neck stand up on end.

"And so it begins," Elzrod muttered and bowed his head.

Malach, Amara, and the other archers who had been hand-picked, lit each of their arrows and fired for the remaining buried explosives. Two of the four arrows made it to their mark lighting the fuses. Both his and another archer's arrow hit some of the front runners setting them alight and dropping them. The momentum of those unfortunate souls took their burning bodies far past the fuses of the devices. All four archers lit new arrows. Malach and Amara took aim for what had originally been Malach's explosive, and the others aimed for the second unlit explosive.

As they fired, the first two explosives detonated. Bodies and pieces of men flew in all directions. Many of the men that weren't killed faltered, their courage all but failing them. Unfortunately, the power of the explosions pushed their next volley of arrows off course, and none of them hit their mark. Getting frustrated, Malach lit his fourth arrow of the day, waiting for his chance to hit the fuse. The enemy archers were now in range, and arrows flew in both directions. He was forced to duck as an arrow bounced off of the wall and flew toward his head, flipping end over end. He stood back up, seeing the other explosive's fuse was lit, and he let his arrow fly, hoping to beat the explosion.

His arrow finally flew true, lighting the fuse only a few moments before the fourth explosive detonated. He turned away, not wanting to add to the horrors he had already witnessed. When he looked up, he took in the battlefield. Now that he was not focused on the explosives, he noticed that some of the men were carrying ladders to lay against the wall. Something large caught his eyes behind the army. A battering ram was slowly being wheeled forward.

The ladders hit the wall, forcing Malach to focus on the matter at hand, and many of the soldiers pulled their swords.

Malach ran up to a ladder meaning to push it off the wall but Ariel stopped him with a hand on his shoulder. "Wait."

Malach didn't understand at first, but as the first enemy soldier's head popped up over the wall, it all became clear. Ariel stabbed the man and shoved the ladder back.

Malach chanced a glance over the parapet and saw the ladder, with a handful of men on it, teeter for just a moment as they worked to push it back against the wall. Unfortunately for them, the body of the top man was hooked on the top rungs and weighed it down on the wrong side.

The ladder toppled and fell. The men who were higher up on the ladders jumped off landing heavily on their fellow soldiers. Those who had not been injured by the ladder or men falling, lifted it once again and set it against the wall. These actions would be repeated hundreds of times over the next few hours.

Twenty or so repetitions of the ladder being placed and Malach pushing it off the wall passed, and the soldiers decided to move it and try a different area. Malach's muscles burned, and he was breathing heavily. However, there was no time to stop and rest. He took his attention off the ladder he had been so focused on and found that not all of their soldiers had been able to push the ladders off. The enemy was on the wall. They hadn't been able to get much of a foothold, but they did have a presence.

Ariel slammed Fury, in the form of a large battle axe, into and through a makeshift barrier the enemy had set in place. Malach ran toward his father to support him, but an enemy soldier climbed over the wall in front of him. He hadn't seen a ladder but didn't have time to wonder about that.

Malach ducked the initial chop of the man's axe and rammed his blade up under the man's armor. He hoisted the soldier up and over the parapet and dropped him off the edge where he had, moments ago, climbed over. Malach looked over the edge and watched as the dead soldier collided with another one climbing a rope. Malach realized that there was a three-pronged hook embedded in the stone next to him, and he hacked at the rope connected to it.

He turned back to see that Skie had made it to his father's side before he had. They had cleared out the enemy and pushed the ladder off the wall. She came running back to him and his father nodded at him. Malach turned back to the battlefield and saw that the ram had been slowly crawling up toward the wall and was now in bow range.

At that instant, he was almost deafened by Elzrod shouting. "Stop the ram! Stop the ram!"

Malach turned his attention away from the men on the ladders and traded Reckoning for his bow. The first volley of arrows killed more than half of the men pushing the ram, and it shuddered to a halt. The demon closest to the ram pushed men toward it and the rest of the troops followed suit. They swarmed it, pushing it along faster than it had been moving before. After the second volley of arrows killed enough men to halt the ram a second time, the enemy changed tactics. A second set of men carrying shields moved in front of those who were pushing.

Malach grabbed Amara's arm, thinking quickly, and shouted over the din of the battle, "shoot for the front shield man and I will shoot the men behind it. If we shoot at the same time, we could kill the man pushing before the shield-bearer can react."

She nodded and nocked another arrow in response.

He took her movements to mean she understood and nocked his arrow. As soon as she fired, he let his arrow loose. Both flew true and had the desired effect. The shield-bearer moved his shield to save himself and the second arrow felled the man behind him.

Malach, through Reckoning, passed their strategy on to Elzrod and he, in turn, passed it on to their archers. Soon they had the ram slowing again, but it wasn't enough. It had covered more than half the distance to the wall in the time that it took to get the word out. Trying to burn it down, he shot the last few of their fire arrows at it. However, it must have been covered in something flame resistant, because as soon as the arrows hit the ram, they extinguished.

Malach turned, searching around him for something to use to stop this thing. If only they had left one of the explosives in reserve for something like this. He watched as the angels took to the sky. They angled toward the ram, but the remaining four demons took flight to cut them off. They intercepted the angels, slamming into them mid-air. They tangled for a moment, cutting and tearing at each other savagely with teeth, claws, and blades. During their struggle, neither demon nor angel could keep themselves in the air and they plummeted toward the ground. They broke off at the last moment, each beating their powerful wings, so they didn't slam into the ground. It was an awe-inspiring sight.

"Stop gawking, son!" Ariel's grabbing Malach's shoulder, startling him out of his reverie. "The angels are giving us a chance to take out the ram."

"How can we do that?"

"You and Amara follow me. I'll explain in a minute." He turned toward the stairs and Malach grabbed Amara's arm, pulling her along without explanation.

"Malach!" She protested, pulling her arm away from him when they had reached the bottom on the stair. "What are you doing? They need everyone at the wall to stop the ram."

"Sorry, Amara," Ariel said. "That was my fault."

"What's this chance you spoke of?" Malach asked.

"Elzrod, is going to continue to command the troops, but you and I will sneak around to the side of the ram where fewer soldiers are guarding the side," Ariel explained. "We should be able to fight our way to the ram and cut the chains holding it in place. If we can do that, they wouldn't be able to use it against us to bring down the gate."

"Where do I come in?" Amara asked without any preamble.

"You need to grab a handful of archers and cover our assault and retreat," Ariel replied.

"Yes, sir," Amara said and ran back up the stairs.

Malach's gaze followed her up the stairs, hoping it wasn't the last time he would see her. He admired her no-nonsense way of taking orders and her calm under the pressures of war. He, on the other hand, was on the brink of panic, knowing that he and his father would be going outside the safety of the wall. He shoved those feelings down and looked back at his father, fighting to maintain his composure.

"Malach," his father looked at him, fire and confidence in his eyes. "You can do this. I wouldn't ask this of you if I thought anything different."

"Thanks," Malach replied, only feeling marginally better.

They headed toward the break in the wall where they could leave the safety of its confines. As they made their way to the breach, they spotted a runner coming from that direction. He recognized Ariel and turned to intercept the pair.

"Sir, there was a band of scouts. . . that found the break." He was breathing hard. "We were able to kill most of them, but one escaped."

"How long ago was that?" Ariel asked.

"Mere moments ago."

"Malach, follow as you can," Ariel was already moving. "I must try and run this man down before he is able to report his findings."

"Go report to Elzrod. He's commanding the troops at the main gate," Malach told the runner and took off after his father.

Malach kept up with his father until they reached the break in the wall. Even without the help of his wings, his father jumped more than halfway up the stairs leading to the top of the wall. Malach watched in wonder for a moment and then started to climb them himself. In the time it took for him to crest the top of the stairs, Ariel was nowhere to be seen. Malach descended the wall with the help of a rope. Once he was safely on the ground, the soldiers lowered Skie down with the same rope. She struggled at first and didn't look comfortable at all but landed on the ground without incident.

Malach moved quickly back toward the main gate, keeping the wall to his left but staying within the tree line. He arrived within sight of the main battle and stopped. He was careful to stay hidden while he waited for his father to group up with him.

He's coming, Malach, Reckoning reported, obviously in contact with Ariel and Fury.

Sure enough, his father appeared beside him, as if out of nowhere. Malach jumped slightly, even with the warning from Reckoning. Skie didn't visibly react, and Malach was a little annoyed. He looked at his father, the man hadn't even broken a sweat. He had to remind himself that his father wasn't a man, but an angel. Maybe they didn't sweat at all? But that was a question for another time.

"I didn't catch the scout," his father reported. "He had too much of a lead on me. We need to destroy the ram still or we will be fighting this battle on two fronts and we don't have the manpower for that."

"What's the plan then?" Malach asked.

"Do you see the area where the troops are waiting to take over pushing the ram?" His father asked, pointing to a group of men that didn't have the weapons drawn.

"Yes."

"That's our point of attack," he said, his voice carrying confidence that Malach didn't feel at all. "We should be able to get past them and to the ram. Once there, you cut the back chain and I'll cut the front. Reckoning will be able to cut through that chain with little resistance."

Ariel pulled Fury from his scabbard and the weapon changed to a large battle axe. It was larger than most men could wield with two hands, but Ariel lifted it with a single hand.

"Stay behind me until we hit that group, and then we will split off."

Malach nodded his understanding and they charged.

No battle cry was uttered, and the sounds of war covered what noise they did make. The enemy, their backs to them, never saw Ariel's axe coming. His first swing was timed perfectly, killing a handful of men in one blow, sending several of them flying. Then, stopping the axe and turning it, Ariel brought it back across, killing several more men. The group scattered in all directions fearing the angel's wrath.

Malach took his chance to strike out on his own. Splitting off toward the back of the ram, he used Reckoning with the grace that only hundreds of hours of practice could yield. Unlike his father, he didn't kill multiple opponents with a single swing. He opted for more finesse to his movements.

He would take on one or two opponents at a time, killing them quickly, before more men could muster a force against him. Skie covered his back, biting and lunging at anyone who got close. He kept his feet and weapon moving, fighting his way to the ram surprisingly easily. He cut through one of the men pushing the ram and slid the second blade into the back of the man guarding him. From there, he climbed up onto the frame of the ram and swung one of his blades at the chain. Reckoning cut right through the chain as though he was cutting through fat.

Time to leave! Malach turned and found that his father was cutting through the front chain.

The length of the ram, previously suspended, came slamming down on the other side of the framing, causing the whole thing to tilt. Malach lost his balance. Instinctively, he reached out for something to grab ahold of and caught himself on one of the timbers, but his momentum swung him around, his back to the enemy.

One of the enemy troops saw the opening and swung for Malach's legs. There was no way that Malach was going to be able to block or jump the blade and he knew it was over for him. The blow never stuck though. The man's blade fell mid-swing, lacking the power to finish the blow. An arrow protruded from the soldiers back. Malach looked up at the wall and threw a quick salute to whichever archer had just saved his life, then concentrated on his escape.

Skie held her ground leaving enough room for him to land safely. As he landed, he cut at a man's knee, toppling him. Malach put a boot in the man's face as he climbed over him, blocking attacks and fighting his way out. Skie fell in behind him, as she had during their assault. They attracted some attention with their assault on the ram, and try as the archers might, they couldn't keep all of the enemies off of them.

Malach and Ariel formed up close to where they had separated. Ariel carved a path as Malach and Skie fought off the enemies that tried to attack them from behind. Despite the battle, Malach found he enjoyed fighting beside his father. It felt right somehow. Like this had been how he was meant to fight. Ariel grabbed Malach's shoulder, and he knew instinctively that they had broken through. It was time to make their escape. He kicked the man he had been swapping blows with, pushing him back against two other men. It gave Malach the space he needed to run.

As he turned, he caught a glimpse one of the demons fighting with Barachiel. It dealt him a terrible blow and Barachiel fell from the sky. He was beating his single functioning wing, trying to fly toward the wall but he was losing altitude fast. Malach was forced to turn his attention ahead of him so he didn't run into a tree as they entered the forest.

He paused for a moment, turning back to witness the fate of the angel. Barachiel impacted the top of the wall, skipping like a stone and disappeared on the other side of the wall from Malach. He looked back at the demon, and it was already on an intercept course with him and Ariel.

"Dad!" Malach turned and shouted above the din of war. "Demon!"

His father turned around, taking in the situation, He pushed Malach out of the way, throwing him clear of the ensuing collision. Malach's landing was less than graceful, but he managed to roll to his feet quickly. He looked on as the demon slammed into his father, picking him up off the ground and flying away with him.

"Get behind the wall!" His father shouted as he was carried away.

Malach did not do as he was told. Instead, he ran along underneath the demon and his father, trying to keep track of them. He caught glimpses of the fight through the canopy of trees. From what he could gather, the demon tried to take Ariel far up into the sky and drop him. However, the next break in the canopy revealed that Ariel was able to grab ahold of one of the demon's ankles. He must have changed Fury into a smaller, more agile weapon, since Malach couldn't see the large battle axe anymore. The trees blocked his view once again, and he ran on.

Malach burst through the trees into a clearing peering up once again. His father had climbed up the demon and was trying to bring it down. He lost sight of them as they lost altitude, plummeting toward the trees ahead of him. Branches cracked and snapped loudly as the two titans broke through the boughs and the ground shook with their impact. He reached the crash site and stopped to take in the destruction they had caused. There was a clear path of broken limbs and dented trees leading to a trough where the two hit the ground. Following it quickly, Malach found them on the ground, still duking it out. Ariel was on top of the demon, grappling with it. Their weapons had been lost somewhere amongst their wake of destruction. Malach changed Reckoning into a battle axe, not nearly as large as the one his father had wielded, but large enough for Malach to need two hands to handle it.

He charged, axe raised and ready to swing. His father and the demon looked up and recognition of his intent lit up in both their faces. His father pinned the demon to the ground while it roared in frustration, struggling to get up. Ariel angled his body out of the way as Malach's axe came down on the demon's neck. Its roar was cut short as the axe separated its head from its shoulders.

Ariel fell back from the demon's still twitching body, exhausted. He was sweating now, which answered Malach's earlier question. He looked down at the now headless monster in front of him. They had been able to kill two demons that day. Even if they lost this battle and had to retreat, at least there were two less of those things in the world.

"Are you alright?" Malach reached out a hand to help his father up, breathing heavily himself.

"Yes," he replied, taking the proffered hand. "Thanks, I'm not sure how that would have turned out if you hadn't helped. I'm at a bit of a disadvantage without my wings."

"No problem. Let's get back behind the wall and see how the rest of the war is faring."

They found Fury and the demon's weapon, which wasn't another hostage Angel Blade, thankfully. They made their way back to the wall, startling the tense guards at the breach. They quickly let the rope down, and Malach had them hoist Skie up first. Then, he and Ariel scaled the wall with the help of the same rope. Once back inside the safety of the wall, they headed back to the main gate. The din of war was gone, replaced by cheers of victory, only to swiftly die down, allowing the moan of the wounded and dying to be heard.

Malach understood this was not the end of the war. However, they had earned a respite and at least a modicum of fear from the enemy. The opposing army would most likely stop within sight of the walls to regroup for the next push. The angels and Elzrod were nowhere to be seen, but they were told where they could find them.

Ariel and Malach found them gathered around a table in a makeshift medical ward. Barachiel lay on the table, still alive, but fading fast. Ariel clasped arms with the other three angels, and they nodded to Malach. Malach got the impression they didn't think as much of him, since he was only half-angel. Or it could just be that they had fought together since the beginning of time and he was simply a newcomer.

Ariel walked up to the table and Barachiel clasped his arm weakly. Malach remained in the background out of respect. Honora and some of the other medics bustled around the room, tending to the rest of the wounded. The fact that Barachiel was so grievously wounded and that none of the medics were working on him meant he wasn't long for this world.

"Ariel," Barachiel addressed him, "I was wrong to say what I did."

"Don't worry about that now," Ariel replied gracefully. "You can apologize once you're through this."

"We both know I'm not making it through this," Barachiel replied soberly. "I felt the death pulse of the demon. Did you get the hellspawn?"

"Malach did," Ariel admitted.

"Death pulse?" Amara muttered from behind Malach.

He hadn't heard her walk up but wasn't startled this time. He shook his head to indicate he didn't know what they were talking about.

"You and Serilda did well with that boy," Barachiel told him. "I wish sometimes that I had dared to do what you two did. Now, I'll never experience that. My jealously soured my heart against you."

"Thank you," Ariel replied. "That means a lot."

"Eloa." Barachiel turned to her. "You are officially in charge of the city. If you can't hold the wall, don't delay long. Save as many souls as you can."

"I won't fail you," Eloa told him, bowing her head.

He caught her arm before she backed away. "Don't fail them."

Barachiel looked past the angels to where Malach was standing.

Ariel motioned him forward.

"Malach," Barachiel addressed him as he moved forward. "I judged you before as I would any nephilim, an abomination and an affront to creation. Please, continue to prove me wrong."

Malach didn't know what to say. He knew that was a big step for the angel to admit that, but he couldn't help but be angry at him for his judgment.

He stepped back from the dying angel and walked out of the room.

Amara followed. "Malach, are you alright?"

"I spent all of my life hiding what I was for this very reason," Malach snapped. "I get judged for *what* I am before they ever see *who* I am. I didn't expect it to come from an angel."

"I'm sorry," Amara said softly.

"Nothing any of us can do about it," Malach replied tersely. "But thanks."

They found a bench and sat for a while in silence before the angels and Elzrod came out of the medical ward.

"Barachiel is dead," Elzrod declared.

There was a moment of silence following Elzrod's declaration.

"We need to get a plan of defense together," Eloa said after the moment had passed.

"Before we get into that," Amara broke in, "what is the death pulse that Barachiel talked about?"

"Angels and demons give off a pulse when they die that other angels and demons can sense," Camael replied.

"Strangely though, I can't feel them," Malach added.

"Most likely because you are only half angel," Ariel said, then turned back toward Elzrod. "And yes, we did kill a second demon, and that kill should also be credited to Malach."

"My father did most of the work," Malach explained, not wanting to take all the glory. "I simply struck the final blow."

"Either way, you two have given us the advantage," Cathetel said, crossing his arms. "For the first time in this battle, we have a chance at winning."

"Not to disappoint you, but our men told us that they didn't kill one of the scouts at the break in the wall," Ariel replied with a scowl. "I failed to hunt the scout down before he returned to the Demon Army."

Malach had almost forgotten about that.

"We have to assume that they will attack there as well as the main gate," Ariel said.

"That was an unfortunate inevitability," Elzrod mused, pursing his lips together. "Ariel, since you are grounded, you, Malach, and Cathetel should defend the break in the wall. Camael, Eloa, and I will hold the main gate. The angels will be able to fly between each site depending on what is needed." He turned to Eloa. "Assuming that's alright with you, since you are in charge of the city's defenses."

Eloa only nodded.

"Where do you want me?" Amara asked, seeming to feel left out.

"You can go wherever you would like," Elzrod replied.

"Right now, I think we ought to get some sleep. The sun will be coming up soon and they might decide to attack at sunrise," Camael said sagely.

"Or they might wait until tomorrow night." Ariel pointed out. "Just like tonight."

"It is possible. We'll have the troops sleeping in three shifts," Eloa told them, taking charge. "We'll also have scouts in the woods surrounding the city, so we'll know as soon as they start to move. Cathetel and Camael," she gestured to the brothers, "you two will take the first watch on the wall. Ariel and Malach," she turned their direction next, "you two will be on the dawn shift. Elzrod and I will take the third watch. Now, everyone who isn't on the first shift go, get some sleep."

The group dispersed, and Cathetel and Camael headed toward to wall. Amara took a few fast steps and fell into step with Malach as they headed toward the barracks. They were being housed in an overflow barracks, and since Honora had been conscripted to the medical ward, Amara found herself alone most of the time in the female barracks.

"Can you come with me to the other barracks for a moment before going to sleep?" Amara asked.

"Umm, sure. Why?" Malach asked. He surprised himself at how nervous he was all of a sudden.

"I need to understand some things about what's going on and about the angels and demons. Remember I only learned they still existed a few weeks ago."

"Yeah, I can, but we will have to be quick," Malach replied. "We both need some sleep. Why haven't you asked before now?"

"I don't know. It never seemed to be the right time before. Now we are in a war against these demons, and I don't have any clue how to react to that or fight them."

Malach followed Amara inside the barracks. It was similar to the barracks he was staying in. There were rows of beds with chests at the bottom for equipment and clothing. Amara sat down on one of the beds beckoning for Malach to sit as well. He decided to sit on the bed opposite her.

"What did you want to know?" Malach asked.

"Back there with the angels, I realized how little I knew about the angels and demons and how little I know about you."

"Well, I'll answer anything I can," Malach replied.

"How much of their power did you gain from your father?" Amara's gaze dropped slightly as if she was thinking.

Malach told her about the things that came with his lineage; his extra strength, quick healing, and the ability to wield an Angel Blade.

"Your height," Amara said suddenly, snapping her head back up to look at him.

"Huh?" Malach asked.

"Your height," she repeated. "You're taller than almost anyone I know, but the angels are even taller, so it stands to reason you got a little of your father's height. The nephilim we ran into was about the same height as you."

"Oh, yeah, I guess that could be something I got from him," Malach responded, he hadn't ever thought of that. He was just the height he was.

"So. . ." Amara started but let her voice trail off.

"So what?" Malach prompted.

"No, nothing," she said, her cheeks growing red. "Never mind."

"No, really, what were you going to say?" Malach asked, growing curious.

"Well, I was wondering," Amara started looking at the floor.

I've never seen her so awkward. Malach thought in the silence.

"Can you have children?" she finally asked. She said it quickly as if she was just trying to get it out before she changed her mind again.

"Ha!" Malach laughed. He couldn't help it. It was such an unexpected and absurd question to him. "I'm sorry," he said once he had stopped laughing. "I didn't expect that question. Of course, I can have children. As far as I know, I am the only half-angel, but there have been many half-demons through the years, and they had no issues procreating, so I assume I won't have any issues either."

"I just had the question pop into my head, so I needed the answer to settle my mind," she explained quickly without looking at him. "Did you really not know that your father was an angel when you were growing up? I mean, his height alone would raise questions, and how did he hide his wings?"

"I didn't realize he was an angel, probably because I was so young," Malach replied, trying to remember all the times he was with his father. "As far as the wings, I don't remember ever seeing him without something covering his back. Maybe that's why he and my mother decided to live in the mountains where it's colder. He would have had more of an excuse to wear heavy furs, which would hide his wings easier."

"That makes sense, but what about everyone else?" Amara asked, nodding. "You might not have realized, but why didn't anyone else?"

"I think people tend to see what they want to see," Malach replied. "As long as my father didn't give them a solid reason to believe he was an angel, they would have justified his height however they wanted to."

"Huh." Amara glanced down again. "That makes sense. When I was taught how to steal and infiltrate buildings, I was taught that if I were to make a noise, to stay out of sight and try to give someone a reason to think the noise was something else. Like placing something on the floor for them to find or something along those lines. People will make their own connections between the noise and the object, even if that object would never make that noise."

"Exactly," Malach affirmed. "I think that's how my father was able to hide in plain sight."

"Well, I think that covers all of my questions," Amara replied. "Oh, one last thing. I heard that angels and demons can somewhat change their appearance. How does that work?"

"I'm not entirely sure," Malach replied truthfully. "The way it was explained to me is they can change certain things about themselves, but they can't change their nature. The only angels who can fully change their appearance are the Arch Angels and Satan himself. The rest can change some things, but they still have to wear a cloak or something that will hide their appearance."

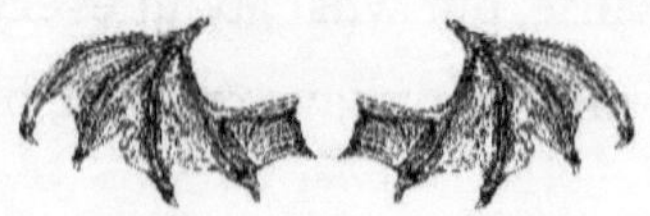

Amara said goodnight to Malach and watched him leave, his tall form receding down the street until he disappeared into his barracks. She couldn't stop thinking back on her trip from Caister to Newaught. The strange man that had forced her into an alliance with him and then paid her in advance. She hadn't seen him again, but now that she knew more about angels and demons, she was almost certain that he had been a demon. She knew in her heart that that alliance would come back to haunt her, even as she hoped that she would never see that demon again. Maybe he would be killed in the war by some angel's—or man's—hand, maybe even by Malach. Somehow, she suspected that she would not be so lucky.

She laid down on the bed with thoughts of the battle that day swirling in her mind. Somehow killing men in a war didn't seem to affect her as much as when she was forced to kill the assassin or any other times she had been faced with the dead. Maybe it was the fact she didn't have to be up-close and personal, letting the arrows do her killing for her. With that thought, she drifted off into a fitful sleep.

Chapter 5

Amara was awakened by Malach gently shaking her. She was happy to see him, his face a welcome sight. At first, she thought she was still dreaming, his dark, deep eyes staring down at her. She would like to kiss him, to feel his lips against hers.

"Amara!" Malach grumbled shaking her the rest of the way to consciousness.

He was real.

She berated herself for such careless thoughts. She couldn't get involved with him. First of all, he would never want to be with her, a thief. Second, even if he wanted to, he wouldn't. He had to find his mother and fight this war. War was no time for feelings, much less love and romance.

She sat up in bed pulling the covers off of herself and grabbing her armor and weapons. Malach had once again turned away from her, embarrassed at her clothing. It's not like she was naked or anything. She always wore her form-fitting shirt and shorts. In Caister, it was the only thing she had worn on a day-to-day basis. Malach had seen her in it before and every time he acted like she was stripping in front of him, like she was naked. Maybe he simply didn't find her attractive. Maybe he couldn't stand the sight of her. He had always stayed fully covered to the point he would have a shirt on, even inside, when the building was stifling with the heat of a fire.

She pushed the thoughts aside. She didn't have time to dwell on them anyway. Malach was either coming to get her for the shift on the wall or because they were under attack. Either of which she needed to hurry for.

"What did you come get me for?" She asked as she finished tying the leather armor in place.

"It's our shift," he said over his shoulder.

"I have my armor on." She rolled her eyes.

Malach turned around smiling at her. "So far, no attack, and all of the city has finished evacuating. They've set up a temporary camp a couple of miles from the city, toward Brightwood."

"Hopefully, they won't have to make that journey," Amara said, purposefully not smiling at him as she brushed past.

"Umm, you alright?" Malach followed her out of the barracks.

"Fine." Amara walked briskly away, not waiting to see if he could keep up.

"Alright," Malach said, seemingly unconvinced but pressing on anyway. "Daziar is going to join us on the wall for our shift, though he has promised Honora that, if the fighting starts, he will fall back to the rear of the army and only fight if necessary."

"I doubt that will happen."

"Yeah, my thoughts exactly." He finally caught up with her quick steps, although his long legs took one step for every two of hers and fell in beside her.

The silence grew awkward, but Amara let it hang on them until they arrived at the broken section of the wall. Malach hadn't told her where they would be spending their shift, and she just assumed that they would be at the main gate. He made it up the stairs first and hailed his father and Daziar. They turned and greeted the two of them. Amara replied to their greeting cordially and walked to their other side putting them between Malach and herself.

She didn't know why she was so bothered with Malach not looking at her. They weren't courting. They weren't even talking about it. How could they in the middle of a war? But it bothered her, nonetheless. Maybe he wasn't attracted to her at all. Maybe they were simply friends and that's all they would be. However, she couldn't help but be attracted to him. Maybe that's what bothered her so much. She had had boys in the past try to make advances on her, but she easily turned them down. Now the young man that she was attracted to seemed to find her very unattractive.

Well, if he doesn't want to even look at me, then I won't look at him either. She folded her arms in front of her.

"What's wrong with Amara?" She overheard Daziar ask Malach.

"I'm not sure," Malach replied softly, leaning in conspiratorially. "Maybe she woke up on the wrong side of the bed? I've never seen her act like this. She's usually very levelheaded and in good spirits."

"What did you do to get her so upset?"

At least one of them has a brain, Amara thought ruefully.

"I don't know." He sounded sincere. Maybe he didn't know, but that didn't make it any better. "I woke her up for the shift. Maybe she needs more sleep?"

"Girls." Daziar shook his head. "We'll never understand them."

Of course you won't, Amara thought to herself. *That would require you to try and understand nuance and emotions.*

"Wait, what are you doing here?" Malach asked Daziar. "Weren't you going to leave with the refugees and Honora?"

"Honora said my burns weren't life-threatening and cleared me for battle."

Amara had a hard time believing that. Daziar's neck was still badly blistered and an angry red color.

Malach stared at his friend, apparently having similar thoughts.

"Fine, I snuck away. She probably didn't even know I was missing until I arrived at the wall."

Malach just shook his head. "She's going to kill you."

Daziar just shrugged.

The morning sun peeked over the tree line to the left. The landscape in front of them slowly changed from a world of shadows and uncertainty to one of illumination and confidence. From the vantage point of the broken part of the wall, Amara could hardly believe they had fought a desperate battle just a few hours before.

Everything now appeared peaceful and happy. She could almost pretend there wasn't a Demon Army camped just a short hike down the road.

A runner came from the main gate. He mounted the stairs and reported to his captain. They talked briefly, and then the runner took off again toward the command post. The Captain made his way over to Ariel and spoke with him. Amara strained to hear what they were saying.

"The army is on the move," the Captain told Ariel. "Although, it appears that their entire army is moving toward the main gate, not the damaged section."

"It's a ruse," Ariel replied quickly. "They would not let an easy entry like this one go unexploited."

"My thoughts exactly." the Captain nodded. "I told the messenger to take word to Eloa to let her know that we will stay on our guard here but to send word if we are needed elsewhere."

"Very good. Be ready for anything."

The word of the attack spread through the ranks, and those who were resting were roused and arrived at the wall in short order. They were all on their guard now, but for a long time, nothing happened. Even after they caught the faint sound of troops marching, there was no apparent attack. Amara was just starting to wonder if the enemy actually knew about the weakness in the wall when a demon was spotted far above their heads. He was well out of arrow range. Cathetel was just arriving at the wall and took to the sky shooting up toward the demon on powerful wings. The angel never made it anywhere near the demon. It peeled off, seeing the angel coming and flew away from the wall.

"That might have been just a reconnaissance flight," Ariel shouted bringing everyone's attention back down to earth. "Stay ready for an attack!"

Amara glanced up one more time and happened to spot something falling from the sky. It was a round object, and it took her far too long to realize was it was.

"Explosive!" She flung herself to the side at the same time the object hit the wall and exploded.

Luckily for them, they were out of range of the explosion; however, others weren't as lucky. The shockwave hit them and shortly after, debris started to fall on their heads. She watched as a splinter of wood the size of her arm impaled a soldier, flinging his now lifeless body backward and off the wall. Daziar had to leap out of the way of a falling timber. It was chaos. The men who had, moments before, been formed in ranks and ready for an attack were now running around like scared rabbits.

"The army is attacking!" Malach warned. He was on one knee behind the parapets, climbing to his feet from where he had taken cover.

He nocked an arrow, the muscles in his arms rippling as he pulled the bowstring back and let his arrow zip away. Amara followed his lead, taking cover behind a parapet and pulling her bow out. It was a good thing she took cover when she did. Seconds later, a volley of arrows flew over the wall and found their targets in the bodies of soldiers who hadn't moved fast enough. Amara saw more than ten men fall around her, arrows protruding from their chests. She spotted Daziar, sword drawn with Skie hard on his heels disappear down the stairs. She assumed he was running to defend the break in the wall.

She moved over beside Malach, feeling a measure of safety next to his strong form. In all reality, she wasn't any safer here than she had been before, but it helped her to get her racing heart under control and to start thinking again. She fired back at the flood of enemies pouring out from the trees and into the gap left by the explosion. The city would be lost soon.

Malach grabbed her hand. "We need to get out of here before our escape is cut off!" He shouted over the din.

He must have been thinking the same thing she was. They headed for the stairs keeping low to not catch an arrow in the chest. Once at the stairs, Amara saw that they were already too late to retreat down them. They continued to run around the top of the wall and soon Malach stood to his full height. They were mostly out of range of the archers on the ground, and if they didn't get ahead of the first wave of enemies, they would be trapped on the top of the wall. No doubt by now the angels had called a full retreat and the troops at the main gate would be escaping even now. Malach could have outpaced her easily and left her to fend for herself, but he didn't.

She stole a quick peek behind her and spotted a few of their troops following behind them; the last few who had made it out of the slaughter. Out of the hundred or so men on top of the wall only this handful had made it out alive.

We aren't out yet, she reminded herself.

As if her thoughts had caused them to manifest, arrows started pelting them from below again as they reach the main gate. They were forced to crouch and slow down. One of the men didn't react fast enough and he caught an arrow in his side. It didn't kill him, however, and two of the other troops helped get him back on his feet. They might be forced to leave him behind soon.

Despite all of this, they made it to the stairs ahead of the enemy. As they descended the stairs, Malach pulled his bow off his back again and nocked an arrow. Amara followed suit. Moments after they had readied themselves, a wave of men turned the corner of a building in front of the small group. The front two men dropped, an arrow sticking out of each. Several of the men behind the first two stumbled over the wounded, and the whole charge was slowed.

Malach darted to his right, down an alley. The rest of the group followed, and they started to make their way to the gate on the far side of the city. If they could make it there before the whole city was overrun, they would be able to escape into the woods. From there, they could form up with the rest of the city.

Malach motioned for Amara to join him at the corner of one of the buildings, "I need you to scout ahead of us. Do you know what direction the gate is?"

She nodded, not trusting herself to speak just yet.

"Good. Keep us moving in that direction, find the safest path through, and don't engage with the enemy unless you have no other choice," he instructed.

She nodded again and moved ahead of the group. She stole down each alleyway, quietly looking around for enemy soldiers. She needed to move quickly to stay ahead of the main enemy force. If they caught up to their small band, they would never make it out alive.

She turned the corner and ran right into three soldiers in Demon Army uniforms. The only thing that saved her was their surprise at her sudden appearance. Her two knives flew into action almost before she realized she was doing it. Two of the soldiers fell with gouges carved in their throats before they even drew their swords. The third blocked her attack with a dirk. His sword came out only a moment after, and she turned aside a stab from his weapon. She ducked, his sword swung only a moment after, and back peddled quickly. A form shot out of the alley she had just passed and slammed the soldier. Malach pulled Reckoning out of the soldier's corpse and picked himself up off the ground.

"You alright?" he asked.

"Yeah. How you get here so fast?" Amara wiped off her knives and sheathed them.

"I heard shouts, so I ran towards you to make sure you were alright."

"Thanks." She smiled at him. "I could have taken him, though."

"I know." He winked at her. "Be careful though. Next time it could be a battalion."

"Yes, sir." She proceeded down the next alley.

She was careful to check around each corner before moving around them. Malach and the group made sure to stay within view of her and she signaled them each time she cleared a corner. They had to be getting close to the back gate of the city. She hoped the enemy troops hadn't been able to get ahead of them. If the commanding officer was even slightly competent, he would have sent a group to control each of the gates in and out of the city.

She peeked her head around the next corner and jumped back. There was a group of soldiers standing in the street. She had jumped back so quickly she hadn't noticed what uniforms they were wearing. She slowly stuck her head around the corner again. The group of soldiers were in Fairdenn uniforms.

She sighed in relief and stepped out, motioning for Malach to follow. She started walking toward the group. One of the soldiers spotted Amara and fumbled with pulling his sword.

"Wait, I'm on your side." Amara put a hand up to stop him.

"How do we know? You're not wearing a uniform." He finally managed to pull his sword.

Malach and the rest of the Fairdenn soldiers rounded the corner and the group in front of Amara let out a collective sigh of relief.

"Sorry." The soldier put his sword away. "We lost our commander and are a little disoriented without him."

"Come with us then," Malach commanded. "We are leaving the city by way of the northern gate. We may have to fight our way out, and the added numbers will help."

"Yes, sir." The soldier saluted.

Amara moved on ahead as the new group joined theirs. With their new numbers, they were able to move with less fear of running into a force they couldn't handle. However, Amara was still cautious. She didn't want to run into an enemy who was even slightly more aware than the first group.

Just when she thought they would never get to the gate, she turned a corner and it was there. She spotted a large number of enemy soldiers milling around the gate and she quickly ducked back behind the building. They could take the enemy, but they would surely lose a few men doing it. Malach and the rest of the soldiers caught up to her.

"I don't think we have a choice," the soldier said after Amara had relayed her thoughts to them.

Malach nodded grimly, understanding what he meant. "But maybe we can bolster our chance at success. Are any of your men archers?"

"Yes, I have two that managed to hold onto their bows, and one who lost his in the retreat," the soldier pointing and then waving the men forward.

"Have two of them fan out to the left and send the other, with Amara and my bow, out to the right. As soon as Amara fires the first arrow, we will charge down the middle."

"Yes, that should confuse them and make them think we have a much larger force than we do," the soldier nodded resolutely.

The troops crept to their positions and made ready to fire. Amara nocked her first arrow but stopped as a war cry echoed through the alley where she was crouching. At first, she was confused as to why Malach, or one of the other men, would attack before she fired an arrow. It all became clear as she spotted Ariel, Daziar, and Skie charging from her left. She quickly let two arrows fly before the three got into her shooting area and charged forward.

Malach and the rest of the group charged out from their alley just ahead of her, and they all converged on the hapless enemy. Ariel had already taken out most of them by the time they had arrived, but the few enemies who had turned to retreat were met with Malach's force and killed quickly.

"It's good to see you three." Malach clasped hands with Ariel then Daziar and ruffled Skie's ears.

Skie walked over to Amara and sat down beside her. She was still a little wary of the big wolf but was starting to get used to having her around, and Skie seemed to like her.

"Good to see you as well," Ariel replied.

"We thought you were goners when the enemy trapped you up on the wall," Daziar said. "How did you escape?"

"Later," Malach promised. "Right now, we have wounded to get out, and we need to regroup with the rest of the city before they get too far ahead of us."

"Right," Amara spoke up. "We need to get out of here before more enemy soldiers respond to the shouting you two did when you charged. I think the whole city might have heard you."

"Well, we didn't know you guys were hidden ready to attack them, or we would have waited just a moment longer." Daziar held up his hands in defense.

"Maybe a battle cry wasn't the best idea," Ariel said sheepishly, "but we thought we would strike fear into them to throw them off balance."

Amara wondered at how human Ariel always acted. Maybe it was his years of pretending to be a human, but most of the time, he didn't act like the rest of the angels.

"Let's get going," Malach said again, a little more insistently.

"I'll round the men up and get the wounded," the soldier in charge said and jogged off to do just that.

Malach and Ariel went to open the portcullis. Amara noticed that the chain had been cut on the wench that raised the gate. It took all of Ariel and Malach's combined strength to lift the portcullis. Even then they were only able to barely get it above their heads. Daziar wedged a fallen sword in the gate so that it would no longer close in the hopes that other soldiers trying to escape would have a better chance.

They kept glancing over their shoulders expecting the enemy to pursue them; however, no pursuit ever came. Amara couldn't shake the feeling that someone was watching them. Once they reached the temporary camp, they stopped for a break and to tend to the wounded. The temporary camp was mostly picked up, but there were still some of the larger things left behind in the rush to leave. There were a few tents remaining, and they used one of these to house the wounded.

Amara helped where she could but found herself wishing Honora had been there, she could have done a much better job. She helped Daziar change his bandages, using a cream that soothed the burns. Then she helped hold down a soldier as Malach and Ariel set his shoulder back into place and wrapped his broken ribs with bandages. The man's screams of pain would haunt her for a while to come, she knew. That was how the rest of the day went for her. Moving from one man to another, helping them survive their wounds. More survivors trickled in throughout the day, and with them, more wounded to tend to. Malach once sent her out for some herbs that would lessen the worst of the pain. Although she was unable to find any in the snow, which still covered everything.

They slept in shifts again; although, Amara didn't sleep much at all. She discovered later she wasn't alone in her unrest. Most of the soldiers hardly slept. When she had caught a few minutes of restless unconsciousness, it was accompanied by hellish nightmares; as if the demons hadn't stopped at assaulting the city but were attacking their minds as well. That thought worried her. She arose well before dawn, intending to go for a walk to clear her head.

"Ariel." Amara caught his arm as he walked by. "Is it possible for the demons to be attacking all of our minds in our sleep? I remember Malach and Elzrod talking about one that had attacked Malach's mind for a long time."

He hummed thoughtfully. "No, I don't think they would be able to attack us on such a large scale. Usually, those attacks are employed on a one-to-one basis. Most likely, it's your mind trying to deal with the horrors you witnessed over the last few days. Some soldiers never recover from what they see in battle, and certainly, none of them forget it."

Amara nodded, thinking about what he had said.

"It will get easier to manage." Ariel put a hand on her shoulder. "Pray it never gets easier to see."

When dawn came, it turned the sky blood red and didn't hold any comfort for her. They were back on the move, carving their path through the woods. Those who could walk did, and those who couldn't were pulled on makeshift sleds. Amara found herself once again in the back of the group alongside Malach and Skie.

She was lost in thoughts about the man walking next to her until she heard herself ask, "why don't you look at me?"

She couldn't believe those words had just come out of her mouth. She felt her cheeks heat up and no doubt they were cherry red.

"What?" Malach asked, stopping in his tracks.

Well, there's no going back now, Amara thought.

"When I don't have my armor on," she clarified. "When I just have my shorts and shirt on. Why don't you look at me?"

"Umm, well. . ." Malach stammered.

"Do you not like how I look?" she prompted.

"No!" he exclaimed quickly but went back to stammering just as fast. "I, umm, well. . ."

"What is it then?" She didn't let up. She didn't want to give him time to weasel his way out.

"I've never seen that much of someone before."

That didn't make any sense to her. "What do you mean?"

"Well, I've been told people, women especially, don't show that much skin unless you're with other women or you are married. Since we are neither, I was trying to give you your privacy."

"But you like what you see, right?" she asked, almost holding her breath.

"Well, yes," he said as carefully as if he was poking a bear.

"So. . .you do find me attractive?"

"Yes," he said a little more confidently. "I do find you attractive."

"Good." She started to walk again. "You know, in Caister, most of the time the women walk around in only a midriff shirt and shorts."

"Really?" he asked, catching up quickly with his longer legs. "Doesn't that bother you?"

"Why should it?" She shrugged. "How do people dress where you're from?"

"The least amount of clothing we wear is a heavy shirt and long pants. I guess the majority of the time it's not warm enough for anything less, but our culture is different. Even if it did get warm enough, I don't think you would see anyone wearing what you do. Even the men don't take off their shirts if a woman is present."

"That's weird," Amara laughed.

"Your people are weird."

"So, you find me attractive," Amara suddenly changed the subject back.

"Well, yeah," Malach said. "But who wouldn't?"

Now, why did he have to go and say that? She internally pouted. *If he wants to court me, he should just go ahead and say something.*

"Um, I know this is going to sound like I'm trying to get out of this conversation." His brow knitting together.

He probably is, she thought, but didn't say.

"But Reckoning just relayed a message that my father wants me up front. I'll leave Skie back here with you. Shout if you need something."

"Fine, but this conversation isn't done."

She swore she caught the sound of Malach sighing as he started walking faster to reach the front of their group. She almost had gotten him to tell her his true feelings, but did she want to know? What if he didn't like her enough to court her? How would she feel then? Instead of the possibility of rejection, he would have actually rejected her.

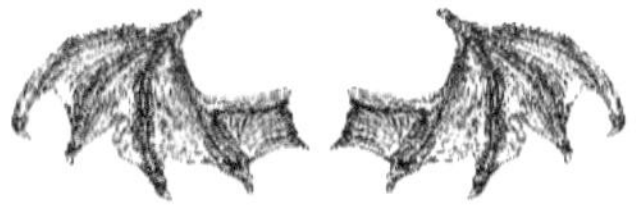

Malach jogged to the front of the line. His father's interjection was perfectly timed for him. Amara was backing him into a corner in their conversation, and Malach would have had to confront his feelings. He honestly didn't know what to think about the fiery, spirited young woman. He enjoyed her company, but he didn't know if it went any farther than that. He had never really had feelings for anyone. Even Honora he only thought of as a friend, and he had known her for most of his life. He did know one thing though, when he was with Amara, he felt happy. Even while nightmarish things were happening, he could joke with her and they could share a laugh. Besides, even if he did have feelings for her, how would they ever be able to court in the middle of a war? He guessed most of mankind had done it, since there were few times of peace in their history, but he had never known anything but peace. He pushed his inner turmoil away as he approached his father.

"What did you need?"

His father turned toward him.

"Are you and Amara courting yet?" His father asked with no preamble.

"What?" Malach stopped short of reaching his father but quickly regained his composer and fell into step. "I mean, no. Why would you ask?"

Did his father know what conversation they had been having? If not, why would he be asking now? Malach had hoped he was getting away from the uncomfortable conversation and had walked right back into it with another person.

"You two seem well suited for each other," his father confided with a smile.

"She was a thief, Dad," Malach protested, trying to find anything to say to get him off the conversation.

"So? Your mother was an assassin." His father snapped back and shot his argument out of the sky like Malach would have shot a bird.

"But she was an assassin for the Angel Army." Malach tried again, but his argument was shot down once more.

"Amara is now a thief and a scout for the Angel Army. I don't see the problem. Besides, your mother was trained and brought up in the Demon Territory to be a weapon for their army." His father looked at him with an amused smile.

"She was?" Malach asked, realizing a few seconds too late that his mouth was slightly ajar. He shut it.

"It's a long story. Remind me to tell you sometime," his father replied. "Do you like Amara?"

He opened his mouth to say yes, but his father cut him off.

"Then ask to court her."

"But what if she says no? And what if I find out my feelings for her don't go any deeper than just friends."

"Then you two just be friends." Ariel stopped and put a hand and Malach's shoulder. "Malach, life can be cut short in a moment, especially with this war starting up again. If you don't take the chances you have now, you may never find true happiness."

His father looked away, taking a deep breath, and when he turned back there was moisture in his eyes from barely checked emotions.

"You're thinking about Mom, aren't you?" It was his turn to put and hand on his father's shoulder.

His father nodded. "Your mother and I had more time than most people get. We had almost two thousand years together. I squandered those years because I was too afraid to tell her how I felt. Too afraid that she wouldn't feel the same way. I only was able to enjoy fifteen years with your mother as my wife, and I would give anything for just one more day with her."

"I understand," Malach said, though he was still not ready to ask Amara to court him. "I'll think about it."

"Don't think too long," His father said in a warning tone. "You might miss your chance."

Ariel started walking again, leaving Malach to think about his words. He didn't start moving again until Amara walked up to him. He fell into step with her, knowing their awkward conversation was about to start up again. He didn't know how to avoid it, so he decided he should face it head-on and be honest with her.

"What did your father want?" she asked as he opened his mouth to say something.

"To give fatherly advice," Malach smiled at her.

"Oh yeah? Are you going to heed his advice?"

"I'm not sure yet," he said truthfully, his smile falling, replaced by a more thoughtful look. "I know where you're going with these questions you've been asking."

"Uh-huh?" She raised an eyebrow at him. "And?"

"I don't know yet what I feel." He shrugged. "And I need time to sort that out."

"Oh." She looked down.

"It's not that I don't find you attractive or that I don't want to be friends," he said quickly, awkwardly reaching out to comfort her. "I just don't know yet what I'm feeling."

In the end, he let his hand fall back to his side, not knowing what to do.

"Well, don't take too long to figure it out." She looked up and poked a finger at him.

To his relief, he could hear the humor in her voice. "Well, you're impatient." He smiled disarmingly at her, in case he read her wrong.

"Darn right I am." She smiled back.

Malach was glad they were still friends, and that nothing had changed just yet. She took his revelation well, but he would have to sort his feelings out soon, she wouldn't wait long. Then she did something he didn't expect. With a little jump, she pecked him on the cheek. She ran ahead, giggling at his dumbfounded look. He smiled. He did like her. He just didn't know if he wanted to be more than just friends.

Daziar ran back to Malach. "Well?"

"Well, what?" His brow furrowed in confusion.

"Did you ask her?" Daziar all but pleaded with him. "Ariel said—"

"Why is it that all of a sudden everyone is interested in my love life?" Malach lamented, throwing his hands in the air.

"I've always been interested in your love life." Daziar poked a finger at him and narrowed his eyes.

"I know. Only a month ago, you were trying to get me to court Honora."

"Yeah," Daziar's frowned. "I've given up on that for both of us. I think Honora thinks of both of us as only friends."

"And rightly so," Malach pointed out. "We are both her friends and have been for most of our lives."

"You know what I mean." Daziar rolled his eyes and shook his head. "I asked again after we left Newaught, you know."

"To court her?" Malach had to consciously keep his mouth closed at his friend's naivety. Daziar had been asking her to court him for several years.

"Yes, to court her." Daziar put his hand on his hips.

"She said no again?" Malach said it more as a statement than a question.

"Yeah," Daziar sighed. "I don't know why."

"Because she doesn't want to settle down yet. Or, and this is a novel idea, she doesn't have those kinds of feelings for you."

"Yeah," Daziar sighed again, looking at his feet, but then perked up. "But you have a chance with Amara, and I'll just live vicariously through your love life."

It was Malach's turn to sigh. He had thought he might get away with not telling Daziar about his conversation with Amara.

"Oh, come on," Daziar pleaded again.

"We aren't courting, I don't know if we ever will."

Daziar was just opening his mouth to say something when the two were interrupted by a call for one of the men in front. Malach inwardly sighed in relief. He was glad he didn't have to explain it to his friend, but he also knew Daziar wasn't going to let it stand like that. Why did so many people have to pry into his business? It might be better if he were to just shout it from the tallest tree. It would at least get the embarrassment over all at once.

The call was echoed by a cheer from the rest of the men. Relief was the general look on everyone's face. They had fallen behind during their conversation and they broke into a jog to catch up.

"What's going on?" Malach asked the closest man.

"We've caught up to the main group. Hot food and shelter for us tonight!" he happily informed them.

Malach sighed with relief. He hadn't relished another night in the snow with little to no shelter or food.

One of the angels lifted off from the main group, and Malach recognized Camael as he got closer. He alighted in front of Ariel, and they spoke briefly. Then Camael headed back. They would, no doubt, stop and have healers waiting for the wounded as their smaller, bedraggled band caught up.

Malach was correct: the main group stopped, and he could see several people waiting at the edge of what was quickly becoming a temporary camp. Malach noted Honora was with the healers waiting for them to arrive. He also spotted men starting fires, which meant they would be cooking food. Malach's stomach growled painfully. It had been more than a day since he had had something to eat. The smell, which wafted out as they got closer, was heavenly.

Malach studied Honora's expression for only a second and could tell Daziar was in for a verbal, and maybe a little physical, beating. He had broken his promise about not fighting. He didn't envy his friend at all.

Sure enough, when they got closer Honora called. "Where is that no good friend of yours, Malach Tresch?"

Malach glanced around him, Daziar had vanished. "Um, I'm not sure?" Malach replied sheepishly.

Worry crossed her face.

Malach held up his hand to calm her, "He was just here. He made it out of the city and is fine."

Her worry was replaced once again by anger, though he knew she was relieved to know they were both alive and well.

"When I find him, he's not going to be fine," she growled.

Malach just smiled.

The group of healers moved forward to meet their group, fretting over the wounded. They stabilized the severely wounded men and accompanied them into the camp. There were still a handful of healers, including Honora, left fussing over those who had smaller wounds and cuts. Malach notice Daziar sneaking around behind Honora while she checked on a shallow cut he had sustained. He didn't even know when or where it had happened, but he had dressed it when they were out of the city. Although, Honora said he had done a poor job at best.

"You know Daziar is trying to get into the camp behind you," Malach raised a hand, leaning in conspiratorially before watching the carnage unfold.

"What?" Honora whirled and looked directly at Daziar.

He locked eyes with her mid-step and froze, as if hoping if he stood still enough, she wouldn't see him. The effect of it was comical. Daziar stood, one foot suspended in the air and a look of pure fear on his face. Honora pounced. He tried to get away, but since he was only about thirty feet away and tired from the battle and journey he didn't get very far. He might have made it into the camp, and therefore able to hide, if he hadn't frozen when Honora turned his way. As it was, he only made it a few steps before she caught him by the arm and then grabbed his ear, dragging him away.

"Ow!" he shouted. "You're going to pull my ear off!"

"It would serve you right, you fiend," she replied. "You broke your promise, and then instead of facing me like a man, you tried to skulk past me."

Malach watched as the two disappeared into the camp, slowly losing them in the crowd, Honora's voice fading as they went.

"I don't envy him," one of the other healers said, walking up to Malach.

"Nor do I," Malach chuckled.

"Let me finish that bandage." The healer was a man a few hundred years Malach's senior, but still well in his prime. He didn't have the build of a warrior, but he was not as soft as some of the refugees Malach had seen.

Malach was still holding his arm up where Honora had been working on it. "Sure."

"Are those two courting?" the healer asked, getting to work wrapping his arm.

"No," Malach replied. "Though not from lack of trying on his part."

The healer nodded knowingly. "There you go. It'll be good as new in a week or so."

"Try a day or two," Malach said. "Being part angel has its perks."

"Part angel, huh?" The healer's eyebrows shot up. "I've never heard of an angel taking a human lover."

"Wife," Malach corrected.

"My apologies." The man bowed his head. "Your parents must be proud."

"I don't know," Malach sighed, unsure of why he was talking to this stranger. "My father is disappointed I have to fight at all."

"But that doesn't mean he is disappointed in you." The healer pointed out. "Anyway, I must be off to check on the other soldiers."

Malach watched the man go thinking about the last thing the healer said. Maybe his dad was proud of him, only disappointed in the situation they were forced into.

Cleared by the healer, he walked into the camp and found himself sitting next to one of the cooking fires. Men who had seen him arrive slapped him on the back in congratulations and sat down next to him asking for his story. Amara soon was sitting next to him, filling in any detail he missed and adding what she had experienced from her perspective.

Soon they were all eating laughing and talking about different stories of prowess and bravery. Malach stayed quiet unless directly spoken to, preferring to listen. Amara finished with a story of how she had killed the monster in the swamps near Newaught. Malach was convinced she had changed some of the details, painting herself in a better light. From what she had told him, she had gotten lucky, and the monster had rolled over and stabbed itself through the brain. She was also lucky that the ground was churned to mud, otherwise the creature would have crushed her. However, he let her have her moment of glory as she told the men the story, as if she had planned the entire thing. She even showed off the tooth that she had taken from the beast, drawing several gasps from the men

"Malach." She nudged him, snapping him out of his thoughts. "Tell them how you killed the demon mid-flight at Newaught."

"No, you can tell the story." He shook his head but was met with a resounding cacophony of shouts that drowned out his reply and any protest he might have voiced.

He told the story of how it had happened. How he hooked the demon and was carried into the air and the desperate struggle, which had culminated with Malach stabbing it through the back of the neck. Then how he had survived the ensuing crash. They all hung on his words, and when he was done, they cheered and hollered.

"If a mere man can do that, we have a chance at winning this war!" one of the men shouted.

"But Malach isn't just a man," Amara said, but her voice was drowned out by the cheers.

Don't tell them, Amara. Malach heard Reckoning in his head, and it seemed Amara did as well.

They need a morale boost, Reckoning responded to what must have been a question Malach couldn't hear. *They will learn soon enough that Malach isn't only a man, but they just lost their homes. They need something to bolster their spirits.*

Amara nodded and stayed quiet as the cheers died down. The men talked for a while longer, but soon they were all called to pack up camp and move on. They were told that the angels wanted to get a few more miles in before stopping for the night. Just in case the Demon Army had sent a force after them. They all pitched in and the group that had come in late were given packs to carry or pulled the wounded on the sleighs.

They trudged along like that for several days. On day two, they did a headcount. Out of the eight hundred troops at the beginning of the siege, only around half survived. During their march, the angels came and went, leaving Ariel or Elzrod in charge. Sometimes, they would leave to scout out the area ahead, other times to make sure they weren't being followed. Eloa left after the first day to warn the Angel Army that Fairdenn had fallen and that they needed to warn any surviving towns to send any refugees to Brightwood. If there were any surviving towns.

The snows came once again, about three days into their weeklong journey to Brightwood. Food was scarce and they lost several of the wounded to malnutrition, cold, or infection. As unfortunate as that was, most who died were the men who couldn't walk. Without those men slowing them down, they were able to make better time. Malach hoped they would make it to Brightwood before they starved.

Chapter 6

Kragen walked through the army camp and their cobbled-together tents. He had been given his assignment shortly after he had seen to the downfall of Whiteshade. He had assumed he would be heading to Fairdenn next, since that was the next city on the docket to fall. Instead, his master, Azazel, had a different plan.

Kragen was pulled from his introspection when he had to sidestep a mule pulling a cart full of arms somewhere. He looked around him. The camp was vastly larger than he thought it would be. Large and small tents rose to all sides of him, some used for sleeping some for gathering, planning, and eating. All of them a patchwork of different materials. Soon they would all be filled with the wounded and dying. War did that to an army. Both sides would lose men, both sides would have wounded, and both sides would have survivors once it was all said and done. However, only one side would be victorious.

An angel flew over Kragen's head, and he tensed. He had been trained to keep his thoughts and identity anonymous, but there was always a chance that an angel might recognize him for who he was. Moreover, his physical appearance could give him away; his six-foot five-inch frame and his jet-black eyes could very well be his undoing.

He peered at the mountain, which housed the angel stronghold. Soon, this would be the war field. This would be the site where everything would be decided. All the celestial beings, all of humanity, and everything in between would fight and die on this field.

His mission had almost failed before it had begun. He had traveled up through the mountains from Whiteshade, through a little backwater town he had been told would have recently been taken by mercenaries hired by the Demon Army. He wasn't supposed to have any issues with them, but when he arrived, they barred him entry and tried to kill him. He had chosen not to utterly decimate the little town, and instead, continued his journey to the Angel Army camp. He would leave them, for now. The Demon Army would deal with their betrayal later. He had barely survived on the supplies that he had left, all but crawling into the camp late one evening. It had turned out to benefit him, lending truth to his lies.

He had been chosen to destroy the enemy from the inside out, and he had no doubt in his mind that he would succeed in his mission. The stronghold would be breached for the first time in history, and the Demon Army would burn through it like fire, destroying everything inside. He was told that the Lord Satan would be returning soon to lead the army, and when he did, he would get the order to set the plan into motion. It would be over before they even knew what was happening.

First, he needed to find a way into the stronghold.

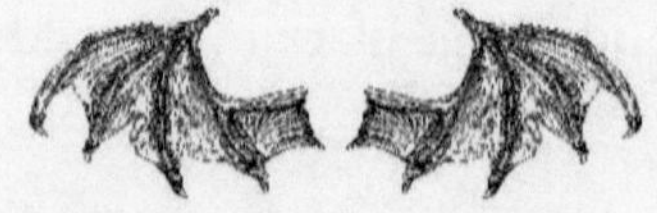

It was almost noon on the sixth day since they left Fairdenn. Malach, out hunting ahead of the main group, spotted Brightwood. The sight of Brightwood surprised him, and he marveled at how quickly they had been able to march across the mountains. They had shaved almost a whole day of their journey by not following the main roads. Even fording the Pangor River hadn't taken terribly long. They had been able to find a narrow spot in the river. The angels had made short work of felling a few trees and lashing them in place for the people to cross.

Through the trees, he could just make out the timbers that composed the outer wall. He moved forward to get a better view of his home. However, his excitement was replaced by an uneasy feeling the closer he got to the town. Something was wrong. He just didn't know what.

He arrived at the edge of the woods before he could put his finger on what was making him feel that way. The front gates that led to the main road were closed. Malach couldn't remember the last time those gates were closed during the day. He stayed inside the tree line and out of sight as he moved around the town trying to gauge why things were so abnormal.

From his vantage point on the hill, he had to strain to peer over the walls, but he didn't see anyone moving around the streets. He decided to climb a tree to get a better view. As he did, his uneasy feeling started to worsen and sour his stomach. He had been right:

there was almost no one in the town at all. He spotted a couple of people walking around the town, but the buildings were starting to appear run down. Maybe most of the people had already left the town, and this was just the people who refused to leave. It didn't sit well with him. Togan, the big blacksmith and Malach's old friend, would have been too stubborn to leave, but there was no smoke rising from his blacksmith's forge.

Things weren't adding up, and he needed to find out what was going on. He headed out to the farm that Honora's father, Arjun, owned. It only took him a few minutes to get within sight of it at a fast jog. The barn was only a smoking ruin, and the house was partially burned and ransacked. He drew Reckoning, senses on high alert as he approached the front door. Or at least what was left of the front door. It lay on the floor, inside the threshold, hacked to pieces by whoever had wrecked the place. He stepped carefully over the rubble, placing his feet purposefully in case he had to fight. No attack came, however, so he continued deeper into the house. He was familiar with the layout of the house, having been there countless times growing up. He didn't see anyone as he moved through the house, but every room was the same; furniture overturned, belongings strewn across the floor. He heard a moan come from one of the back rooms and he rushed to investigate.

There was a lot of fire damage in the back part of the house. He wasn't sure how it hadn't spread to the rest of the house, but he didn't question it too much. He peeked into what had been Honora's room. There was a heavy beam that had fallen from the ceiling. He spotted movement below the beam.

"Johm!" Malach rushed forward.

The man seemed almost unconscious as Malach worked to free him. The beam was pinning him to the floor and there was no telling how long he had been there. Malach had to use all his considerable strength to lift the beam. He hefted it up, enough to wedge a few spare pieces of debris underneath. It gave him enough space to pull Johm out by his ankles. Moments after Malach had pulled the man out, the beam crushed the debris and slammed back to the floor. He turned Johm over and held his head as he put his water skin to the man's lips. Johm came around enough to take a small sip.

"Johm?" Malach lightly slapped his cheek, trying to keep the man conscious.

"Malach," the man croaked, his eyes flitting open.

"Johm, what happened?" Malach asked quickly. "No, never mind that. Where are you hurt? Let's get you patched up first."

"Malach, I'm not going to last long." Johm coughed, blood dribbling out of his lips.

He looked down at the Johm's ruined legs and stopped. "Don't talk like that, Johm. We have healers with us who will fix you right up."

Johm saw through his thinly veiled lie. "Malach, Brightwood has been taken."

"I noticed," Malach replied.

"Listen!" Johm suddenly gripped Malach's arm tight to emphasize his point, but he fell into a coughing fit, spraying blood with each cough. When he got his coughing under control, Johm continued. "They hit us out of nowhere. Maybe fifty of them. I was able to help everyone get off of the farm, and I even took a few out before they set the house on fire. I knew that the town wouldn't be able to repel the force that attacked us."

"Do you know who it was?" Malach asked. "Do you know what happened to the town?"

"No, I don't know who they were. Arjun said they would head toward the Angel Army," Johm told him. "We had heard rumors of the Angel Army had set up their camp a few days walk from here."

"You just hang in there. I'm going to go get help," Malach said.

Johm held tight to Malach's arm not allowing him to leave. "Don't leave," The man ordered. "I'm not long for this world. I will be gone by the time you get back."

"Johm. . ." Malach's voice caught in his throat, clogged with emotion.

"Stay here, please," the man pleaded, as his familiar gruff demeanor melted away. "I've never had anyone in this life Malach. Arjun and his family treated me like I was a part of theirs. I. . ." his voice faltered. "I don't want to be alone at the end."

A single tear rolled out of Johm's eye. Malach counted him as a friend and had known him for most of his life. He couldn't bring himself to deny Johm's last request. His vision blurred, as tears rolled down his own face now too. He didn't wipe them away, letting the cold streaks linger. He sat there with the man, long after Johm had breathed his last breath.

Malach didn't know how long he stayed by Johm, but sometime later, self-preservation and better judgment prompted him to move. The group of soldiers and refugees would walk right into a trap if Malach didn't warn them. He carefully wrapped Johm's body in the tablecloth that had been lying on the floor as he had entered the house and hoisted the big man over shoulders. He carried Johm's body back the way he had come, retracing his steps through the woods and back to the group. The snow-covered ground made his journey back all the harder, but he was resolute in his grim task. He would see that Johm got a proper funeral. Then he would kill the men responsible.

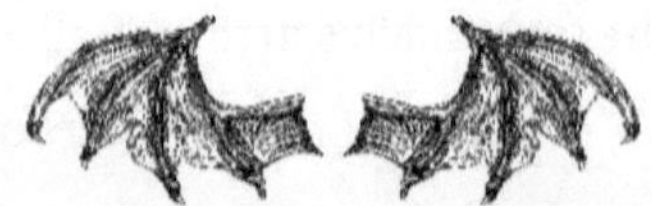

Amara arrived at the edge of camp just in time to see Malach walk into the midst of the group who had stopped to watch him approach. He was carrying a wrapped body. They all stared at him as if he were some morbidly fascinating sight, as if he were the dead man walking into their midst, not simply carrying one.

We left so many dead on the journey here, and so many more in the city, Amara thought. *Why would Malach carry this one back with him?*

She moved up through the crowd to get a better view. He laid the body down on the ground with great care and a certain amount of reverence. He looked up and around, his eyes coming to rest on her. She could see that he had been crying.

That sent a shiver down her spine and she took a step back.

This man, who was so emotionally cut off since she had met him, had cracked. The hard shell he wrapped around himself falling away to reveal the boy underneath. Her heart broke for him, but before she could free herself from the crowd to comfort him, Honora and Daziar had joined Malach.

"It's Johm," Malach told them, his voice cracking anguish.

"What happened?" Daziar choked on his words as well

Honora burst into tears and fell to her knees in the snow.

"He was killed saving the only family he knew," Malach knelt, hugging Honora close, as fresh tears spilled down his face.

Daziar moved to join the hug, even as Malach extricated himself to meet his father, who was just arriving. Amara moved forward with Ariel. Even with the tears in Malach's eyes, she could see a fire burning in them that wasn't there before.

"Malach, what did you find at Brightwood?" Ariel asked, cold and impersonal.

Malach seemed to draw strength from his father. He wiped his eyes and took a deep breath letting it out slowly. He straightened and held his head high once again. The shell was back, though tentative and frail. "A force has taken the town. Johm told me before he died that he thought most of the town made it out. Arjun had plans to head to the Angel Army with the rest of the town."

"Then we skip the town, and go straight to the camp," Ariel turned to address the crowd.

"No!" Malach almost shouted at his father, shattering the silence that hung over the crowd. "I'm going to kill the hellspawn that did this." Malach pointed to Johm's body lying on the ground.

"Malach, I understand how you feel," Ariel turned back to his son, trying to comfort him. "I want them dead too, but we will lose men if we attack the town."

"Then I'll do it on my own!" Malach shouted at him.

His emotional armor was once again broken but this time by anger, an anger which brought with it the desire for revenge. There would be no stopping him now. Even if he did have to do it on his own. Amara moved to Malach's side against her own instincts and spoke quickly. "What if Malach and I sneak in and open the gates tonight. We could charge the town with maybe a hundred troops and take them without a fight."

"That might work," Daziar spoke up, his arm around the still sobbing Honora. Brightwood isn't big enough to support too many troops. There can't be that many."

"No," Ariel stated with finality and turned away. He ordered the group to set up a temporary camp for the noon meal.

Amara watched as Malach balled his fists and gritted his teeth so hard she was afraid he would break one. He stared in anger at his father. She understood where Ariel was coming from. After all, the need for survival was one of the first things she was taught in the Shadows. Ariel wasn't just making the decisions for him and his son, but for the hundreds of people with them.

A thought struck her. Why was she so on board to throw her life at an enemy that meant nothing to her? She turned and looked at

Malach. Was it because of her feelings for him? The ramifications of that thought hit her like a charging demon. These feelings would put her into more situations where she could die. They were why she stood on the wall in Fairdenn, they were why she would go with Malach into Brightwood. She decided at that moment she could live with the consequences of those feelings. She *would* go to Brightwood with Malach to avenge his friend.

Everyone. Amara jumped as Reckoning's voice popped into her head, and she watched as Honora and Daziar, started as well. *Elzrod would like to see you at the back of the camp. Please bring Johm's body, and we will hold a vigil for him.*

Malach relaxed his muscles slightly, and he helped Daziar reverently pick up Johm's body. Everyone parted as they made their way through camp to where Elzrod was sitting with several other men. They set Johm's body carefully on the ground and joined Elzrod.

"I've been in contact with your father," Elzrod stated. "He said he would allow us to camp here for the day to hold a vigil for your friend. He also said he would allow a funeral pyre for him after dark, when the smoke can't be seen. We believe we are far enough away from the town the light of the fire will not reach it. He asked that we take the body back a mile or so to be sure."

"Johm wouldn't care about a funeral," Malach dismissed Elzrod's words with a swipe of his hand. "He would want us to kill the snakes that did this and take the town back."

"I realize that Malach," Elzrod said in a low tone. He didn't move, but his words carried all the weight they needed to quiet

Malach. "That's why these men are here. They have volunteered their services to take back the town."

"Against my father's command?" Malach sat back, studying the men surrounding them for the first time.

"Yes, but I will only take volunteers," Elzrod replied. "I think, however, the town will provide us with more than justice for your friend. It should still have supplies there that will be vital to our survival. It would also be helpful to take it and provide ourselves with the staging ground we have lost."

"All that is fine by me," Malach replied, steel once again entering his voice. "I just want to kill the bastards."

Amara looked at Malach, a little shocked. He had never been like this as long as she had known him. Granted that was only a month or so, but he was always the voice of reason and logic, cool and calculated. Here he was, angry, rash, and dark. She wasn't sure she like this side of him.

"I'll stay at the pyre," Honora bowed her head. "I will honor Johm there while you obtain justice for him."

"Fine. We will leave a few men with you as well, in case there are any issues." Elzrod agreed. "Until nightfall, I suggest you get a little rest."

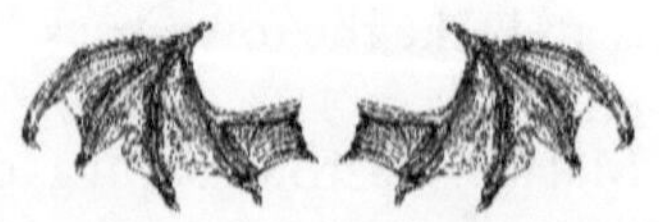

Malach, Daziar, and two other men carried Johm's body on one of the sleds they had used for the wounded. They had fashioned four handles on each side for them to hold. They carried him for a way until Elzrod called for a halt. Four men and the ladies that had come including Honora would stay behind and build the pier, lighting it once they were finished. The rest of the men would head for the town, hopefully making it in enough time for Amara and Malach to sneak in and open the gate before the first light of morning crested the horizon. They had almost fifty men volunteer, not including Malach, Elzrod, Daziar, and Amara, which meant they would at least match the supposed number of the group that had taken the town. Skie, of course, would have to stay with Elzrod until they regrouped with Malach. Their plan hinged on the element of surprise. If Malach and Amara were found out before they had a chance to open the gate, they would be forced to retreat.

Malach and Amara would run ahead of the main force so they could start their part of the plan before they lost the cover of night. Malach knew a spot they could climb over the wall with little difficulty; however, it was on the opposite side of the town than the gate they would need to open. They agreed they should check along the wall closer to the gate in the hopes of finding a more direct point of ingress.

They stole through the night, leaving the cover of the trees, making a mad dash toward the town. They reached the wall and paused to listen for any signs that they had been seen. After a few moments of continued silence, they decided they were in the clear. They started moving down the wall, away from the main gate. Amara checked for handholds that they could climb up, and Malach kept his eyes peeled for any guards that would be patrolling the wall.

They were about halfway to the place Malach's climbing spot was when Amara stopped them to check for the umpteenth time. She motioned to Malach. She thought they could make it to the top of the wall, so she started climbing. When she was almost halfway up, she motioned for him to start his ascent. He started up, watching where Amara put her hands and feet, following her lead. It didn't take long for Malach to catch up to her with his superior height and strength. She pulled herself up to the top edge of the wall and peered over. Malach stopped behind her as she looked around.

She gasped and tried to back down, stepping on Malach's head.

"Oomph!" Malach let out an involuntary noise.

"Move," she hissed. "There's a guard coming."

"Fine." He started moving down. "Just don't step on my head again."

She shushed him as she pressed her body against the wall.

Malach followed her example, getting as close to the wall as he could. He heard the heavy footfalls of the guard walking down to the wall toward them. As the guard got closer Malach tried to slow his breathing and not make any undue noise that would give them away. Amara stepped down one more step, right onto Malach's fingers. Malach stifled his yelp and grit his teeth. She didn't let up the weight on that foot. The guard stopped almost directly above them. Malach tilted his head up but couldn't see the guard past Amara's body. His fingers were throbbing in timing with his quickened heartbeat and his arms and leg started to burn. Seconds stretched into minutes and finally, the guard started walking again. By the time the guard had passed, one of the muscles in Malach's forearms had locked up painfully and he was positive his fingers were broken. She finally, mercifully, took the pressure off his fingers and he felt the rush of the blood returning to them. He let go of the wall and shook out the muscle, allowing it to release. Then finished the climb and rolled over the top of the wall.

"What's wrong?" Amara asked, grinning at him. "Can't keep up with a girl?"

"You stood on my fingers!" He held up his hand for her to see and made sure he could still move each one.

"You shouldn't have had them there," then added, "but I am sorry."

Malach nodded his acceptance.

"You were having more problems than those fingers," she verbally jabbed at him again.

Malach turned her around and started ferrying her down the walkway.

"My muscle locked up. You know most people don't climb walls every day of their lives like you."

"Aren't you supposed to have super strength or something?"

"That doesn't mean I'm all-powerful," Malach retorted under his breath.

Amara stifled a laugh, but Malach heard a little of it escape anyway.

"Laugh it up, but you're not being a very stealthy thief."

Amara allowed Malach to have the last word, as they quickly descended a set of stairs, leading to the ground. They moved as quickly as they dared. First light wasn't far off. Luckily, that also meant it was the darkest part of the night, less likely that they would be spotted.

Amara and Malach were almost to the gate when he got careless. He turned the corner on the last street and stopped dead in his tracks. Two guards were sitting in front of the main gate around a small fire. Malach had expected them to be on top of the wall. Luckily, their backs were to Malach. Amara grabbed his arm and pulled him back behind the building.

"What now?" she asked.

"We wait. Hopefully, they will leave to patrol soon."

"What if they don't?" Amara looked around the corner again.

"If we don't have a choice, we will kill them and open the gate." Malach crouched down, trying to still his beating heart. *How does she do it? She is so calm and collected. I feel like a small child, sneaking out of my room to get a midnight snack.*

They hunkered down, keeping close to the wall and to each other for warmth. They kept an eye out for the two guards to leave but they never did. One of the guards was extremely overweight and Malach wondered if he had done anything in the battle. He looked better suited for the rich, soft lifestyle than that of a soldier. It made sense he wouldn't want to stand on the wall for very long.

The first light of the morning started to show up in the sky and Malach decided it was time to move. He tapped Amara on the shoulder and motioned for her to take the high road above the guards' heads. He would take them head-on, bringing all their attention to him, giving her the opportunity to get the gate open. They would have to hold out until the main force got to them. He figured it would be about ten to fifteen minutes before they got to the gate, which didn't sound like a lot of time, but when you are fighting overwhelming odds, that was pretty much an eternity.

Just as Amara was leaving the cover of the building, the two guards started to rouse themselves. Malach grabbed the back of her leather armor and hauled her back behind the building. They pressed themselves up against the wall. Malach wished he could just melt into it. They waited but no shouts came from the direction of the guards. Malach chanced a glance around the corner to find, no guards at all. They had moved from their place around the fire and were nowhere in sight.

He moved carefully around the corner, pulling Amara along with him, this time by her hand instead of her armor. He liked the feel of her small warm hand in his. He shook his head to clear his thoughts. He needed to focus on the task at hand. He let go of her, confident she would follow him now, and stole toward the gate. It was a simple thing, having only two heavy beams securing the two large doors. It wouldn't hold up against an all-out assault but would stop most smaller forces long enough for the citizens to either escape or rally a force large enough to fight off the invaders. Malach imagined the gates hadn't been closed when the city was attacked, since the assault came during the middle of the day and without warning.

They reached the gate without being spotted and lifted the first heavy beam from its place barring the doors. They were just starting to lift the second of the two beams when Malach heard voices on the wind. He dropped the beam and pushed Amara into the gatehouse, following close behind her.

The gatehouse was more like a storage room for the beams, and although not very big, had a small supply of weapons. Malach had to squeeze in close to Amara to get the door to close behind them. Malach turned around in the small space and peeked through the crack he had left between the door and the frame. He watched as the two guards came back around the corner and started walking toward their fire again at the front gate. Malach prayed, to anyone who might be listening, that the two guards wouldn't see the beam they had already removed that was now propped against the wall off to the side. The two guards were oblivious to it, however. They made their way to the fire and sat down again. Unfortunately, they sat down just as they had been before, facing the main gate and the gatehouse where Malach and Amara were hiding.

Malach turned around to consult with Amara careful not to make a lot of noise. Now her face was directly in front of him, though she only came up to his chest level. She blinked at him a little surprised at their closeness.

"Please tell me that is Reckoning's handle and not what I think it is," Amara's cheeks flushed red.

"It is!" Malach hissed, his cheeks starting to burn at the suggestion.

No, I don't believe it is. Reckoning piped up mentally.

Malach sent a mental image of a rude gesture to the blade and turned around again not wanting to face Amara. He moved an empty sword rack from beside the door to give them a little more room and looked back out at the two guards.

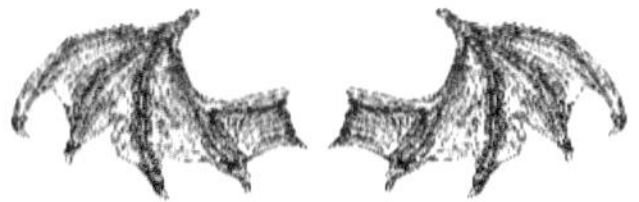

Even standing behind Malach, Amara caught the voices of the two guards. They didn't seem to care how loud they were nor who heard them.

"You know, when we took this job, I didn't think it was going to be so boring." She thought the first voice was the thinner guard by how he sounded.

"I know. We were promised battles and blood," the large one replied. "Now we just sit at a fire all night guarding this gate against no one."

"Yeah, the only excitement was when we first got here," the first guard said. "You know, I got to set fire to the barn. Unfortunately, we had to move on before I could get the house burning well enough to burn it to the ground with that idiot of a farmhand in it."

"I would have enjoyed hearing him beg for his life and scream as the fire took him," the second added.

Malach's fist clenched, and Amara could all but hear his teeth grinding together. She slipped her hand over his clenched fist to try and comfort him. His muscles relaxed but only slightly. He shifted and she was able to see out through the crack in the door.

The thinner guard scooted his chair around the fire to escape the smoke that had blown into his face. His back was almost to Malach and Amara when he finally settled.

"I know," the first continued. "And then, when we caught one of the elders in their Counsel Hall, I think the boss felt great satisfaction gutting that impudent whore. She just wouldn't keep her mouth shut."

Malach exploded in a sudden and violent rage. He burst through the door, throwing it off its hinges, and let out a guttural war cry. Amara stared in shock as he barreled toward the thinner of the two guards. Before they knew what was happening, Malach wrapped his hands around the man's head and twisted it to the side. A loud pop reached her ears as the bones in the man neck broke and he slumped to the side. Malach continued his charge toward the larger guard and swatted away the sword the guard had managed to level in his direction. He held onto the man's wrist and slammed his shoulder into him. The guard twisted away, trying to get free, but Malach held on. Malach pulled hard on the man's arm, and it stretched. Another popping noise sounded as the man's arm and shoulder separated. The guard was forced to drop the sword and he let out a pained scream. Malach picked him up bodily by his armor, and he struggled weakly to get free of Malach's grip. Malach turned and slammed him down onto the still burning fire, sparks and embers flying in all directions. He held the guard there by his leather chest piece allowing the flames to lick at the man's clothing.

"You will join the screams of the damned, you spawn of hell!" Malach roared.

Amara didn't want to watch this anymore, but she couldn't tear her eyes away, she wanted to leave but her legs wouldn't budge. The flames burned through the man's heavy furs and starting in on his skin. And he did scream, unearthly screams. They barely sounded human. The screams echoed through the previously silent night bouncing off the mountains surrounding the valley. The smell of burning flesh made her turn and wretch.

Once she got her faculties under control, she turned back to see several half-dressed men stumbling out of some of the buildings. They quickly took in what was happening, pulled weapons, and charged. Malach ended the man's suffering by stabbing Reckoning through the man's heart and released his hold on the burning corpse. He turned to face the men coming his way. He seemed oblivious to the burns on his own body. When he pulled Reckoning out of the man, the weapon had changed into the form of a large wicked looking battle axe, instead of his normal staff weapon.

No! Reckoning's cry of protest sounded in Amara's head. He was so desperate for Malach to listen he must have projected it to her as well.

What else had he said to Malach already? She pitied the blade. Malach had told her about what he had been through, and this must be dredging up bad memories for him.

Malach's first swing took the front three men's heads from their shoulders before they could bring their weapons to bear. Not that the second group was any better off for getting their weapons up. Reckoning seemed to pass through the metal almost as easily as though flesh. The sight of the carnage in front of them slowed the charge of the rest of the men but to their credit, they didn't stop.

Malach waded into them, and Amara finally was able to tear her attention away from him and back to the gate. By now their force would have heard the screams and would no doubt be headed their way, but she had to get the beam out of its housing and open the gates or the two of them would surely die.

She moved to the wooden gate and tried to lift the heavy timber enough to slide it out of the way. It was too large for her: she needed Malach's strength. She looked back and spotted more men heading their way. Although there was a growing pile of bodies at Malach's feet, she knew he wouldn't be able to take on the whole force. She could see that he was bleeding from several wounds already, though none looked immediately life-threatening. No, she would have to figure this one out on her own. Luckily, this beam was the lower of the two. She would have never stood a chance if it were the higher one.

She got her back underneath one side of the beam and used her legs to push up with all her might. After a couple of agonizing moments, it hadn't budged. She studied the gates and they appeared to have bowed in, trapping the beam against the housing it set in. She set her shoulder against the doors. They slowly moved back out, releasing the beam, so then took her place under it again. Another few moments of pain and burning muscles, the beam was up and out. While holding the beam up she was able to push the gate out far enough that the beam wouldn't fall back into place, and with a heave, she sidestepped out from under it, letting the wooden behemoth fall. It hit the ground with a thump and stuck fast. One side of the gate swung free of the beam, but the other wouldn't budge. Someone else would have to move it.

Amara turned her attention to the battle going on behind her. Malach was still swinging his axe, letting out guttural, pained, angry shouts as he did. She didn't know how long he was going to be able to keep that up, but she knew she could help him. She threw two of her throwing knives as she started her charge toward the fray. One was blocked by its intended target, but the other found its home in the eye socket of a man, he dropped to the ground without another sound, dead before his body came to its final resting place. Amara ran toward Malach as he swung his axe down, bending at the waist with the momentum and weight of it. She took her chance to vault off his back leaping into the air and loosening more throwing knives at random. She hit the ground on the other side of the main force with her back to a wall and pulled her long daggers, ready to face any opponent that came her way.

However, most of the men weren't looking at her at all. They weren't even looking at Malach. They were looking at the large she-wolf that had bounded through the open gate. She was a sight to behold with her coat alight, the cold light of the moon refracting off her snow speckled pelt. Her hackles were raised, showing her white incisors and the fur along her back bristled menacingly. She tore down the street, barreling straight into the middle of the forces that would have soon overwhelmed them. Several men lost their nerve at the sight of the savage beast tearing into their companions and started to flee. They were met with Amara's knives. As Malach and Skie ripped at the front lines, Amara stopped any who fled in her direction, killing a few besides that. When the main force finally arrived, it was all but over. They helped clean up the few stragglers who remained, and the fight for Brightwood was over.

Malach's blood lust wasn't satisfied, however, and he grabbed one of the few surviving enemies dragging his body over to the fire that he had burned the other man alive in. He savagely kicked what was left of the burnt man out of the way and held his newest victim just out of the flames reach. There wasn't much left of the fire, but the coals would easily ignite the furs the man wore.

"Where is your leader?" Malach growled dangerously at the man.

"I-I don't know," The captive groveled, devolving into a pitiful mass of tears and spittle as he pled for his life.

"You do!" Malach shook the pathetic, hapless man.

"Last I saw, he was at the council chambers, but that was hours ago. Please, don't kill me!"

Malach shoved the man into the embers but didn't hold him there. The man rolled out of the fire, shedding his already burning furs as Malach turned and walked away, murder in his eyes.

Amara caught up with him, "Malach, what do you plan to do?"

"Kill the coward that did this," Malach growled.

Skie caught up and walked beside Malach.

Amara thought she could see the same anger and rage in the wolf's eyes as she saw in Malach's. As if the she-wolf was feeling that same thing and was as intent on getting revenge. Amara shuddered. She didn't like Malach like this at all. She didn't think this was righteous fury anymore, just debased anger and the desire for revenge. It didn't fit Malach's character, and she didn't like to see him like this. She followed him anyway. Maybe she could reason with him once he had a few moments to cool off.

They passed through the doors of the Council Hall and into the main chamber. Amara took in the sight of the large hall. It was mostly empty, except for a raised platform where, she imagined, the elders would have sat to judge or discuss the topic at hand. Four of the chairs were empty but one held a body. The elderly lady sat slumped over, her unseeing eyes staring vacantly at the door they had just entered through. Malach walked up to the body and closed the eyes of the old lady, lifting her frail body from the chair and laying it on the ground, reverently crossing her arms across her chest and whispering something that Amara couldn't hear. Skie nudged Malach's head, as if to comfort him in his time of loss.

If Malach's rage had subsided at all on their walk over here, it had rekindled and burned twofold now. He stood, hefting Reckoning onto his shoulder, a dangerous light in his eyes as he strode out of the main room and through a door behind the raised platform. Amara followed quickly. She turned the corner on the door and saw that Malach and Skie had sped up, climbing a flight of stairs. She spotted them again just as they disappeared around the corner of a set of stairs that turned right, about halfway up. She took the stairs as fast as her legs would carry her, trying desperately to catch up with him. She made it to the top and nearly ran into Malach's back.

She peered around him to see a wiry man with one eye missing, standing at the end of the hall. His sword was drawn. Off to either side of the hall were sets of closed doors, and behind the man was a window. They were more than two stories up by now, and there would be no escaping through the windows without severe injury.

"Are you the man who led the attack on this town?" Malach's voice seemed to be much calmer, but Amara could still hear the angry in it.

"Yes." An evil grin spread across the man's face.

"Why?"

"Because I was hired." The man shrugged. "And because you took my eye. Imagine my disappointment when you weren't here. But now you show up, and it's time for me to take my revenge."

"The eye I took from you was a warning and a chance to change," Malach growled. "One I never should have given you. Who hired you?"

"There's a war on, boy. Think about it, and the answer will present itself."

"Why kill Elder Maria?"

"The old hag?" the man cackled. "Because she talked back-"

Malach roared and charged, not letting the man finish whatever else he was going to say. The man put his sword up to guard against Malach's attack, but it was a futile gesture. Reckoning passed straight through the blade, biting into the man's shoulder. Malach put a boot into the man's chest, kicking him off the blade and defenestrating him. Amara heard a cry as the man fell, but it was cut short as he, no doubt, hit the ground. Malach took a step forward to peer out the window the man had just passed through. He nodded to himself, seemingly pleased with the man's demise, and Reckoning slowly changed back into a knife.

Malach passed Amara, pausing as if he wanted to say something to her but instead kept walking. Skie followed Malach, but it was some time before Amara could get her feet to move. She was unnerved by everything she had witnessed this morning, and she needed time to sort out her feelings and emotions. She felt like she didn't know Malach at all. She thought she had figured him out. This angry, vengeful side scared her. Maybe he would calm down now that he had avenged his friends.

She sighed. She should go make sure everything else was finished. She might be needed somewhere else.

As she passed by the counsel chairs, she noticed the old lady's body had been removed. She wondered at how Malach could go from a merciless killer who would burn a man alive, to such a soft and gentle person who would remember to pick up a body to take to the funeral pyre. She walked out into the cold morning to see the soldiers of their army piling the bodies outside the front gate to be burned. She spotted Malach coming out of the building. His gaze was haunted, and he appeared gaunt and weary. He had burns on his arms from holding the man in the fire and cuts all over his body that he was feeling for the first time.

Daziar found him and pulled him away from the group of men. He checked Malach over for any wounds that were life-threatening and Malach just stood there. He stared off into nothing, and it seemed like he wasn't fully present. Amara went over to see if there was anything that she could do, but Daziar stopped her.

"He needs some time, Amara," Daziar told her.

"What's wrong with him?" Amara peeked around Daziar as Malach plodded away from them and sat on the step of a building.

"I've only seen him like this one other time, when we were kids." Daziar turned, following her gaze. "You know he lost his parents when he was young, and they were presumed to be dead, right?"

"Yeah."

"He didn't say a word to anyone for a week when that happened," Daziar told her. "Mom said he had retreated inside his own head. I didn't understand it at the time, but I think that's how he learned to cope with loss. This will be the first time since then he has lost someone that he's known since childhood to anything other than old age or sickness."

"What can we do?"

"Give him some time. He'll pull through."

"You didn't see him," Amara shook her head, turning to Daziar. "How he fought. It was like he didn't care what happened to him, and he didn't care about anything else. Daz, he held a man in the fire until he burned to death. It was a frightful sight to behold."

"Malach takes any attack on those he calls friends personally," Daziar replied. "Just be glad you are among those he calls friend. I wouldn't want to be on the receiving end of his fury, righteous or otherwise."

Daziar left her standing in the street, checking on other men who had sustained injuries and even laughing and sharing battle stories with a few of the men. Amara decided to not heed Daziar's advice and walked over to Malach. She sat down next to him and put her hand on his knee. He turned to her with his still vacant eyes. Tears were silently falling from them. She didn't say anything to him simply let him know she was there, she was with him. Skie was on his other side with her head resting on his other knee. They sat like that for a while watching the sunrise over the mountains.

"I don't feel any better," Malach said suddenly with little to no emotion in his voice. "I thought I would feel better after I avenged Johm and then Maria, but I just feel empty and tired."

Amara didn't know what to say to him. She had no idea how he was feeling and wasn't about to pretend she did, so she just sat there with him.

"Is this how it's always going to be?" he asked the cold morning sun.

Amara thought he might be asking her, but she didn't know. "I hope not."

He spun his head to look at her. "I had a chance to kill that man a while back, but I spared him."

"Mal..." But she let her voice trail off, unsure of what to say. "I hope one day we have peace again. Then we can settle down somewhere and have families, and you can be a hunter again. Maybe I can pick up a skill that's not illegal."

He smiled at that last part, and life seemed to enter him again, albeit only a little. Amara smiled back, glad to see the warmth returning to his eyes. She was a little afraid she wouldn't see that in him again until after the war.

"I hope we get that chance together," Malach replied.

She lifted her head to look him in the eyes and he leaned down and kissed her. It wasn't like she imagined it was going to be, but it was full of warmth, and it made her heart flutter. That was enough.

He broke off the kiss all too soon, in her opinion, and smiled once again at her. She thought she might love this man. He had a few different sides to him, and one, in particular, was a bit scary, but she liked the normal side to him, and it seemed to be coming back.

"Does this mean we are courting?" Amara asked.

"If you want it to,"

"Then, yes." Amara sat up straight, a grin crossing her face. "Yes, it does."

"Come on. We have to get things ready," Malach said, standing up and upsetting Skie's head from his lap where she had fallen asleep.

The she-wolf glared at Malach, but he ignored her. They walked toward the center of town, Amara and Skie flanking Malach on either side. Daziar came and clasped arms with Malach.

"What are we getting ready for?" Amara asked.

"For the refugees and the rest of the soldiers to join us in the newly reclaimed Brightwood," Daziar answered before Malach could. "They've already sent a message to the camp, letting them know what happened. I bet everyone will be surprised and excited!"

"Good," Malach said. "Although, I'm a little worried about how my father will respond to the news."

"Malach, no matter what he has to say to save face in the front of the men, he can't be anything but proud. If we had known you two," he nodded toward Malach and Amara, "would be such a deadly pair, we wouldn't have worried about the gates or the reinforcements. When we got here, there were only a handful of enemies still standing. We didn't lose a single person tonight."

"Most of that was Malach," Amara admitted, and she meant it. She had only seen the angels fight like that in battle.

"Don't be so modest," Malach replied. "I know you killed your share of them too."

"Well, if you two are done patting each other's backs, we do have work to be done." Daziar jammed a thumb over his shoulder and turned to walk in that direction. "You know, because of you two, I didn't get to kill a single bad guy."

Malach chuckled and shrugged. "Should've gotten here sooner."

Chapter 7

Malach, Amara, Daziar, and Elzrod moved through the town, helping where they could. Pulling a cart of supplies or repairing a hole in a wall or roof to get the town ready for the refugees. It was some time around noon when the main group arrived. The bodies had been cleared out of town and set to burn, but the snow and dirt still ran red in testament to the battle that had taken place the night before. Ariel strode in the gate and spotted the four of them. He started moving in their direction.

"Let me do the talking, Malach," Elzrod muttered out of the side of his mouth.

Malach didn't have time to answer but agreed it might be the wisest decision.

Ariel walked up to them scowling. Malach remembered the disappointed and slightly angered face from his childhood and couldn't help but smile at the memory. It was the wrong thing to do.

Ariel noticed the smile and misinterpreted it as insubordination, "Do you think what you did was funny, Malach?"

"Don't get onto Malach," Elzrod stepped forward and slightly in front of Malach. "It was my idea and my plan."

"It was foolish," Ariel turned on the older man. "You could have been all killed."

"But we weren't, Ariel," Elzrod pointed out, meeting his gaze. "Not one of our men were killed, and very few were injured. We have your son to thank for that."

"Malach?" Ariel glanced at him.

"Yes," Amara cut in. "You should have seen him. He took on the whole of the enemy troops to allow me to open the gate."

Ariel studied Malach, his conflicting expressions seemed at war to control his face. As if he couldn't decide whether to praise him for his courage or berate him for being so foolish and disobedient. In the end, he dismissed the whole thing not saying anything either way. "Well, we do have a new outpost for vetting troops and refugees now. Have we found any supplies?"

Malach's heart sank as his father turned to Elzrod to get a report.

"Not as many as we had hoped for." Elzrod motioned for Ariel to walk with him. "Depending on how many people decide to stay here, we will have to leave most of the supplies we found so those people can survive the winter."

"That's unfortunate, though not unexpected." Ariel nodded. "At least they will have proper shelter for the harsh winter."

Malach couldn't help but wonder what kind of shelter his mother had or if she was freezing in some dungeon somewhere.

"When are we going to be leaving to rescue Mom?" Malach cut off whatever his father was about to say next.

His father deflated visibly, appearing wearied and older, and the few wrinkles on his face deepened. "Soon, son."

"You said that in Newaught." Malach pushed.

"I know," his father sighed. "But we have an obligation to make sure these people are safe."

"Let someone else make sure they are safe," Malach gestured to the refugees. "We've done our part. How much longer do we need to stick our necks out for strangers when our own family is in the hands of the enemy?"

"Walk with me." Ariel gripped Malach's arm and steered him away from the group.

"We need to see this through," Ariel told him when they had walked out of earshot of the group.

"No, we need to go find Mom." Malach pulled his arm out of Ariel's grip.

"Just a few more days." Ariel faced Malach, locking eyes with him. "Besides, if we get to the Angel Army, they might have more information on where your mother is being held."

"It's been weeks since we heard about where she was being held." Malach emphasized his frustration with a swipe of his hand. "How much longer will we wait? How much longer can we wait?"

Ariel ran his hand through his hair roughly. "Not long, son, I know how you feel, but as you said, it's been weeks since we heard anything. Would you rather leave now, only to find she's been moved by the time we get there? The wiser move is to make sure our information hasn't changed, resupply, and then set out to find her."

Malach growled, turning away from his father and running his own hand through his hair. He turned back to Ariel. "Fine, but as soon as we know if they have any information or not, we go," Malach agreed reluctantly.

"Deal," Ariel nodded. "Son, we will get her back."

"I hope you're right." Malach stalked back toward the group, still frustrated but knowing his father's plan was probably the smart one. Ariel followed, after a moment,

The group stood there in awkward silence as the two rejoined them. Ariel spoke first. "Since the other angels have already flown to inform the army of our plight, we need someone to stay here to help set up the outpost and get Brightwood back in working order. As much as I hate to say it, the best one for the job is me."

Malach threw up his hands. That would delay the mission even more.

Ariel glanced at Malach but didn't say anything. "Elzrod, plan accordingly when you chart our journey to the Demon Territories. The rest of you need to go and report Brightwood's recapture to the army and let them know to send supplies and manpower to hold it."

"I ought to stay here to care for the wounded," Honora spoke up, motioning to the wounded being carried into the town. "As much as I want to go see my family, I'm needed here. Mal, Daz, make sure my family knows I'm alive and well. I really wish we knew they all made it out safely."

Malach and Daziar nodded.

"What about the rest of the soldiers and refugees?" Daziar put his hand out palm up. "I mean, where are they going? They can't all stay here; the town won't hold them all."

"Good question." Elzrod ran his hand over his beard in thought. "The simplest solution would be to let them decide. Obviously, some of the soldiers and all the healers need to stay. However, any refugees who are able should be taken to the camp."

"Good." Ariel nodded. "I will work with the former Captain of the Guard to pick the soldiers who will stay here. Elzrod, you take Daz, Mal, and Amara and gather the people to let them know what the plan is."

Unsurprisingly, the refugees did not like being told that they couldn't stay in Brightwood, but to Malach's relief, no one put up much of a fight. Some of the older refugees were allowed to stay in fear that they wouldn't make the arduous journey over the mountains. By that night, they had an understanding of how many people would be staying in Brightwood and the number of supplies they would need to survive until more supplies could be sent.

As for the group traveling over the mountain, they would still have to work on gathering some supplies along the way and rationing the supplies they had. Malach knew this would only get harder and harder to find food as the winter dragged on.

How are they feeding the whole army? Malach mused.

This far up into the mountains, with most of the cities taken by the Demon Army already, they would be hard-pressed to make it through the winter without taking casualties from malnutrition and cold. He figured he would find out when they got there; no sense worrying about it right now.

Malach took off his heavy furs and laid them out to dry. Then he laid down on his mat in the building that he was assigned to. This would be the first time he had gotten to spend the full night in warmth without being on guard or being pulled from his bed to face some danger or another since Newaught. He was going to enjoy this.

They woke the next day, strapped on their packs, and headed out. The last time Malach left Brightwood, there was a big group sending them off, almost a celebration. This time, however, it was the opposite. Instead of the big group seeing a few people off, it was the big group leaving. Ariel and Honora were the only two people who saw the group off on their journey.

"Remember to change your bandages at least once a day," Honora reminded Malach for the twentieth time that morning, and she wouldn't stop checking each wound as they had made their way to the gate.

"Honora, enough." Malach pulled her away from him by her shoulders, setting her at arm's length. "Most of these are scratches and will heal by day's end."

"Yeah, and what about my burns?" Daziar literally pushed his way into the conversation, elbowing Malach to the side a little. "Don't you want to check those one more time?"

"Your burns are healing fine." Honora frowned at him, knowing he just wanted her attention. "A few more days of applying the salve I gave you, and they will be gone."

"We will make sure your family knows you are safe." Malach changed the subject. "You just make sure you *are* safe until they get back here."

"I will." Honora hugged him and then Daziar in turn.

"Take care of yourself, son," Ariel clasped arms with Malach once he had extricated himself from Honora's hug.

"I will, and I'll be back to start our search for Mom."

"She would be so proud of you." His father's normally stern features softened. "As proud as I am."

Malach smiled at him, but he didn't know how to respond, so he nodded and turned to leave.

They had been able to take a few horses in the evacuation, before the battle started at Fairdenn, and now they would be taking most of the animals to the Angel Army encampment. Every one of the civilians was able to ride, and even a few of the men; although, most of them rode double, children astride behind or before them. They would be able to make better time without the wounded and the weak slowing them down. Malach imagined that they would still have to lead the horses through some of the deeper snowbanks.

Malach mounted up behind Amara. She was small enough they wouldn't have to trade places to take turns guiding the horse, and he enjoyed the closeness for more than warmth. She had the same horse as back in Newaught, and Malach remembered from her story: she had taken the horse from the guard in Caister. She named him Shasta, and she had been taking care of him since. He was strong, sturdy, and ready to take them anywhere. He nudged the horse into movement and their journey began.

It was an extremely uneventful journey, and for that, Malach was grateful. The first two days, they saw nothing but wilderness and snow. On the third day, however, they crested the top of a ridge to see a large encampment spread out before them. The sight before him filled him with hope. Amara gasped at the sight.

There were thousands upon thousands of tents in the valley below. Beyond the field of tents, there was a massive fortress, built into the side of a mountain. He didn't know how many people were there, but it seemed to Malach like everyone in Angel Territory had already arrived at the encampment. Malach quickly reminded himself that not everyone had been lucky enough to make it. They had lost so many on their journey, but even that couldn't stop him from feeling hope swell inside him. Maybe they did have a chance in this war after all.

To the west of the mountain, there was a large lake with an emerald green hue to it. It looked to have a layer of ice covering its surface, but they would still be able to pull fresh water from it for the army. To the east, there was an expanse of land that was cleared of trees but there were also no tents, or any other structures, set up on it.

"Is that where they are going to expand to when the army grows?" Amara asked looking in the same direction as Malach.

Malach chuckled. "You *are* a city dweller aren't you. Where do you think food comes from?"

"The market of course." Amara shrugged. "Wait. . ."

Malach laughed even harder. "No, before it can go to market it has to be grown. That's set up for farmland. Of course, nothing is growing right now since it's the dead of winter."

"I knew that."

"Sure, you did," Malach replied, still chuckling and shaking his head at her. "The market."

"Hey, don't shake your head at me. I just didn't think about it."

"Uh-huh," Malach replied, unconvinced.

Amara crossed her arms but didn't say anything else.

They started down the ridge, following a path that was not well used. It switched back on itself several times, and Malach thought it must be a game trail instead of the road, which would have been used by most to get to the encampment. About halfway down the path, Elzrod contacted the angels at the encampment to let them know they would be arriving in a few hours. He was allowed to vouch for Malach, which meant they would be able to walk right into camp without giving up their weapons or being searched. Everyone else, however, would be subjected to the search and would have to give up their weapons for a transition period or until they left.

They made it to the encampment about an hour before dark, and there were three angels waiting for them. Malach recognized Cathetel and Camael, although he didn't recognize the third angel, who was female. Cathetel immediately took Elzrod and Malach away from the group while the other two angels helped the new soldiers and refugees get settled.

"Malach," Cathetel addressed him, ever serious. "We have found where your mother is being held."

Malach's heart swelled, his father had been right in sending him to the encampment. There was news that would help them find his mother. He felt a little foolish for his outbursts at his father now. He would have to apologize to him later. He noticed the expression on Cathetel's face and his heart plummeted twice as hard as it had jumped.

"What's the news, Cathetel?" He crossed his arms, bracing himself for the bad news.

"She is alive," Cathetel held out a reassuring hand, "but she is being held at the demons' main compound."

"Great." Malach didn't understand why that was bad news. "Then let's go get her."

"Malach," Elzrod turned to him, "that is the area they will be staging their army."

"Your point?" Malach asked, crossing his arms again. He understood the implications and why they would refuse to allow Malach and his father to try and rescue her. He wouldn't let that stop him.

"Have you seen this camp?" Elzrod waved a hand at the massive camp, his voice low and calm. "From what we know, the Demon Army is much larger than this, and they will all be there. I don't think we could ever get in without getting caught, much less get your mother, who will most likely be injured, out. We need to think about this logically."

Malach let out a groan of frustration. He recognized the reason behind Elzrod's words, but he wasn't ready to just give up. "What do we do? You saw what they did to my father while he was in captivity, I can't leave my mom to suffer a similar, or worse, fate as he did."

"I understand how you feel-"

"Do you?" Malach clenched his fists. "I'm having a hard time believing any of you understand how I feel. I am going to find my mother and save her or die trying. You can either help me or get out of my way."

"Malach, I've talked this over with your father." Elzrod put a hand on Malach's shoulder. "I promised him I would help you two until the end. I want you to calm down and think about this. Your temper is getting in the way. What good will it do anyone if you were to rush into this and get yourself killed? We will do what we can and take this rescue as far as we are able, but you have to understand there are limits to what we can do."

"I just don't see how you can do anything about it," Cathetel cut in before Malach could reply. "Malach, take some time to think about it. I think you will come to the correct conclusion."

"I've already come to the correct conclusion," Malach snapped at the antagonistic angel. "I don't need any time to think about it. Elzrod, I will go through Hell to get my mother back. I know you have your limitation, but I don't share the same responsibilities or reservations. When you stop, I will continue until my family is safe."

Elzrod sighed and shook his head but let the matter drop. They continued farther into the camp, passing rows and rows of tents that each held a large number of troops. As they got closer to the fortress, the tents started to change from the large tents, which held many soldiers, to smaller tents that would only hold a few people in each. Malach was about to ask Elzrod about the change, but the old man beat him to it, almost as if reading his mind.

"The smaller tents are for the soldiers that came here with families. They don't want to stay in the bigger common tents that the single men and women would fill." Elzrod explained.

"How many women are soldiers?" Malach asked, he had only seen a few guards at Newaught that were women. It seemed to him most women decided to pursue different careers than the more combat-intensive ones the men gravitated toward. There were no laws against women taking those careers. In fact, they were given the same training as the men growing up.

"We have about half as many female soldiers as male," Cathetel answered for Elzrod. "However, in the training programs that we have here in the encampment, there are three times as many women being trained than men."

"It should start to even out the longer the war draws out?" Malach asked.

"Correct." Elzrod nodded.

They walked past the small tents and into a section that had even larger tents than the first section. Malach wondered again at the reason for the difference. Once again, he didn't get the chance to ask.

Cathetel predicted the question this time however and started explaining, "These tents are the mess where the meals are served and the medical tents for any injuries, from sprained ankles to stab wounds. The other tents are housing for the refugees who do not have families and cannot take up arms yet. We have one for the children, orphaned by the war, one for the elderly, who cannot bear arms anymore, and one for those who have been injured past the point they can fight, but no longer need medical attention. Also, we set up one of these for the people of Brightwood. They all insisted they stayed together. They didn't want to lose each other after losing their town."

"How many people from Brightwood made it?" Malach asked, trying to mitigate his hope in case there was bad news.

"Most of the people of your town made it," Cathetel replied, as stoic as ever. "I heard there were a few casualties when they were attacked and a few more on the way here, due to the harsh weather in this land. After we are done in the fortress, I will take you to your people, and they can go home if they like."

"Thank you," Malach replied, genuinely. "What are we going to be doing in the fortress?"

"Michael has requested you and Elzrod to join him and the rest of the angelic hosts to talk about our current situation and the future of the army," Cathetel told him

Malach noticed the angel's fist clenched, and he got the feeling Cathetel wasn't happy Malach was invited to the meeting.

"*The* Michael?" Malach raised an eyebrow, ignoring the angel's tone in favor of the significance of the request and who was requesting it.

"Yes," Cathetel growled, it sounded like he was grinding his teeth, but Malach couldn't see the angel's face from where he was.

"Do I need to change or do something to get ready?" Malach glanced down at his dirt and blood-encrusted clothes and tried to brush some of it off, which didn't help. He didn't want to meet the Archangel Michael without cleaning up.

"No time," Cathetel insisted. "I was told to bring you immediately upon your arrival."

"Don't worry, Malach," Elzrod told him, trying to reassure him. "None of the angels will take offense to our appearance. They know the road we have walked to get here."

Malach nodded and they continued in silence.

They approached the massive front gates. They were made completely out of iron and were thicker than Malach was wide. The Demon Army would be hard-pressed to get through those and breach the fortress beyond. As they entered through the open gates, they walked into a large, rough-cut cave. It may have, at one point, been a natural cave system, but it had been carved out to accommodate an army. The ceiling was high above their heads, and the angels would have plenty of room to fly above them.

Past the gates there were hundreds of feet of solid rock before the fortress itself started. The smooth stone blocks of the fortress wall seemed out of place in the rough-cut cavern. The unevenly rounded ceiling of the cave made it look as if the fortress had been buried by the mountain and then tunneled into from the outside. They entered through a much smaller gate, and the walls and ceilings grew much closer. The part of the fortress that could be seen from the outside was only a fraction of the actual fortress that lay below the mountain. The feel and design of the walls and columns reminded him of the Shadows' lair.

Reckoning? Malach decided to ask the blade and see if he knew. *Was the construction of the caverns under Newaught of angel design?*

Very astute of you, the blade responded. *It was, in fact. Although your father and I visited it once during the construction, our travels never lead us back there until we fled Newaught some weeks ago.*

Why didn't you mention it then?

You didn't ask.

Malach sent a mental image of him rolling his eyes at Reckoning.

He got a mental image back of Reckoning shrugging sheepishly.

They wound their way through several halls and stairways, all the while heading up. Malach couldn't figure out where the transition from underground tunnels to above-ground halls was but eventually, they walked out of a doorway into the sunlight. Malach had to shield his eyes until they adjusted to the bright light. Eventually, they did, and the sight before him took his breath away.

They were standing on an open-air terrace overlooking the encampment. The sun was almost touching the mountain tops, and it set the landscape ablaze with its orange glow. The snow, normally a bright white, looked like it had been ignited, and its beauty was a sight to behold.

In contrast with the beautiful scene was a group of bickering people, souring the moment. Malach peered closer and as his eyes continued to adjust, he found himself not looking at people, but angels. In the middle of the terrace was an ovular table with chairs scattered around it. The chairs might as well not have been there, since every angel was standing and pouring over a map laid out on the table. All conversations ceased when Malach, Elzrod, and Cathetel were noticed.

Elzrod moved forward and was greeted warmly by many of the angels who had been standing around the table. One angel, who was much larger than the rest and in full golden armor, waited patiently until the rest had greeted Elzrod then moved forward.

Elzrod and he clasped arms.

"I see your mission was eventually successful." The angel glanced Malach's direction.

"Yes. It took me some time to find the boy, but I did," Elzrod chuckled.

The angel turned and stepped up to Malach, "Malach, I am Michael."

Malach didn't know how he should greet the legendary angel but made a snap decision to kneel. It was a mistake. Even as he was kneeling Michael picked him up, so his knees never touched the ground, and set him back on his feet.

"We only kneel to one Being, Malach," Michael told him kindly, "and, though I appreciate the reverence, I am not that Being."

Michael reached forward and clasped Malach's arm, signifying he was an equal.

"Is this your wolf companion?" Michael asked, glancing down at Skie. "May I pet her?"

Malach shrugged. "You will have to ask her."

Michael crouched down on one knee, so he was eye to eye with Skie. "You are beautiful, my dear. You look as if you come from the line of the dire wolf."

Michael did something odd then. He paused as if listening to her, and she yipped and let out a light growl.

"I did know a dire wolf, but that was a long time ago. I do miss my friend greatly, however. Would you mind if I pet you?"

Skie barked once and bowed her head slightly.

Michael ruffled her ears and chuckled. He looked back up at Malach. "You have a rare companion, Malach. She is probably one of the last of her kind. Though I suspect, from what she told me, she is only part dire wolf. Take care of her, and she will always be by your side."

Malach realized his mouth was agape a moment later and shut it quickly. He longed to ask Michael questions about Skie, but the archangel ushered Malach and Elzrod forward. Cathetel took his leave, apparently not invited to this meeting. Michael motioned to two unoccupied seats, but Malach didn't think they were actually supposed to sit in them, since everyone crowded around the table were all standing.

"As I was saying," a female angel, who was just a large and impressive as Michael, spoke.

"That's Gabriel," Elzrod whispered in Malach's ear. "She's-"

"*That's* Gabriel?" Malach interrupted. "But she's…well, she's a she."

"Yes," Elzrod replied with forced patience. "She is, and she's been pushing to strike back at the enemy."

"Good, I'd be happy to see the Demon Army put in their place."

"From what I understand it's not good. The Demon Army most likely won't attack us here until spring, which will give us more time to train and bring the rest of the army to bear. If we strike back, we invite an early assault."

Malach nodded his understanding and turned his attention back toward the debate. Michael sat down, while the rest of the angels argued, patiently waiting for them to finish what they had to say. Gabriel had a few angels supporting her plan, but the majority favored Michaels's plan of waiting.

Michael held up his hand and the table went silent. "I'm sorry to cut everyone short of what would be the hundredth time we've argued this, but instead I would like to hear from our newcomers." All heads turned to Elzrod and Malach, each with a different expression.

Malach breathed a sigh of relief as Elzrod stood up. He told them of the journey, from the flight from Newaught to the battle at Fairdenn and ended with the reacquiring of Brightwood.

When Elzrod was finished, Michael leaned back in his chair and studied Malach. "Malach, you were the one who confronted and killed the leader at Brightwood, correct?"

"Uh, yes, sir," Malach replied, stepping up beside Elzrod.

"Did he say anything to you before he died?" Michael asked.

"He told me he was hired," Malach replied.

Michael waited for a moment, but when Malach didn't offer any more information, he prompted, "Did he say by whom?"

"No sir, only that because of the war, it should be obvious," Malach told them. "I assume he meant the demons."

"See!" Gabriel pounded the table with her fist causing Malach to start. "Malach and his group fought back and were successful. We should be learning from their success and courage."

"These were untrained and undisciplined men they faced, and they had no support from the demons like the other cities that have been taken did," Michael replied calmly.

"Michael's right," Malach blurted before he could stop himself. He liked the idea of getting payback, but the smarter move was to be patient. "The men we fought in Brightwood were much less skilled than the men we fought in Fairdenn. I was able to kill many of the men in Brightwood without much of a fight."

Gabriel threw up her arms in frustration. "I thought you would be on my side. You seek revenge, do you not? I thought, after your rage filled rampage through Brightwood, you would be more willing to act. Looks like you are just a scared as the rest of these cowards."

"That wasn't my finest moment," Malach muttered, balling his fists and working hard to keep his anger in check. "I might want revenge against the demons, but I can keep my desire for it in check long enough to see that attacking now would cost more men than it's worth."

Michael smiled and nodded at Malach, then addressed Gabriel, "please, sit down." And then to the group still standing, "that goes for everyone."

They all took their seats. Some of the angels having to walk over to their chairs to bring them back to the table. Malach wondered if they were thrown that far away because of the tempers in the room. He had imagined angels would be more, well, angelic. They seemed like children, bickering over who got to play with which toy, except with superhuman abilities. All of them, except for Michael. He seemed to always keep his head about him, not allowing himself to get out of control.

"Now, let's talk about this like civilized angels." Michael closed his eyes and rubbed his forehead. "We have been over this a hundred times, and a hundred times we have concluded we will wait until spring, when the snow melts, to start our offensive. Now, Raphael, where are we at with our research into the new weapons the demons had demonstrated?"

"The explosives they have been using to get past our walls were the easiest to reproduce," an angel to Malach's left replied. "It was just a matter of mixing the right amount of each substance. The cannons and powder guns are a little harder to reproduce, but we have been making headway."

"Good, keep working on those and start production of the explosives," Michael instructed. "Gabriel, I need you to take five of our angels and go to Brightwood. That town cannot fall."

"Trying to get rid of me, are you, Michael?" Gabriel sneered.

"Not in the least," Michael replied coolly. "We cannot lose Brightwood again. It is one of the last towns we have left, and we need it if we want to take in any more refugees. Also, you might get your chance for a little action. If the demons get word that we have taken it back, they might try for it again."

"If it's any help," Malach interjected. "My cottage just outside of town should be unoccupied. You and your angels could stay there during your time at Brightwood."

"Thank you for your offer, Malach," Michael nodded at him. "I'm sure that would give them the anonymity they need to get things accomplished without too many interruptions yet be close enough to deal with any issues that arise. Now, the last thing on the table is the issue of Lanifair Harbor. Since Fairdenn was taken, the land route to Lanifair is cut. Also, since Newaught was taken, we have no way of getting to it by sea, but it is the only port city we have any rights to. However, we don't have warships, and we can't gain any supplies through it, I think it would be in our best interest to continue with our plan of evacuation. With the simple change of bringing them here instead of Fairdenn now that the city has fallen. Thoughts?"

A female angel that Malach didn't know spoke up, "If we abandon the town, we allow that port to be used by the enemy for moving troops and supplies into our territory. It is true that we can't use the port at the moment for our own gains, but I think giving up the city is a mistake."

"And what about the citizens?" Elzrod extended a hand, as if to physically push his way into the conversation. "If the port becomes an important city to the demons to move troops and supplies to support their army, they will attack the city and kill all who are there.

Not only the soldiers, but the citizens as well. It will be expensive to defend this city, between the troops and the supplies. I think if we decide to defend the city, we need to evacuate any who cannot fight and leave only soldiers and healers."

"I think that makes sense," Michael nodded slowly, one hand stroking his chin. "Allowing the demons to take the city without a fight would be short-sighted, thank you two for your valuable input. This is all, of course, under the assumption that it hasn't already fallen. Elzrod, would you be willing to take command of that post and oversee the evacuation and fortifications?"

"Unfortunately, I have a prior commitment to young Malach and his father," Elzrod replied.

Malach spun his head to peer at the old man, but wisely kept his mouth shut.

"You can't seriously be talking about finding Serilda!" Gabriel objected. "That's a suicide mission."

"I have promised Malach and Ariel that I will do whatever I could to get Serilda back," Elzrod confirmed Gabriel's suspicion. "You know me. I'm not going to get us all killed."

"Elzrod," Michael leaned forward. "We need you here with the army."

"You know the Demon Army won't attack here until spring, and you have many angels who would do a fine job defending Lanifair Harbor. We will be back before the snow melts."

"You can't promise that!" Gabriel brought her fist down on the table once again. "You have no idea if any of you will ever come back."

Elzrod sat forward to lend emphasis to his words but was interrupted by Michael. "Elzrod, are you serious about attempting this insane rescue mission?"

"Yes, I am."

"Fine," Michael sighed and sat back in his chair. "You have my blessing,"

"What?" Gabriel objected, and Malach was afraid that the table would splinter under the assault of her fist.

"Promise me one thing," Michael stared directly at Elzrod locking his in his gaze and ignoring Gabriel. "Promise me that if it gets too dangerous, you will come back."

"That's fair, but your interpretation of too dangerous and mine might be different."

"I'll trust your judgment," Michael nodded once slowly, finalizing the conversation then turned his gaze on Malach. "Malach, you are more important to our cause than you think. You need to come back from this. If you don't, the demons will either kill you or turn you."

"I understand you want to make sure we get back safely, but I don't know why I am so important?" Malach asked.

"How many demons have you been able to kill since you first learned about them?" Michael answered Malach's question with a question.

"Umm. . . I'm not sure. We killed two at Newaught, one on the road to Fairdenn, and two more at the battle of Fairdenn,"

Malach replied counted them off on his fingers as he recalled the deaths. "But I didn't kill them all myself."

"You were, however, the catalyst of their deaths. The number you counted off is more than have been killed in the past two thousand years after the main war was ended," Michael replied. "And even before that, there were only one or two demons or angels killed every few years. Whether you like it or not, God has obviously blessed you, and whatever side you choose will make a big difference in the coming battles. We know we will eventually win the war: God has prophesied that end, but you could save or doom hundreds or even thousands of souls, depending on your choices."

"No pressure," Malach muttered under his breath.

"You are the only child of an angel and a human, and that is significant," Michael continued, either having not heard Malach's muttering or choosing to ignore it. "We need you to come back alive so you can help us win the war."

"Believe me," Malach replied. "I will do my best to stay alive, but I will do whatever it takes to get my mother back."

Michael nodded. "Then it's settled. Elzrod, Ariel, and Malach, along with any other humans willing, will go into Demon Territory and find Serilda."

"Then who will go to Lanifair Harbor?" Gabriel asked.

"You will. I will send Cathetel and Camael, along with two other angels you choose, to defend Brightwood. Anahita will lead them," Michael replied. "You will go to Lanifair, with four of our numbers, to defend and evacuate the city. That will leave about twenty angels here to defend the fortress if something happens that we don't anticipate."

The female angel who had spoken earlier simply nodded.

Malach leaned over to Elzrod and asked, "Is that all the angels who are left?"

"So it would seem. We've lost two, including Barachiel, since I left to find and train you," he replied.

Most of the angels nodded in agreement, which seemed to signal the end of the meeting. Many of them stood, walked to the edge of the terrace, and took flight. Flying out to the camp in their respective directions to go about the business they had been charged with. Michael nor Gabriel stood to leave but stayed seated at the far end of the table from Malach and Elzrod.

Malach stood. It was time for them to go and find his friends from Brightwood. He was dying to know that they were all alright and to tell them what had happened at Brightwood; although, they, no doubt, would have heard about it already. Daziar wouldn't be able to keep his big mouth shut. Elzrod stood to follow Malach, but Gabriel jumped to her feet and quickly blocked Malach's path.

"Malach," Gabriel addressed Malach but looked at Elzrod as she did, "may I speak with you?"

"Uh, yeah." Malach nodded.

Gabriel led Malach away from Elzrod and toward the edge of the terrace. Malach didn't feel safe standing on the edge of the open terrace, not because he thought Gabriel would do anything, but he just wasn't a fan of being that high up without something to hold on to. He stopped short of the edge and Gabriel stopped a couple of steps later, looking back at Malach questioningly.

She turned to Malach, "Are you alright?"

"Yes," Malach smiled nervously at the archangel. "I just don't have wings like you do if I were to fall."

Gabriel nodded thoughtfully. "I wanted to talk to you about the possibility of striking back against the demons."

"I won't go against what Michael has said here in this meeting. Striking back at this point I believe would be a mistake." Malach shook his head, growing wary of the angel's motives. "I think Michael is right to wait until spring."

"That's all fine. I'm not talking about fighting to take back our cities, although I still stand on my belief we should do that as well." Her anger seemed to have subsided since the heated debate at the table. "We have the ability to make explosives now. I can get you enough to make a few of them, which I think would be of great help on your quest to rescue your mother. However, if you get the chance, I want you to plant one in the heart of the demon's compound where it will do the most damage."

"I can do that," Malach smiled, liking the idea of getting some payback against the Demon Army. "Why didn't you bring this up with the rest of the angels?"

"Because not all of them agree with me," Gabriel admitted.

"You mean most of them don't. Especially, Michael. Why?"

"They think it will cause the Demon Army to attack early. I think it will slow them down, not speed them up."

"I'll do it. Even if they speed up their attack, I doubt they could march their whole army over the mountains to attack us before the snow melts anyway."

"My thoughts exactly. I'll make sure you have the necessary training and materials before you leave." She turned and flew off the terrace without another word.

Malach walked back over to Elzrod.

Michael was talking with him as Malach approached. Catching sight of Malach, they both fell silent and turned toward Malach.

"Am I interrupting?" Malach asked.

"Not at all," Michael replied. "Elzrod was just catching me up with where you are at in your training. You've already bested Storm?"

Malach nodded.

"Very good. Most people take years to do that." Michael praised. "I knew you would be a big piece in the war. You have already saved many people and I suspect that you will save many more before the end of all this."

"Michael was also giving me all the information we have about where they are holding your mother and what we might run into along the way," Elzrod told him.

"Malach," Michael said seriously, "this is going to be a long shot at best. To even make it to the demon compound, you will have to cross most of the known world. Once there, you will have to sneak past one of the largest armies in the history of mankind, and then you will have to escape across all of demon territory, not to mention any of our territory still owned by the demons. I implore you to reconsider."

"Michael," Malach replied, as serious as he could be. "I appreciate the concern, but I can't stay. I would never be able to live with myself knowing I didn't make every effort to get her back. It's not a good chance, but it's still a chance, and as long as there is even a small hope, I have to take that chance."

"I understand." Michael bowed his head solemnly. "No harm in trying." He raised his head. "Malach, please be careful and come back to us safely. I was serious when I said I think you are a key factor in this war."

"I will do my best, sir," Malach replied. "I've been dying to ask; how did you talk with Skie?"

"Wolves and other creatures don't normally have full thoughts, but dire wolves were the exception," Michael explained. "I knew a direwolf for many years and learned how to communicate with them. I would love to teach you sometime; however, it would seem neither of us has the time now."

"I'm tempted to try and convince you to teach me now, but I will have to be patient. Thank you for explaining."

Michael nodded his farewell, and Elzrod motioned for him to walk out the door.

Elzrod followed Malach, bidding farewell to Michael. They wound their way down, back through the fortress. Malach supposed they were backtracking to the main gate, but if he was honest, he was unequivocally lost. Elzrod either already knew the way, or he had memorized the twists and turns as they went up. Either way, they soon arrived at the large metal doors and out into the sunshine.

"Michael told me where they have housed all the people from Brightwood," Elzrod told him turning to there right after exiting the large doors. "I'll take you there now. I'm sure you are ready to reunite with them."

"I would like that," Malach followed him, eager to see his friends again.

As they walked up Malach recognized Togan, working beside the tent where he had set up a grindstone. He had two piles of various weapons sitting on either side of him. As Malach and Elzrod got closer, Togan finished with the axe he was working on and set it in the much neater of the two piles. He reached over to get another weapon as a young man that Malach didn't recognize dropped an armload of weapons into the pile. Togan pulled his hand back quickly before he lost a finger to the falling blades.

"Boy!" He yelled angrily. "How many times do I have to tell you-"

"Don't listen to this old, crusty lump of ore!" Malach shouted, cutting the big man off.

Togan jumped to his feet, inflating to tower over Malach, "How dare y-" he started to bellow, ready to crush whoever had disrespected him, until he saw who it was.

He cut his rebuttal short and rushed forward. Malach had his hand out to clasp the big man's arm, but Togan slapped it aside and engulfed Malach in a bear hug, lifting him off his feet. Togan nearly crushed him with his exuberant embrace and several of Malach's vertebrae popped under the pressure. Togan deposited him about as gently as he had picked him up, showing Malach the biggest smile he had ever seen on the man.

"Good t' see ya alive, Malach," Togan said. "Daziar said you were alive, but nothin' beats seein' the proof to the words."

"It's good to see you too, Togan," Malach replied, returning the man's broad smile with his own. "We feared the worst when we found out Brightwood had been taken. I'm glad you and the rest of the town survived."

"I hear its safe t' return thanks t' you," Togan replied. "I also heard you took all the ruffians on, single handed."

"Don't be ridiculous," Malach replied with a mischievous grin. "I used two hands."

The large man let out a bellow of a laugh at Malach's comment, and he saw a few heads peek out of the tent in their direction. It wasn't long before the whole town was out, congratulating him and thanking him for defeating the men that took Brightwood. He was able to extract himself from the throng of people and ran directly into Arjun.

"Malach, is Honora alright?" He grabbed Malach's shoulders with both hands and all but shook him. "I haven't been able to talk with anyone yet."

"She's fine, Arjun," Malach assured him, gently pushing the man back and off him. "She stayed behind at Brightwood to care for the injured."

Arjun breathed a sigh of relief and, as if his worry for his daughter was the only thing keeping him up, sat down on a nearby chair. "Thank you, Malach. I'm so glad you were with her. When we heard the news about Newaught, we feared the worst. I knew when we heard you were alive that she would be too. I just had to know for sure."

"You know I wouldn't have left her behind."

"I know. When you're a father, you will understand."

If I ever get the chance, Malach thought.

He never considered having children. He'd never even courted anyone. However, now that he had feelings for Amara, he was a little sad. Thanks to the demons and this war, he might not ever have the chance to have children.

Arjun stood up. "I have to go tell Zahra. Thank you, Malach, we owe you so much."

"You don't owe me anything, Arjun." Malach smiled at his happiness.

Arjun walked away and disappeared into the tent. He was only gone for a couple of moments when Togan approached. Malach was already tired of everyone thanking and offering something in return for his heroics, but he would suffer the man his audience.

"Elzrod tells me you're plannin' on rescuin' your mother," Togan stated. "I'm comin' with ya."

"Togan," Malach took a step back, caught off guard by his bluntness. "I'm not going to stop you, but you know that there is a very real possibility that we won't be coming back,"

"I understand the risks, Malach, but that's why you'll need my war hammer along for the ride," Togan replied. "My skills do not lie in stealth an' infiltration, but I'm mighty handy if it comes down t' a fight."

"I would be honored to have you along with us," Malach said clasping arms with the man. "Thank you."

"Who else is in our party?"

"Elzrod, Daziar, Amara, Ariel, you, and myself."

"Honora isn't coming?" Togan's brow furrowed.

"I'm not sure. She hasn't said, but I hesitate to put her in harm's way." Then he added, "she should be here with her family."

"Then you need a healer, unless you fancy settin' broken bones or carin' for other injuries."

"No, I don't relish the thought of doing anything like that. Nor, I think, does anyone else."

"Then I will have Marena come with us."

"The maid at the tavern that you were always making eyes at?" A suspicious smile slowly crossed Malach's face.

"One and the same," Togan said jovially. "I took your advice asked her t' court me."

"No, did you?"

Togan nodded an affirmative.

"Good for you! See, I told you that was a good idea." He was happy for the big man. "I didn't know she was a healer."

"Her mother was," Togan told him. "Growin' up she would help 'er so she knows a lot more than people give 'er credit for. She is also very handy with a bow."

"Well, we will have three bowmen, or women, along for the ride. Have you met Amara yet?"

"She a bit of a spitfire, isn't she?" Togan gave him a knowing look, indicating he had.

"Yes, she is," Malach chuckled. "She was a part of the infamous Shadows."

Togan's eyebrows when up in shock. "She was? She seems like a normal person."

"Just because she was a thief all of her life doesn't mean she's not normal," Malach defended her.

"I'm sorry, I meant no offense," Togan apologized. "You just expect someone who's been a thief all their lives t' be a little nasty and suspicious. She's not either of those."

"No, she isn't," Malach chuckled. "Although, I know what you mean. She, I dare say, is a knife master and a decent shot with a bow."

"Good. Well, I need t' go tell Marena to pack her things. I'm sure you will want to be ready as soon as possible." Togan said.

"Yes, and I'm sure Elzrod will want to get the party together in the morning to talk about what we will be doing and our road into Demon Territory. I will send word when I know where and when."

"Good, I will see you again soon then."

"Togan, before you go, could you point me to where the Wervines would be?" Malach asked, intending on seeing his adopted family.

"Mal!" Two very familiar voices shouted from behind him.

Togan smiled and left without another word.

Malach spun just in time to catch the two girls, who were like sisters to him. They had both grown since he had last seen them, and they almost knocked him over with the combined force of their collision with him.

"Emy! Marla!" Malach exclaimed, hugging the girls close.

Emmeline and Marletta were Daziar's sisters, and Malach had grown up living with them. Behind them, Jenari and Daniel, Daziar's parents, strode up behind the girls and joined the embrace. They released him and Malach glanced around searching for Daziar. He was nowhere to be seen.

"If you're looking for Daz, he went with a man named Elzrod," Jenari told him. "He seemed to know him."

"Elzrod has been helping us since Newaught," Malach nodded, reassuring them. "It's great to see you all!"

"We were so happy to find out that you all were safe," Jenari fidgeted with her hands. "I worry so much about you all."

Emmeline and Marletta knelt and loved on Skie, who almost looked like she was smiling.

"Daziar told us you aren't staying?" Daniel crossed his arms.

Malach always had a hard time figuring out what Daniel was feeling. "Unfortunately, that's correct."

"Do you have to go so soon?" Emy wined.

"My mother is being held by the demons, and we know where. I can't just leave her."

Daniel nodded as if thinking, "I wouldn't expect any less."

"But, please, be careful." Jenari fretted, fidgeting with her hands again. "I would be devastated if anything happened to either of you."

"We will be," Malach promised.

"And don't be gone as long," Emy stamped her foot for emphasis.

"Yes, ma'am," he chuckled.

An angel alighted next to Malach. He recognized the angel from the meeting. Raphael was the only angel he had seen who had four wings. Each of the angels seemed to have different types of wings. Cathetel and Camael's wings seemed to be made of metal. Raphael's four wings looked more like what Malach had envisioned, white feathers and a strong, muscular frame. He wondered for a moment what his father's wings had looked like.

"Malach," He addressed him. "Gabriel asked me to give you a crash course on the explosives, as well as outfit you with the pieces needed to create a few small devices. Is this a good time?"

Malach looked over at the Wervines, and Daniel nodded.

"As good a time as any," Malach replied. "Lead the way."

Raphael led him and Skie back into the fortress in the mountain, but instead of going up, he took Malach down a flight of stairs and into a maze of corridors all its own. He led Malach through several turns and down a spiral staircase. They were far under the fortress now, and the air felt damp and musty. He smelled the earth around them, and it was much warmer than it had been outside. Raphael stopped when they reached a heavy metal door.

"Before we go in, no open flame beyond this point," Raphael took a lantern with glass panes to allow the light of a single wick, which he lit. "But I'm sure I don't have to tell you. You've seen, firsthand, what this stuff is capable of."

Malach nodded solemnly, and the angel pushed his way through the metal door.

Inside were a number of metal parts and pieces strewn about on several tables. Behind them were barrels, lots of barrels, stacked floor to ceiling. The smell of sulfur hit him and made him want to turn and leave. The barrels must be holding the powder used in the explosive devices. If the empty space to the right of the barrels was any indication, they planned to have hundreds more soon.

Skie plodded over to one of the stacks of barrels, sniffed it, and sneezed.

Malach could swear she made a disgusted look.

She looked up and him and shook her head as if trying to shake off the smell, then plodded to the corner farthest away from the barrels. She laid down and put her head on her paws but continued to study Malach and Raphael.

Raphael was already on the other side of one of the tables waiting on him. Malach shut the metal door carefully. He felt very uneasy in this room. He walked to the table facing Raphael, and the angel started to inform him about the properties of the powder. He went so far as to tell him how to make the stuff, if he was ever in a situation that called for it. Raphael also showed him how to put everything together in different ways for different kinds of blasts.

If I remember half of this, I will be surprised, Malach thought most of the way through Raphael's instruction.

Don't worry, Reckoning told him. *I will remember it all.*

Wait, you mean I didn't have to listen to any of this and you could have just remembered it for me? Malach asked incredulously.

Well, yes, Reckoning replied, *but you need to know this too. There might be a time where you need it in a pinch and don't have time to consult me.*

I guess you're right, Malach sighed.

"Am I boring you?" Raphael asked.

"No!" Malach lied. "I was just talking to Reckoning."

"Good, he will assist you if you forget anything," Raphael nodded.

"Do you and the other angels talk to your blades often?"

Raphael's brow furrowed. "We do, although, after thousands of years of being with your blade, you have less and less to say. It tends to be more sporadic and tactical and less banter."

Which is why it's fun to have someone new to talk to, Reckoning told him. *Don't tell any of the angels this, but they can be dull and boring most of the time.*

Malach covered a laugh with a cough. *Your secret's safe with me.*

"Hmm," Raphael sounded thoughtful. "I seem to have kept you too long. Night has fallen, and you will need to rest for tomorrow's journey. I have taken the liberty of packing the supplies you will need for three explosives." The angel handed him a set of heavy saddlebags. "God's speed."

"Thank you." Malach nodded at the angel and whistled to Skie.

She immediately got up from her corner and quickly moved to his side, obviously ready to leave the acrid smelling room.

Reckoning guided him through the maze and back to the surface. Malach set the saddlebags down to take stock of their contents. There were several different containers for the powder to go in, each designed to direct the blast in different directions. Below those were containers that, no doubt, contained the powder. The amount of powder he was carrying in those saddlebags was awe-inspiring and slightly terrifying.

He closed the saddlebags and glanced up at the camp. The fires were starting to burn low, and only a few people were tending them. He walked into the Brightwood tent to find a place to sleep. The tent had been sectioned off by hanging strips of cloth to allow at least a modicum of privacy. He passed row after row of these 'rooms' until he started to see some of them with the flap open. He glanced into some as he passed, and they still had personal items in them, so he kept moving. Eventually, he found one that didn't have anything in it and moved in. He pulled back the heavy fur blankets, laid down on the bedroll, and was out in seconds.

Chapter 8

The next day, Malach had found they had taken his things to a singular tent within the soldiers' area of the camp. He retrieved them, dropped them off at his room, and headed to the mess tent. Elzrod had told him that morning they would be meeting there, directly following breakfast, so they could be on their way by noon with all the supplies they needed. Malach had also found out that about half the previous occupants of Brightwood would be headed back to the town. The other half decided to stay in the war camp for various reasons. The elders and those with children made up most of the half staying, not wanting to put them through the harsh journey back through the mountains.

Malach made it to the mess tent and entered. He spotted Togan, Amara, Elzrod, and Marena sitting at a table, already digging into plates of food. Grabbing a plate with his breakfast ration, he headed their way, sat down next to Amara and starting tucking into the food himself.

"Are you ready to hike back over the mountains?" Amara asked.

Before Malach could respond, Elzrod spoke up, "we won't be going with the main group."

"We won't?" Togan asked.

"No," Elzrod replied. "We will need to move much faster than they will, if we expect to get back here before the snow melts."

"How are we going to do that?" Amara asked. "It's not like we have wings or anything. The fastest we can move is on the horses, and they will only save us a few days."

"And only if the weather holds," Malach pointed out.

"You forget that the Pangor river runs all the way to the Great Divide," Elzrod replied. "The army has a fleet of small boats and canoes moored in the Emerald Basin that I have been permitted to take."

"Wouldn't taking the horse for the whole journey be faster than taking the river for half the journey?" Marena asked.

"It would, if we could take them the whole journey," Elzrod replied.

Daziar walked up to the table and sat down, "What are you all talking about?"

"Let me just explain everything now that we are all here," Elzrod pulled out a folded piece of paper, which turned out to be a map. "We are taking the canoes down the Pangor River to Angelcross. Since we haven't heard anything from them since the war started, we suspect that that outpost is under demon control. If possible, we will liberate Angelcross and, at the least, we will have to take back the equipment we need to ford the Great Divide. Once across, we will travel to Kargod, where we can procure some horses. Then we will cut through Ragewood forest and into the Demon Compound."

Malach looked around at everyone. Most were nodding their heads in agreement. Daziar continued to shoveling food into his mouth.

Is he even breathing? Malach thought. He shook his head and brought his mind back to the matter at hand. "How are we going to meet up with my father?"

"Anahita is going to be headed to Brightwood ahead of us. In fact, she left this morning and should be arriving there before we leave. Ariel will meet us where the road crosses the river." Elzrod pointed to the spot on the map.

"Sounds like a plan!" Togan leaned back in his chair.

"Thank you," Elzrod folded his map, pushed his chair back and stood up. "So pack, say your goodbyes, and meet me at the Emerald Basin at midday."

Malach finished his breakfast and got up. He was already packed since he never unpacked the night before. However, he did need to grab a few supplies before he headed to the basin. The hardest part about the day would be waiting for everyone to meet him so they could depart.

Amara came running up behind him, "Malach,"

Malach turned.

"Are you headed to the Basin?" She asked.

"Not just yet, I just have to grab some supplies," Malach replied. "I didn't unpack last night, I assumed we would be leaving quickly."

"I didn't unpack last night either, so that's all I need, too. Why don't we get what we need and head to the basin together?" Amara suggested.

"I would like that," Malach smiled, genuinely happy that she wanted to spend time with him.

He held out his arm to her and she took it smiling. They walked to each of their tents respectively and picked up their packs. Malach experienced an uneasy feeling as they exited the Brightwood tent, and it caught him off guard. He glanced around and saw a young man watching him from a little way away. As soon as Malach made eye contact with the man's black, cold eyes, he stood to his considerable height and briskly walked away. Malach bolted after him tearing his arm away from Amara as he did.

"Malach?" Amara called after him.

He didn't answer. This man was a nephilim and Malach knew it. He had gazed into those same cold black eyes back in Fairdenn. There must be another spy, and he needed to find him before he disappeared into the crowd. He turned the same corner the man had and caught sight of a dark cloak disappearing around another tent. Skie caught up to him and passed him seeming to know who he was chasing.

"Get him, Skie!" Malach directed her and she took off ahead of him, her powerful legs a blur under her.

He pushed his way through the crowd, a myriad of complaints and indignant shouts following him. He turned the corner and caught sight of Skie. She had slowed and was sniffing the ground trying to find the scent of the man. Malach stopped beside her, and she peered up at him. She had lost the nephilim in the confusion of all the other smells and he was nowhere to been seen.

"It was a good try, girl," Malach knelt next to Skie and ruffled her ears as he continued to scan the crowd.

Amara came running up, finally catching up to them. "Malach, what was that all about?"

"I saw a nephilim," He stood.

"Are you sure?"

"I'm certain. He was taller than me and had black eyes."

"Sounds about right. We should tell the angels."

Might I remind you two, not all nephilim are working for the enemy, Reckoning told them.

"But he did run," Malach said out loud so Amara could hear his reply to the Blade.

You have a point, Reckoning agreed. *I will report it, and we can let the angels take care of it from here.*

"Reckoning is probably right," Amara said as they walked to get their supplies. "I mean he was in the heart of the camp, he had to have passed the same inspection we did to get in."

"You're probably right." But he couldn't shake the feeling that those cold black eyes were still watching him.

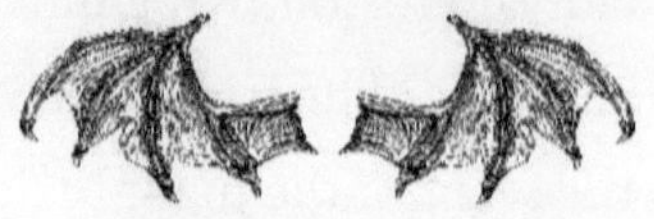

Kragen peered out from the shadow of a cluster of tents as Malach and his two companions walked away. He had gotten extremely lucky. He had been briefed on all the angels and on Malach Tresch and his wolf companion before he left on this mission. He spotted Malach and Skie and followed them to ascertain how much of a threat they were. Malach had been credited two demon kills before Kragen had arrived at the camp, and if the rumors were true, he had killed three more at Fairdenn.

He had underestimated Malach and was spotted. He had also underestimated the wolf. At a single command, the wolf had known exactly what Malach wanted it to do and had hunted him down. He had just barely gotten out of sight before the beast barreled around the corner. Cold, calculating death glowing in its eyes. The huge wolf hadn't been able to decipher his scent from the throng of people in the camp.

He didn't know how long Malach and his friends would be around, but he couldn't afford another mistake like that. No doubt they would report this to the angels, and they would be on high alert for anyone fitting his description. He needed to lay low for a while until they grew complacent once again. He headed to the tent of refugees he had been staying in. He grabbed his fully packed bag and headed out. Staying out in the open like this with the rest of the refugees would draw too much attention. His mistake had cost him his warm bed, but he was going to make sure it didn't cost him the mission.

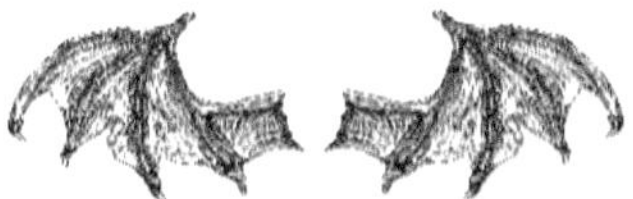

Amara and Malach acquired the supplies they needed and headed for the basin. It wasn't a long walk, but they were in no hurry. Skie moved along ahead of them sniffing at various things and seeming to try and pick up the scent of some prey. Soon, she left them altogether heading for the tree line not far away.

"So, what's your plan after this is all over?" Amara asked as they walked.

Malach lifted his head and took a moment to respond. "I always thought that I would go back to Brightwood, live my life out hunting. Now, I don't know. What are you thinking?"

"I don't know either." She turned her head to gaze off into the distance. "I had planned on going back to the Shadows in Caister, but I doubt you would want to join me there." She turned back to study his reaction. Part of her hoped he would join her, another part of her understood he never would.

"Would, you really want to go back to the Shadows?" Malach didn't look her in the eyes and fiddled with Reckoning's handle, which stuck out of its sheath.

"Well, unless something better came along." She raised an eyebrow and smiling suggestively as he turned to finally glance her way. He was so nervous and shy sometimes. She thought it was kind of cute.

"I guess there's hope for you yet," Malach grinned.

"I think I would have to have something exciting to do every day, though," Amara continued, turning serious again. "Maybe you could come with me to Newaught or Caister. We could get a boat and you could be a hunter of the ocean."

"You mean a fisherman?" Malach raised an eyebrow at her. "I don't think that's something I would enjoy."

"Oh." It was Amara's turn to study her feet.

"I'm sure we can figure something out,"

Malach put an arm around her shoulders, and she instantly felt secure and reassured. Everything would work out in the end.

"I sure we can." She smiled and snuggled into his warmth, putting and arm around his waist.

As they approached the basin, Amara could see the lake was covered in several feet of solid ice at the bank, the ice extended out onto the body of water. However, she could tell that it wasn't fully covered. There was a point where the ice gave way to the water, and she could see there were boats moored out beyond where the ice stopped. To her left, there was a dock extending out to the center of the lake, even past where the boats were moored, so they could be safely reached. It wouldn't be much longer, and the basin would be completely covered in ice and the boats would be stuck fast where they were. Just in front of the dock were stacks of canoes; some bigger, some smaller, tied down on wooden structures to keep them off the ground.

These must be the canoes we will be using, Amara thought.

Malach must having been thinking the same thing, for he steered them over to the stacks. He dropped his pack at the base of one of the structures to study one of the canoes. She could see that the canoes were built well and would be able to take a beating if they were to run it into something along the way or take fire from enemy archers. That, unfortunately, meant that it was going to be very heavy. If they had to carry these canoes over some obstruction, it would slow them down considerably. She had no idea how fast they would be able to go, but Elzrod thought they would go much faster than on horseback over the mountains.

"Have you ever been on a boat?" Amara asked.

"Uh, no," Malach replied honestly.

"It's not too hard," she assured him. "There is a bit of a learning curve, but I bet you will pick it up quickly."

"So, you have?" Malach cocked an eyebrow at her.

"Yeah, living in a port town, I've had several occasions to go out on the ocean. I've been in something kind of like this, but I imagine it will be different on a river than out on the ocean."

"Most likely, but I'm sure your experience will come in handy."

"I guess we will find out. I've never been up in the mountains in the winter, though, so that has been an experience."

"That means you've never been out on the ice?" He grinned at her, which told her he had something in store for her.

"No, I haven't," she replied with little trepidation, unsure of what he had in mind.

"Then leave your pack here. You're going to love this."

She did as she was told and followed him up the bank to a place where the basin pushed out into a shallow pool that had frozen solid. He took a bough from an evergreen tree and walked out onto the ice, setting to work clearing the snow. After about fifteen minutes, he had cleared a large, somewhat circular area. He tossed the branch onto the bank and motioned for her to come out onto the ice.

She carefully moved to the edge of the bank but didn't know how best to continue. He took one of her hands and gently pulled her out onto the ice. As soon as her second foot lifted off the ground, the foot on the ice tried to slide out from under her. She braced herself for the sudden and inevitable impact, but it didn't come. Instead, she felt Malach's strong arms around her and the warmth of his body on hers. She opened her eyes and gazed directly into his. He caught her. He righted her on the ice but still held both of her hands to steady her. They moved around the ice slowly, allowing her to get used to the slippery surface. She found, after several near falls, she enjoyed it. To her horror, Malach let go of her hands and let her stand on her own two feet, so to speak. She flailed her arms, trying to keep her balance and managed to save herself. After a few more moments of fright, she was able to skate around without fear of falling. Although, she wasn't as graceful as Malach.

"We used to do this every winter as children," he told her, as he passed her for the umpteenth time. "Honora even got us all these things she called skates that made it much easier to maneuver. She was much better at it than Daz and me. She used to do jumps and twists. We were never able to get anywhere close to doing those."

"I will have to get her to teach me, if I ever get the chance," Amara leaned into a turn a little too much and lost her balance. She was able to save herself from falling, but she was by no means graceful. "Well, if you do this in Brightwood, maybe I could come to live there after all."

"Really?" Malach asked, skating over to her.

"Yeah, I mean as long as we take a trip down to Caister every few years to see Lawdel. And that's if we survive the war."

"Fair. For now, let's just enjoy this while we can," Malach replied, taking one of her hands and skating with her, out to the middle of the ice.

They skated for several hours, and Amara improved quickly. She was skating almost as well as Malach as the other members of their party started to arrive. Malach skated off to greet his friends, but Amara wasn't finished yet. She wasn't sure she ever wanted to be finished.

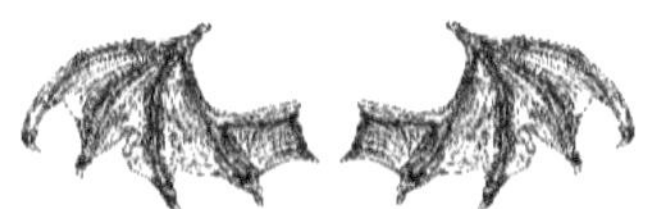

Finally, they spotted Elzrod coming down the road toward them. Malach and Togan started to take the largest of the canoes off the structures. They had three canoes on the ground, ready to be put in the water by the time Elzrod walked up. Elzrod studied the three canoes for a moment.

"One more canoe, if you don't mind," Elzrod told them.

Malach looked at him quizzically but proceeded to do as he was bidden.

Once the fourth canoe was on the ground, Elzrod explained himself. "Each of these canoes can hold the weight of three people, but we will need to pack our supplies into them as well. Also, we will be picking up Ariel along the way, so he will need space for him and his supplies. Since Amara and I are the only people here with experience in boating, we will be in two of the canoes alone. One we will load down with the extra supplies and the other will be open for Ariel when we get there. Malach, you and Daziar will take one of the other canoes. Which leaves Togan and Marena in the other."

Elzrod explained how the canoes would work and how to steer and manage them. "Be careful not to tip the canoe. If you do, the frigid water will send your body into shock. It won't take long for you to lose consciousness if that happens. There are parts of the river that will be moving faster and could get dangerous. Make sure you don't strike a rock during these parts, or it could send you into the water."

"Large amounts of danger and death. Anything else?" Daziar threw up both of his hands and shrugged.

"One last thing," Elzrod put a finger in the air. "There is a large section which has never fully been explored. We don't know what we will encounter during that section of the river. However, if our crossing during our flight from Fairdenn is any indication, then there shouldn't be anything we can't handle."

They moved the canoes out to the end of the dock and one-by-one, slipped them into the water, tying them to the dock. Elzrod and Amara carefully climbed into their respective canoes and loaded most of the supplies.

"I'll get in back of ours, as I'll be able to pick up steering this thing rather fast." Daziar climbed awkwardly into the back, almost tipping it several times and flopped down hard on his seat.

"You'll probably be needin' one of these then, don't ya think?" Togan held out the paddle that Daziar had forgotten to load onto the canoe.

Daziar blushed and took the paddle.

Malach waited until he was certain Daziar was settled, not wanting to be thrown out of the boat by his jostling. He had to work to coax Skie into the boat and she didn't seem very happy once she was in there. It only had to rock for a few moments and Skie decided laying down would be much safer.

Once they had all settled in, Togan added a couple extra paddles into Amara's canoe, just in case. Marena climbed into her canoe, taking the front seat and Togan started to untie each canoe. They didn't go far since there wasn't any real current, and Togan was able to untie his canoe and slip into it quickly, without any trouble. They each pushed off from the docks, following Elzrod as he effortlessly, and gracefully paddled toward the mouth of the river.

Malach paddled, with strong, even strokes, alternating sides every so often. Daziar, however, didn't seem to have grasped the explanation Elzrod had given them. He would paddle on one side of the canoe until they were well off course, and then, almost frantically, change side and paddle heavily on the other side of the canoe. This resulted in the canoe making a winding, zigzag path through the water. Their path was so wide, in fact, there was no way they would get down the river without running aground on one bank or the other.

"Hey, Daz," Malach called back, trying his best to stay patient. "Try paddling once or twice on one side and then repeating the same thing on the other."

"I got it," Daziar replied stubbornly. "Just getting the hang of it that's all."

"Well, get the hang of it quicker. We are being left behind."

It was true. The other three canoes were almost to the mouth of the river, and Malach could tell Elzrod was trying to slow down a little for them. The current, however, had a mind of its own and grew stronger the closer they got to the river's mouth. There was only so much they could do to slow their progress.

"Do you want to come back here and do this?" Daziar retorted.

"I can give it a shot if you want," Malach replied, trying to defuse the frustration that was evident in Daziar's tone.

"No, I don't," he replied tersely, and Malach could all but see him pouting, even though he didn't turn his head to look.

Malach shook his head and continued to do his best to keep them on track.

The canoe started to straighten out slightly. Daz had somewhat taken his advice, even if he wouldn't admit it. They entered the mouth of the river and started to pick up speed, which made the canoe's meandering path all the more dangerous.

Malach called out rocks and obstructions as they came and prayed to God, if he were listening, they wouldn't hit them. They got so close to one rather large rock, Malach braced himself for the waters icy touch. Instead, they slid by it, scraping the side of the canoe along the rock and leaving small furrows in the wood. He let out the breath he didn't fully realize he was holding.

Daz let out a triumphant whoop, pumping his fist still clutching the paddle, "See? I have everything under control."

It didn't make Malach feel any better. The fact his friend was barely able to navigate the perils of the river and still believed he was in control was frightening.

About midday, they finally caught up. The rest of the group had stopped in a wide part of the river which had a nice sloping bank. Throughout the day they had been able to catch glimpses of the other canoes in the places the river straightened out. There hadn't been any splits in the river so far, which he was grateful for. They hadn't been in danger of getting lost, but he didn't like being so far behind. If Daz wasn't able to steer them around something and they left more than a scrape on their canoe, the others might not even know it.

They ran their canoe aground, and Skie bailed out as soon as the nose hit the bank. Malach hopped out and pulled the canoe farther up the bank, out of the current. Daziar disembarked, and they walked up to the rest of the group.

"Glad you two finally decided to join us." Amara grinned at them.

"If Daziar wasn't trying to run us into every rock and obstruction along the way, we might have gotten here sooner," Malach said, not totally joking.

Togan guffawed loudly at the look of indignation on Daziar's face, which only deepened with Malach's comment.

"It's not as easy as it looks, Mal," Daziar replied, crossing his arms defiantly.

"Isn't it?" Malach raised an unconvinced eyebrow. "Togan seemed to manage it."

"Then you try it," Daziar replied, starting to get genuinely upset. "When you run us into something, we will see who is laughing then."

"It won't be you," Elzrod pointed out. "You will be cold and wet with Malach in the river. However, I think it would be a good idea if you all switched. It would give everyone a chance to steer before we get to the rapids tomorrow morning. That way, if something did happen to one of us, we would all have experience."

"You mean it gets worse?" Daziar shoulders slumped.

"Yes, it does," Elzrod nodded solemnly.

They all settled down around a small fire, warming themselves and eating the midday meal. Once they were done, Elzrod doused the fire and they all climb into the canoes. Malach had to pick up Skie and forcibly put her in the boat this time. He held her while Daziar shoved them off the bank.

To Daziar's dismay—however, unsurprising to the rest of the group—Malach turned out to be the better of the two at steering. He kept them relatively straight and never once got too close to an obstruction in the river. Even Skie felt comfortable enough to stand up and peer around at the bank gliding by them. Daziar sat at the front of the canoe for a while, not paddling but simply pouting, muttering to himself how this part of the river must be easier to navigate than the stretch that they had traversed this morning.

Malach had to eventually break the silence to get Daziar to paddle again. "Hey, Amara, isn't this part of the river a little calmer than this morning."

"I think it's a little hard-" she started to say but cut herself off as she caught Malach's look. "A little hard to tell, but the river seems to be a little straighter and the current not as fast," she amended.

Her words had the desired effect, and Daziar perked up a little. A few minutes later, he picked up his paddle again.

The things you do for friends, Malach thought.

I find you humans to be odd at times, Reckoning said out of the blue.

You and me both, Malach thought back ruefully.

The rest of the day was uneventful, other than a short water war between Togan and Marena. Although, they stopped before anyone got too cold and wet. Malach hadn't ever seen the big man so happy, and he was glad for it. They also passed under the bridge the army used to get people from Fairdenn to the camp.

"This is as far as the army has scouted the river," Elzrod informed them. "From the bridge until we reach the crossing south of Brightwood is unknown to us."

As dusk started to settle in several hours later, they pulled their canoes up onto the bank, and Malach could hear rushing water coming from downriver. It seemed a lot louder than the sounds that were coming from upriver where they had just passed. He decided to scout the river ahead. He stood and Skie all but leaped up from where she was laying.

"I'm going to scout the river ahead," he declared to the group.

"I'll go with you," Amara stood as well and followed him out of camp.

They made their way through the dense underbrush, the rushing water growing louder as they went. They were forced to stray away from the river itself to get around a tangle of briars, but they worked their way back once they were able. What they found took their breath away, both from fear and from awe.

The river turned into a canyon over the span of only a few hundred yards. The result was the river turning into a flume, funneling the water, and shooting it down at a steep angle. The flume was straight as an arrow, and it looked deep enough for a canoe, but Malach wasn't sure he wanted to go down it. If something were to go wrong, it was going to hurt.

"This is going to be incredible!" Amara jumped up and down, clapping her hands.

"Umm, I'm not sure that's the word I would use," Malach tore his gaze away from the flume and looked at her. "More like terrifying, or insane, or extremely stupid."

"Don't be so worried. Just imagine how fast we'll go!"

"Believe me, I am," Malach replied and headed downstream once more. He wanted to see how far this thing went.

They didn't have to walk too far to get a better view. He pushed through the underbrush only to have his foot fall into thin air. He caught hold of a bush he had been pushing past and held on for dear life as he started to plummet off the cliff. A surprised shout escaped his lips as he peered down at the long drop awaiting him. Amara grasped his arm, and with her help, he pulled himself back up. Once both of his feet were planted on solid ground he collapsed, breathing heavily as much from fright as from exertion.

Amara however peered out over the cliff and whistled low and long, "That would have been a long drop."

"It's the sudden stop at the end that had me worried," Malach retorted. "Thanks, Amara."

"No problem. What kind of person would I be if I let my suitor fall to his death?" Amara smiled at him. "You have to look at this. It's beautiful."

Malach got to his feet and moved carefully toward the edge of the cliff. This time he made sure his feet were always in contact with the ground. He got past the bushes and branches blocking his view and gaped at the sight before him. They were above all the trees in the valley below, the Pangor winding through it like a blue snake. They could see for miles, and it was all covered in snow, which made it even more beautiful as the setting sun reflected off it. The expanse was wild, untouched by any beings, and undamaged by any war. Malach sat down next to Amara who had already taken a seat. They admired the sublime landscape in silence, taking in its beauty.

"Couldn't we live here?" Amara asked her voice fill with awe.

"I would love that. We could build a house a little back from this cliff and clear out a view. We would wake up to the beauty of this wild land and each other."

Amara leaned over and rested her head on his shoulder, and he put his arm around her waist. "That sounds amazing, Mal."

Malach had never heard her use his nickname, and he liked the way it sounded when she said it.

He was content. If only he knew his mother was safe, he would have stayed. War be damned, consequences be damned. It would be many years before anyone would find them here. He and Amara could live long, happy lives and have as many kids as they wanted. They wouldn't have to fear what battles they would have to fight or horrors they would have to witness. No, this was paradise.

Malach glanced over in the fading light and was brought back to reality by the sight of the flume. It was at such a steep angle that it ended in a pool at the bottom of the cliff with only a small drop. Furthermore, they could watch from here as each canoe went down to make sure everyone made it safely down and to know when the previous canoe was out of the way.

Amara broke into his thoughts, suddenly, with a warm passionate kiss. He started at first but let himself relax into it and returned the kiss. He became aware that his heart was racing, and he was feeling something he had never felt before. It was a kind of heat, but he wasn't embarrassed. He loved Amara, more than he had loved anyone. He wanted this woman to be by his side for the rest of his life, and he would fight for that future.

She broke off the kiss and gazed into his eyes. "Mal, I love you."

"I love you too," he pulled her in for another kiss.

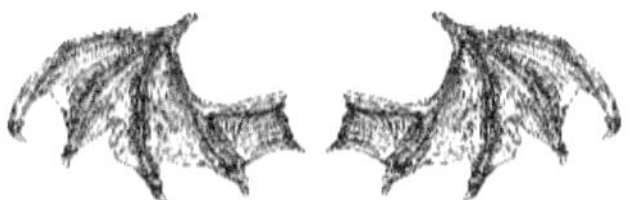

Malach and Amara walked into the camp shortly after the light from the sun faded completely. All eyes turned to them as they entered. They didn't say anything but awkwardly took their spots by the fire.

"How was your evening?" Togan grinned mischievously.

"Togan," Marena scolded, slapping him on the shoulder.

"Fine," Malach replied, unfazed. "We scouted the river ahead and we are in for a ride tomorrow."

"What do you mean?" Elzrod asked.

He relayed what they had found and the cliff he had almost fallen over. He explained there was no way down for miles, and they wouldn't be able to go around the flume of water unless they wanted to leave the canoes behind. He also informed them of his plan to make it as safe as possible by having a lookout watch the end of the flume and report using Reckoning and Storm to relay messages.

"I vote we don't go at all," Daziar suggested. "We are only a day into this trip. Why risk it when we can just backtrack for a day and take a much safer route over the mountains?"

Malach didn't like the idea of wasting all that time. They had used the river to save time in the first place. If they quit now, it would put them several days behind.

"Malach," Togan leaned toward him. "Do you think the flume is safe enough to traverse?"

Malach paused to think before he answered, crossing his arms, "I wouldn't suggest going if I didn't think we could make it. However, it's not without danger. One wrong move, and you could end up in the freezing pool below or worse, injured and caught in the flume itself. Although, I think it's worth the risk."

"That's good enough for me," Togan grabbed the ladle and stirred whatever stew they were cooking.

"Well, if Togan's going, so will I," Marena put a hand on Togan's shoulder.

Malach nodded his thanks at their support then turned to Daziar. "Daz, if you want to go back, that is up to you, but you will be the only one. Everyone else will be headed down the flume tomorrow."

Daziar thought about it for a second and Malach wondered if he was going to go back this early in their mission. "Fine," he finally agreed. "But if we all die tomorrow, I get to say I told you so."

Elzrod nodded thoughtfully. "If I knew this is what we would face by traveling this direction, I might have chosen a different path for us. However, since we stand to lose many days going back, I agree. We should push forward. I suggest that Amara be the first to go down the flume. Once she is down and we have the report from Malach, Togan and Marena will follow and able to assist if she needs help, then I will go, and last Malach and Daziar. That way we keep communication open as long as possible."

They agreed and filled their bowls with the stew. Once finished, they went to their separate tents to sleep for the night. Malach decided, no matter what happened tomorrow, he would push on toward the goal of saving his mother. Even if he had to walk alongside the river the rest of the way there, sopping wet.

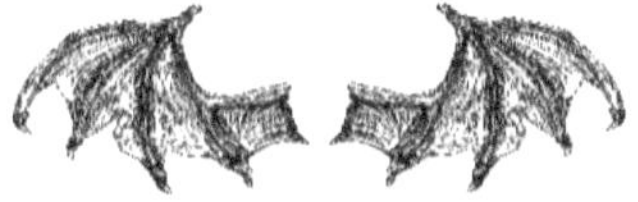

Amara woke before the light of dawn was even a glimmer on the horizon. She tossed and turned for a bit but couldn't fall back asleep. She left her tent, deciding to take one last look at her and Malach's clifftop view.

She pushed her way through the underbrush. However, it was a bit easier, since they had already trampled their way through it twice. She got close to the cliff and slowed down, careful not to make the same mistake Malach did the day before. The scenery unveiled before her was even more breathtaking than the prior evening.

She sat down, dangling her feet once again over the edge. She really did love the view and the ambiance of the area. She wished she could stay here with Malach. She had never once thought about having children before meeting Malach, but now she knew beyond a shadow of a doubt that, if they survived this war, this would be their future.

She pulled out the amulet from around her neck. She hadn't thought about it in a long time. The amulet had been found with her when she was a baby. It was a silver chain with a silver setting in the shape of a claw. The stone set into what would be the palm of the claw was a deep, blood red. It had an otherworldly ambiance about it, and if she looked closely, she could almost see something swirling inside. She held it closer, but the swirling seemed to stop. She wondered if it had been a trick of the ever-growing light. She had thought about selling it once or twice. It would have fetched her a high enough price to feed her for a few months. But it had never felt right, so she had kept it all these years.

Maybe one day she would find her parents, or at least find out what happened to them. Lawdel thought the pendant had to have been given to her by one or both of her parents, and he told her it meant they loved her. If they had loved her, though, she wouldn't have been left on the streets to die in the cold. For a long time, she didn't care if she found them or not. Now, however, since helping Malach find his father, she couldn't help but wonder what her parents would be like.

The sun peaked over the horizon and lit up the valley below; slowly at first, leaving some of it in the shadow of the mountains, but the light seemed to speed up as the sun rose. Amara sat and watched it move across the valley until the direct sunlight struck her. Her pendant flashed, startling her and almost making her drop it off the cliff. She managed to hold onto it and brought it up to her face to study it. Somehow since the initial flash, it had grown dark instead. Not refracting the light or focusing it in any way but darkening the stone from the color of fresh blood to a deep, dark blackish-red. It reminded her of something, but she couldn't quite put her finger on it.

Skie walked up beside her and plopped down, laying her head in Amara's lap.

She quickly looped the pendant over her neck and dropped in down her shirt. It was uncomfortably hot against her skin, but once it was out of the sunlight, it started cooling.

Skie glanced up at her as if she could sense Amara's discomfort.

"It's nothing," she lied to the big wolf. "I just wish we could stay."

Skie plopped her head back into Amara's lap and closed her eyes.

Malach appeared out of the underbrush. He spotted Amara and Skie and sat down with them. "Everyone is ready to leave."

"Alright." She took one last look at the valley, not wanting to ever forget the sight in front of her.

"I'm sorry we can't stay." Malach was watching her.

"I know." Amara didn't take her eyes off the valley.

"We will come back." He stood and held a hand out to help her up. "I promise."

"I'm going to hold you to that promise, Malach Tresch," she warned, taking his hand.

He hauled her to her feet and pulled her close. So close she could feel the warmth radiating off his body. He leaned down and kissed her softly, pulling her into his warm embrace. He held her for a fleeting moment, and she wished it would never end.

"We have to go, everyone is waiting, and you get the pleasure, or terror, of going down first."

Amara's stomach twisted all of a sudden, and she wished she hadn't been so vocal about wanting to go down the flume. At first, she was excited, but now the time to go down was upon her. She wasn't sure she really wanted to do it. She was committed, however, and everyone expected her to go first. The closer they got to the camp, the more her stomach twisted. They arrived at camp, which wasn't anything more than a clearing next to the river now, and everyone was looking at her, waiting for her to get in her canoe and go down the flume.

It's going to be fine, she told herself. *Malach wouldn't let you go down it if he didn't think you would be alright. Besides, Togan and Marena will be coming down behind you if something does go wrong.*

"Are you ready, Amara?" Elzrod motioned to her canoe with his hand.

The solemnness that hung in the air made her feel like she was being led to the gallows, but instead of being an unwilling prisoner, she was walking there of her own free will. She managed a nod and plodded over to her canoe. Her pack and things had already been placed in it.

"It's going to be fine," Malach said quietly in her ear.

She turned and flashed him what she hoped was a cocky grin. "Of course it is. This is going to be fun!" But she didn't fully believe her own words.

She carefully got into the canoe and picked up her paddle. Malach gave her one last nod and then headed back for the cliff to watch and relay information. She hated to see him go but understood it was for her own safety.

To her shock and amazement, Skie hopped into the canoe in front of her. She took courage from the large wolf, gritted her teeth, and pushed off from the bank. She paddled out into the current that would take her to the mouth of the flume and glanced behind her one last time. Togan and Marena were already climbing into their canoe and Daziar was loading supplies into his.

Good, she thought to herself. *They will be ready if something goes wrong.*

She turned to face the river ahead, readying herself for the plunge. It took what felt like an eternity for the mouth of the flume to come into view. Maybe it was just her nerves that made it feel that way. She finally spotted it, even as she was almost upon it. From where she sat in the canoe it just appeared to be a little dip in the stream until you considered what was beyond it. Clear blue skies with only a few wispy white clouds.

Amara gulped and maneuvered her canoe so it was pointed directly at the middle of the flume. There was no going back now. Even if she wanted to, she was in the strong current, and she would not be able to paddle her way free before going over. Every moment that passed, every foot she got closer to the flume, the more she wanted to jump out of the canoe and swim for shore. She would never make the swim; however, her body would go into shock, and she would drown before she made it to shore. No, her best chance of survival now would be to ride this out. She would go down the flume and into the pool waiting below. Although, hopefully, not into its icy cold depths.

The leading edge of her canoe nosed off the edge and the hull scraped, jarring her to a stop. Skie was knocked off her feet and landed with a thud. Amara would have been thrown as well had she not been bracing for the plunge. They teetered there, stuck, the nose of the canoe sticking out into open air and the water rushing by her. It took her a moment to process what had happened.

The canoe had scraped along a stone shelf or rock under the water and ground to a halt. As the water rushed around her, it started to turn her canoe, first to one side then the other. If she didn't act fast, she might end up going down the flume *outside* of the canoe. She lunged forward, jerking the canoe, hoping to move it just enough to push it over the edge but it barely budged. She tried again. It wasn't working and the rocking of the canoe was getting worse.

She stood up and put her leg out of the canoe and, before she could talk herself out of it, plunged her foot in. The water came up to her knee and filled her boot. She pushed hard on the stone shelf. The lessened weight and force of the water jolted the canoe forward under her. Her foot acted as an anchor, holding one side of the back of the canoe long enough to turn the back end. She was able to get most of her body into the canoe as it went over the edge. The back of the canoe slammed into the rock and the impact flung her the rest of the way in. Her head crashed against the forward seat, and Skie yelped from underneath her body. She almost lost consciousness but fought through the darkness and brought herself back to her senses. She must not have lost too much time. The rock walls on either side of her flew by.

She pushed herself off of Skie, who let out a small wine. Amara ignored the wolf and raised her head to see what was in store for them. The little pool of water rushed up to meet her. She ducked her head and hugged Skie close just as the canoe shot out of the flume and hit the water with a mighty splash. Moments later she was showered with the freezing water that the canoe had sprayed into the air.

She sat up from where she and Skie had taken cover and took stock of her situation. She glanced around the boat, but it didn't seem to have any holes or have sprung any leaks. Skie whined at her again, studying her head. Just about the same time, a massive headache split her skull. She dropped her head into her hands and moaned. Something warm and sticky coated her hands, and she knew she was bleeding. She also knew no help was coming soon. Togan and Marena with their boat sitting much lower in the water would be bashed into the shelf and most likely tipped into the water. She needed to warn Malach.

Despite the pain that now coursed down her neck she stood up in the boat and wave her arms over her head hoping Malach was still watching. After a moment she made a cutting motion across her neck. She motioned in the Shadows' wordless code, warning him of the rock shelf, but even as she was, the world was going dim at the edges. She sat down hard, missing the seat and thumping into the bottom of the canoe. She was vaguely aware of Skie licking her face and head before everything went black.

Chapter 9

Somewhere, in a dark dungeon in Demon Territory, Serilda lay in filth and squalor. Her clothes, little more than torn rags, hung from her emaciated body and she had little more energy than to crawl over to the bowl of slop the guard had pushed through the cell door and eat it. She wasn't chained, not anymore. They had taken those off many months ago when she had lost the strength to even pull on them. She was a fighter, but even now, she was considering the wisdom of staying alive. Her husband was most likely still imprisoned or dead, and they had told her they had killed her son. Even going as far as to bring his head before her and rolling it out of the bag at her feet. She had killed the human that had been with the demons in a fit of rage, bashing her head into his and going for his throat with her teeth. She really wanted to kill the demon that was tormenting her, but she knew that she wouldn't have a chance in hell at that. He would have swatted her away like a gnat.

She had stopped eating after that. Until she thought she would sleep and never wake up. But the demon couldn't allow that. She awoke choking on food. Chicken, of all things. Good, warm cooked meat, and her body had taken over. She ate until there was nothing left. Then she threw most of it back up, and even then, she ate it again, uncaring that it tasted like bile. The next day was the same. Her body's own instincts betrayed her, and soon, she was eating again.

After a few days, they had relegated her back to the slop again, not wasting the good food on her. She wished she could just die. Unfortunately, she had no means by which she could realize her demise. If only they would bring her blade back to her. If she could just connect with Fang, they could end this together, the way it started.

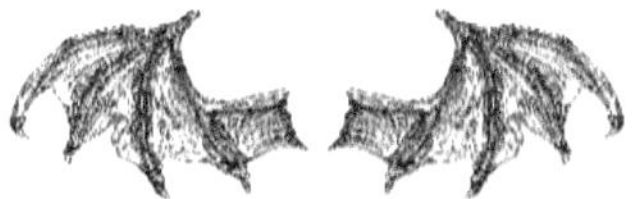

Malach watched as the canoe shot through the opening of the flume and skipped across the small pond, sending a spray of water out in front of it. He couldn't tell from where he was if Amara was even in the little craft much less if she was ok. He peered closer holding his breath involuntarily. Amara sat up and Malach let out the breath in a relieved rush.

Amara made it fine, Malach mentally told Elzrod.

Good, we will send Togan and Marena as we planned, came the reply, Malach could tell he was relieved as well.

He turned his attention back to Amara to see her waving her arms at him, she made a series of motions at him but all he really understood was the cutting motion she made across her throat.

"Don't send anyone else!" Is what it told him.

Wait! Malach shouted mentally.

What's wrong? Elzrod asked.

I'm not sure, Malach replied and told him what he had just seen.

That sounds like a version of the old demon hand signals they used to use in the war. Elzrod replied. *Can you send me a mental image of what you saw?*

How do I do that? Malach asked.

The same way you send words, Elzrod instructed. *Just picture what you saw and send that.*

Malach concentrated sending him the motions she was doing exactly as he remembered them.

That all you remember? Elzrod asked. *You didn't see any of the more subtle movements?*

I'm sorry I didn't see every little move of her fingers from a half-mile away, Malach retorted.

We will have to work on that, Elzrod replied, quite serious.

Hurry, Malach implored watching Amara collapse in the canoe. *Amara's just passed out. Luckily, she is still in the canoe.*

Well, there was something about a shelf, but I couldn't see much, Elzrod mused. *She definitely doesn't want us to come down because of whatever it is.*

Malach wasn't willing to wait for Elzrod to figure it out. He sprinted back through the woods and before anyone could stop him got into his and Daziar's canoe. He paddled it out of reach of anyone onshore and ignored their warning cries. Soon he was around the bend and away from them. He moved toward the bank once again, trying to stay out of the main current so he wouldn't get sucked into the flume. He steered into a back current that was coming off one side of it and paddled hard to beach his canoe on the bank. He watched the entrance to the flume looking for any danger that the water might hide. He almost paddled out to it and then decided against it.

Malach, Elzrod's voice called in his head. *Malach, don't do anything stupid.*

Have you ever known me to do anything stupid? Malach asked getting out of the canoe onto the bank. *Don't answer that.*

Malach, if you end up getting yourself killed, you won't be able to save her. Elzrod warned.

I won't get myself killed, Malach replied. *But I can't sit around talking about the problem when Amara needs my help.*

Malach walked around the bank toward the mouth of the flume. The glare of the sun off the water lessened as he did, and he could see a rock shelf just under the surface. That must be what Amara meant. He could tell that it wasn't very wide, and he thought he might be able to break through it with Reckoning. He would have to do it in the water though. He would not be able to reach it from the bank.

Without a second thought, he waded into the freezing water. He sucked in a breath as the water came up past his waist. He wouldn't have much time before his body went into shock. He let the current hurry him along, trying not to lose his footing. He reached the shelf and carefully climbed up onto it. The current nearly swept him off and the air felt colder than the water as he exposed the parts of him which were now sopping wet. Widening his stance, he changed Reckoning into a large hammer and took his first swing at the shelf. The water slowed the hammer before it hit the shelf and he didn't do as much damage as he was hoping.

Malach, Reckoning said urgently. *Change me into a pickaxe. I will have less resistance in the water, and you can break the shelf away quicker. Elzrod and Daziar are already on their way to assist you.*

Malach didn't answer but took the blade's advice. His next swing made contact with a hard, jarring impact. It wouldn't have been as bad, but Malach's hands were over-sensitive from the cold. He took another swing, and a piece of the rock shelf broke away and was sent down the flume. Malach was aware of his teeth chattering uncontrollably and couldn't remember when they had started. His third swing broke off another chunk, which followed the first down the flume and out of sight. He had made the shelf deep enough, but he had to widen it or the canoes would still be caught. Malach's fourth swing had much less strength behind it and he had to take a fifth swing to break off the third chunk of rock. That wasn't a good sign. His muscles were growing numb, and he was losing strength in his limbs. He already had lost almost all the feeling in his legs and feet. Two more swings slammed down and the gap widened again.

He glanced up to see Daziar and Elzrod turn the bend on the stream. The gap was wide enough now a canoe could fit through. He just had to get back to the bank and get warm. He took one last swing for good measure and then put Reckoning away and waded back through the frigid water. Weariness started to set in about the time he made it back to the bank. His eyelids were heavy, and he could barely keep them open. He fought the current to make it to the bank and finally pulled free of the water. He clawed his way up the bank and laid down. It was over. He had done what he needed to get the party down the flume to help Amara. He could rest now.

Malach closed his eyes and felt a sharp pain on his cheek. He brushed at it with one hand trying to wipe away whatever the nuisance was. All he wanted to do was sleep. Another sensation of pain, this time accompanied by the sharp sound of flesh slapping against flesh. Someone had slapped him. Anger boiled in his belly sending new warmth to his limbs. He opened his eyes and tried to swing at whoever had hit him, but his right arm wouldn't respond. He couldn't really feel it.

He peered down to his right. He was still on the bank but farther up from the water. Heavy blankets had been piled on him and a fire was just being started. His wet clothes had been stripped off of him and tossed to the side. He noticed Daziar to his left. He must have slapped him. He lifted his left arm and, after freeing it from the blanket with quite a bit of effort, slapped Daziar back.

Daziar barely flinched at the feeble attempt at revenge and smiled broadly at his friend. "You hit like a girl."

"Don't let Honora hear you say that," Malach mumbled back. "She would make sure you knew how hard girls could hit."

Daziar chuckled, "Good to have you back, Mal."

"I didn't go anywhere, just closed my eyes for a second."

"It been almost a half-hour. We thought we had lost you for a second."

"Amara!" Malach exclaimed, remembering why he had risked his life. He tried to get up.

"Elzrod went down the flume to help her," Daziar put a hand on Malach's chest. He didn't have to push to keep Malach down, however, the furs were doing *that* all on their own. "If there is anything to do for her, he will do it."

Malach relaxed, resting his head back down on the ground. After a few more moments his legs and arms started to burn as the feeling and circulation started to return to them. Togan and Marena had come down the river and Togan soon had a roaring fire warming him as well.

"We'll spend the rest of the day and night here." Togan declared. "Tomorrow we'll join Elzrod and Amara."

Malach thought that sounded like a good plan. He didn't think he would be able to go anywhere until he recovered a little. He just wished Elzrod or Storm would send word about how Amara had faired. Since he wasn't a full-blooded angel, he would have to wait for Elzrod to make the connection.

Reckoning, Malach thought, *if you hear anything from Elzrod wake me.*

Or I could just tell you in your dreams so you could get more rest, Reckoning replied.

Sounds good. Malach replied.

"Hey, Daz," Malach called.

"Yeah?" Daziar looked up from the fire.

"Don't you dare slap me again." He pointed a finger at him. "If you do, you'll get more than a little slap back."

Daziar grinned at Malach. "Sleep with one eye open then."

Malach drifted off into sleep.

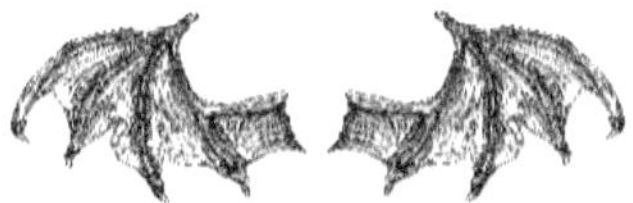

On the downward side of the flume, Amara was fairing only slightly better than Malach. She was similarly wrapped in as many blankets as they had on them and her head was bandaged. Elzrod told her she was lucky, since the cold slowed her blood loss and Skie laid on top of her to keep her warm. Apparently, when she hit her head, she cut it open. Elzrod had to shave her hair to sew up the wound. He had given her some herbs for the pain, but she still had a massive headache.

Elzrod kept her awake for a while, telling her about what had happened and what Malach had done to allow him to get to her before she bled out. If he had stopped to think and figure out a better way to get to her, she would most likely be dead. She owed him her life yet again. Although in some ways they owed her their lives for warning them about the shelf. Maybe they came out even on this one. She would have to wait until the morning for the rest of them to come down the flume. Then they would continue their journey. Hopefully, the rest of their trip down the river would be less eventful and less painful.

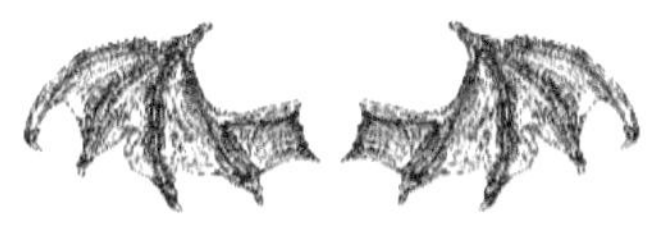

Malach and Daziar came down the flume first the next morning. Malach was still wrapped in furs, not allowed, by Marena's orders, to do anything and Daziar whooped and hollered the whole way down. Daziar seemed to have a better grasp on how to steer the canoe today.

Amara could tell by the look on Malach's face he didn't like not being able to participate in the paddling.

His face brightened to a smile when he spotted her, however, and then changed to worry at seeing her bandages. "Are you alright?"

"Better than you, lunatic!" she called back, happy to see he was still breathing. "I heard you tried to turn yourself into an ice sculpture."

"Something like that," Malach chuckled. "I see you went head-to-wood with your canoe and the canoe won."

"Yeah," Amara moved a hand to the bandages. "I guess I don't have as hard of a head as you do."

They heard a roar of laugher coming from the flume and they all turned to watch Togan and Marena shoot down it. Togan was in the front of the canoe and when it hit the pool, the wave of water it caused was massive, almost reaching the bank where Amara was standing. The momentum of their canoe brought them right to where the rest of the party was, needing only a few paddles to correct its course. Togan was still laughing like a child when they ran aground.

"My only wish is t' return t' the top and be able to do that a second time!" he bellowed jovially.

Everyone shared in his mirth, laughing along with the large man. Amara and Elzrod climbed into their canoes and the group started down the river once again. Skie stayed with Amara, standing in the bow of the canoe as if she was captain of the small vessel. Amara had to keep leaning to peer around the wolf so she wouldn't run into anything.

Around midday, Malach couldn't take it anymore, he unwrapped and freed himself of the furs. Ignoring the protests of the rest of the party, he took up a paddle and set to work. He would not be dissuaded. He tired faster than he normally would and had to take rests along the way.

That afternoon, they passed under the trees the angels had felled on their flight from Fairdenn. The trees had slowly sunk into the bank on either side of the river, and they had to duck low to not crack their heads on them. A few hours later, Elzrod called a halt, and they set up their camp for the night.

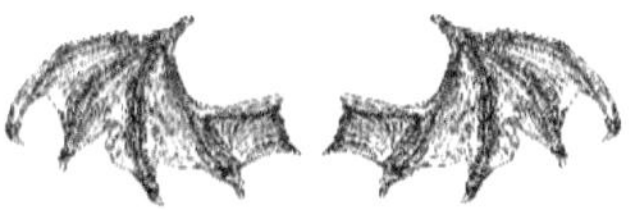

With another day on the river behind them and only a half a day to go, the small group set out the next morning with vigor. Elzrod contacted Ariel and found that he was already waiting at the bridge, and he would be ready to go when they arrived. They were ahead of the schedule Elzrod had placed on them. Malach didn't know how it would affect them coming into Angelcross, but in his opinion the faster they could get to his mother, the better.

Daziar pulled his paddle out of the water and set it down in the canoe rolling his neck and stretching his shoulders. "Mal, can I talk to you?"

"Uh, yeah, Daz. Is something wrong?" Malach pulled his own paddle out of the water and turned around in his seat.

"I know how important this is for you," Daziar started, and Malach didn't like where this was headed. "I would never stop you or do anything to hinder you from finding your mother. . . but I don't think I'm supposed to be here."

"What do you mean?" Malach asked.

"I don't know what my part in this war is, but since we left the Angel Army I don't feel right." He shrugged. "I don't think my path is the one you are on. I'm afraid that I will simply hinder your journey to rescue your mother."

"Daz, I know we've had a rough time lately, but you know you are my brother in everything but blood. If this is about what happened in Newaught-"

"No," Daziar cut Malach short. "You were in the right in Newaught, and I deserved much worse than what you did. To tell you the truth, you shouldn't have had anything to do with me after I betrayed your trust. I just don't think I'm supposed to be here. My path lies elsewhere."

"Then, when we get to the bridge, you head back to Brightwood and find your place in this war," Malach replied with a heavy heart. He didn't want Daziar to go, but he understood how he felt and would let him find his own way. "I will see you again when we return with my mother."

"Thanks for understanding, Mal," Daziar picked up his paddle again.

"You know Honora is going to yell at you for staying," Malach didn't envy his friend one bit.

"I suspect she will do more than that."

They caught up with the group and paddled their way around a bend in the river. The bridge, which was supposed to be there, was just a burned-out husk. Malach pulled out his bow and strung it even as he saw Amara and Marena doing the same. Amara quickly dropped to the back of the group, since she was the only archer who didn't have a partner in the canoe with her. She managed to keep up with them mostly but had to keep switching out her bow for the paddle and back again. He didn't see anyone at the bridge, but he continued the scan the tree line along the banks. Ariel appeared beside the bridge, and all bows turned toward him.

Malach dropped his bow and called, "what happened?"

"Another band of mercenaries," he called back. "We were able to turn them back. Although, with the promise of supplies from the army, we decided that burning the bridge and setting a watch would be in our best interest."

"Very well," Elzrod replied. "We will meet you on the other side of the bridge."

Ariel disappeared back into the woods and the group paddled to the other side of the bridge where the bank didn't rise so steeply. The group, with Ariel's help, moored the canoes but didn't pull them out of the water. Daziar got out of the canoe and pulled out his belongings, shoulders slumped.

"Where are you going?" Amara asked him. "We aren't resting here. We need to keep moving."

"Daziar has decided his path leads him somewhere else," Malach told the group. "He has decided to stay and help hold Brightwood."

Elzrod nodded his agreement, as if he foresaw this coming. Togan and Marena seemed to be fine with the decision as well and didn't say anything. Ariel turned to Daziar and clasped the young man's arm, pulled him close, and whispered something into his ear.

"Coward," Amara said quietly, crossing her arms.

Malach turned to her and shook his head quieting her.

She bit down another retort, but he could tell she was still upset.

Malach turned back as Daziar walked a little farther up the bank. Ariel handed his pack to Malach and he stowed it between the seats. He leaned to help counter the weight of his father as he climbed in. They pushed off from the bank and headed down the river once again. Malach turned around and saw Daziar watching the group leave. His friend hung his head and walked up the bank. His friend was not a coward; however, Daziar didn't seem to be feeling the same way. The next bend in the river blocked his view of Daziar and he turned to face forward.

"He'll be fine, Malach," Ariel told him. "He's doing what he thinks is right, and you have more than enough allies for the challenges ahead."

Malach smiled at his father and nodded. He would be ready for what was ahead, and he *did* have everyone and everything he needed to get his mother back. He had already liberated his father with similar numbers, and they would do that same for his mother.

"The hardest part of the river is over," Elzrod told the group, cutting into Malach's thoughts. "It should be easy from here until Angelcross."

"How far is that?" Amara asked.

"We will leave the river a half a day's walk from Angelcross, which leaves us with two more days on the Pangor," he replied.

Togan groaned loud. "I'm ready t' be out of these blasted things and on my own two feet!"

"I thought you were enjoying yourself," Marena turned around to look at him, confused.

"I liked that flume we went over, but I'm tired of all the slow-movin' water we are havin' to paddle through now."

"Flume?" Ariel asked.

Malach filled him in on their journey thus far. Ariel was disappointed he hadn't been able to experience the flume, even though both Malach and Amara had been hurt in the experience. Elzrod remembered it was time to change Amara's bandages, and they lashed their canoes together temporarily for him to do that. Her wound seemed to be healing well, and the bleeding had slowed to a light oozing.

"We will have to find you a new hairstyle once that is healed, Amara," Marena commented. "I can help with that when the time comes."

"Thank you, Marena," Amara smiled.

Malach turned to Togan and rolled his eyes.

Togan mouthed the word "women," agreeing with Malach's sentiment.

"You won't be joking when Amara looks stunning and you want to win her hand," Marena replied, having seen some of the exchange between the men.

Togan and Malach looked around sheepishly and Amara and Marena laughed at their discomfort.

Elzrod and Ariel just shook their heads.

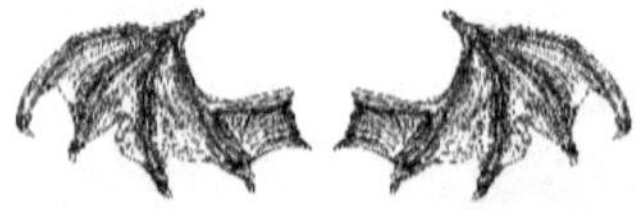

Daziar watched as the river swept the canoes around the next bend and out of sight. He hung his head and walked up the bank. Maybe he was a coward, like Amara had said. Maybe he just didn't want to face the hard challenges that Malach would face on his path. He shook his head to clear the negative thoughts. No, he wasn't. What Ariel had told him gave him hope, and he would find his place in the war where he could do the most good. This was one of the hardest choices he had made in his life, and even though he didn't know exactly where his own path lay, he knew it wasn't with Malach this time. He climbed the bank and found a group of men building a watchtower for the outpost at the river. He approached the man who appeared to be in charge.

"Pardon me," he said, politely interrupting a conversation the man was having with one of his workers. "I was wondering if you could spare a horse?"

"What fer?" The man asked gruffly, not liking to be interrupted.

"I need to get back to Brightwood to check in with the angels there," Daziar replied.

"Oh." The man studied Daziar with a little more respect. "Unfortunately, I only have a couple mules for pullin'. You will have to make yer way on foot."

"Got it," Daziar sighed, disappointed but resigned, and not at all upset with the man.

It seemed, for the next couple of days, his path would be the road to Brightwood. From there, he would try to find his place in this war. Maybe he would be needed to defend Brightwood. His small town had become a large piece in the war, and he would see it held. He trudged down the road, still feeling defeated, like a dog returning home with his tail between his legs.

Chapter 10

Amara peered out of the underbrush at the outpost of Angelcross. She was laying in the cold snow and even though the snow wasn't as deep as it was in the mountains, it was still cold. Skie was on one side of her and Malach on the other, both close enough for her to feel the warmth radiating off of their bodies. Ariel and Elzrod were on the side of the compound that housed the gate, and Togan and Marena on the side opposite of Amara and Malach. Directly opposite of the gate was the sheer cliff of the Great Divide, the canyon dividing the demon and angel territories.

The wall wasn't much more than eight-foot-tall, roughly cut logs lashed together and set into the ground. She had scouted the outpost the night prior and found it was indeed under demon control. However, there wasn't a demon posted there, only a small squad of men.

It was obvious they thought Angelcross would be the last place the enemy would attack. There were only two men on guard each night walking the camp. They rarely even looked out to the woods to watch for any enemies.

The plan was to infiltrate the camp and incapacitate or kill the enemy. Then they would get the supplies for the specially made ballista, which fired a large grappling arrow over to the other side of the canyon. They would be able to climb across the ropes to the demon territory. There was no way they would be able to climb over safely with any of the enemy troops still conscious. They would be taking no prisoners on this mission.

Amara wasn't sure she was comfortable with killing the soldiers. She hadn't said anything about it when Elzrod and Ariel had been laying out the plan. Everyone else was perfectly fine with it, but she didn't know if she could follow through. She had killed in self-defense and in a fair fight, but this was different. This night, she would become an assassin.

Malach and Amara observed as Ariel and Elzrod made their way calmly up the path toward the outpost. The guard noticed them when they were only a few yards from the front gate. The hapless man nearly fell off his stool.

"That's our cue." Malach moved, quiet and low toward the wall, Skie trailing him silently. Amara wondered how the wolf always seemed to know what was going on and what to do. She followed quickly, knowing Togan and Marena would be doing the same on their side. There were several buildings, but only three would house the enemy. Two for the troops and one for the captain, or whoever was in charge.

Amara heard the guard at the front gate challenge Ariel and Elzrod rather loudly and hoped it would not rouse any of the troops sleeping. It did draw the second guard out of the middle of the compound and to the front gate. Now they would be able to move more freely around the buildings. Malach and Amara slipped into the first building they came across and Amara spotted Togan and Marena doing the same at the second building.

She turned forward and took in the building she was walking into. It was one of the main barracks.

Skie sat at the door waiting for Malach and Amara to accomplish their grim task. Malach moved down the row of cots to one end of the room and cover the first man's mouth while simultaneously sliding his knife across the man's throat. From the threshold, she didn't hear anything.

She peered down, studying the face of the sleeping man who was to be her first victim. He was young, not much older than her. She glanced back up at Malach but turned her head as he killed a second man. She couldn't do it. She could kill a man standing up, but she couldn't kill a man who didn't have a chance to defend himself. She rushed outside and ducked into the shadows, her breath coming in ragged gasps as if she had just run for miles.

Only a few moments later Malach came out of the building and joined her in the shadows. "Are you alright?"

"I can't." Tears started to flow down her cheeks. "I can't. . ."

"It's alright," Malach replied, wrapping one arm around her.

"I'm not an assassin." She looked up, studying his face for the frustration or anger she feared. "I can't."

"It's fine," Malach smiled, reassuring her he wasn't angry. "Why don't you go get the supplies, and we will finish this up."

She nodded her thanks, wiping her eyes, and got to her feet. Malach stole back into the building. She ran over to the supply building and glanced toward the front gate. Elzrod's eyes tracked her, drawn by her movement. They were still deep in conversation with the two guards, which was their job for the night. She slipped into the supply building and started searching around for the special arrows and lengths of rope they would need to get across. She found them and grabbed four of the long shafts. The arrows were almost as long as spears and she underestimated how heavy they were. She lost her balance as she spun to leave. She had to let go of the heavy arrows to keep from falling and impaling herself on them. They fell to the floor, the sound of their clattering echoing off the walls and breaking the silence painfully.

She froze, listening for signs the guards had heard. She heard a shout that was cut short, no doubt by Elzrod or Ariel's sword. Then a second, which, to her ears, was little more than a choking gurgle. As if someone was trying to shout with a slit throat. Several more shouts erupted from the direction of the barracks, and Amara quickly ran out of the supply building, leaving the arrows where they lay. Malach and Togan backed out of the barracks, facing off against several soldiers who had obviously survived the assassination attempts. She didn't see Marena and feared the worst for her. She didn't have much time to dwell on the thought. Three more soldiers came out of the building behind the first three. There must have been a lot more soldiers sleeping in there than in the first building they entered.

The soldiers exited the building spreading out to either side of Malach and Togan. They didn't realize it was a mistake. Amara's knife cut deeply into one's neck and on instinct, he pulled it out. His blood flowed freely, and he quickly expired. Skie jumped another soldier from behind clamping down on the man's neck and shoulder. His screaming and thrashing didn't take long to subside. Several of the soldiers glanced her way, following the trajectory of her knife, and Togan, with his hefty battle hammer, took the chance to swing it at their knees. He hit the first one and Amara heard a pop and a snap as the soldier's left knee caved unnaturally to the side. However, Togan's hammer didn't stop there, grinding the man's knees together and sweeping him off his feet. He let out a scream of agony, his head hit the ground, ending his misery. Elzrod and Ariel were jogging toward them and they now outnumbered the soldiers. They started to retreat back into the building at the sight of reinforcements. One of them cried out in pain, a sword suddenly sprouting out of his chest. Marena pushed the man off her sword. Amara was overjoyed to see she was alright. The last three soldiers decided that they would rather fight than be taken prisoner but were quickly cut down by the group.

"Well, that didn't go as planned," Elzrod sat down heavily on the ground, his breath coming in white bursts.

"No plan survives first contact. You taught me that." Malach reminded him.

Elzrod chuckled, "That I did."

"It was my fault," Amara admitted, kicking at a loose rock on the ground. "I dropped the ballista arrows and alerted them."

"Well, it went better than I thought it would," Ariel reassured her. "Let's get those arrows and make this crossing."

Malach and Togan retrieved the arrows and large coils of heavy rope. Elzrod took one of the arrows, tied one end of the heavy rope to it, and set it aside. He repeated this for the other arrow and length of rope. He picked them up and carried them to the two ballistae.

"These two ballistae are set here in case there was ever a demon invasion," Elzrod explained patting the arm of one of them like it was a fond pet. "This is where the Great Divide is thinnest. We hoped we would be able to shoot a couple out of the sky if they ever tried to fly over. However, we didn't anticipate they would take Newaught so easily."

"I don't think anyone saw that coming," Ariel agreed. "We also anticipated this being a good place to start our own invasion if there came a time for that."

"But how did you expect to do that since there is no way across?" Malach peered down at the long drop to the ground below and took a couple of steps back remembering the other long drop which almost ended his mission early.

"That's where the Ballistae come into play," Elzrod replied. "They aren't just here for defense but to set up a system to get across the divide."

"How come the demons haven't set up something on the other side?" Togan squinted at the other side of the divide where only trees were visible.

"Most likely they didn't waste their time since they had something else planned," Ariel told him. "In hindsight, we should have realized what it meant and started figuring out what they were actually planning."

"Better for us that they didn't," Marena stated.

"So how do we plan on getting across?" Amara asked, fearing she already knew that answer.

"I'll show you," Elzrod spun, glee evident in his voice.

Amara had never seen the old man so happy.

He picked up one of the arrows and loaded it into a ballista, careful to keep the rope out of the pulleys and workings. He tied off the rope to a metal ring set into the ground and walked to the back of the ballista to take aim. It took him just a few moments to line up the shot. He pulled the trigger. The ballista heaved the arrow out and over the divide, the rope trailing after it like a long tail. It hit just below the ledge on the other side, driving the tip of the arrow deep into the earth, almost all the way up to where the rope was tied off.

Elzrod reloaded and took aim a little higher and loosed the second arrow. This time it pierced all the way through the trunk of a tree and stuck fast. Elzrod and Ariel pulled the ropes taut and secured them, the lower one to the metal ring set into the ground, the higher one to a metal ring set into a post at about head height.

"Now we cross," Elzrod stated simply.

"We what?" Amara asked, thinking she had heard wrong.

"You hold on to the top rope and step out onto the bottom one and cross," Elzrod explained in more detail.

"Umm, no," Amara replied, glanced around the group for support. "You have to be joking."

"He's not joking," Ariel replied. "I'll go first."

Ariel stepped out onto the ropes without hesitation. He got a little way out and the rope started to have more slack. Luckily, there was little to no wind blowing or it would have been near impossible to get across. As it was, the farther out Ariel got the more the ropes swayed and moved. Ariel glanced down a few times at the dizzying drop to the ground but kept moving. He made it to the other side and motioned for the next person to go.

Elzrod fashioned a sling for Skie, and they secured it to her. Then Malach and Elzrod attached her to the top rope and Malach was able to pull her behind him as he made his way across. Skie tolerated this mode of transportation, but Amara could tell she was not happy about it. The height didn't seem to bother Malach either; although, unlike his father, he never glanced down even once. He and Skie arrived on the other side without incident. They had a little problem getting Skie off the rope as the knots had tightened because of her weight. However, they soon had her off the ropes and onto solid ground. She walked well away from the cliff's edge and glared at Malach as if she blamed him for the ride over the chasm.

One by one, each of the group made the tense, precarious climb across the ropes and each time they made it across. Once, on Togan's crossing, a gust of wind had knocked him off balance and he had found himself horizontal staring at the ground. After a few tense moments, he was able to right himself and continue on to the other side.

Finally, only Elzrod and Amara stood on the angel's side of the Great Divide. Her turn had come. She tried to act the part of the confident and brave person she normally was. Unfortunately, as she got to the edge of the divide and slid her foot out onto the rope, she froze. One foot on the solid ground one foot suspended in the air. She could no more go back than forward.

Elzrod came up behind her for support, "You've climbed across ropes between buildings before, right?"

"Ye-yes," she stammered out.

"This is no different. One foot in front of the other, and you will be across in no time. I'll be right here in case anything goes wrong.

She was able to tear her gaze away from the ground below and affixed it on Elzrod. His kind, confident gaze gave her strength. She turned back to the other side of the divide and spotted Malach waiting there for her, motioning her to come to him. She set her other foot onto the rope and started to slowly make her way across. A stray thought that Elzrod might have abandoned her sent her head spinning. She found he was only a couple of steps behind her. The motion caused her to lose her bearing and she had to hold fast to the rope as her top half swung out over the chasm. She pulled herself upright, quickly hugging the rope in a death grip, her breaths coming in gulps and her heart pounding out of her chest.

She waited for a moment to allow herself to calm down. A few more steps and she would be halfway across. The ropes swaying more than ever. She glanced down between her legs and froze. The ground was so far down. If she fell, she would be screaming for a long time before she hit the ground.

"Amara, look up," Elzrod commanded. "Don't look at the ground or you won't make it across."

She closed her eyes and forced her head up again. She felt the rope they were standing on drop suddenly. She screamed involuntarily and held on to the top rope with all her strength. She was still standing on the bottom rope though. It hadn't dropped but a fraction of an inch, but that was enough for her legs to freeze once again.

"Not to alarm you," Elzrod said much more calmly than she thought he should be. "but it seems that the arrow the rope is connected to is starting to slip out of the cliff side. We might want to move this thing along."

"It's what?" Amara asked, very much alarmed.

"It seems to be coming loose, if you would kindly start moving again, we need to get off this rope."

"What?" Amara turned her head to see the arrow that was embedded in the cliff slide only by an inch or so and felt the rope drop again. "What do we do?"

"Move!" Elzrod shouted.

She did just that.

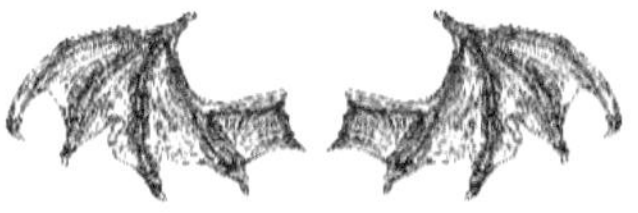

Daziar walked into Brightwood, the familiar sights and smells comforting him. This was his home, and he was happy to be back, but it was a bittersweet moment. The almost three-day walk didn't relieve any of the guilt he felt over leaving Malach. For all he knew, he left him to face the whole of the Demon Army alone. And why? Because he didn't feel like going? Or worse, because he was a coward? He felt defeated and weak.

"Daziar?" A voice asked, snapping him out of his thoughts.

He looked up and spotted Honora.

Why did it have to be her that I saw first? he thought. "Uh, hi, Honora."

"Why are you here?" she asked, eyes wide. "Is something wrong?"

"No," Daziar replied. "My path no longer led where Malach's did and I decided to come back."

Slap!

Honora's open hand hit his face with enough force to turn his whole body and tears sprung into his eyes. "You did what!?"

"I came back," Daziar straightened just in time to be on the receiving end of Honora's other hand, turning his body the other way. "Would you stop that?"

"Would you stop being a moron?" She was almost shouting now.

Heads of curious onlookers were now turning their way and Daziar pulled Honora over to the awning of a building.

"Keep your voice down," He hissed at her. "I tried to go with him and help. I really did. But I couldn't. I couldn't sleep. I didn't have any peace about it. I talked with Malach, and he agreed with me that I shouldn't go if I didn't feel right about it."

"Of course he did!" Honora threw her hands in the air. Her volume was much lower, but the disappointment and anger were still very evident. "You two are like brothers, and he isn't a jerk. He would have told you just about anything was fine. Now he's out there facing the Demon Army without one of the only people he trusts in this world! The only other person is me, and I didn't go when I had the chance!"

She's not really mad at me, Daziar realized, in an uncharacteristic moment of clarity. *She's mad at herself for not going with Malach in the first place.*

"I can't believe I'm not out there with him," Honora's shoulders slumping.

Daziar could see tears forming in her eyes. "Honora, he's not alone," Daziar tried to comfort her even though he was feeling the same way. "He's got Elzrod and his father. Who, I might add, is an angel. It's not like they are going to let anything happen to him."

"I know." She turned her head, trying to hide her tears. "I just don't know if we will ever see him again, and that scares me."

"We'll see him again," Daziar moved closer to give her a hug.

She pulled back quickly, "Of course we'll see him again. I don't know what I was thinking. I'll talk to you later."

Honora turned and walked quickly away. Daziar eyes followed her, not really understanding what had happened. She turned down a street and disappeared from sight.

"That was odd," a voice said from behind him.

He turned to see the most stunning woman he had ever laid eyes on. She had a slender body with form-fitting silver shining armor. She had blond hair that was so light it was almost white, glowing in the sunlight, and her eyes were the brightest and most intense blue that Daziar ever saw. As her wings unfurled behind her, Daziar thought his heart might have stopped. Her wings glowed almost like tendrils of light instead of something solid. He hadn't seen any other angel's wings like it.

"Uh, are you just going to stand there gawking?" she asked in a perfectly melodic voice.

Daziar realized his mouth was open and shut it quickly. "Oh, I, um, I-I'm Daziar," he managed to stammer out.

"I'm Anahita," and she smiled a smile that seemed to light up the world around Daziar. "But you can call me Ana."

"I'm Daziar," He repeated himself before he could think about what he was saying. "I mean, umm, well, uh welcome to Brightwood!" He kicked himself mentally. *Stupid. Welcome to Brightwood? How dumb can you be, Daz?*

"Thank you!" she said, to Daziar's relief. "I noticed you just arrived, and I came to welcome you!"

"Oh, thank you. I used to live here," Daziar explained. "So, I guess I'm used to being the one welcoming people."

"Then welcome back! Where did you live? I will see if your old house is available."

"My parents should be back. I would assume they are living there again."

She proffered a map with names scrawled on it and asked, "Name?"

"Wervine."

"Yup, it looks like your parents are living in a house here." Ana turned the map around to show him. "Is that your old house?"

He quickly studied the map. "Yes!"

"Wonderful, then you will have no problem finding your way."

Yep, Daziar thought glumly. *She definitely can't wait to get away from me.*

"I will be seeing you around town," she smiled at him again, which gave Daziar a little hope. She turned and walked away back toward the gate.

Daziar made his way to his parent's house. By habit, he didn't knock but opened the door and walked in. He was greeted with a familiar sight and it comforted him. His mother was in the kitchen bustling around making dinner for his family. While Marletta set the table.

"This house is already occupied," he heard his father shout from the direction of the bedrooms. "You will need to find out which house they have put you in because we are all full-"

His father cut himself short as he turned the corner and saw his son standing at the front door. Marletta had already stopped setting the table and was looking at him as well. His mother turned around to see why her husband was at a loss for words and burst into tears as she found out. She ran around the counter and hugged him, crying into his chest.

"Daz, how?" His father asked, open-mouthed.

"My path didn't follow Malach anymore," Daziar said with much more confidence than he felt, but that mantra was starting to get old to his ears. "My place is here helping my family, town, and the Angel Army."

His mother pulled away from him but held him at arm's length to get a good look at him. "I'm so glad you are safe," she managed to squeak out before losing her voice to tears again and hugging him.

His father, having gotten over the shock, scowled at him.

Daziar almost expected a scolding. The way he used to, when Daziar and Malach had gotten into trouble.

Instead, "You're sure you're supposed to be here?"

"Yes, Dad, I talked with Mal about it too, and he agreed," Daziar told him. *Am I sure? If I can't even believe myself, how will anyone else?*

"Then welcome home, son," His father didn't smile, but he did stop scowling, which was the best Daziar could have hoped for.

"Where is Mal now?" Emmeline bounced up and down eagerly.

"Hopefully, close to Angelcross, where they plan on crossing the great divide to enter Demon Territory," Daziar told them.

"I overheard one of the angels talking just after Ariel left," Marletta studied the floor and kicked at one of the floorboards. "They said that Angelcross had been taken by the Demon Army."

Daziar's heart sunk in his chest and he felt guiltier than ever. They were most likely there right now fighting to survive and continue the mission he abandoned. He sighed heavily and sat down in one of the chairs around the table.

"Daz." His mom put her hands on his shoulders. "They will be fine. They are all strong, and they all have each other to help."

"You've made your decision," his father told him. "Good or bad, you can't go back now. You just have to do that best you can, moving forward."

"Thanks, Mom, Dad." Daziar smiled at them even though he didn't feel too much better. "I think I'll just go to my room and get things settled."

He stood to go but his father held up a hand to stop him. "Uh, about that. We didn't think you would be back so soon and, well, we kind of gave up your room to another refugee."

"You did what?" Daziar asked, appalled.

Before his family could explain any farther the front door opened and Auron stepped into the house. He stopped in his tracks at the sight of Daziar. No one said anything for several very uncomfortable moments.

Auron finally spoke up. "Hello, everyone. Not sure what is going on, but I have some good news. They had located where the demons are keeping my wife and many other prisoners. If we can free them, we should be able to convert a few hundred of the Demon Army soldiers to our side."

"What is he doing here?" Daziar asked as if Auron hadn't said anything.

"Daz!" his mother scolded. "He is our guest, no one would take him in, so we did."

"Mom there is a reason that no one would take him," Daziar replied. "He was an enemy soldier and could turn on us at any moment."

"I would never do such a thing," Auron held up his hand in protest.

"Oh yeah?" Daziar challenged, standing and advancing on the man. "Even if your wife was threatened again? That's why you're here, isn't it? The Angel Army kicked you out of their camp and sent you here 'cause they don't trust you."

"Uh, they didn't kick me out, but they didn't trust me either, but I wouldn't ever harm your family," Auron put his hand over his heart. "You have my word."

"Your word means less than a pile of horse droppings to me," Daziar growled between gritted teeth.

"Daziar Wervine," his mother scolded him again. "Auron is our guest and you will treat him that way."

"But Mom-"

Daziar started to protest but she cut him off, hands planted firmly on her hips. "But nothing. Auron has had a rough time of it lately, and he is trying to make up for what he's done. You will treat him with respect."

"No," Auron stopped Jenari from saying any more. "He's right. He has no reason to trust me and my word shouldn't mean much to him. Daziar, I would ask you to at least give me a chance to gain your trust. I intend to rescue my wife, and I already have the support of the angels and your friend, Honora. I simply ask you to trust them if you can't trust me."

"Honora is in on this plan of yours?" Daziar leveled a finger at Auron's face.

"Yes." Auron nodded slowly.

"Then I'll go too," Daziar declared. "If only to protect her if it's a trap."

"I would be happy to have you with us," Auron beamed. "I know from the road to Fairdenn you are a fierce fighter."

"Flattery will get you nowhere," Daziar warned. Although the compliment had made him happy somewhere down deep inside, he didn't have to let Auron know.

"Daziar," Daniel spoke up, "You can either sleep in your old room with Auron or you can sleep in the sitting room on the floor. We have brought the extra bed in from the stables in case another refugee was in need of it."

"I would rather sleep on the floor," Daziar crossed his arms.

"Fine," Jenari replied, obviously unhappy with him. "But if you want to eat my food you will sit at this table with the rest of us and at minimum be cordial to our guest."

"Fine," Daziar replied.

"What was that?" Jenari wagged a finger at him.

"Yes ma'am." His tone was that of an unrepentant child.

"Good. Go clean-up for dinner. You're filthy from the road."

Daziar walked out the door. He picked up the bucket sitting outside and filled it with as much snow as he could stuff in it. He then went inside and dug it out into a pot that was sitting on the stove and watched it melt. Once most of the snow was melted, he pulled it off the stove, grabbed a cloth, and walked outside once again. He dipped the cloth in the water and scrubbed at his face and hands. Once he was finished, he dumped the water out and stalked back inside.

Dinner was mostly silent and very awkward. Not much was said other than the occasional, "Please pass the bread," or "Could you get me more soup?" When the meal was finished, they all helped clean up dinner, and it wasn't long before they are retired for the night.

Chapter 11

Malach watched as Amara and Elzrod started across the ropes. He wasn't sure it would hold two people but Elzrod wasn't worried so he trusted it would. A sharp grating noise assaulted his ears and made him cringe.

Amara screamed.

He ran to the cliff side and peered down at the arrow. He could tell it had slipped out a little, showing the discoloration from the dirt where it was embedded. He glanced up at the two forms still on the rope. They didn't seem to be moving. Another grating noise drew his attention back to the arrow. It slid out more.

Elzrod shouted something he couldn't make out.

Malach laid down, reaching out to grasp the arrow shaft. Ariel understood what he was doing and grabbed his ankles to give him some leverage. He pulled against his father and pushed the shaft back into the mountain trying to hold it in place. The rope started to bounce more and more as Amara and Elzrod got closer, and it got even harder to hold. Despite Malach's efforts, the shaft inched out and then again just a few moments later.

"I can't hold it!" he shouted, not daring to take his concentration away for even a minute.

The head of the arrow finally broke loose Malach held tight to it trusting his father's strength to keep them on the cliff side. Several wood splinters bit slowly into his hand as they slid down the shaft, drawing blood and slicking up the wood making it harder to hold.

Malach let out an involuntary, guttural yell. Some of his vertebrae popped as they were stretched.

Two feet appeared at the end of the rope. As they disappeared over his head some of the weight left, giving him some measure of relief. The second set of feet appeared and disappeared, and he let go of the arrow. Some of the splitters broke free of the shaft, still piercing his hand. Others took pieces of flesh with them as the arrow fell away.

Malach was hauled back onto the cliff and Togan, Ariel, Malach, and Skie all landed in a heap. The others must have come to help at some point in the whole ordeal. He was so tired. Every part of his body felt like it had been stretched and he wouldn't have been surprised if he had gained a few inches in height. His hands throbbed and burned.

He pulled out some of the large splinters he could find in all the bloody mess.

Togan pulled a leg out from under Malach and stood. "Let's not do *that* again."

Malach laughed in spite of the pain, but he wholeheartedly agreed with the man.

Elzrod cut the other rope and let it fall into the chasm.

They all got to their feet and moved into the forest. Malach assumed this was Ragewood Forest. They set up camp not far into it and Marena helped him remove the rest of the wood splinters from his hands and bandage them.

What will we find in here? He didn't sense anything unusual, and it appeared to be a normal forest.

Amara told him on their way down the river it was mostly unexplored. Which meant there were a lot of wild rumors about what they might find in it. But first, they would make their way to Kargod to acquire horses. Their path would then lead them deep into Ragewood forest, around the town of Ragewood, to the only demon compound they had an approximate location to. He felt like they were going the long way around, but this path would lower the chance they would be caught. Especially since Ariel and Elzrod were two very recognizable figures to the demon's and their informants.

"Thanks for saving me and Elzrod," Amara broke the silence, startling Malach out of his thoughts.

"You know you don't have to thank me. I know you would do the same for me."

"I know. I just want you to know I am grateful." Amara squatted down in front of him and gently turned his hands over, studying them. "How are your hands?"

"They will be fine in a few days. How is your head healing?"

"Slower than I would like, but Marena said we would be able to leave the bandages off here in a few days and style my hair shortly after. I should be fully healed by the time we make it to the demon compound. Elzrod says I'm healing faster than he thought I would."

"That's good to hear," Malach motioned for her to sit with him. Neither of them was tired with all the excitement, so they talked long into the night.

Malach couldn't remember falling asleep, but the next morning, the light stuck his face, and he woke up to find Amara's head on his chest. Someone had draped blankets over them to keep them warm. Her arms were wrapped around him and her face was relaxed and peaceful. It was such an uncommon expression on her face, but one which suited her well. Ariel walked over and Malach carefully extricated himself from under Amara's sleeping form. He walked away in silence with his father.

"You love her, don't you?" Ariel asked when they had walked a little way away.

"Yes," Malach nodded thoughtfully. "I think I do. How did you know you loved Mom?"

"When I realized I could live a hundred lifetimes and never be happier than when I was with her." His father gazed into the distance.

"What do you think of Amara?"

His father turned back to him and smiled. "She is a lot like your mother. Strong, no-nonsense type, but fun-loving and has a good sense of humor. She sees what she wants and takes it, and I think she has her sights set on you." Ariel chuckled.

"So, you like her?"

"I'm not sure yet," Ariel turned away again. "There is potential in her for darkness still, but I think only time will tell."

Malach was about to ask what he meant by that when they heard Elzrod calling for camp to be cleaned up.

They ate a cold breakfast as they walked. They would reach Kargod sometime late afternoon. Togan, Marena, Amara, and Malach would enter town, hopefully in time to find and purchase some horses. Malach would have liked fewer people to venture into Kargod. They would draw more attention with more people, and if any of the demon informants were to take notice, it could doom their quest there and then. However, it would raise more questions if one person were trying to buy six horses.

It took them until almost dark to travel to Kargod, and the four barely made it in the town before they closed the gate. Unfortunately, they would have to wait until the next day to purchase their mounts. They found a tavern called The Devil's Horns and went inside.

Togan purchased them rooms and a meal while Malach went with the girls to a table in the corner out of the way. The tavern was filled with the undesirables of the town, and there were more than a few unabashed stares at the two women. At least until Malach or Togan caught the eyes of the one staring. No one wanted to mess with either of the fierce-looking men though. They would want even less to do with the two women if they knew anything about them.

They ate mostly in silence, not knowing who might overhear any idle talk. After a while, they decided to retire to their rooms. However, some of the patrons had other ideas. As they started to head to their rooms, several men on the other side of the tavern stood and quickly moved to cut them off from any escape. There were at least ten of them.

"Look what we have here," the one, who was clearly their leader, said.

Malach spotted the tavern owner out of the corner of his eye look up from wiping down the counter and quickly look back down. *No help there,* he thought.

"We don't want any trouble." Togan raised his hands disarmingly. "We only want t' retire t' our rooms for the night."

"Well, then you will be needing to pay for protection for the night." The man cocked an eyebrow at them.

A few of the men around them chuckled.

"We are more than capable of protecting ourselves," Amara spoke up from behind Malach.

Malach didn't know whether to applaud her courage or be frustrated at her not—so—subtle challenge to these obviously abrasive men.

Togan held up his hand to silence them. "We're weary travelers made homeless by the war. We have very little money and not much of worth," Togan lied.

"I don't believe you." The grimy man grinned evilly at them. "So either hand over your money, or I won't be able to protect you from these men that wish to do you harm."

"I don't think ya heard me." Togan calmly pulled out his war hammer. "We don't have any money for you."

Malach, Amara, and Marena followed Togan's lead pulling their own weapons out, although Malach pulled out his bow, not wanting to draw attention to the fact he had an Angel Blade. Malach notched an arrow and took aim at the leader's head. It was so close to the man's face that he had to go cross-eyed to look at the tip of the arrow. It wouldn't be easy to fight in close quarters with a bow, but he would hopefully be able to manage it well enough. Marena drew her full-sized sword and Amara, long knives.

"I'm not sure if anyone could miss at this range, so I don't think it matters to you how good of a shot I am," Malach told him.

Skie growled from under the table, not bothering to stand up yet. Several of the men were caught off guard, not having seen her sitting under the table, and jumped back in alarm. The man Malach had at the end of his arrow didn't dare move, in case it caused the arrow to be loosed.

"Now that ya have the idea," Togan said, "you are goin' t' let us retire to our rooms and you nor your men will bother us the rest of our stay here."

The man nodded slowly, and the group walked by the men to the stairs leading to the rooms. Malach, kept the man at arrow point rotating with him until he was on the side with the stairs and whistling to Skie to let her know that it was time to come with him. She padded slowly between the men, the ones she passed closest to held their breath, no doubt hoping the she-wolf wouldn't attack them. She padded past Malach, rubbing against his leg almost cat-like as she ascended the stairs. Malach dropped his bow and headed up the stairs.

"Do you think they will attack tonight?" Malach asked Togan as he caught up with the group.

"I think we sufficiently frightened them for t'night," he replied thoughtfully. "Hopefully we will be outta town before we have t' deal with them again."

"Still, we might want to take turns on watch just in case," Marena spoke up. "Amara did challenge them, and they won't take to that kindly, especially from a woman."

"They challenged us first," Amara mumbled, crossing her arms.

"True," Togan didn't react, as if he hadn't heard Amara. "I'll take first watch."

They didn't have any issues from the group of ruffians the rest of the night, as Togan predicted. They didn't even see any of them as they exited the tavern and headed to the stables they had seen upon entering the city. They were able to purchase four of the horses they needed and two mules at the stables. The man they dealt with told them they would be able to acquire the other two horses they were needing on the other side of the town at a second stable. Marena and Amara took the horses out of town and back to where Elzrod and Ariel would be waiting.

Malach and Togan walked through the market on the way to the other side of the town and bought the supplies they needed, then haggled with the stable master for two more horses. They had to pay more for these since they were both large, black war horses. Malach had no idea how the army hadn't commandeered them for the war, but it was possibly because Kargod was a small, removed city from the main road. The size of the horses, however, would accommodate Togan and Ariel's size and weight.

Their return trip didn't go quite so smoothly. The men from the night before were waiting for them on the main road. Malach glanced behind them, noting six more men had cut off the only points of escape. They were trapped. Skie growled menacingly and it was apparent most of the men were reluctant to attack them simply because of her.

"Gentleman," Malach spread his arms wide and winked at Togan. "I thought we settled this last night. We appreciate your kind offer of protection; however, we aren't in any need of it. Thank you."

"We ain't here to offer you protection this time," the leader replied. "We are here to kill you and take what money you have. Then, when we are done with you, we will hunt down your two lady frien-"

The man never got to finish his speech, as Malach put an arrow between his eyes before the man had even realized the bow was out. No one moved, the ruffians shocked into silence at the death of their leader. He nocked another arrow in the midst of the silence. It didn't take them long for one of them regained his wits enough to give a war-whoop. From the one cry, chaos erupted and Malach sent three more arrows into the crowd of men headed toward them. The horses bucked and one kicked out, catching the closest man directly in the face dropping him. It proceeded to stomp down on the man's fallen form shattering bones audibly. He wouldn't be getting up ever again. Malach pulled Reckoning, not having any choice but to use the blade to defend himself. He heard the tale-tell sounds of Togan's hammer slamming into a body behind him. Togan had engaged the men at their rear, leaving Malach and Skie to deal with the ones in front.

Malach turned his attention back just in time to deflect a swing aimed at his neck, he took the momentum of the swing, allowing the other end of his pole weapon to come up to impale one of the charging men on the end of it. Malach weighed their skill against his as he engaged with the first few men. If he kept his cool, these men wouldn't stand a chance. He blocked, cut, stabbed, and countered gracefully in the middle of the four men, slowly wearing them down with small cuts, being careful to only take chances which wouldn't allow his enemies any openings.

Finally, one of the men made a fatal mistake. Malach burst into action smacking the weapon out of the man's hand with one side of his staff and whirling to bring the other side across the man's throat, cutting a large furrow through his neck, almost separating his head from his shoulders completely. The whole time Malach never stopped moving, quickly dropping back into a more reserved stance and parrying the attacks which came his way. The remaining three men were warier now. They realized now they would have to work for this kill.

Malach could still hear Togan fighting but couldn't take his eyes off his own fight to check on the man. He had gained a few small cuts of his own by this point. He took the offensive and rushed the man to his right. He was able to deflect Malach's weapon but didn't anticipate the follow-up roundhouse kick. He was unconscious before he hit the ground. Malach turned quickly to see Togan's hammer slam into the head of one of the remaining men, crushing it like a ripe melon. The last man, now covered in the gore of his companion, decided it was in his best interest to flee, and Malach and Togan watched him run, turning down an alley and out of view.

"Nothin' like a good fight t' get your blood pumping in the morning, eh, Malach?" Togan hefted his hammer, resting it on his shoulder. He didn't have a scratch or cut on him.

"Something like that," Malach grumbled. "But now we have to go find our horses.

They departed to the moans of the men who were still alive behind them, leaving them to writhe on the ground in their pain.

One of the horses hadn't run very far, the one who had stomped the man to death. The other, however, had gone clear to the other side of the town, stopping only when one of the guards near the gate had caught it and calmed it down. Malach and Togan found it with the guard and had to explain what had happened.

"That band of thugs has been plaguing this town for a long time," the guard explained, handing the horse's reigns to Malach. "They mostly leave the townsfolk alone now, but any travelers are usually accosted by them. You two did us a favor taking care of them. I doubt they will give us any more trouble for a while."

"We appreciate the assistance with the horse." Togan nodded. "And we're glad we could help, even if it wasn't somethin' we were lookin' t' do."

They mounted up on the horses and headed out of the town, happy to put it behind them.

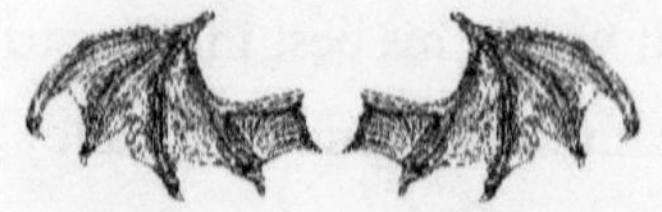

Daziar stood in the council room with Honora, Auron, Anahita, and Eloa. They were huddled over a map planning their own rescue mission. They had been able to confirm there were more than two hundred women and children being held at a camp near Lindow, just inside the Angel Territory borders.

"Why would they keep them in Angel Territory?" Honora asked. "You would think they would keep them much farther away from possible rescue."

"They must be keeping them close, in case they need to leverage them to keep the soldiers in line," Eloa explained. "Just to make sure everyone understands the plan let's go over it once more."

"We all know the plan, Eloa." Ana rolled her eyes.

"I'm going to go over the plan once again," Eloa said more forcefully.

"Fine," Ana replied, crossing her arms. "But you can't make me listen."

Daziar became more smitten with this woman by the minute. He realized he was staring at the beautiful angel and turned away quickly. He wasn't fast enough, however, and she caught his eye as he turned away. His eyes moved to the next face he could find to hopefully convince Ana he wasn't staring, and his eyes stopped on Honora. She was already glaring daggers at him. He was taken aback by her intense gaze. Was she mad at him for staring at Ana or for leaving Malach? Or both? He decided to look at one of the only people in the room he didn't have to worry about, Eloa.

"Honora will infiltrate the camp and blend in with the prisoners, spreading the word there will be an opportunity to escape," Eloa reiterated for the third or fourth time. "Honora will give the signal, and Ana will bring her small force to bear against them, pulling the guards to the east side of the camp. Meanwhile, Honora and the prisoners will overpower the guards and escape out the west side. Daziar and Auron will be waiting to help them. Once the prisoners are safely away, Ana will break off their attack, making the guards think they have won. With all luck, they won't even know there has been a prison break until it is too late to catch up."

"I have a question," Auron raised his hand.

Ana sighed.

Eloa glared at her, and then looked back to Auron. "Yes, Auron?"

"What if the guards aren't fooled long enough for the prisoners to get away?" He glanced at Ana sheepishly.

"Then Ana's force, Daziar, and any of the prisoners able to fight will hold them off while Honora leads the rest to safety," Eloa answered.

"Yes, that sounds like a good plan," Ana cut in. "Can we go now?"

"You know that patience is a virtue," Eloa admonished.

"I know," Ana cocked her head to the side to look at Eloa. "We've been cooped up at the Fortress for the better part of two thousand years. Only Ariel and a few others got to go do anything of interest during those times."

"What do you mean?" Honora's brow furrowed. "No one had seen any angels or demon for so long we just assumed that you didn't exist. When we found out otherwise, I assumed that you were just laying low in the mountains all this time. Ariel and others were out in the world that whole time? How did they not get spotted and found out?"

"Ariel and his task force were sent on many missions over the last two thousand years. They have been very active." Ana shook her head as if she was annoyed. "The only beings allowed on his task force were the angels who had trained in stealth and the Blade-Bearers, since they were human. If they were ever found out, it would have meant the end of the peace. As weak as we were at the end of the war, it would have meant the end of us. The only way we made it through was putting up a facade that we were still stronger than the demons."

"Yes, and we can only assume when Ariel and Serilda were captured they found out how vulnerable we still are," Eloa finished Ana's story for her.

"That's why the demon who attacked Malach was up in Brightwood in the first place," Honora reasoned. "It just happened to find Malach on its search for the army."

"That's what we think," Eloa nodded her affirmative. "Although, it could have been up there for Malach, since he was Ariel's son. We don't really know."

"This is all really interesting," Auron interrupted. "But shouldn't we be getting ready to leave? We have a long way to travel, and in the snow, which will make it even longer."

"Yes," Eloa replied. "Have a safe journey, and may God bless your mission."

The group filed out of the council room and into waning daylight. They would be leaving before the sun came up in the morning, and they had a few things to get done before they left. Auron and Honora split off from Daziar and Ana, leaving the two alone in the street.

"Hey," Daziar started, kicking a rock with his foot. "Umm, if you needed any help with some of the things you need to do before we leave, I could help you."

"Daziar!" Honora called from down the street. She had her hands on her hips and appeared, to Daziar, to be in the mood to yell at someone. Namely, him.

"Seems like you might have more on your plate than you think," Ana chuckled. "Thanks for the offer though."

She smiled her intoxicating smile at him and walked away. All thoughts except the beautiful angel's face left Daziar's head, and he must have grinned like a halfwit.

What was I even doing before she smiled at me?

"Daziar Wervine!" Honora yelled in a threatening tone.

"Oh, right," he muttered, his spirits plummeting faster than a rock thrown down a well. He turned and trudged over to where Honora was waiting for him. "What?"

"Are you making eyes at Ana?" She poked him in the chest.

"What?" Daziar asked again, this time alarmed that he might have been found out.

"You are! You are falling for her! First, Malach swooning all over that thief and now, you over an angel?" She threw up her hands in exasperation. "You know she's way out of your league right?"

"What?" Daziar asked for the third time, realizing now that he was repeating himself. "I don't have eyes for Ana."

"I saw you practically drooling over her."

"I was not!"

"You know she has lived for thousands of years. She will never see you as anything more than a child."

"You don't know that."

"Oh, so you do like her." She smirked.

"No! Yes. I don't know," Daziar sighed, he had been outsmarted. "Fine, yes, I think she is the most beautiful being I have ever seen."

"I see. She is beautiful, but don't get your hopes up. She most likely won't want any kind of romantic relationship with you."

"You never know. Ariel married a human," Daziar pointed out.

"Ariel and Serilda knew each other for almost two thousand years before they married and had Malach, and you don't have that kind of time. Unless, for some reason, God chooses you as a Blade-

Bearer, but that's about as likely as him coming down and smiting the Demon Army."

"Yeah, yeah." Daziar frowned. "It's not like it's against their laws or anything."

"No, but you saw how the other angels acted around Ariel and Malach, like Ariel was less than them. Would you be willing to put her through that? She would lose all standing she has with her own kind, if she ever even agreed to courting you.

"Fine, I'll think about it more before I do anything."

Honora sighed and changed the subject. "What do you have to do to be ready to leave?"

"Just get a couple of things. I never unpacked my bag."

"Good, then you can help me." She turned and walked away, expecting him to follow, no doubt.

That's a bit presumptuous. He followed her anyway.

They walked through the town to Togan's old house, which was connected to his shop and forge. Togan had told Arjun to take his house and take care of it on their return to Brightwood. The whole Reybella family was staying there, including Jecrym and Kath. They walked in and were greeted by Kath. Daziar and Honora filled her in on the mission they were about to embark on.

"I was about to go to the general store where the angels have set up their distribution of food and supplies," Kath told them. "If you want, I can add the things you still need for your mission to my list and get them for you."

"That would be wonderful. Thank you, Aunt Kath," Honora listed off the things she still needed, and Daziar added the few things he needed to the list as well.

Kath walked out the door, and Honora lead Daziar to the room she was staying in. Daziar didn't realize Togan had such a large house. He wondered why until he entered the room Honora was staying in.

There were pieces of metal everywhere, each in a different state of completion or deterioration. Some were projects that had been abandoned, and some looked like Togan had worked on them just yesterday. He noticed an old sign that he recognized from where it used to hang over the entrance to the Reybella's farm. Togan had replaced the sign ages ago and brought the old one back here, most likely to reclaim the metal. However, it seemed the sign had been forgotten and the rust coating it had nearly finished its job of eating the sign to nothing. It was a sad reminder of the once grand farm. It would be many years before it would be the way it had been.

"Are you going to stand there gawking or are you going to help me?" Her voice broke Daziar from his trance.

"Sorry," he apologized. "I was just thinking about your family's farm."

"I try not to." Her eyes started to tear up, and she glanced down at the sign he had just been studying. When she spoke again, however, there was no trace of emotion in her voice. "Come on. Help me pack."

Daziar did, packing the things Honora handed him, although he vetoed some things she would not need on the mission. She did insist on having her handheld mirror with her, and Daziar caved, reasoning it would not weigh enough to matter anyway. He just shook his head at her as she carefully put it into a pocket on her bag where it wouldn't be broken.

"You never know when you'll need to fix your appearance." She wagged a finger at him

He just shook his head at her all the more.

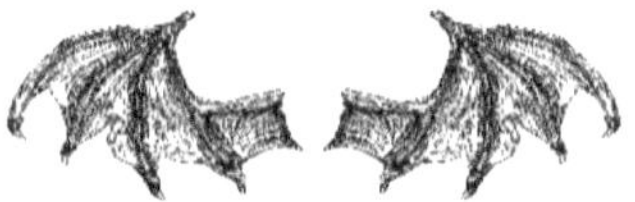

Malach and Togan arrived at camp to find the group packed and ready to ride. Malach handed the large horse over to his father and they mounted up. They informed the group what had happened in town, and everyone agreed it would be best to put as much distance between Kargod and them as possible.

Malach took up the rear, mostly because his horse was lazy. He had to keep urging it forward with his heels and slapping it with the reigns. This was going to be a long journey.

Elzrod soon joined him, slowing his horse to plod alongside the lazy horse. "Malach, can I talk to you?"

"Sure?" Malach replied, kicking his horse once again to keep it moving.

"Back in Brightwood, you seemed to be dealing with something. Reckoning told me he was worried about you still."

"What did he say?"

I told him you recognized the leader of the mercenaries. Reckoning spoke up.

Malach nodded. "I did. I let that man live when I knew he wouldn't stop preying on the weak. He killed Elder Maria, and if I hadn't left him alive-"

"Someone else would have led the attack on Brightwood, and people would have died anyway," Elzrod cut him off. "If you blame yourself for every death, you will destroy yourself with guilt."

Malach stared at the old man. "Did Reckoning tell you I blamed myself?"

"No, I've seen men go insane with guilt. I don't want to see you fall to that same fate. You need to learn that not everything is your fault. You can't and won't save everyone and blaming yourself for those deaths won't help you be better or stronger in the future. It will make you bitter and hateful."

"But what if-" Malach tried again but once again, he was cut off.

"There will always be 'what ifs.' Don't dwell on the 'what ifs.' Understand what you could have changed and what you couldn't have. Then learn from the situation and do better next time."

"I'll try," Malach mumbled. He didn't have any other arguments to throw at the man. There was truth in Elzrod's words, even if he didn't like what was being said. He wanted to hold onto the pain and anger and let it fuel him forward, but it wasn't healthy.

They were well into Ragewood Forest by the time they made camp. Something was off about the forest. Malach could tell even Skie was unnerved by it. However, no one could point out what specifically made them feel uneasy. Skie wouldn't lay down next to Malach like she normally did but paced nervously. She made lap after lap around the camp, always peering into the woods as if searching for something. She stopped and growled here and there, a warning to whatever was out there that the camp was her territory, and she would defend it. Malach studied Skie, feeling her tension as if it was his own. He had a hunch they wouldn't be sleeping much for the next few weeks.

They made it through the night with their normal watch rotation. Skie had finally settled into a restless sleep next to Malach. The next morning there were dark circles under everyone's eye, and everyone had reported having uneasy dreams and hearing sounds that woke them up multiple times during the night. Their dreams had been different, but the sounds they heard had been all too similar. No one had seen anything while on watch, but everyone heard the scratching and skittering of something just out of sight.

Their unease lessened as day broke, and the sounds they heard during the night seemed to burn away with the light and warmth of the sun. The snow was melting more and more with every day and every mile they traveled away from the mountains. Malach still couldn't shake the feeling of being watched. Was it just his imagination? He felt like he was not the hunter anymore. They were the hunted, stalked by an unseen predator.

He rode up between Elzrod and Ariel. "I feel like we are being hunted," he whispered conspiratorially.

Elzrod grunted affirmative.

Ariel nodded slowly. "Don't say anything more. We will spread the word and be ready tonight."

They continued in silence. Their unseen stalker, remaining unseen, and Malach remaining on high alert. Several times, the hairs on the back of his neck stood up, and he turned to see nothing around him. Once, he thought he had spotted a shadow moving out of sight but the breeze moving through the trees making the shadows of the leaves dance. He couldn't be sure it was anything other than his own eyes playing tricks on him.

The snow had lessened even more and continued to get thinner the farther south they traveled. The temperature also got warmer, and they were able to shed some of their heavy furs. Now the snow lay in patches and a carpet of leaves littered the ground.

"If the snow is melting here, won't the snow be melting in the mountains?" Amara asked.

Ariel chuckled. "No, it will be several months before the snow melts up there. Even only as far north as Lindow, there will still be inches of snow and ice being kept cold by the winds of the plains and the cold air coming down from the mountains."

"Don't worry," Elzrod stretched and yawned. "We have a couple of months before the passes are accessible to a large army and their war machines."

"Oh." Amara's cheeks grew red.

"Not every place in the world has the same climate," Marena added haughtily.

Everyone turned her direction. Malach had never heard her say anything rude before.

"Sorry," Marena quickly apologized. "I didn't mean for it to come out that way."

"We are all tired," Ariel interjected. "Maybe we ought to call it a day and set up camp."

They spent another almost sleepless night in Ragewood forest. Some in the group were starting to grow irritable with the lack of sleep and long treks during the day. Togan was having the most issues, needing to dismount and walk some of the time because of the growing sores from long days in the saddle.

"We can't keep goin' like this!" Togan shouted in frustration.

"Do you need a break?" Elzrod lifted an eyebrow at the big man.

"No, I need it t' end," Togan replied. "I need t' get a good night's rest and I need t' be off this beast for more than an hour each day."

"We have another week and a half at the least," Ariel replied patiently. "And if we turn back we will have at least two days back to Kargod. You will have to endure."

"Don't tell me to endure, your kind has much more stamina than the rest of us." Togan's nostrils flared in anger.

"I apologize," Ariel held up a hand to calm him. "I simply meant to point out that no matter which way you go, you will be riding for a while."

"Argh," Togan turned and punched a tree.

"Enough of this. We need to talk about what's going on." Marena glanced around at the group. "We all feel it, even Skie. Someone or something is watching us. I think if it was a demon or a scout they would have already left to report and I still feel eyes on me even now."

"There are stories of monsters in the forest," Amara spoke up. "Most are so fantastical they can't possibly be true, but there are a few that could be what we are experiencing."

"Monsters?" Togan raised an eyebrow and snorted.

"Please, tell us what you've heard," Elzrod held up a hand to silence Togan's outburst. He and Ariel were the only ones who didn't seem to be feeling the effects of sleep deprivation.

"There are several stories of a monstrous spider that has attacked different parties who venture too far into the woods," Amara explained. "Also of large snakes that have drug men into lakes or other bodies of water. I think those might be the most likely."

"This could also be explained by normal animals following us," Malach spoke up, siding with Togan and not buying into hearsay. "Wolf packs have been known to follow travelers for days, judging whether or not they can take down the whole group or if they should leave for easier prey, especially in the winter when food is scarce. Also, some larger cats will do the same."

"I've heard several reports of seeing the ground move from angels flying over Ragewood," Ariel spoke up. "I trust the word of the angels who have reported this. I just assumed it was some trick of the light or terrain."

"Hmm," Elzrod stroked his white beard, which had been growing since they left the Angel Army. "That doesn't really narrow it down."

"Giant spiders, large water snakes, normal predators, or the ground itself," Togan counted off the list on his fingers. "That's the best we have? Can we rule anything out?"

"Not much," Elzrod shrugged. "However, snakes don't usually stalk their prey for several days; whereas we might need to be careful around bodies of water, I don't think we need to worry about them in this instance. We haven't heard any wolves since we crossed the Great Divide, so I think it's reasonable to rule them out as well."

"That leaves the larger feline predators, giant spiders, and the moving ground," Marena listed off the revised catalogue of creatures.

"Has anyone caught any kind of sight of what is following us?" Amara asked.

"Unless Skie has, I don't think so," Malach shook his head. "I thought I saw a shadow move in the forest the first day, but it could have just as easily been the shadow of a tree branch moving in the wind."

"Then there is nothing to do but wait and stay alert," Ariel stated, ending the conversation.

They spent their third night in Ragewood just as uneasy as the previous two nights. They got up the third day to continue their trek. None of them felt any more rested.

"Would you keep your horse from running into mine?" Amara snapped at Marena.

"He won't listen to me. He just wants to run into your horse's shoulder," Marena pulled heavily on the reigns to try and pull her horse away.

"You can control your horse. You just need to show him who's in control!" Amara shouted.

"What does that mean?"

"It means you're too demure to take control of him!"

"I am not! I've been handling him just fine until today."

"So you're saying you're just incompetent?"

Marena kicked out at Amara but missed, instead catching the horse in the ribs.

It bolted, almost dumping Amara off the back with the sudden movement.

She was able to get it under control and started back toward Marena, fire in her eyes.

"Enough!" Ariel shouted putting his horse between the women. "This doesn't help anyone. If you can't get along, Marena, you can join me up front with Togan, and Amara, you can go back and ride with Malach.

The two ladies moved to their respective ends of the procession. By the time they stopped for the noon meal, they had cooled down enough to apologize to each other. Malach decided it was time to figure this enigma out. He slipped away quietly, only Ariel noticed his movements and nodded his approval. Malach moved back the way they had come and climbed a tree. He pulled his bread out and started eating. He still needed lunch after all. There he sat waiting and watching, completely still except for his chewing.

What he saw made his blood run cold. A spider crawled down a tree to his right. It wasn't at all what he would consider monstrous, but it was larger than any Malach had seen. Its leg span was at least twice the size of Malach's hand if he spread his fingers as wide as they would go, and it was an orange-brown color with a few black markings on its back. It scuttled quickly under his tree and passed him headed for the group. Moments later two more of the same size and color spiders came out of the same tree and followed the first one.

Malach sat perplexed. Three spiders following their party through the woods for three days now. Was it even possible? Had those spiders been watching them this whole time, or was it a coincidence these three spiders crawled out of a tree and skittered toward his friends?

He jumped out of the tree and landed softly.

Reckoning, Malach thought. *Have you seen anything like this?*

No, he replied. *If they are doing what you think they are doing, that means they are smart. Smarter than others of their species.*

What does that mean? Malach asked.

It means we are in trouble, Reckoning replied, genuine worry in his voice. *If these things have been in this forest for who knows how long, and if they have the same number of offspring as other spiders... well, it means there are a lot of spiders running around out here.*

If they are smart and have numbers behind them, we need to get out of this forest right away, Malach followed the spiders careful to remain unseen.

Let's take care of these three and then talk with Elzrod and Ariel about where to go next, Reckoning suggested.

Malach nodded and unslung his bow.

Two of the spiders came into view just starting to run up a tree not too far from where they had stopped for noon meal. Malach pinned one's head to the tree with an arrow. Its eight legs scratched and scrabbled at the tree, trying in vain to free itself as it died. The other turned toward Malach, its front pincers clicking. There was intelligence in its eyes and a drop of venom dripped off the end of one of its fangs. Malach pulled a second arrow and fired but it jumped to the side and the arrow struck the ground harmlessly. The third spider descended from the tree on a web. It was an eerie sight, but it didn't stop Malach from taking a shot at the thing. It dropped quickly, and the arrow cut through the web it was descending on, it hit the ground and Malach heard a slight crunch. It didn't stop it from getting back up, but it was dragging one leg uselessly.

The spider who still had full use of its limbs skittered off into the woods, away from Malach. He tried to follow it but the one with the bad leg got in his way. He stopped, facing off with the creature. They circled each other Malach didn't know how fast the thing was, so he was wary of it. All of a sudden, a knife pinned it to the ground. Just like the one he had pinned, it tried to free itself until it finally died, its legs curling inward toward its body. Malach glanced up and spotted Amara leading the charge with the rest of the group behind her.

"Are you alright?" she asked.

"Yes." He nodded. "Thank you."

"What is it?" Togan was peering down at the creature from a safe distance.

"Some kind of arachnid," Elzrod was studying the one on the tree.

"How many are there?" Ariel quizzed Malach.

"I only saw these three, I'm not sure if there are more out there or not."

"Hopefully, we can get a good night's sleep now," Togan poked the dead spider with a stick.

"I'm not so sure this is going to get any better," Elzrod's face was screwed up with worry.

"How do you know?" Amara asked.

"I'm not sure I want to know," Malach shuddered.

"The color for one," Elzrod pointed at the spider on the tree. "Usually, males are the brighter colored, and then the pedipalps seem to be enlarged, which only happens to the males."

"The what?" Amara brow wrinkled in confusion.

"The pedipalps," Elzrod repeated, smiling as he explained. "See these little legs next to the mouth. The ones too short for walking? These are pedipalps. They use them during mating to-"

"Oh, enough of that," Marena shuddered and walked around unable to stand still. "Why is it a big deal what gender they are?"

"Because most male spiders live much shorter lives than the female," Elzrod replied. "Most of the time the females are much larger and more dangerous than males."

"We need to leave, then." Amara's eyes widened with fear. "If there are more and bigger things like this out there, then I don't want to be anywhere near them."

"Most likely, these were just like normal spiders," Ariel reasoned. "They are all over the place, but they are just looking for their next meal or to mate."

"You're telling me these things are all over the place?" Marena pointed at the spider, then glanced around her as if trying to make sure none of the creatures were sneaking up around her.

"Well, yes, but I think you are missing the point," Elzrod put his hand on her arm to calm her. "They were following us because they wanted their next meal, nothing more."

"We will need to watch for more of these things. It isn't normal for spiders to follow you for three days," Malach pointed out. "They usually stay in one place and catch things in their webs."

"Hmm," Ariel hummed thoughtfully. "Maybe this species is more of a hunter than others. Their size alone would allow them to be more of a predator. I think we need to keep moving. We might not run into any more, but the quicker we get out of this forest, the better."

"Fine, but if these things come after us again," Amara wagged a finger at Ariel, "I'm not going to be happy with you."

They walked back to the horses and mounted up. They drove the horses the rest of the day but didn't feel like they were being hunted anymore. Everyone slept well, and Ariel stood watch for most of the night, not needing the sleep.

They all woke the next day feeling refreshed and rejuvenated. The day went by much faster and better. By the end of the day, they were worn out from the ride, but they were in much better spirits. They even laughed and joked around the fire that night. When they retired to their tents, they all felt hope once again.

Chapter 12

Kragen had found his way into the Stronghold. Even after a decently accurate description of him was posted all over the camp stating he was wanted for questioning. He had avoided the search patrols by leaving the camp. He had taken shelter in the shadow of the stronghold. Ironically, he was safer the closer he got to his enemy.

He snuck in each night to find the food and supplies he needed. It was on one of those trips he noticed there were a few carts headed toward the stronghold. He followed them discreetly until they were rushed through the gate to the stronghold. The carts weren't even searched, from what he could see. The gates closed behind them, however, cutting off his view of the carts. He waited for a few hours until the carts came back out. They were empty. Which meant the barrels and crates were still inside the stronghold.

He had followed the cart back to their point of origin but to his disappointment, they were not loaded up again. Only stored away until they were needed next. It took a few more nights to find out the delivery schedule and then a few nights after that to arrange for an empty barrel to be loaded onto the cart. On the night the carts were to be rolled into the stronghold, there was an extra barrel loaded.

The carts rolled for a few minutes and then a few minutes more. It took longer than Kragen remembered, and he was worried they might be going somewhere other than the stronghold. He was about to pop the lid open to look out, but he heard the boom of the gates closing behind the carts. He was in.

Only another minute or two of movement and the carts came to a stop. The crates and barrels were unloaded, including the one he was in. Now he was sitting in the dark, waiting for the sounds of the workers to die away. He would soon be able to leave the barrel and find a weakness to exploit from within.

The sounds of the carts receding reached his ears. It wouldn't be long now and he would be in a position to carry out his mission. He pushed on the top of the barrel and to his horror, it didn't budge. He pushed harder but it didn't even wiggle a little. The workers must have put something on top of the barrel. And from the amount of pressure he was putting on the lid, it was heavy. He wiggled and squirmed his way around to put his feet against the lid. He pushed with all his considerable strength. Nothing.

Kragen sighed and righted himself inside the barrel. He pushed the rising panic down and pulled his knife. He whittled away at the side of the barrel for a long time. He had to stop a couple of times as someone walking by. Finally, he broke through the wall of the barrel, and fresh air spilled in.

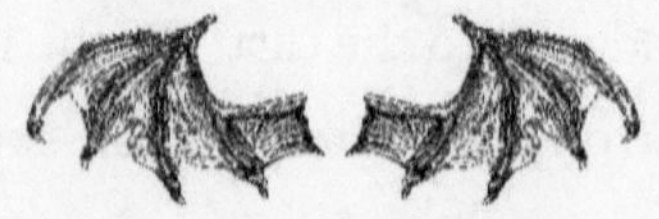

"Malach, we have to go." Togan woke Malach in a rush.

Malach glanced around. It was still dark, but he heard people rushing around the camp. Something was wrong.

Togan pulled him to his feet and the world swam before him. He almost had to sit down again, but his vision cleared in the next few moments. He followed Togan out of the tent, picking up his pack as he went.

"What's going on Togan?" he asked, still confused.

"Leave the tents!" Malach heard Elzrod shout from somewhere to his left.

"Mount up!" Ariel called from the same direction. "We need to get ahead of them."

"What's going on?" Malach shouted again, this time to anyone who would answer him.

"Spiders!" Amara all but screamed on the edge of panic.

That one word was enough for Malach and he was instantly wide awake. He ran for his horse. Her nostrils were flaring in fear, and she wanted to run, pulling at the rope tying her down. Malach caught her head and calmed her, then quickly saddled her before she spooked again.

As soon as he got the lead rope untied from the tree, the horse pulled Malach off his feet as it reared. He hit the ground and rolled away, knowing that the horse's hooves would be coming down on top of him. The hooves thumped into the ground beside him and Malach sprung to his feet. He leaped up into the saddle and kicked the horse to go, fumbling with the reigns and pulling the lead rope up out of the way of the horse's already thundering hooves. Luckily, the horse had followed the others, and Elzrod came into view up ahead to his right. He turned his horse. He stole a glance behind him but couldn't see anything in the darkness. As he caught up with Elzrod, the rest of the party came into view including Skie. He was happy to see they hadn't lost anyone.

Elzrod, what's happening? Malach asked mentally.

Spiders. Togan saw only a few of them at first, and then, all of a sudden, there was a flood of them, Elzrod replied.

I can't see them. Malach turned in the saddle taking a longer look this time.

I think we got ahead of them, but it's hard to tell. Elzrod replied. *They should have been able to overrun us with how quick they are. I'm not sure why they didn't.*

Malach turned to his left and then to his right. Off to the right, he could just barely make out movement in the darkness. He squinted, straining to make out more than just shadows. A mass of legs moved between the trees. He didn't know how far ahead of them the spiders were, but he needed to tell Elzrod and Ariel.

They are on the right! Malach mentally shouted.

"Left!" he heard Ariel bellow from the front of the group.

All of them veered to the left at the command and continued their breakneck flight through the woods. Malach watched Marena duck under a low hanging branch and flattened himself against the horse just in time to miss being taken off his seat. Once again, he spun his head around. There were no signs of the spiders anymore, maybe they had lost them. Ariel pulled up on his reigns hard and his horse skidding to a halt. The rest of them followed suit. Malach didn't understand why until the front runners turned right to head back south.

Ahead of them were spiders in webs spanned between trees. They had been lying in wait. These spiders looked much larger than the three they had previously fought. However, because of the lack of light, Malach couldn't tell if they were actually larger or if his eyes were playing tricks on him.

Two more times they almost plowed into one of these traps and two more times the keen eyes of Ariel saved them. The spiders weren't barely outpacing them, they were well ahead of the group. They were pushing them farther into this trap.

"Their herding us," Elzrod was breathing heavily.

"What do we do?" Marena asked.

"If we keep going forward, we will run into whatever trap they have laid for us," Ariel shook his head. "But if we stop and fight, we have to deal with the horde behind us."

"What if we go through one of the web barriers they have set up?" Amara suggested, she seemed to have calmed down in their flight instead of giving into the panic.

"How?" Togan asked.

"They have only a few spiders on each of them and our swords should be able to hack through them," Elzrod nodded, agreeing with Amara.

"Let do it," Malach said, setting his jaw. "I'm tired of running where they want us to run."

"We are headed mostly south right now, so let's break through the next barrier and try to get past the main force of them," Ariel suggested.

They all agreed and kicked their horses into a canter. When they came across the next web barrier, they headed straight for it. The spiders didn't seem to expect a head-on attack, and they were able to cut a few from the web before they reacted at all. Malach and Togan dismounted to defend the group from the spiders. While Amara and Marena worked on one side of the web, Ariel and Elzrod worked on cutting the other side. Malach stabbed one spider after another, trying to keep them all in front of him so they couldn't get behind him and either attack him or any of the others. He still didn't know what would happen if one of them sunk its fangs into him, but he didn't want to find out. He had killed ten or more of the creatures when the call to move came from Ariel. He took one more swing at the closest spiders, forcing them to jump back and mounted up.

His horse started moving before he was even fully seated, following Marena's horse directly ahead of him. He was glad for the movement as the spider only missed by inches, lunging at him and the horse. It managed to get two of its legs on the rump of the horse but was slung off, due to its momentum. They spurred their horses into a gallop once more, and Malach thought for sure they were free. He kept glancing around him watching for any signs of pursuit, but they quickly left the remaining spiders behind them, and there was no sign of any others in any direction.

"Did we lose them?" Togan asked.

"Just keep going until we are far away from this place," Elzrod shouted over the wind and sound of horse hooves beating against the ground.

Ariel, who had outpaced the group, disappeared. Before Malach could react, his horse fell throwing him clear of the saddle. He hit the ground hard but didn't go very far. Something sticky clung to his clothes and hair and he struggled to get up. He checked behind him to find his horse. Huge spiders appeared as if out of thin air and swarmed the horses who had fallen. These must be the females, as they were a dull greyish brown color and three times the size of the males.

Malach was finally able to get his feet under him, but the webs clung to him, making his movements sluggish and awkward. He managed to kill the first two spiders who came for him. He turned to see if anyone else was up and fighting and spotted Amara fighting three of the things. He moved to help her but his legs wouldn't budge. He glanced down to find them wrapped in the webs. He must have done it himself while fighting the spiders. He cut one leg free and started working on the other. He checked on Amara just in time to see one of the spiders sink its fangs into her arm. She screamed and stabbed it in the face.

Malach finished cutting free his second leg and started her way. One of the spiders got in his way and he batted away a hairy leg, stabbing it directly though one of its eight eyes. Its thrashing propelled its soon to be corpse out of his way. He moved forward but the webs started piling up on his legs again. One of the spiders finished wrapping Amara up. He wasn't going to make it. He cut at the webs at his legs again.

He felt a stinging pain in his arm and looked up to find one of the spiders had latched on to him. He shook his arm, dislodging the smaller male spider and sending it flying. It landed on its back and was stuck in its own web. It thrashed around for a moment until it was able to gain its feet again. He felt another piercing pain in his leg. He tried to stab the spider biting his leg, but his arm had gone numb and Reckoning slipped from his fingers. He grabbed at it with his good hand and stabbed down at the spider. He was able to kill it, but he had to pry its fangs from his leg. He started moving back toward the edge of the webs. If he could get clear of them, he had a chance to get away. His leg started to go numb and he tripped, falling into the webs. The spiders seemed to have been waiting for the venom to take effect, and when he fell, they sprang. Malach changed Reckoning to a short sword and stabbed up at the creatures descending upon him. He was even able to kill a few. One after another sank their fangs into him and pumped him full of their venom.

This is it, he thought as his vision started to grow dark. *This is how I die. This is where my story ends.*

The last thing he remembered was being wrapped tightly in warm material. Securely swaddling him like a mother would a baby. It cut the bitter chill of the night air and he was grateful. He let his eyes close and felt at peace. He was so tired. He let his weariness take him into sleep's wonderful embrace.

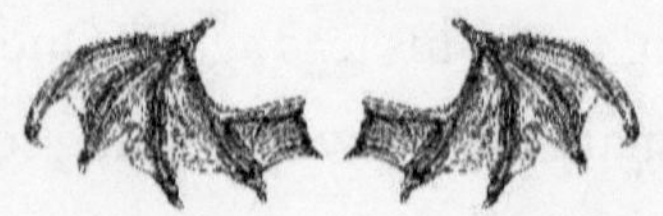

Serilda woke to a boot kicking her in her already broken ribs. She cried out involuntarily in pain, coughing, and tasting blood in her mouth. Maybe this was it. Maybe they would kill her, and it would be all over.

"Get up, maggot!" The man shouted, another blow from his boot connected with her hip this time.

That didn't hurt nearly as bad, but she knew if she couldn't find her feet, the abuse would keep coming. She struggled to all fours and then used the chains on the wall to lift herself to her feet. The man grabbed her roughly by her hair and pressed his body against hers.

"You know, you're a pretty thing," he said into her ear. "If I wasn't ordered to leave you alone, I would have had you by now. But it's only a matter of time before they let me have my – oomph!"

Serilda reached back and grabbed the man's groin and squeezed as hard and she could manage.

The man jumped back pulling from her grasp and yelled, nursing his privates.

She turned around, grinning maniacally at the pain she had caused.

He met her eyes, rage evident on his face. Enough rage to kill her. He pulled his sword and advanced on her, "I'm going to kill you, you-"

"You will do no such thing!" a commanding voice said before the man could strike her down.

Serilda's heart sank. She was so close. She almost had the death she desired.

"Put your weapon away before I end you," the voice commanded again.

A different demon than the one she had seen previously walked into the room holding something wrapped in a cloth. The man reluctantly did as he was told but sent a wad of spit flying at her. The foul substance fell short of her face, the intended target, and hit her on her almost bare chest. She didn't react in the slightest even though she wanted nothing more than to wipe away the slime.

This demon commanded more respect than the other one who had been torturing her, and for good reason. He was one of the Seven Lords of Hell. As such, he could change his form much more drastically than other demons. Right now, he was a handsome man she had met many, many years ago, on the streets of Yargate Port. He still had horns like any demon, but his were much smaller and less pronounced. He could hide his wings totally and his claws almost looked like normal human hands. If she wasn't looking closely, she could almost forget he was a demon.

He reached out and grabbed the man by his neck and lifted him from the ground. "Next time you even hint at disobeying an order, you will find that I can cause you immeasurable pain." He flung the man out of the cell door and out of Serilda's view. The demon then turned to her.

"Azazel, it's been a long time," Serilda said.

"Ciarán, you were always my favorite pupil," Azazel crooned.

"That's not my name anymore." Serilda scowled.

"But it is still who you are."

"I left that life when I left both armies,"

"Yes, with your little pet angel," he said with disgust. "You even procreated with him, resulting in that abomination you call a son."

"Abomination?" Serilda barked a laugh. "And what do you call those things you sire?"

"Oh, the nephilim? They are abominations as well," he admitted. "But I give them a purpose. Much like a little whelp, I pulled off the streets a couple of thousand years ago. Do you remember her?"

Serilda ground her teeth together.

"The shivering, starving, naked, little girl whom I clothed, fed, and trained to be my assassin."

"You abused me, raped me!" Serilda shouted, anger bubbling over as she railed against the chains holding her to the wall. "Then you killed my child in front of me! You are nothing more than a monster who deserves to burn for eternity!"

"I have a gift for you, my dear Ciarán," he crooned, his change in tone giving her mental whiplash. "I think you will find it most enlightening."

The demon unwrapped the buddle and showed her what it contained. It was her blade, Fang. But that meant they had managed to turn it against her. A new kind of torture would begin now. The kind which wouldn't ravage only her body, but her mind as well. If there was any hope left in Serilda, it left her. Truly her only escape would be death and yet they wouldn't ever allow that. No, she would be tortured until the end of the war, or until she died of old age a few centuries from now. She would be tortured by one of her closest companions, one who had vowed to her she would see her dead before anything like this would happen to her. Fang had broken her vow.

Chapter 13

Daziar, Honora, and Ana lay on a ridge in the snow watching the camp below them. The slog through the almost impassable mountain roads had taken much longer than they thought, but they had reached Lindow. Other than the heavy snowdrifts they had to traverse, and Auron almost falling off the side of a cliff, the journey had been uneventful. Now they watched the prison camp, trying to figure out a way they could get Honora inside without getting her killed.

Ana had with her what she called a *spyglass.* Daziar marveled at the invention, but she seemed to think it would be commonplace very soon. The spyglass was a metal tube that telescoped in on itself for easy storage. Daziar didn't fully understand how it worked, but there were some glass pieces inside that made things faraway look very near.

With as far away as they were from the prison camp, Daziar doubted the guards would see them, even if he stood up and jumped up and down, waving his hands, but with the spyglass, they could clearly see everything happening in the camp. All they had to do was wait and watch, and soon, they would be able to move Honora into position and free the prisoners.

Daziar originally liked the plan, reasoning Honora would have the best chance of getting into the camp. She would play the role of the helpless daughter of a Newaught council member who was reported to be resisting the demon regime. It would be an unfortunate scare for the man, but it wouldn't be long before he would get word it wasn't truly his daughter. Now, however, Daziar had started to change his mind. He had started thinking of all the possible ways this could go wrong. Arjun, who had insisted he would be coming on the mission, had started to get to him. The whole journey Arjun had been arguing with Honora and Ana about the role Honora was playing. After a couple of weeks of listening to him, Daziar was worried. Honora, however, was still committed to the original plan and wouldn't be swayed.

The three crawled back down the snowdrift they were hiding behind, making Daziar shiver as the cold snow seeped up and through his heavy furs and armor. The snow seemed to have a mind of its own, seeking any opening in his clothing and reaching its cold fingers in to steal his warmth. Even though he had grown up in the snowy northern mountains, he still didn't like it.

Ana's words broke the silence, "I think it's time."

"I agree," Honora nodded. "We've watched long enough. We need to act soon or we might miss our chance."

"Honora, are you sure you are alright with doing this?" Daziar asked.

"Yes, and neither you nor my father can stop me or talk me out of it." She poked him with a finger to emphasize her point. "I need to go get ready. I have to look like I've been running through the woods for weeks and need help."

Honora got to her feet carefully, making sure the snowdrift concealed her from the prison camp. She walked down the drift and into the small camp they had made, Daziar followed quickly. There were no fires. Since they were so close to the enemy, they didn't want to risk the smoke giving away their position.

Honora pulled out her handheld mirror and started getting ready to play her part in the ruse. She started by steaking her face with dirt and making it look like she had been crying. She then clumped her hair and messed it up, deliberately putting tangles in it. Daziar was sure she would have to cut off half her hair to get all the tangled knots out of it. She took off her outer furs revealing the ripped, worn, and dirty ones below. She shivered as the cold bit at her exposed skin, the last thing she did was swap out her boots. The ones she put on had holes worn in them, and she would be risking frostbite if she had to stay in them for more than a few hours. They hoped the Demon Army would clothe her better once she was in their camp. They wouldn't want their valuable new prisoner to come to any harm until they needed her to. She set off at once without talking with anyone and already starting to look very cold.

"Good luck," was all he said as she passed him.

"T-t-thanks," she chattered back, handing him her handheld mirror. "T-take care of t-t-that. I'll w-want it back w-when I return."

Nothing else needed to be said. Daziar and Ana would be watching if anything went wrong. Honora struck out west, taking a roundabout way to the prison camp to conceal the direction she came from. They didn't want the Demon Army to find their camp. He put her mirror into his pocket.

I hope she'll be alright, Daziar thought as Honora got smaller and smaller as she jogged away.

Daziar grabbed some of the cold porridge offered to him and sat down, shoveling it into his mouth. It would be a while before Honora showed up at the prison camp, but he'd be daft if he wasn't going to be waiting and watching when she did. He finished the bowl in record time and got up to head back up the snowdrift. Arjun chose that time to come out of the tent he was staying in.

"Daziar," Arjun called, catching sight of him.

Daziar stopped and waited for him to walk over to him.

"Do you know when Honora is going to be headed for the prison?"

Daziar didn't want to be the one to tell Arjun, but obviously, Honora hadn't thought to tell him she was leaving. He took a deep breath. "She just left,"

"What?" Arjun almost shouted.

Several of the soldiers shushed him. His voice could easily carry to the prison and no one wanted to get caught.

"I had assumed she talked with you this morning about her leaving, but she just changed to her rags and left for the camp," Daziar started, guiding the man toward the ridge. "Come with me, and we will wait at the top of the snowdrift to make sure she makes it safely inside."

"That strong-willed daughter of mine will be the death of me."

He followed Daziar back up the snowdrift and they dropped to their bellies in the cold snow, crawling the last few feet. Daziar stopped beside Ana who had remained at the top of the drift, keeping an eye on Honora's progress. She glanced at the pair and turned back to her spyglass.

"You know she isn't going to arrive for some time, right?" Ana told them after a moment.

"We do," Arjun replied for them. "But I want to be here when she does. If anything happens to her, they will have my axe to deal with."

Ana narrowed her eyes at Arjun. "I expect them to rough her up a bit. I don't want you blowing our cover just because one of them hits your daughter."

Arjun ground his teeth together and her words. "So be it, but if I have the chance to kill any who touch her when we attack, you'd best believe I will take it."

"I'd be disappointed if you didn't." Ana grinned at him.

The three fell silent waiting and watching, each lost in their thoughts. Daziar rolled onto his back where the furs were thicker and where the snow couldn't get through as easily. He closed his eyes against the bright sun and allowed his muscles to relax. Before he knew it, he was being shaken awake by Ana.

"She's approaching the prison."

Honora was cold. She didn't think her short walk through the snow would cause her to be so cold. However, since she did it in torn up and wholly inadequate clothes, she lost her heat quickly. She was almost to the prison, though, and she hoped—no, she prayed—they would react the way she expected. Her feet were wet where the melted snow had seeped into her boots, and her toes had gone numb with the cold a half hour ago. She could barely feel the rest of her feet. She needed to keep moving. Hopefully, they would at least put her someplace where she could dry her feet.

As she approached the prison, one of the guards came out to meet her. She acted like she didn't notice him but just kept trudging along, slowing her steps and dragging her feet to give the appearance she had been walking for a while. She didn't have to fake the shivers and chattering teeth though, those came naturally.

"Halt!" The guard commanded her.

She jerked her head up trying to look surprised as if this was the first time, she had noticed him. He was only about ten paces away and had lowered his spear. She thought about putting her hand up in a sign of surrender, but she was too cold to do anything but hug herself.

"P-p-please," she chattered her eyes half-closed. "H-h-help."

She collapsed to the snow, and it was all she could do not to jump back up. The sudden shock of the cold, wet snow jolted her body, there was no way she would have ever been able to fall unconscious. The guard stood where he was for a few long moments and she internally begged the man to pick her up soon or she really would freeze to death. To her relief, the guard called back to his companion and walked over to inspect her. He searched her person quickly and found the knife on her belt that she intended him to find. He took it and picked her up and tossed her over his shoulder. She stayed as limp as she could, hoping he wouldn't notice the involuntary tensing of some of her muscles.

The guard turned toward the prison. Her head bounced up and down on the man's back and she soon had a headache. She hoped this would be over soon. She noticed a change in the sound and heard a few shouts around and above them. They must have been passing through the gate and under the single guard tower. She heard a tent flap move and heavy fabric brushed against the side of her face and the air became altogether warmer.

The guard hefted her off his shoulder and roughly set her down on what might have been a bed roll. Her head bounced off the ground. Luckily, there had been something semisoft to cushion the blow or she might have actually lost consciousness.

"You fool," someone spat at the guard, and he recoiled away from whoever it was.

"Sorry, sir," the guard apologized smartly, and she heard his boots click as he snapped to attention in front of someone, most likely his superior officer. Her head throbbed all the more, and she winced involuntarily.

The officer must have noticed because he said, "Leave us, I want to question her alone."

"Yes, sir!"

She heard the guard leave quickly. She wouldn't be able to hide the fact she wasn't unconscious for much longer. She made a show of waking up, holding her throbbing head, which helped her growing headache marginally. She didn't like her treatment so far; however, he *had* brought her to a warm tent, and she *was* starting to get feeling in her fingers again. Nothing yet from her toes, but if she could stay in the tent for a little longer the feeling should return to them too.

"I'm sorry for your treatment up to this point," the officer said.

She lifted her head for the first time and gazed straight into beautiful green eyes. It took her so off guard, she stumbled back a bit. The man in front of her wasn't at all what she was expecting. He was indeed an officer, but he didn't look vicious or cruel as she had expected. He wasn't fat and creepy or small and slimy, either. He looked normal. . . kind, even. He looked at her with what might have been genuine concern on his face, and he had a hand extended to her to help her to her feet.

"It's alright." He put his hands out to reassure her. "I'm not going to hurt you."

"Y-you're not?" She didn't have to fake the confusion in her voice. She was genuinely perplexed at his demeanor.

"No." He shook his head. "I'm here to help you and all the other refugees."

"The what?" Honora's brow furrowed. Nothing he said made any sense. Maybe she had been hit on the head harder than she thought.

"The refugees." He smiled. "That's what you are right? You have been displaced by the war. I would say possibly from Fairdenn, judging by the direction you were coming from. Is that correct?"

"Uh, yes," she told him. It was what she wanted him to think anyway, so she played along.

"Please, allow me to get you some warm clothes." He moved to an ornate wardrobe, which looked terribly out of place in the tent. "I'm sorry about your home. I know our army was the one that attacked, and you most likely think we are the monsters here."

She nodded, dumbfounded as he helped her to sit up on the mat.

"I assure you, we are not all monsters," he continued, draping a warm blanket over her shoulders.

Then he did something she never would have expected in a thousand years. He unlaced her wet, muddy boots and removed them gently from her soggy, still numb feet. After he had gotten them off, he dried her feet and started rubbing the feeling back into them. They burned as the circulation started to return. The officer then moved to help her take off her soaked outer layer and laid the blanket back over her. She sighed deeply as the warmth of it took away her shivers, and she let her guard down for only an instant. The officer moved away from her and to a table. He turned around and something gleamed in his hand. She recoiled quickly, ready to fight.

"Woah!" The officer put up his hands and showed her a small hairbrush with metal filigree inlaid into the wooden handle. "I'm not going to hurt you." He smiled disarmingly.

He set the brush aside, easing her back down onto the mat and replacing the blanket she had flung off her with her sudden movement. She allowed him to do it, but studied him the whole time, suspicious. He went over to the fire and took a pot off a hook where it had been hanging, pouring the steaming water into a smaller bowl. He stuck a finger in the bowl seeming to test how hot the water was, and he didn't recoil. He moved over to her and set the bowl down behind the pillow that was meant for her head.

"May I wash your hair?" he asked.

Honora was absolutely baffled by the man's action and only nodded her affirmation, mouth agape. She slowly turned her back on the man and laid her head on the pillow. He gently pulled her hair out so that she wasn't laying on it and started to clean the hair she had just dirtied not an hour before. Once, he got up, threw out the water, refilled his bowl and continued to clean her hair. The warmth of his hands and the water made her want to relax but she fought against it, trying to stay alert and aware of what was going on.

Maybe that's his ploy. Her thoughts were coming slowly, almost as if he had drugged her. Her eyes widened. *Had he? No, she was just that tired.* She relaxed again.

The officer, no doubt, would get her to let her guard down and tell him anything he wanted to know. But that didn't make sense. He didn't know she was anything more than a refugee, did he? She decided to let this play out and see what happened, besides it did feel *so* good. After he was done washing her hair, he dried it with a cloth.

"What is your name?" The officer asked.

He asks so innocently I almost believe him. "Akila," Honora lied. *And the questioning begins.*

"Akila," the officer repeated, as if trying out how it felt on his tongue. "That's a very pretty name."

"Thanks." She was still determined to not give away any information.

"I will leave you to change and brush your hair." He sat the brush next to her. "I have laid out some warm clothes for you that should fit well enough. I will be waiting outside let me know when you are finished."

That was it? No other question?

He left the tent and a gust of the cold wind rushed in as he left, making her shiver. The wind was cut off when the heavy flap closed behind him. She was alone. She still didn't know what to think. This was not at all how she thought this meeting would go. He was obviously the one in charge, as indicated by the reaction of the guard, but for the past few moments, he had played the role of a servant. She couldn't wrap her head around it. She turned to find there was indeed a pile of clothes lying on the table folded neatly and off to the side was a makeshift wall to give her privacy. She shrugged to herself and walked over to change out of the rags she wore.

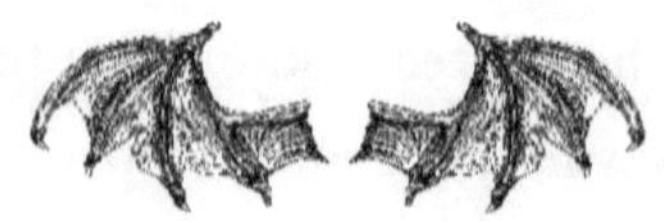

"What's happening?" Arjun asked for the tenth time in half as many minutes.

"She is still in the tent," Ana growled, grinding her teeth in annoyance. "The guard just came out, but she isn't with him."

"If she doesn't come out of the tent in the next few moments, I'm gonna-"

"You're gonna what?" Ana cut him short and then continued, not allowing him to answer her question. "*You're* not going to do anything. We all knew what was going to happen, and I won't allow you to risk the safety of this mission or Honora. She's been in there less than two minutes and you're already prepared to ruin our chances of getting all the prisoners out safely. If you can't stay calm up here, then you will have to go back to the camp and wait there."

Daziar was dumbfounded. He had never heard anyone talk to Arjun like that before. Arjun opened his mouth once as if to protest and closed it, turning back to the prison. They waited and watched in tense silence, and Daziar felt very uncomfortable being between the two of them. Soon there was movement at the tent they had taken Honora into but Daziar couldn't tell anything from where they were.

Ana watched through her spyglass giving commentary as she did, "An officer has stepped out, but there is no sign of Honora."

There were all silent for a few minutes, pensively waiting.

"There she is," Ana announced.

Arjun let out a long sigh of relief.

"She has new clothes on, and her hair has been cleaned. It looks like everything is going according to plan."

"What do you think they said in there?" Daziar asked.

"Most likely they talked about Honora's supposed father," Ana didn't take her eyes off Honora. "The officer is probably plotting how best to exploit the information he now has."

Daziar nodded thoughtfully. "What now?"

"We wait." Ana finally torn her eyes form the spy glass and collapsed it. "And watch for Honora's signal. Who wants to take first watch?"

"I will," Arjun replied, almost before Ana got the words out of her mouth.

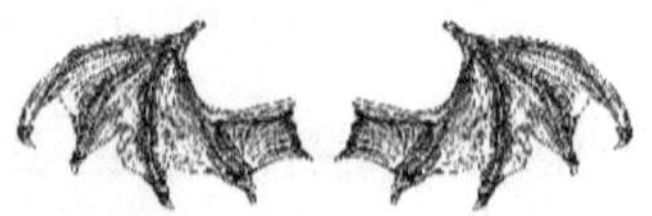

Honora changed out of the dirty, worn clothes and took the hot, wet towel provided for her. When she had wiped her skin clean as best as she could, she dressed and pick up the hairbrush. The officer wasn't at all what she had expected. Nothing about her arrival here had been what she expected. She didn't have to ask for clothes, he provided them for her. She didn't have to demand some way of cleaning herself, it was already ready. Almost as if they had been expecting her, but that was crazy.

I didn't even tell him my story about my father! She realized and silently berated herself for her oversight.

She would just have to figure out a way to slip it into her conversation later. But why was the officer being so kind to her? Why would a prison camp commander care for a refugee? A terrible thought struck her all of a sudden and she looked down at her clothes. Whose clothes had these been? A prison camp wouldn't be equipped to take in refugees, so these clothes must have been taken off a corpse. She had the sudden urge to vomit but managed to keep the bile at bay. No, she couldn't get complacent, she couldn't start trusting these people just because they were kind in the first few minutes of her stay. The other shoe would drop, and she would be just another prisoner in what would undoubtedly be inhumane conditions.

She took a deep breath and steeled herself to what would come next. She walked purposely outside with her head held high. The cold wind hit her like a punch to her gut. It stole her breath away and she hunched over hugging herself for warmth. The officer walked up to her and she flinched away from him. He paused and then continued what he was doing. He put a warm blanket over her shoulder helped her wrap up in it. It helped but it didn't shut out the wind.

"Come with me," he told her and started walking away before she could reply.

She jogged to catch up with him and she almost had to continue jogging to keep pace with his long brisk stride. "Where are you taking me?" She asked, having to work hard at distrusting him.

"To your tent," he told her. "You will be staying with several other women refugees. It's not the most comfortable, but at least you will have a warm tent and a place to lay your head. We are supposed to be receiving more supplies any day now, and then we will be able to provide more than one meal a day."

She couldn't help but notice the pain in the man's voice. He seemed to truly care if the people here had what they need and whether or not he could provide it. The officer led her to a large tent. He opened the flap for her, and she could feel the warmth spill out of the opening. He ushered her inside and followed her in, closing the flap behind them.

Several women glanced up at them as they entered, and Honora felt self-conscious and nervous. The women all looked clean and had warm clothes on. They were a little gaunt, but with only one meal a day, anyone would be. Honora wondered if the officer and his men were only getting one meal a day as well. She doubted it, since they all looked healthy and well-fed. After a cursory inspection of the newcomer, women went back to what they were each doing and didn't pay much more attention to her or the officer.

"There should be bed space in the back of the tent," the officer told her. "Just take any empty bed roll and make yourself as comfortable as possible. I'm sure you can find out any information you want to know from the women here, but if not, please feel free to come to my tent and ask me."

"I need to get a message to my father. He will be wanting to know that I am safe." She grabbed his wrist as he turned to leave.

"Who is your father? I will find him and send a message if I can." the officer turned back to her.

Honora told him her father was an official in Newaught, and his eyes widened though he didn't say anything. She told him her father would be searching for her and would do anything to get her back. She worked at sounding more important than she was so he would put her with the prisoners instead of the refugees. She reasoned there must be both at this camp, and she would need to find the prisoners if she was going to break them out.

The officer promised again to send word to her father and exited the tent. Honora turned to the women to see they were studying her once again, this time with suspicion in their eyes. She was put off by their glares but did her best not to let it show. She walked past them farther into the tent to find where she would be sleeping.

"Hey, whelp," she heard one of the ladies call to her.

She ignored the lady and kept moving.

"Whelp," came the call again but again she ignored it.

A boney hand grabbed her upper arm, squeezing painfully and turning her around. She looked into the eyes of an older lady with white hair and bags of skin hanging from her face. "Didn't you hear me, whelp?"

Honora turned away from the lady's foul breath. "I heard you, but I don't answer to whelp. My name is Akila," she replied defiantly.

Honora's head snapped to the side as the woman's free hand slapped her roughly.

"Listen here, whelp," the women spat at her, "you will answer to whatever I call you. I'm in charge around here."

"Give it a rest, Gretchen, you old hag," another voice came from behind Honora. "You aren't in charge."

Honora dared to take her eyes off the volatile woman and turned to find out who the other voice belonged to. Another elderly lady was standing a few feet behind Honora with her hands on her hips and jaw set. She was shorter than Gretchen, and her hair was a silvery grey. She had deep laugh lines like her face was used to smiling but at the moment she wasn't wearing one.

"Why I never," Gretchen sputtered.

"Yeah, you never," the smaller woman took a step forward. "You never lift a finger to help anyone but yourself, you never encourage anyone, you never greet anyone with kindness, and you never will be in charge, so stop acting like it!"

Honora couldn't help but smile at the little spitfire of a woman and Gretchen released her hold on Honora's arm. Honora turned to look back at Gretchen the smile turning into a smirk.

Gretchen turned and stormed off in a huff.

Honora let out the breath she didn't realize she was holding.

The smaller lady didn't say anything else just turned and walked away.

Honora didn't know whether to follow her or to find her bed, hopefully far away from Gretchen. The lady stopped at the end of the hall of makeshift walls she turned and motioned for Honora to follow, as if she already should have been. Honora moved quickly to follow the lady and who didn't wait for her, turning the corner and continuing out of sight. Honora broke into a fast jog to catch up, having to pull up the skirts she wasn't accustomed to wearing or she risked tripping over them.

She turned the corner just in time to see the lady disappear again heading deeper into the tent. She turned the corner, however, this time she could see to the back of the tent. There was a hall of makeshift walls reaching just over her head, but she could easily see the little lady and she continued her brisk walk down the hall. She caught up with the lady about halfway down the hall and almost ran into her when she stopped at one of the little rooms without warning.

"Sorry," she apologized, lightly out of breath.

"For what?" The little lady gave her an odd look, but then pressed on. "This can be your room. I know it's not much but it better than sleeping in the snow."

"Thank you," Honora said. "And thank you for your help with Gretchen. Horrid woman."

The lady smiled at her, "You're welcome dear, but Gretchen isn't so bad after you get used to things here. She just thinks she can boss around the new people. What's your name?"

"I'm sorry," Honora apologized realizing how rude she had been. "My name is H-Akila. What's yours?"

"I'm Rose. It's nice to meet you, Akila."

"And you as well," Honora bobbed her head. "How long have you been here?"

"Just a few weeks," Rose replied. "Before then, most of us were in our homes in different towns."

"Where are you from?" Honora asked.

"Fairdenn," Rose told her.

"I was there when it fell!" Honora blurted before she could stop herself. "I mean, after I fled from Newaught, I saw the destruction of the city."

Rose narrowed her eyes at Honora and didn't say anything for a few moments.

Honora was on the edge of panic. Had she just blown her cover already? Should she just spill her guts and swear Rose to secrecy?

"Terrible, wasn't it?" Rose deflated, no doubt, remembering what she had lost.

"Yes, it was," Honora replied, mentally sighing. "I didn't see any refugees though. I assumed that the townspeople had all gotten away or were killed in the fighting. How did you end up here?"

"Most left when they called the evacuation of the city," Rose replied. "Except those who couldn't, the sick, or the wounded. I stayed behind to care for them, knowing if I died, no one would miss me. I don't have any living family, so I cared for the sick until the Demon Army swept through the city. I assumed we would all be put to the sword, having heard the terrible things the Demon Army did in the olden days. But when they arrived, they brought healers to tend to the wounded and sick. They took the wounded soldiers to a prison and we were moved here."

"I thought this was a prison when I first spotted it," Honora picked up on the word prison. Maybe she could fish from some information. "I was going to pass it up and try to make it to Lindow, but I just didn't have it in me in this cold."

"Poor thing, you must have been scared to come here. What a shock you must have had when you arrived," Rose empathized.

"It was definitely not what I expected," Honora nodded. *Rose isn't going to tell me anything, either because she doesn't know anything or because she doesn't want to tell me for some reason.*

"I will let you get settled here," Rose gestured to the open room. "Evening meal will be served at dusk, but don't worry I'll come get you here so you know where to go."

Rose walked away.

What am I going to do until the evening meal?

Rose said to settle in, but Honora didn't know how she needed to go about doing that. She presumed she should stay here. If she had walked all the way here from Fairdenn through the cold and snow, she would be tired. She laid down on the cot and rested her head on the somewhat soft pillow. It was a bit lumpy and well worn. It wasn't dirty, however, and she was grateful. She laid there, trying to plan what she was going to do next. Maybe at the evening meal, she could find out where they were holding the prisoners. Rose wasn't going to tell her anything but maybe one of the other refugees know something and was willing to talk about it.

She wondered why the refugees wouldn't have just been moved back to Fairdenn by now, or even another city like Lindow. What did the demons have up their slaves? Maybe she would be able to find the answers to these questions soon.

She stayed in the little room for several hours, pretending to be asleep anytime someone walked past the open doorway. Finally, it was Rose who walked up and knelt next to her. Honora continued to pretend to stay asleep until the woman shook her gently.

"Akila," Rose said softly. "Akila, time for evening meal."

"Huh?" Honora cracked one eye trying to appear groggy. "Oh, alright."

"You must have been tired to sleep all afternoon like that," Rose smiled sweetly. "I know your road has been hard, but you will have an easier time here."

"Thank you." Honora smiled back at Rose. Honora sat up and got to her feet.

Rose led her to the entrance of the tent. She tightened her grip on her cloak and wrapped it more securely around her. Honora mimicked her and wrapped her own cloak tighter around herself. Rose opened the flap and a blast of cold air hit her, causing her cloak to billow up and away from her body, stealing her warmth. She drew in a sharp breath and pushed out into the winter weather.

It seemed like there was always wind blowing on these plains, to some degree, and a person never knew when it was going to change directions or intensity. The wind was blowing much harder than it had been only a few hours before, picking up the top layer of ice and snow and blasting it into their faces. The weather had turned into a blizzard, except, as far as she could tell, there was no new snow falling. To make things worse, it was still bright and sunny. The snow in the air reflected the sunlight, blinding her to the point that it was still painful with her eyes closed. Rose grabbed her wrist and together they fought against the cold wind. Rose all but drug her into another tent and closed the flap. Honora opened her eyes and Rose secured the tent flap.

Honora took in her surroundings. There were groups of people sitting on blankets on the ground in the tent. Which made sense, since there were no tables or anything to sit or stand at. To Honora's right, there was a serving area where some ladies, she didn't know if they were refugees or volunteers, were serving food. Rose started walking toward the serving table. As they moved down the table, Rose greeted every server by name and introduced Honora, as Akila, to every one of them. Honora would never be able to remember all of their names but politely thanked them for the food, even though it wasn't much to look at. The food put on her plate was an oatmeal, of sorts, with little to no taste and a flat piece of stale bread that tasted almost the same.

Rose steered her toward a blanket in the tent that had only one other occupant. The rest of the refugees seemed to give this woman a wide berth, and there was plenty of room around her for Rose and Honora to sit. They approached the woman from behind and Rose lightly put a hand on her shoulder so they didn't startle her. The woman turned to face them and stood. As she got up, her size shocked Honora. She just seemed to grow until Honora was afraid her head would reach the top of the tent. The woman had to be a giant.

"Akila, this is my good friend Vadis," Rose introduced them. "Vadis, this is Akila."

Vadis made a series of hand motions and grunts in response and which had Honora perplexed. She turned to Rose to see if the women had understood any of it.

"Oh, Vadis is a mute," Rose explained. "We have started to figure out a way to communicate with hand motions. It's a slow process, but we can now get more ideas across to each other."

Honora glanced back up at Vadis, who had a silly grin plastered on her face and was nodding emphatically. From Vadis's expressions, Honora didn't think a whole lot was going on behind her slightly too far apart eyes. She didn't think Vadis would have any information she wanted but at this point, she was trapped and had to sit with these two.

"Vadis says she is very happy to meet you, and she hopes that you would consider being her friend," Rose translated the hand motions then added quietly. "The poor dear doesn't have very many friends, in fact, I am the only one who will get anywhere near her. I think everyone else is scared of her."

Honora nodded. *I'm not too sure I want to be near Vadis either*, she thought and immediately felt a little guilty.

Rose sat down and Honora sat, although reluctantly, with her. It took Vadis several moments to descend to a sitting position due to her awkward moments and sheer size. The three ate in silence for a while. Honora dug into the bland food, trying to keep up the appearance of not having eaten in a few days.

"Slow down, dear," Rose reach and hand out to her as if to physically stop her from eating so fast. "I know you think you need to get food in you right away, but if you eat too quickly, it will revisit you before it's supposed to."

Honora slowed down, trying to look a little sheepish. "Sorry," she said through half a mouthful.

Vadis grunted to get Rose's attention and made several hand motions.

"Vadis said that, if you are that hungry, you can have the rest of her food as well," Rose translated.

"Oh." A pang of guilt shot through her. Now she'd done it. She wasn't really hungry, and this woman who only received one meal a day had offered to share her food. "Umm, no, I couldn't. You already have so little."

Vadis made several more motions.

"She says, 'but you have so much less,'" Rose translated and Vadis slid what was left on her plate over to Honora.

"She insists." Rose smiled. "Besides, I heard we will be getting two meals a day soon."

Honora didn't know how to get out of accepting the offering from the big woman, so in the end, she took the plate and tried to eat it. The guilt she felt seemed to make the food stick in her throat, and she had to force the rest down.

Rose and Vadis conversed with their hand motions while she ate. Rose also spoke her side of the conversation aloud so Honora could mostly follow the conversation. They talked about the gossip of the camp and Honora slowly realized Vadis might know more than she previously assumed. Vadis, it turned out, was ignored but the majority of people, since she was mute and therefore, was privy to a lot of private conversations. Since Rose had taken the time to learn to communicate with her, Vadis told Rose everything. If anyone knew anything about the prisoners who were supposed to be here, Vadis would. Now all she had to do was figure out how to get that information without asking outright. She didn't want to tip off the wrong people to what she was doing.

Rose and Vadis finished their conversation before Honora could find a way to ask and they stood. She figured she would just have to ask another time. She needed to signal Ana anyway.

The wind had died down a little bit and the sun was much less intense. She still didn't want to spend too much time out in it. Vadis and Rose pushed out of the tent and Honora followed, stopping to strap the tent flap down and letting Rose and Vadis get ahead of her a little.

She pulled out a green handkerchief and held it up to her face as she tried not to let the wind carry her forward too fast. Ana, or someone, would be watching for her to give a signal. She had a green, red, and blue handkerchief she would raise to signal how things were going. Green for 'everything was fine', red for 'something is wrong, come rescue me' and the blue one would let them know she was ready to escape. If she showed the blue one, the plan was to attack the following dawn. If they didn't see anything from her they would wait until the next check-in and then attack, if she didn't give an all-clear signal. She put the handkerchief away and caught up to Rose and Vadis.

She ducked under the tent flap Vadis was holding open for her, and the warmer air thawed her exposed skin. She followed the ladies to one of their rooms where Vadis produced a deck of cards. Rose motioned for them to sit and they did. They played card late into the night, laughing and enjoying themselves until it was time for Honora to retire to her little room.

She laid down in her bed happy. Truly happy. She hadn't been so content since her time in Newaught. She had expected this whole experience was going to be terrible and uncomfortable. She hadn't thought she would find any friends here. Just people needing her help. These people had done more to help her than the other way around so far. Making sure she was safe and well-fed, even when they weren't. She fell asleep with a smile on her face.

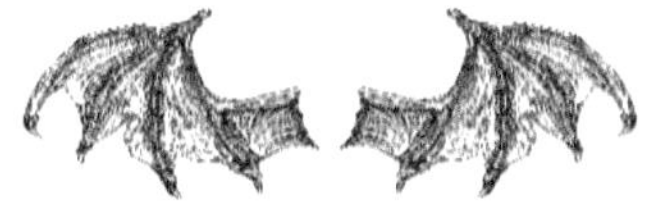

Daziar and Arjun paced the camp, waiting for word Honora had signaled them letting them know how she was doing. Auron had taken the watch after Arjun, but it hadn't helped the man calm down. His nervousness had been contagious and not long after he started pacing, Daziar hadn't been able to sit still and joined him.

"Would you two sit down?" Ana asked, but it was more of a command.

"I can't sit still." Arjun shook his head, not making any motion to comply with Ana's command.

"Well you're driving me up a tree," she complained.

"If you can't beat 'em, join 'em," Daziar replied from his path on the other side of Ana.

"You two are going to wear a hole in the ground halfway to Hades by the time the mission is over." Ana threw her hands up. "And I'm going to make you climb out on your own."

Daziar deviated from his path and sat down on the rock where she was sitting. "What do you suppose we do to whittle away the time."

Auron came running down the hill as fast as he could in the snow. To his credit, he didn't shout, but he was excited. He got to the camp and put his hands on his knees to recover from the run.

He needs to get into better shape if that's all it took to get him that far out of breath, Daziar thought.

"Honora gave the all clear," he finally forced out between breaths.

"The all clear to attack?" Arjun asked putting a hand on the hilt of his axe.

"No," Auron gave the man a confused look. "The all clear that she is alright."

"Oh," Arjun dropped his hand. "Good, I'm glad she's alright."

"Arjun, we have to trust she has everything under control," Ana reiterated for the tenth time that hour.

"I know. I wish you would stop saying that."

"Then you need to heed my words and actually trust your daughter," Ana told him a bit forcefully, standing up for emphasis.

Arjun was about to retort, which undoubtedly would have led to an argument between him and the angel, but Daziar interrupted, "Alright, let's all take a breath. We won't do Honora any good bickering amongst ourselves."

"Your right," Ana sitting back down.

I am? Daziar thought. He had been the voice of reason for once. *Excellent.*

"Um, this might not be the time for this," Auron spoke up nervously. "Could we light a fire and actually have something warm tonight? I'm tired of nearly breaking my teeth on half-frozen bread and cheese."

"No!" Arjun, Daziar, and Ana said all at once.

"Alright, fine," Auron held up his hands and back up a step. "I'll just go back up the hill and continue to watch until I lose visibility... or my fingers."

Chapter 14

Malach woke up disoriented. It was almost pitch black, but there was a slight glow coming from somewhere. He was wrapped tightly in some sort of material, but his face was mostly uncovered. The tug of gravity didn't seem right. He was being pulled up. Or maybe above him was down?

His memories came back in a flood, filling him with terror. The spiders had him, they had wrapped him in this cocoon. It wasn't any fabric that held him tight—it was their webs. He was hanging upside down from a cave ceiling and the floor was below him. The weird feeling of gravity made sense now. The glow he was seeing was from some kind of luminescent moss clinging to the walls, floor, and ceiling. He struggled to break himself free. His limbs were still numb and weak from the venom the spiders had pumped into him.

To his left was another cocoon. Much larger than his and roughly horse shaped. With any luck, the spiders would feed on the horses before any of his friends. He struggled again to break free. The tightening of his muscles seemed to move the venom out of his limbs giving him some of his strength back. He tried again to free himself but was unable to break any of the strands. As he regained feeling in his hands, however, he realized that Reckoning was still at his fingertips. The spiders had wrapped them up together. Malach tried to send a message to the blade but got nothing in response.

It must be a side effect of the venom, Malach thought. *Something about it is blocking my communication with Reckoning.*

Malach hadn't realized how much comfort he had taken from being connected to Reckoning or how much he had come to rely on him. No matter what trouble he got into, he could always count on Reckoning to have a plan or idea to get him out. He had to push the panic down to think clearly.

He struggled to get at the blade's handle. It was just out of reach and he couldn't free himself enough to grab it. He heard scuttling sounds coming from an entrance to this larger room and froze. Moving only his eyes, he caught sight of one of the spiders crawling into the room. To his left, the horse started to struggle, starting to come to its senses, and the spider moved quickly up to the ceiling and onto the horse cocoon. It took every bit of his self-control not to shout or struggle to get free at the terrible sight. He managed to stay still watching in terror as the spider sank its fangs into the horse's neck and the animal's struggling slowed, ceasing altogether after a few moments.

Malach heard a whimper behind him, and he instinctively turned his head. He froze, realizing his mistake, and shut his eyes, consciously forcing his muscles to go slack. Moments later, he felt his cocoon jolt as the spider climbed onto it. He nearly screamed at what would come next. The spider slowly descended the cocoon until it was, no doubt, face to face with Malach. If he opened his eyes, he would have stared directly into all eight of the spider's beady orbs. He forced his breath to stay calm and even, knowing it was his only chance of escape. The next few moments stretched into an eternity. The spider, finally, mercifully, started to move back up his cocoon and onto the ceiling. Malach didn't dare make any kind of move or even open his eyes until the small scratching sounds of the spider's legs faded to silence and even then, he waited.

"Malach?" It was Marena. "Malach, are you awake."

Malach dared to open one eye scanning the room for any creepy crawly but there weren't any. He opened his other eye and took stock of the surroundings once again. The spider had spun his cocoon and he was now facing the opposite way. He could see several more cocoons. Only one was human-shaped, the rest appeared to be various other animals. Marena face stared out at him from the human-shaped cocoon. Fear shone in her eyes.

"Marena," he whispered almost inaudibly for fear of being overheard. "Do you know what happened to the others?"

"No," she replied just as quietly. He thought he saw just the slightest shake of her head. "The last thing I remember is being thrown from my horse. I must have hit my head on the way down. How about you?"

Malach told her what he had seen but the recap didn't help either of them to figure out where the rest of the party had been taken.

"We need to get out of here. Any plans?" Marena asked.

"Reckoning's in here with me," Malach informed her. "But I'm wrapped too tight to reach the hilt."

"Can't you just tell him to change into something bigger and sharp?"

"I'm not sure why but I think something about the venom blocks my mental communication with Reckoning. Hopefully that will wear off soon."

"I don't think we should wait for that."

"What about you?" Malach asked. "Any way to get free?"

"No, my sword is wrapped up with me in its sheath, but somehow, the hilt is pointed toward my feet so there is no chance of getting it out."

"Then keep an eye out for those spiders. I'll try to get it out, but last time I moved too much, one of those things came to check it out."

"How do you expect me to watch the whole room? I can't move."

"Right..." Malach said feeling foolish. "Uhh, just tell me if you hear or see anything."

He tried again to mentally and physically reach Reckoning. He didn't get any reply from the blade, so he focused on reaching for the hilt. He got his longest finger on the hilt and tried to hook it and pull it closer. He couldn't tell if the blade actually moved or if his mind was playing tricks on him. Although, as soon as he got a second finger on it he knew he was making progress. He was able to pull it closer and get a full grasp on.

"I got him," Malach whispered in triumph.

"Good. Either shut up and wait or hurry because I hear one of them coming," Marena replied.

He didn't want to wait, so he started cutting through the cocoon. It took him much longer than he had anticipated, but in the end, he was able to cut a small hole which loosened the webbing around his arm.

"Malach, hurry," Marena urged.

He sawed at the webbing as hard as he could, slowly cutting down the side. With each pass of Reckoning over the cocoon, Malach was able to move more. He glanced up at his feet and spotted the spider scuttling across the ceiling. He cut quicker.

The spider arrived at his cocoon and starting down the thick strands of webbing connecting him to the ceiling. The web finally started to tear from his weight and he grabbed a handful of the cocoon to stop himself from plummeting to the floor below. His feet fell past his head causing him and the cocoon to swing. He used the momentum to bring his sword hand around, stabbing up toward the spider. It hadn't seen the attack coming and couldn't get out of the way in time. Malach's sword went into its face up to the hilt, the tip exiting out the back of its body. It went limp and, as Malach dropped the tip of the sword toward the ground, it slid off his blade. It made a slight squishing noise as it landed, and the noise caused a shudder to go down Malach's spine.

The strength in Malach's arms hadn't fully returned since the spiders had bitten him, and he was already starting to lose his grip on the webbing hanging by one hand. He wiped the spider's gore from Reckoning and stuck it between his teeth. His teeth protested painfully as he clamped down on the sword, hard enough for it not to slip away from him, and he had to make sure he didn't cut his tongue on the sharp blade. He reached up and grabbed hold of the webbing, giving his tired arm a reprieve.

He turned to the cocoon Marena was encased in and used his body weight to start to swing. Once he had it going, he reached out, trying to get a good hold on her. It took a couple of tries, but he was finally able to grab ahold of her cocoon. Once he was satisfied with his grip, he let go of the webbing he had been wrapped in and held onto Marena's gossamer prison. His momentum swung them both, and Malach studied the room to make sure no other spiders had come to check on them.

"I think I'm going to be sick," Marena moaned.

"Sorry," Malach apologized sympathetically.

Soon they stopped swinging, and he carefully cut into the cocoon, careful not to cut too deeply as to hurt Marena. It took him several minutes to cut a large enough hole in the cocoon for Marena to get her hand loose and help him. Soon she was free and hanging from the webbing as well.

"Now what?" She peered down at the ground.

It was far enough down he didn't want to risk jumping, but not so far that they would be killed if they ended up having to take the plunge. He looked around and realized that some of the cocoons hung much lower than others. If they could get over to one of those they should be able to climb down safely.

"Help me swing this."

They swung the webbing they were hanging from until Malach could reach the webbing which had wrapped him and climb back onto it. Marena gave him a confused look until he swung over to the cocoon which held one of their horses. He wished he could take the horses with him, but he didn't see how, and besides, they couldn't wait for them to wake up. They needed to save the rest of the group. He found where the horse's heart would be and slid Reckoning between the horse's ribs. He felt a slight shudder but knew it hadn't felt any pain. It saddened him to do it, but it was a better fate than what awaited it if he didn't.

A thought struck him, and he decided to check for his saddlebags. He climbed back up the horse and cut into the cocoon. He was in luck. The saddlebags were there. This had been his horse.

He wrestled the saddlebags out, trying not to think about the horse too much. He slung the bags over his shoulder and started climbing down again. He climbed to the bottom of the cocoon and hung as far down as he could. He glanced down one more time to make sure he wasn't going to land on a stalagmite and let go. He landed hard and his knees buckled, which caused him to crumple onto the hard stone. Reckoning went clattering away from him into the darkness.

He laid on the ground for a moment, taking stock of his limbs to make sure he didn't have any worse injuries than a few bruises. Marena swung over to the horse cocoon. He rolled over and pushed himself up getting to his feet. His muscles protested, stiff and tight, but he managed to move out of the way. Marena had a similar experience and ended up almost in the same position as Malach; on her back on the floor with the wind knocked out of her.

"Well, that wasn't fun," she said when she had regained her breath.

Malach helped her up off the floor. She was almost as stiff and sore as he was. He didn't know if it was an effect of the venom or being held in those cocoons for so long. For that matter, he didn't even know how long they had been in the cocoons.

"Help me find Reckoning," He said. "I lost him when I fell."

They groped around in the dark, searching for the blade. He wished he could communicate with the blade. He could have him change into something larger to give them a better chance of finding it. He crawled a little farther into the darkness and almost fell into a hole in the floor he couldn't see. His hand brushed against the side of the hole and came away wrapped in sticky webs.

"Ugh." He tried to shake the webs off and then wiped his hand on the stone floor to break them loose.

"Found him!" Marena declared from Malach's right.

He turned to her and heard a scritching noise from behind him at the same moment.

"Behind you!" Marena cried.

He jumped to the side as she rushed forward. The spider had leaped at him, and Marena skewered it in midair. The spider curled around the blade as it died, and Marena had to push it off with her boot.

"Thanks," Malach said, climbing to his feet.

"Something tells me you will be returning that favor before we are out of this mess," Marena held the blade out, pommel first. "But you're welcome."

"Any idea which way is out?" Malach took Reckoning from her.

"None."

Most of the tunnels they found were too small for them to fit in or only large enough for them to crawl. He didn't fancy being in one of those if they came across any spiders. Finally, they found one tunnel large enough for them to be able walk through. Malach had to duck, but Marena could stand up straight. It was also the only tunnel the spiders could have gotten the horse through, so it stood to reason that it was the way out. They would have to search for the others along the way. He wished they had a torch. The moss didn't give off enough light for them to see much more than about ten feet in front of them.

Malach felt a tingle in his mind, but he still was unable to reach Reckoning. Hopefully, it was a sign his ability to communicate with the blade would return soon. The came into another room, this one not near as tall at the one they hung in. He didn't see any fresh cocoons. In fact, the only things he did see were skeletons and husks of animals, and some humans, long dead. They passed through the cavern and back into the tunnel. There was a clear path worn along the tunnel floor and he was wary of coming upon a spider unawares in the dark. They walked for what seemed like miles, never seeing a spider or any other fresh cocoons. Malach was worried that they would never see any of their friends, or the light of day, again.

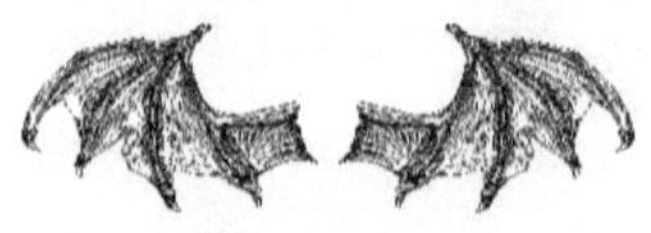

Amara awoke upside down and wrapped in webs. She watched as two or three spiders, she couldn't tell how many as they kept entering and exiting her field of vision, skitter around the room she was hung in. She kept very still, not wanting to draw any attention to herself. Maybe the spiders would leave, and then she could get herself out of this situation.

As she waited, she kept an eye out for anything useful or for any of the others who might be hung there with her. Suddenly, she felt the cocoon shake and gasped involuntarily. The world around her slowly turned

A cloaked figure came into view. She couldn't believe what she was seeing. The spiders seemed to fear the man, giving him a wide berth. She must be dreaming. No one would have been able to get past the sea of spiders she had seen when they were fleeing through the woods.

"Greetings, Amara," the figure said in a deep, gravelly voice.

It was a voice she recognized, though. Where had she heard that voice before? Maybe at Newaught? No, before she had gotten to Newaught. The stranger from the woods. The one who had pressed her into service. He must be a demon. The lumps under his cloak were the horns and spike he could not hide. Her mouth went dry. Was he here to kill her for turning on him? Would he try to make her betray Malach? Or was he here to take her away from this place?

"What do you want?" she asked, careful to keep her tone neutral.

"I wanted to check in with my little spy," he replied happily, as if they were having this conversation over a dinner table, not in a cave full of monsters. "You have done well for yourself. I knew, the first time I saw you, you would do great things for me."

"What do you mean?" Amara narrowed her eyes at him.

"You are in with the half-angel and his father," He told her. "When I first conscripted you, I had hoped that you would rise through the ranks of the Shadows in Newaught and be a valuable asset to me there, but this!" He motioned around them. "You were able to convince the angels you are trustworthy and have gotten close with them."

"I won't betray him," she spat. It was the wrong thing to say. She had just lost any leverage she had over the demon. "I know you're a demon," she said quickly, trying to gain some of her composure back and put him on the defensive.

The demon pulled back the hood of his cloak, revealing his hideous face. "Good for you, but you are mistaken."

"No, you are most definitely a demon."

"Oh, not about that," he chuckled, "about you betraying your little abomination."

He sounded so confident. Amara didn't know what to say so she stayed silent.

"If you and your *friends* make it out of here alive, then you will betray Malach and turn him over to me. If you don't escape the spiders," he shrugged, "then it won't matter anyway."

"Cut me loose," she shouted at him, starting to struggle to free herself, "and we will see whom I betray."

"That fire will get you a lot of places," the demon chuckled, backing up from where she hung. "But struggling like that will only bring the spiders down on you."

She peered up at the ceiling to see one of the spiders descending onto her cocoon and she felt a slight sting on her leg. She fought to stay conscious, but in the end, the venom overtook her.

As she started to slip back into unconsciousness, she heard the demon speak. "You will bring Malach to me," he said. "And when you do, you will have your just rewards."

Then the darkness took her once again.

Malach and Marena stopped to rest. They were both feeling the pangs of hunger but neither of them had any food to eat. It had all been in their packs, and who knew where those ended up. They waited in silence. He didn't know if she preferred the silence as he did or if she just didn't know what to say, but he didn't offer any conversation starters himself. Besides, he didn't want to draw any unwanted visitors with their voices.

They both got up again a few moments later and started walking. There had been a few forks in the main tunnel, and they had stayed to the right each time. Neither of them had any recollection of the trip down, so Malach decided they would stay consistent and hope for the best. They walked out of the tunnel into yet another room and again there was nothing there.

"How can there be this many rooms in the tunnel system and yet none of them have anything in them?" Marena asked, "or any way out?"

"Maybe we took a wrong turn? The skeletons have been getting older and older the farther we walk. Maybe we ought to go back and take a left at the first fork."

"That is a long way back, and if we are wrong, then we could be in these caves even longer.

"If we are right and don't go back, we run the same risk," Malach pointed out. "All indications say the spiders don't come this way often. To me, it seems like we are going in the wrong direction. Even if there is a way out ahead, it won't mean much, since I won't leave anyone behind."

"How do we know the others were taken? Maybe they were able to make it out of the spider's trap."

"I'm not sure if any of them *could* have made it out of that trap. I saw all of the horses fall, since I was in the back of the group, and that means we all fell into the webbing."

"Fine. We search until we can't anymore," Marena replied. "But I don't think any of them would want us starving in these caves. We need to find a way out as well."

"Of course." Malach nodded. "Even if we are forced to leave, I am coming back."

"And I'll be right there with you."

There was a fire in her eyes, telling him she would keep her word, and Malach was glad she was with him. If he had been alone, he would be in much worse spirits.

They backtracked until they found the most recent fork in the cave system. They decided to follow it for a little while to see if there was any indication of the way out or of their friends. They came upon another room full of bones, none looking any newer than the ones they had already come across, so they went back farther, repeating this process several times. They found a spider in one of the tunnels. It recently died from a wound made by a sword. Malach was hopeful they might have found a path out of the cave, but the next couple of caverns held no other indications it was their way out. Malach kept count of the forks they passed, and they were almost back to the cavern they woke up in. He was starting to lose hope when they walked into a room littered with bodies, most were spiders that lay dead or dying, some wrapped in webbing, some already eaten. There was a husk of one of the war horses as well. Malach could tell its neck had been broken, presumably from the fall.

They searched but, luckily, didn't find any of their friends among the bodies. What they did find were two packs of supplies. They pulled out some of the food and both felt renewed after getting something in their stomachs.

"You know, I've heard rumors about you in Brightwood," Marena told him, chewing on the best tasting stale bread either of them had ever eaten.

"Which ones?"

"That you lived with the wolves and that's why Skie follows you. I didn't believe them, of course. When I asked Togan about your family, he told me I would have to ask you."

And there it was. Everyone wanted to know his whole life story, but he guessed he had just been tromping through spider-infested caves all. . .day? Or was it night? Either way, he figured he could answer a few of her questions.

Malach summarized how he had been raised by Daziar's family and how he had met Skie. "How about you?"

"I used to live in Lanifair. I moved to Brightwood with my parents because I wanted to be the blacksmith for the town."

"Really?" Malach asked brows raised. "You, a blacksmith?"

"Yes, but when I got there, Togan had already set up shop with his family, and the town didn't need, or want, a second blacksmith."

"Did you talk to him about it? He always talked about getting an apprentice, but no one ever asked. And you know him, he's too gruff to ever really ask anyone."

"I didn't at the time. Then, my parents got sick so most of my time was spent taking care of them."

"Where are they now?" Malach asked and immediately regretted it.

"They died about fifty years ago." She studied her bread. "It seems like yesterday we were out on the harbor in Lanifair. We used to go for walks on the docs there."

"I'm sorry."

"It's fine. They were at a ripe old age of about five hundred and eighty. After they passed, I stayed in Brightwood. Togan is going to teach me to be a blacksmith, once we get back."

"Well, I'm glad you found each other. Togan has been on his own for a long time, and he seems happier with you than I have even seen him."

They sat for a moment, and Malach was ready to get up when Marena broke the silence again. "You know, he looks at you as his own son."

"I've been told," Malach smiled.

"He's proud of you."

Malach was getting uncomfortable now.

Marena continued anyway, "he came with you on this quest just to ensure you make it through alright."

"He didn't have to." He didn't like the thought of Togan putting his life at risk just for him.

"He wanted to. I know how much you mean to him, so I wanted to as well, no matter what happens."

"You love him, don't you? I mean, I know you two are courting, but you really love him."

"Yes." Marena nodded, smiling. "And you love Amara."

"Umm. . .yeah, I guess I do," he replied, feeling awkward again.

"Not everyone would go back into danger for someone."

"She would do that same for me."

"I've seen it. In the way you look at her and how you act when she's around."

"Let's go ahead and get moving," he said, trying to ignore what Marena said and stood up.

"Alright," she seemed content to let the matter drop.

They hefted the packs onto their backs and moved out. They found more spider corpses as they went. This must have been the way they came in. They didn't find any of their friends, dead or alive, so they decided to backtrack to the next fork, which, Malach believed, was the first one they had come across on their way out. If only they had taken the right path, they wouldn't have wasted all that time. Malach still didn't know what time it was or if it was day or night. It all looked the same down in the caverns.

As they walked down the right side of the fork, they started to hear the scritch-scritch of the spiders moving around. They readied their weapons. Malach tried to contact Reckoning for the first time in a while.

Malach, Reckoning sounded far away or muffled, but Malach could finally hear him. *What's happening?*

Malach started filling him in on what had happened so far and where they were at. In the middle of his explanation, one of the spiders came around a bend in the tunnel. Everyone froze, the spider seemed too surprised to react quickly, and Malach attacked first.

It moved at the last moment, and he only lopped off its front two legs. It stumbled back, trying to get away from him, but it couldn't. He plunged Reckoning down into the spider's head, pinning it in place. It struggled until its remaining legs finally curled up. He pulled his sword free and glanced around, hoping the noise hadn't drawn any of the other spiders.

Everything was quiet.

Nothing moved.

Malach let out a sigh of relief. Too soon. The scritching of hundreds of spiders' legs started all at once. Down the bend in the tunnel, the silhouettes of the first spiders came into his view and there were countless more behind them.

"Run!" Malach shouted, and they both took off down the tunnel, the horde of spiders hard on their heels.

He was finally able to change Reckoning's form back to his pole weapon as they ran. They wouldn't be able to outrun the spiders for long, as tired as they already were, but he was hoping to make it to where the tunnel narrowed to make their stand.

It sounded like the spiders were only a few feet behind them. He didn't dare turn to look with all the bones, rocks, and other debris littering the ground. He had to focus where he was stepping so he didn't trip up. The narrowed tunnel came into view, and he skidded to a stop directly in the opening, turning and cutting two of the front running spiders in half. Marena, not knowing his plan, stopped only after she realized he had turned to fight and ran back to him, covering his left flank. And they fought, knowing if even one of the spiders got to them, they most likely wouldn't ever wake up again.

It wasn't long before they had a pile of spider bodies lying at their feet. The bodies slowed the surviving spiders, and they were able to ease their frantic swinging. Malach spotted a light behind the sea of legs and wondered if he might be delusional.

"Do you see that?" Marena asked, confirming Malach wasn't the only one seeing it.

"Yeah, keep fighting though," he shouted back, separating yet another leg from a spider who had gotten too close.

The light flickered and Malach recognized it as the light from a torch. Maybe they would make it through this after all. The light got brighter and brighter. Soon the spiders stopped attacking altogether, turning toward the light coming around the bend in the tunnel. Malach had to overt his eyes because of the brightness.

"Malach!" Ariel's voice called out. "Malach, you have to fight your way to me!"

"I can't see!" he shouted back.

"Then follow my voice," Ariel shouted. "The spiders have all their attention on us."

Malach trusted his father, but it wasn't easy to let go of his fear and start climbing the mound of spider corpses. As he got closer, his eyes started adjusting to the light, and he was able to make out shapes. He swung the blade of his weapon at the shape of a spider between him and his father. He miscalculated how far away it was and clubbed it with the pole instead. It flew against the wall and out of Malach's sight. He heard the satisfying, crunching splatter of the thing hitting the wall. It wasn't going to be coming after him again.

He reached his father and felt a hand on his arm, guiding him forward. Now the light of the torch wasn't directly in his face, he could see clearly once again. They moved forward. Elzrod fought off a few spiders, but the majority of the horde cowered away from them. Malach and Marena joined the fight, and once again, the spiders turned and fled. They had won, for now.

"Are you two alright?" Elzrod asked.

"Fine," Malach replied for both of them. "We were able to get free off the webbing and have been wandering the caverns looking for everyone. How did you two manage to escape?"

"We were never taken," Ariel shrugged. "When the spiders bit us our healing ability saved us from the venom. The spiders didn't expect that, and we were able to fight our way free. Since then, we have been looking for where they took you."

"I noticed that it took more bites to take me down than the others, but the first one slowed me enough I couldn't fight off the rest," Malach mused. "I didn't think about you two having superior healing abilities though."

"Have you found Togan and Amara yet?" Marena asked.

"Yeah, and what about Skie?" Malach asked. "Do you know where she is?

"We have not found Amara or Togan yet," Elzrod didn't turn toward them, keeping an eye out for any spiders returning. "You two are the first we've found. However, Skie managed to evade capture and would be here with us, except she wouldn't allow your father or me to lower her into the cavern. I think crossing the Great Divide was too fresh in her mind."

Malach was relieved to hear Skie was alive.

"We've been through a lot of the caverns," Marena informed them. "We think Togan and Amara are farther in the spider's nest."

"That's unfortunate," Elzrod replied. "Is that what you two were trying to do when we found you?"

"Yes," Malach replied. "I think we were doing a great job on our own, but if you two want to come along for moral support, I think we can allow that."

"Well, that's very kind of you," Ariel grinned.

Marena rolled her eyes at them. "Let's go get them."

"I agree," Elzrod said. "We should attack before they've had a chance to regroup."

"Good idea," Ariel nodded, and they started moving down the tunnel as a unit. "Did you two see anything before you retreated?"

"Nothing," Malach shook his head. "We never got close enough."

"Wait a moment," Malach stopped them. They had arrived at the tunnel which would lead them to the horde of spiders. "I have something that will cover our retreat. He pulled ingredients of the explosives out of his pack there was a list of what to and how much to mix and Malach quickly set to work.

"Where did you get that?" Ariel narrowed his eyes.

"Gabriel," Malach replied absentmindedly.

"For what?"

"I'll tell you after we get out of here alive."

He poured the mixed powers into an oblong-shaped container manufactured with a fuse already set in the top of it. Malach popped the cap onto the little container and set it off to the side of the tunnel. It was a directional charge and he set it facing toward the direction they would be retreating from to provide the maximum amount of spider casualties.

"That will cover our escape if we need to use it," Malach explained.

"Good thinking." Elzrod patted him on the shoulder.

They continued down the tunnel. They arrived at the bend Malach and Marena had first seen the spider and continued around it, unchallenged. They entered a smaller room where the ceiling wasn't far above their head and found three cocoons, all human-shaped. Malach turned the first one around and was met by a gruesome sight. He jumped back in shock and revulsion as the cocoon slowly turned back around. Once his breathing was back under control, he moved forward and, steeling himself, he turned it back around to face him. The man, or what was left of him, hadn't been old, but his face was shriveled and wrinkled almost beyond recognition. The husk was not near as old as the ones he had seen, and some of the skin on its face hadn't fully dried and shriveled yet. Malach could make out enough of the man's features to know it wasn't Togan and he sighed in relief. He moved to the next cocoon and was met with a similar sight. Again, the husk was not one of his friends. He got to the third one and was met with welcome sight. Togan's sleeping face appeared as he turned the cocoon around.

"Dad, come help me!" he called.

Ariel handed the torch to Elzrod and walked over.

He supported the man's weight as Malach reached up with Reckoning and cut the webbing holding the cocoon to the ceiling. Togan's body dropped, and Ariel caught him before he hit the ground. He lowered Togan to the ground safely and started cutting open the webbing free. They had him unwrapped. There were several red marks on him, but one was much more recent than the rest.

"They must have bitten him again when he woke up too early," Malach pointed to the fresh fang mark. "They would have done the same to Marena and me if I hadn't gotten free and run it through."

"I'll take him back to the tunnel entrance and out of danger," Ariel replied.

"Alright." Elzrod nodded. "We will continue and try to find Amara."

Ariel picked up the big man and slung him over his shoulder and walked out with little more effort than a farmer would have with a sack of potatoes or grain. He turned the corner and moved out of sight.

Malach turned back to find Elzrod and Marena were already headed into the next tunnel. He hurried to catch up and found this tunnel was not tall enough for him. If they had to fight while they were in this tunnel, he would be severely limited. He walked just behind Marena as the tunnel twisted and turned. Elzrod burned through most of the webbing that would have hindered their progress, but some of it still brushed against and wrapped Malach's limbs and got in his hair. He wanted to have a long bath after this to get all of the sticky substance off of him. They heard the scritch-scritch noise of the spiders moving up ahead.

Malach readied himself for the onslaught of spiders, but it never came. They turned another bend in the tunnel and found a spider with only three legs left on its body slowly dragging itself down the tunnel. It turned as Elzrod caught up to it and tried to defend itself, but it wasn't quick enough. Elzrod ended its life.

They entered the next cavern and stopped in their tracks. Spiders lined the walls and ceilings, and Malach could see several sets of eyes peering out of tunnels at them. No one moved. The spiders stared; their prey turned predator. He spotted Amara in a cocoon, hanging from the ceiling off to their right. It would only take him a few moments to get to her and cut her out, but there was a spider clinging to the webbing which wrapped her. He could tell she was still sleeping, so she wouldn't be able to help them in any way.

"Amara is to our right," Malach mumbled out of the side of his mouth.

Elzrod gave a slight, almost imperceptible nod and slowly handed Marena the torch. Malach watched as he slid his foot out to the right and then slid the other to join it. He slowly and carefully started making his way toward Amara's cocoon. Malach didn't know if he should join his mentor or stay where he was. A few of the spiders shifted nervously and if he moved as well, it could set them all off.

Elzrod was almost halfway to Amara and some of the spiders had even backed up to give him room. The spider on Amara's cocoon hadn't moved yet, but it didn't seem to have the support of its friends either. Maybe they would make it out without having to fight after all.

As Elzrod moved ever closer, the one spider guarding Amara raised its front legs defensively and showed its fangs. It was clear it wouldn't give her up without a fight. Quick as lightning Elzrod moved forward and swung Storm up at an angle. The spider died without even knowing what had hit it, and Storm cut through all but a few of the strands of webbing holding Amara to the ceiling. The last few strands failed from the extra load they bore, and Elzrod grabbed Amara with one arm. With his other, he fought off the spiders who reacted to his attack. Malach and Marena burst into action cutting a path through the few feet separating them from Elzrod.

"Malach," Elzrod shouted, "take Amara and run. We will be right behind you."

Malach did as he was told and hefted her over his shoulder as gently as he could. He used Reckoning to start cutting a path back through the spiders while Marena and Elzrod defended the rear. He cut past the last spider and took off at a dead run. Marena and Elzrod didn't follow right away, and the light of the torch started to fade, but it didn't take long for them to catch up. He was slowed by the low tunnel and the weight of his precious cargo. They ran past the dead three-legged spider and then out into the first cavern. They didn't stop there. They could hear the spiders dead on their heels.

He passed the explosives and called, "Remember to light the explosive!"

Marena leaned over and lit the fuse as they rushed by. They didn't stop to make sure it would cover their retreat but continued their flight from the caverns. Elzrod ran out in front of them and lead the way, through the tunnels unfamiliar to Malach.

The explosion shook the ground under their feet. Malach was forced to slow to keep his footing but fortunately, none of them fell. A crack shot its way up the tunnel wall and out onto the ceiling.

"Run!" he urged. "The cave is collapsing!"

Sure enough, the first rocks started to fall from the ceiling and the three of them redoubled their efforts. Malach glanced up and found the one crack had turned into many and the cracks had outpaced them. Soon rock started falling in front of them and they had to duck around them.

Amara stirred and squirmed in his grasp.

Great, Malach thought. *Of course, she would wake up at this moment.*

"What's happening?" Amara asked groggily.

"Can't talk," Malach replied over the crashing of the rocks. "Concentrating on not dying."

"Why can't I move?" Amara asked, the first signs of panic sounding in her voice.

"Spiders," Malach said, grunting as he ran around a boulder the size of a horse that had just landed in front of him. "Cave in!"

"Hey, put me down," she commanded him. Clearly, she wasn't grasping the full gravity of the situation.

Malach didn't listen to any more of her protests and concentrated solely on not getting crushed by the cave in. Finally, he started to pass the cracks still weaving their way across the ceiling. Malach wasn't going to take any chances. He kept up his pace for another few hundred yards before slowing to a walk. They seemed to have passed the point where they were in danger. Elzrod and Marena were up ahead, having left him behind with Amara. They were both sprawled out on the floor still breathing heavily.

Malach set Amara down, gently laying her on the floor. He cut her free of the webbing until she was able to wiggle her way out and start working the feeling back into all of her limbs. Malach flopped down next to the others and worked on slowing down his breathing.

"That was invigorating!" Elzrod exclaimed.

"That's one word for it," Marena grumbled.

"Did anyone see Ariel and Togan in all that?" Malach asked.

"No," Elzrod replied turning serious. "Ariel must have moved farther out before the explosive went off."

"What did I miss?" Amara asked, still unable to stand up because of the venom.

"Oh, not much," Malach replied. "Just fighting through hordes of spider and blowing up the caverns as we fled for our lives. That's all."

"Oh, well, if that's all," Amara said on the verge of laughing.

"We probably ought to move farther away from the cave in, just in case," Marena suggested, pointing at the small cracks still slowly inching along the ceiling.

They all got up, except Amara, who still couldn't walk. Malach picked her up and carried her farther out of the tunnels. They spied torchlight ahead and soon arrived at the spot where the two men sat. Malach set Amara down and helped her prop herself up against the wall.

"That sounded eventful," Togan said as Marena wrapped him in a hug and squeezed him hard.

"A little bit." Malach nodded, grinning.

"I thought it would be wise to move farther out of the reach of the spiders to set Togan down and let him recover," Ariel told them.

"It was a good thing you did," Elzrod replied. "That whole section of tunnels collapsed."

"Do you think the spiders will be able to get out?" Amara asked.

"I'm sure they have another way t' get out," Togan replied, "For the few moments I was awake, I saw a honeycomb of tunnels leavin' the room I was in."

"I doubt they would come after us," Ariel said, seeing Marena and Amara's worried faces. "They will be licking their wounds for the next few days."

"Do spiders even have tongues?" Amara asked, her smile returning to her face.

"Ha!" Malach laughed loudly but was cut off by a glare from his father. "Sorry."

"Let's get moving," Marena motioned around at the cavern. "I don't want to be in this place anymore.'

"I second that," Togan agreed, getting shakily to his feet. "I'm good t' go."

"So am I," Amara stood up but overcorrected and almost fell flat on her face.

Malach caught her and helped her along.

The party started walking out of the tunnels, and it wasn't long before they started to feel fresh air on their faces. Not long after that, they saw the light of day coming from farther down the tunnel. Amara started running ahead of the group.

"Hurry up!" she yelled back happily. "We are almost there!"

"Amara, wait!" Ariel called after her.

They all ran forward to catch up with her. She ran through the opening at the end of the tunnel and froze. She craned her neck up at the ceiling staring at something they couldn't see. Malach was second to the opening, and he spotted why she had stopped. They had walked into a circular room with sheer walls on all sides. As they rose, they angled in, doming the roof. Part of the roof had caved in and there was an opening.

"Incredible," Togan said when he came to a stop next to Malach.

"Is this where we were brought down?" Marena pointed at the opening.

"Yes," Elzrod nodded, "and it's how we made our entry as well."

"Now we just have to get back up," Ariel said and added. "This kind of thing was a lot easier when I had my wings."

They walked over to the rope and Elzrod tested it to make sure that it was still secure. Skie, undoubtedly roused by the movement of the rope, poked her head over the edge, peering down at them. Malach was happy to see her furry face and beamed up at her.

She panted happily at him and yipped.

"I missed you too, girl!" Malach called.

One by one they climbed up to the opening and out into the light. Malach got up to the top, and Skie tackled him, licking his face with excitement at seeing him alive. Finally, it was Togan's turn. The hulk of a man struggled to climb up the rope. Regardless of all of his muscles, he just couldn't make it up. In the end, they had him tie the rope around his waist and hauled him up. It took all of them to get him out through the opening.

"Let's *not* do that again," Togan said, once he was on solid ground again.

Chapter 15

Honora scrubbed her cloths over the washboard. She stood in the main refugee tent in what she would have considered a nightshirt. It was a plain brown color and fell to her ankles. The tent was warmer than outside, but without her warm clothes on, there was a definite bite to the air.

The heavy tent flap opened, blasting Honora with cold air. The thin nightshirt didn't even slow down the cold wind. She dropped her clothes in the washtub and hugged herself until Vadis closed the flap and secured it. She turned and spotted Honora for the first time and her eyes widened. She made the motion for sorry, then walked over, and hugged Honora.

It was always awkward for Honora, but Vadis liked to give people hugs. Honora just smiled and endured it. The large woman didn't ever seem to notice it made others uncomfortable though and therefore kept on doing it. This time, however, was less awkward for Honora, mostly because Vadis was warm, and she was now extremely cold.

"It's alright," Honora told her in her ear.

Vadis released her and straightened, allowing to cool air to reach Honora skin once again.

Over the five days, she had spent at the refugee camp, Honora was starting to learn some of the motions Vadis and Rose used to communicate. Rose and Vadis had told her it was fine to just talk back to Vadis, but Honora needed to know what the motions meant to understand her.

At one point, she had asked about the other tents in the compound, playing the part of a curious girl but received a simple answer in response. One of the smaller tents was for the few men who weren't prisoners of war but also unfit to join the Demon Army. There was a tent for the soldiers who were guarding the refugee camp. Then there were several others for things like first aid, mess hall, storage, and several small tents for the officers. Nothing was mentioned about any prisoners.

She didn't know how much longer she could stay before the messenger came back with word from her supposed father. She needed to find some information about them soon or she would have to leave. The refugees, however, would stay. She realized quickly these people were better off here for the moment. As much as she hated the Demon Army, they were actually taking care of these people. She had originally feared they were only told they were refugees, but she truly believed if they wanted to leave, they would be allowed to.

Only a few moments passed during Honora's musings, and Vadis was just turning to go back to whatever she was doing. "Vadis?" Honora called to her before she left.

Vadis turned back to her with a questioning look.

"I need to talk with you and Rose soon. Would you be able to find her for me while I finish washing my clothes?"

Vadis nodded and smiled but there was concern in her face and she motioned, *is everything alright?*

"Yes," Honora nodded and smiled reassuringly.

Vadis smiled back at her again, but Honora could tell she wasn't fully satisfied with her answer.

She will have her answers soon, Honora thought, turning back to her washing.

It was time to come clean with the two women. They had become good friends to her in such a short time. She couldn't leave them without telling them the truth. She had snuck all over the camp and didn't think the prisoners were here any longer. With that knowledge, she decided this would be her last day here. They would have to search out where the prisoners had been taken and try again at another camp.

She finished with her clothes and hung up the last piece of clothing in the small room she slept in. Vadis knocked lightly on the wall next to the entrance. Honora turned and smiled at her. She would miss Vadis and her innocence. Vadis motioned to Honora to follow her to Rose's room. She did, and they were soon sitting with Rose.

"What did you want to talk to us about?" Rose asked just as concerned as Vadis.

Honora told them everything, only leaving out the parts about her friends being camped nearby for their safety. She thanked them several times during her story for the extraordinary kindness they had shown her, and she told them she would be leaving tonight. She ended her tale by asking them honestly if they knew anything about the prisoners.

Vadis was crying softly by this point and Honora was afraid she had hurt the woman's feelings. Rose was sitting silently and staring past Honora. All of a sudden Vadis hugged Honora which took her by surprise.

Rose smiled sadly. "She is going to miss you."

"I'm going to miss you both," Honora replied.

"I understand why you lied," Rose said sadness still in her voice. "That doesn't change the fact you did lie to us. You took advantage of our kindness."

Vadis pulled away from Honora and cocked her head at Rose inquisitively.

"I'm truly sorry," Honora apologized.

"I heard there was a group of political prisoners here before they repurposed this camp for refugees," Rose said, she looked like she had aged by years in the last few minutes. "I heard there was a large escape attempt, but I didn't hear how successfully it was."

"Thank you." Honora smiled.

"Now that you have your information, it's time for you to leave."

"Rose, I never intended to hurt you-" Honora started to apologize again, but Rose cut her off.

"But you did. Now it's time for you to leave." She motioned to the door.

Tears sprang to Honor's eyes as she stood and did as Rose asked. Her head hung low in shame as she walked away. She heard Vadis's grunts and knew she was most likely motioning to Rose about what had just happened. She knew she didn't deserve their friendship, but she had hoped for it. She glanced back before going around the corner of the makeshift wall and spotted Vadis sticking her head out from Rose's room. Honora smiled, waving at the woman and she smiled back. Honora didn't go back. Rose had made it clear she was not welcome.

She trudged back to her room and sat heavily on her bed roll. She would wait for sundown and escape. It should be relatively easy, since the few guards posted wouldn't be looking for refugees escaping. She would take word back the prisoners weren't here. But then what? Would they pack up and return to Brightwood? They didn't have any information about what had happened after the escape. Were they taken somewhere else? Were they all killed? Did any of them escape? Instead of answering questions, Rose's information had just created more.

Honora sighed. Maybe Ana would be able to sort some of this out.

"How's our little spy doing?" a smug voice asked from the door.

Honora jerked her head up to see Gretchen standing in the doorway watching her. "Pardon?" Honora asked, pulling herself together enough to try to keep her cover intact.

"You heard me." The lady scowled. "You have been sent here to spy. Now get up!"

"No, I've done no such thing." Honora tried to look perplex and confused.

"Rose told me everything."

Gretchen made a motion and two other ladies appeared next to Gretchen. They squeezed through the door to pick Honora up, one on each arm and escorted her down the hall. She glanced over her shoulder as they pulled her out of the tent to see Vadis and Rose watching them leave. She knew Rose was hurt, but she never thought she would betray her to the Demon Army.

The cold wind tore at her nightshirt and bit her to the bone. Gretchen and the two women didn't care, though, and they dragged her to the officer's tent. They didn't even pause when they got to the tent. The officer was only dressed from the waist down and was working on shaving the stubble off of his face. He turned around to see who had entered, obviously perturbed.

"What's this all about?" He barked.

"We found a spy," Gretchen said, and the two women pushed Honora forward roughly.

Her knees hit the ground unable to keep herself from falling. She hugged herself shivering.

"Why would there be a spy in a refugee camp?" The officer raised an eyebrow.

"She thought this was a prison camp," Gretchen answered.

Honora's stomach twisted. Rose *had* betrayed her.

"What proof do you have?" The officer's scowled deepened.

"She admitted it to one of the women in our tent," Gretchen proclaimed, puffing out her chest.

The officer squatted down in front of Honora seeming to judge her. "Is this true?"

Honora almost denied it but there was no point. Rose would just corroborate Gretchen's story. The truth would come out in the end.

"Yes." She straightened her spine and held her head high. "I was sent to find out what I could about some prisoners who were supposed to be here. Now that I know they aren't I will be on my way."

The officer chuckled at her, "How do you plan on leaving? Do you think I would just let you walk out the front gate?"

"Well, I had hoped you wouldn't want the trouble, and you would just let me go, so yes, the front gate will do fine," Honora sneered at him.

"Ha! Brazen, aren't you? I wouldn't let you go, even if I wouldn't be executed for it. You are going to be my ticket out of this frozen hell."

Her idea had been a long shot and she knew it.

"No, I will take you to Newaught. You will face trial as a spy, be executed, and I will be congratulated, maybe even promoted. The sad thing is, if you had come to our camp only a few weeks before, you would have found the prison camp you were hoping to find."

"What happened?" Honora asked, maybe she could get the information she needed and the others would be able to rescue her.

"Wouldn't you like to know?" He stood and turned away from her. "Thank you for bringing this one to me." He turned around with some pieces of parchment in his hands. "Please take these to the mess hall, and they will give each of you extra food for the week."

Honora almost couldn't blame the women for turning her in for food. Since being at the refugee camp, she had been constantly hungry. Even though they had started giving them two meals a day, they weren't really large enough to fill them up.

"Thank you," Gretchen smiled, and Honora preferred the scowl.

The officer turned his back on Honora and finished dressing, then started packing a bag for the road.

"Are we leaving today?" Honora asked, trying not to sound as alarmed as she felt.

"Yes, we have plenty of daylight left, and I mean to get a few miles in today."

"But you need to get previsions for the road, and you won't be able to stay up all night to make sure I don't escape, so you will have to find another man to come along."

"The good thing about being a lieutenant is you have plenty of people to get things done for you. I realized you were hoping to escape tonight, however, I will have to insist you come with me."

Honora's heart fell, the last of her hopes dashed. She would just have to trust her friends would come after her and rescue her.

It didn't take the lieutenant long to get the things he needed together, even a couple of guards to accompany them on the trip to Newaught. They at least covered her in dry clothes and furs, so she didn't freeze to death before they got to Newaught.

Honora found herself only a few short hours later with her hands bound, trudging through the snow between two hulking men. She had tried to chat with them when they first left the refugee camp, hoping to work some information out of them but only got a few noncommittal grunts in response, so she quit trying. It was almost dark now, and she knew that her friends would be following them. She had decided to try and see if she could get a little more information out of the lieutenant before they rescued her. She had managed to wrap the green handkerchief around her neck and hoped that her friends would understand not to attack yet. The lieutenant finally allowed the group to stop, and the three men started setting up a camp. Soon there was a fire and several tents erected to stave off the cold.

"So, Lieutenant," Honora addressed him after they had eaten and he had a little mead in him. "You mentioned that the refugee camp had been a prison just a few weeks ago?"

The lieutenant was quiet for a time and when Honora thought that she wouldn't get a response he said, "What's your real name?"

"What?" Honora asked, taken aback at the abrupt change in topic.

"Your real name?" he repeated and then explained. "You gave us a fake name when you entered the camp. What is your real name?"

"How do you know that I didn't give you my real name?" Honora trying and failing to cross her still bound arms.

"Because you would be a lousy spy if you did." One side of his mouth rising into a sneer and the two lunks chuckled at his statement.

"If I give you my real name, will you tell me what happened to the prisoners?"

"How will I know that you told me the truth?"

"The same way I will know you will tell me the truth," Honora narrowed her eyes. "There's no reason to lie anymore."

The lieutenant thought about it for a moment. "Fine. You first."

"Honora Reybella,"

"Honora," The lieutenant said her name slowly, his eye flitting to the left. "Weren't you last seen with the half-angel Malach?"

Honora's eyebrows went up involuntarily in shock.

"You were!" The lieutenant leaned back, a smug smile firmly planted on his face. "I'm going to get a promotion for sure after I deliver you."

One of the large guard's head snapped around suddenly, searching the darkness outside of the firelight for something.

"What is it?" The lieutenant sat up quickly.

The large man just shook his head still searching the darkness.

All of a sudden there was a shrill cry mixed with a guttural noise, somewhere between a shout and a growl, as two figures flew past Honora. The larger of the two figures slammed into the guard, knocking him down close to the fire. His hand fell into the fire and he added his pained cry to the cacophony. Honora jumped up and put a shoulder into the lieutenant as he stood. He had his sword half-drawn, and the impact sent it flying out of his hands. He fell backward into the snow. She froze, unsure of what more to do with her hands tied. She spotted the guard who had been standing, holding one of the figures off the ground.

It was Rose.

She had her back against the soldier and his large hand was just under her chin, no doubt one swift motion would snap her neck. Vadis was still wrestling with the second guard whose sleeve was singed and hand already blistering. She slammed a fist into his temple knocking him unconscious.

"Don't move, or I'll have Boris break the old lady's neck," The lieutenant threatened.

"Boris?" Honora rolled her eyes. "That makes sense."

The lieutenant retrieved his sword and forced her to her knees in the snow. She glanced at Vadis, who seemed ready to charge the lieutenant and shook her head. The large woman caught her look, and the fight went out of her.

"Now that that's over," the lieutenant sighed. "Boris kill her."

Boris' muscles tensed in preparation for the kill.

Honora heard a whistle and a thwump.

The man stopped what he was doing. An arrow protruded from Boris's eye, but he didn't fall right away. There was no doubt he wasn't living anymore, but it was almost as if his body hadn't realized it yet. They all stared at him until Honora heard a second whistle. She dove to the side, slamming her shoulder into the ground, unable to brace herself with her hands still tied. She rolled onto her belly and crawled quickly behind the cover of a rock. She heard several more arrows streak into the camp and heard a grunt of pain. After only a few seconds, the arrows stopped, and she chanced a look over the top of her rock. Rose and Vadis were both peering out from behind whatever cover they had found, and there was an arrow sticking out of the guard Vadis had knocked out and another sticking out of the lieutenant, who was still very much alive. Before Honora could fully grasp what was happening, Daziar and Arjun came charging in, battle cries on their lips.

"Wait!" Honora held up her hands as if to physically stop them.

Both men slid to a stop, confusion plain on their faces.

"I need him alive!"

"Honora!" Arjun rushed over to her and cut her loose. "Are you alright?"

"I'm fine. Check on Rose." Honora pushed him away, guiding him to take care of the other two women first.

Daziar helped Rose to her feet then turned to help Vadis. She already stood up and he came face-to-chest with the tall woman. He looked up at Vadis, who smiled down at him. Daziar was dumbfounded at her size and he didn't hide it well.

"Daziar," Honora chided. "It's not nice to stare."

Honora turned back to the lieutenant to see he was no longer laying on the ground. She glanced around quickly and spotted his silhouette struggling through the snow. She heard a whoosh as something passed over her head. Ana landed on the other side of the lieutenant, blocking his escape. She led him back to the camp and tied his hands with the same leather thong that had been used to tie Honora's.

Ana sat him down in the snow. "What information do you need out of this piece of filth?"

Honora walked up to the lieutenant, "What happened to the prisoners at the camp?"

The lieutenant spat at her feet in response.

"Oh, come now," Honora cooed, even though anger sprung up inside her. "You were going to give me that information just a few moments ago."

"That was before your people attacked and killed my men," The lieutenant replied. "Now I won't tell you anything."

Honora groaned, turning an accusatory glare on her father and Daziar, "If you two would have waited just a few more minutes I would have gotten the information we needed."

"It wasn't us who attacked first," Ana defended them. "We just responded to the commotion these two made." She pointed to Rose and Vadis.

Honora turned her glare on Rose and Vadis, but their bewildered looks stifled her wrath.

"We didn't know." Rose shrugged sheepishly. "We thought you were in trouble. When Gretchen boasted that she had overheard our conversation and turned you in as a spy, we decided to come rescue you. Well, it was mostly Vadis' idea."

Vadis smiled broadly at Honora, and there was no way she could stay even slightly upset at the two. "So, you didn't tell Gretchen that I was the spy?" she asked.

"No!" Rose's eyes widened. "Is that what Gretchen told you?"

"Yes, and I believed her since I knew I had hurt you both with the lies I told," Honora nodded.

"You did hurt us, but Vadis reminded me that the only lies you told were to keep you safe and that the real you was the friend we came to love over such a short time."

Vadis motioned but Honora couldn't discern their meaning.

Rose translated. "When we heard you were being taken to Newaught, we snuck out of the camp to come rescue you."

"Thank you." Tears welled up in Honora's eyes. "Thank you both. You are true friends."

"We came after we heard the commotion," Daziar reiterated what Ana had said.

"We saw your signal and thought you wanted us to wait," Arjun put in. "Against my better judgment, we did."

Honora nodded her understanding.

"What did you find out about the prisoners?" Auron walked out of the darkness with the rest of the soldiers following him. "Can we go save my wife?"

"I haven't found out as much as I had hoped," Honora studied her feet. "The camp is not a prison camp anymore. Something happened, and it is now a refugee camp. I was about to simply sneak out and report when I was caught. Now, however, I'm glad I did get caught. I found out that our intel was correct, and it only recently turned into a refugee camp. I was working on finding out what happened to the prisoners when Rose and Vadis so kindly interrupted."

"I will get the answers out of him," Ana declared. "Arjun, if you will lead everyone back to our camp and get everyone warm. Feel free to make a fire. I don't think we will have any company tonight."

"I think I will stay," Daziar said. "In case Ana needs any help."

Ana didn't say anything, and Daziar seemed to take that as permission he could stay. Honora didn't want to think about what Ana would do to the lieutenant. She tried to put those thoughts out of her head as her father led her back to the camp.

It wasn't very far from where the lieutenant had set up his camp, and Honora marveled at how quiet they must have been to set up camp this close. They got to work digging a shallow pit for a fire, while others gathered the few flammable things they could find. A couple of the men thought ahead and brought back the fuel the lieutenant and his men had gathered. Soon they had a meager fire going and the three ladies were wrapped snuggly in furs. Honora was glad for the fire. Even though it wasn't very large, it would mean they got to eat warm food for the night.

Honora was pleased Rose and Vadis were here with her, and when the food was passed around, she motioned for the two women to be served first. They ate until they were full and then had another portion each. Vadis, who, despite her apparent age, acted much younger, laid her head down on Rose's lap and fell asleep.

Ana and Daziar walked into the camp not long after—without the lieutenant.

Daziar must have noticed the worried look on Honora's face because he said, "We didn't kill him."

"No, the coward just about passed out after you left, we had to wait for him to come back around before we could question him." Ana grabbed some of the food they were cooking and sat down. "He didn't take much convincing. He is still tied up and now unconscious, no doubt he will wake up and head back to his camp tomorrow and act like nothing ever happened."

"Huh," Honora snorted. "He sounded so tough when he was in control and safe. What did you learn?"

"Most of the prisoners we able to get away, but they don't know where they went," Daziar fixed himself a plate and sat next to Ana.

"Right," Ana nodded mouth half full of food. "They were able to recapture a few of the prisoners but most disappeared. They knew that the prisoners were headed toward Newaught, no doubt trying to seek refuge, but that somewhere along the way, they vanished without a trace."

"Vanished?" Honora watched the two horsing down the food like there was no tomorrow. *They are two peas in a pod, aren't they?*

"The tracks just stopped," Daziar talked around his food as well. "They couldn't find any trace of the prisoners anywhere."

"How could that many people simply disappear?" Rose piped up.

"Not without help," Ana pointed a finger at the woman, nodding approvingly. "I will send a messenger back to the angel army in the morning to find out if they know anything about it. Until then, we need to continue on to Newaught to see if we can find any trace of them ourselves. Someone has to know where they went."

"Rose and Vadis ought to be taken back to Brightwood or the Angel Army," Honora declared. "They need a warm bed and food. They have been through a lot and need to be somewhere safe."

Ana thought about it for a moment, "They can go back with the messenger. I will send two men along to keep them safe."

"Are you and Vadis up for that?" Honora turned to Rose, concerned it might be too arduous a journey for them, mostly for Rose.

"That shouldn't be a problem," Rose smiled. "We've been through much worse and now we have full stomachs and warm clothes to help us on our way. Thank you, Honora."

"No, thank you. You and Vadis risked everything because you thought I was in danger. You didn't know I had friends nearby to rescue me, which made your actions all the more courageous. This is the least I could do for the two of you."

Rose nodded graciously, and Honora was sure she spotted a tear slip down the old woman's face. She didn't say anything: she didn't want to embarrass Rose in front of everyone.

The messenger left that night. He would be able to move much faster on his own and the two women needed sleep. They retired to their tents and in the morning said heartfelt goodbyes, wishing each other luck in their journeys. Vadis would have had a hard time saying anything though her tears even if she had the use of her voice, but she was able to sign her feelings and words to Honora, with the help of Rose translating, of course.

Honora watched as the group of four left, hoping their paths would cross again. She wished she could go with her two new friends, but her path led elsewhere. She would miss them.

She turned toward Newaught and steered her thoughts toward the mystery ahead. Where had the missing people gone? She knew Auron was worried about Prinna, but the main group of prisoners had to be their top priority. Hopefully, Prinna had escaped with the main group and had not been recaptured. Only time would tell and only if they managed to find the missing people.

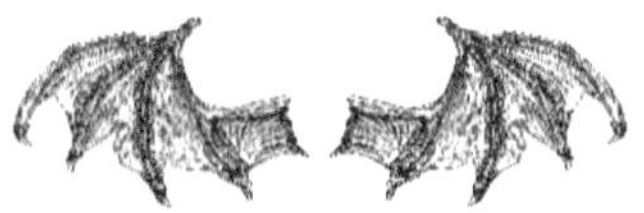

Kragen sat in the darkness, waiting for the last person to leave the kitchen. His stomach made a noise, and he studied the rotund cook to see if he would have to kill the man. The cook didn't seem to notice, so he stayed still. He was glad he didn't have to waste the energy to kill the man. He was already too weak from lack of water and food.

He had been stuck in the barrel for almost two and a half days. He had been woken by the workers pulling the barrel off the top of the one he was in. It had taken all of his self-control not to burst from the barrel to alleviate the painful cramps then and there. He waited, however, until the sound of the workers' footsteps dwindled. He had been so stiff and cramped he had to tip the barrel over to crawl slowly out of it. He laid himself straight on the floor, resting and stretching his muscles. He didn't wait there long though; he had a job to do, and there was no telling when the workers would come back to find him in this pitiful state.

He had mustered his strength and sat up. It took all he had left to right the barrel and replace the lid. He had to crawl into the shadows. He rested for a few minutes, trying to regain enough strength to get up.

The workers had finished moving the barrels and doused the wall sconces before he was fully rested. He had stood up on wobbly legs and moved through the stronghold's halls. It must have been some hour of the night or early morning, as there were few people roaming the halls. He had followed his nose more than anything to find the kitchens. Now he was waiting for one blasted man to leave so that he could eat his fill and drink until his stomach sloshed.

The man finally left, and Kragen didn't wait. He moved out to the leftover chicken from someone's feast the night before and tore into it like a wild animal. He found a glass of leftover wine and guzzled it, not caring it had soured. Then he found a jug of water and upended it into this mouth.

"What are you doing?" a man's voice called, and Kragen froze.

The cook had returned.

"If you are in need of food and drink, I have freshly cooked ham for breakfast," the man said kindly.

Kragen didn't know what to do as the man moved quickly to one of the ovens and pulled out a large ham, placing it on the counter with his back to Kragen and starting to cut it.

"I won't have anyone eating cold chicken for breakfast in my kitchen. Please, sit. I will bring the plate to you. Would you like some juice with your breakfast, I have-"

The man never got to finish. Kragen couldn't take the chance the man would tell anyone about this encounter. He ran his knife across the cook's throat and pulled him away from the counter. There was a large garbage chute on one side of the kitchen, and Kragen moved to it, pulling the body with him. He opened the door to the chute and a blast of hot air slammed into his face.

Good, Kragen thought. *It leads to a furnace. No one will ever find the body.*

He moved back to the plate of ham and picked it up. Blood had splattered onto the ham but Kragen almost didn't notice and surely didn't care. He took his plate of food and stole out of the kitchen to find a more private place to fill his stomach.

Something evil, or simply dumb luck, lead Kragen down a few flights of stairs until he stopped and a heavy metal door. It opened on well-oiled hinges and he slipped in, shutting it behind him. A familiar and pungent, sulfur smell assaulted his nose. He had stumbled on the success of his mission. He smiled a cruel smile and, as his eyes adjusted to the light, he surveyed the stacks of barrels. So much gun powder all in that same place. His stomach rumbled again, and he sat on one of the barrels. As he stuffed the ham into his mouth, he savored the flavor of it and the slight iron taste of the man's blood. This was a sign, a sign from Azazel. He would succeed and they would drink the blood of their enemies.

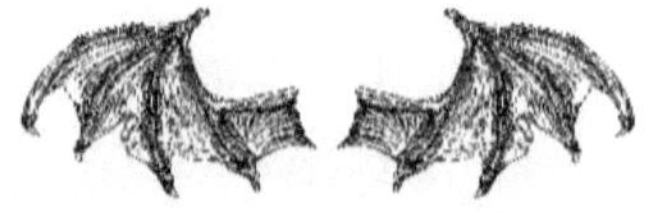

Amara and the group made good time away from the spider's nest, even though they were tired from their ordeal. None of them complained about their pace. They all wanted to get as far away as they could. Even when it started to get dark, everyone agreed to push on. The moon was high in the sky before they finally couldn't go any farther. Since they had left all of their tents when the spiders, attacked they had to craft makeshift lean-tos for the night. The two women in one, Ariel and Malach in another and Togan and Elzrod in the last.

As tired as they all were, it turned into another sleepless night with the horrors of the spider caves still fresh in their minds. They got up the next morning and took down camp sluggishly.

Having lost the horses, they wouldn't be able to make the journey in the same amount of time, and having lost most of their supplies, simply rationing the food wouldn't be enough. They took turns hunting, but the range of the spiders had to be immense. They didn't see sign of another living thing the first day and still hadn't seen anything by noon the next day. They were running dangerously low on food.

Amara couldn't get thoughts of the demon out of her head. He couldn't seriously think she would betray Malach or the rest of the group. She would never do it. Should she even say anything to the rest of the group about it? How did he know where to find them?

A thought struck her for the first time. Had she dreamt the whole thing? It made sense. The venom might have induced the dream and her mind had taken the demons she had seen and the stranger from the woods and combined the two. Had the stranger back then even had horns? The demons didn't even know they were in Ragewood. If they did, they would have sent more than just one demon to talk to her.

She breathed a sigh of relief. That had to be it. The demon was all in her head. Right? Yes, it was the only explanation that made sense. She held her head high, confident there would be no more surprises until they got to the demon compound.

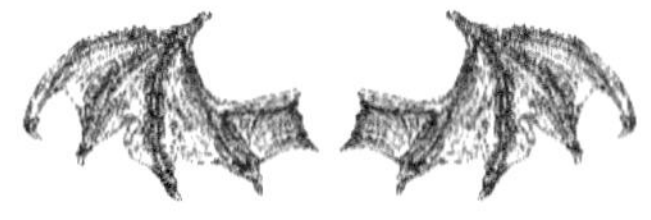

Finally, on the fourth day after their escape, they saw signs of living animals again. Fresh droppings from what looked like a small deer. Malach and Ariel decided to track it to see if they could bring it down, but a few miles later, they decided to call off the hunt, afraid of losing their way in the woods. Malach was able to bring down a rabbit on their way back but they only got a mouthful each off the scrawny thing.

Each day it seemed to get better, and they hoped they were past the worst of it. They were able to start bringing down more game and stave off hunger. Skie brought back a small doe, and they were able to fill their bellies once again.

Marena had helped Amara shave the rest of her hair on the side where her head injury had occurred. Then they styled her hair, leaving it long on the top and side with a braid separating the shaved and long hair. Malach liked it, thinking it made her look more like a warrior.

"I think we are about two weeks from the demon compound." Elzrod showed them the map that night around the fire. "Right about here,"

"I see you added the spider caves on your map," Togan pointed at the map.

"Yes," Elzrod beamed. "I hope to update all of the maps once we get back to the army in the hope that we will be the last group to come into Ragewood Forest unaware of the dangers it holds."

"What are we going to do when we get to the demon compound?" Amara asked quietly.

Amara had been quiet since they left the spider caves. Malach wondered if there was something wrong. Maybe it was just the horrors they had witnessed, but maybe it was something else? He would have to find time to talk to her about it to see if he could help.

Amara continued, "the plan was to rescue Serilda and escape on the horses, hopefully outpacing any pursuit. Now we don't have horses."

"As I was saying," Elzrod said cutting of Ariel's response, "we have another two weeks' journey to the demon compound. However, Ragewood City is only a day out of the way. Since we have lost our supplies, we need to restock, and we might be able to acquire a few horses as well."

"Do we have enough money for that?" Malach asked.

"It depends on how much they are selling for," Elzrod replied. "If they are as much as they were in Kargod, no."

"Then maybe we shouldn't *buy* them," Amara replied.

"We need horses to make our escape," Togan said missing the point Amara was trying to make.

"She means *steal* them," Malach said his tone hard. "Any other time I would say we ought to acquire them honestly, but I think she's right."

"Really?" Amara asked, a little shocked that Malach would agree with her to steal anything.

"Then it's settled," Elzrod said. "Togan and Marena will buy the supplies we need and Malach and Amara will steal the horses. We should be there sometime tomorrow."

As they made their way to Ragewood city, something about stealing the horses didn't sit right with Malach. He understood why they were stealing them, and he accepted they didn't have much choice but the people of Ragewood were innocent. They weren't soldiers who chose to fight, they were just people how wanted to live their lives, they just happened to live in Demon Territory.

He sighed as he walked.

"What's wrong?" Amara asked.

"Nothing." He kicked a rock on the path and sent it shooting off into the woods.

"Really? Sounds like somethings wrong."

"I don't like that we are stealing from innocent people," Malach crossed his arms.

"You will kill soldiers in their sleep, but you don't want to steal some horses?" Amara threw up her hands in exasperation.

"Soldiers choose to fight, like we do. I don't have a problem fighting them because we are doing what's right."

"Oh," Amara turned on him. "That's why you don't want me to go back to stealing after the war?"

"Amara, I was a guard at Newaught." Malach held up his hands to ward her off. "I grew up protecting myself and others against bandits and highwaymen. Of course I don't want you to go back to stealing. We would be at odds if you did."

"I see," Amara crossed her arms and set her jaw. "So if I were to go back to the Shadows, you would turn me in?"

"No," Malach replied but Amara wasn't listening.

"And what about my friends? Would you turn them in? My adopted father? What about him?"

"Amara, that's not what I meant. I just meant that we have totally different backgrounds, and we just have to figure out how to make it work."

Amara didn't say anything, simply walked a little faster and passed Elzrod and Ariel, taking the lead.

Ariel watched her stomp past him and glanced back at him.

He shrugged and Ariel slowed letting Malach catch up with him.

"What did you say to her?" Ariel asked, lowering his voice conspiratorially.

"Nothing." Malach shrugged.

"Obviously, you said something she didn't like."

"I told her I didn't like that we were going to steal from innocent people. She somehow thought that meant I would turn all of her friends in after the war for thievery."

"Would you? If she or one of her friends committed a crime right in front of you after the war was over, would you turn them in?"

"Uh, well, I mean they committed a crime." Malach put his hands out palms up in front of him as if gesturing to the hypothetical crime in front of him.

"Then she is right." His father shrugged.

"I would hope once the war is over, they wouldn't have to steal."

"Malach, most thieves don't just stop stealing, even if they can make their money doing something legal. If you can't accept where she came from or accept her friends for who they are, then maybe you should rethink a relationship with her."

"What?" Malach's eyes widened.

"Just think about it." Ariel walked back up to Elzrod.

They stopped for the day just after noon, but they didn't set up a full camp in case they had to leave quickly. Togan and Marena continued on toward the town to purchase their supplies before the heist. About mid-afternoon, Malach and Amara headed toward the city to meet with Togan and Marena. Amara still was giving Malach the cold shoulder no matter what he said to her or how many times he tried to apologize. Soon, he just let the matter drop, and they walked in awkward silence.

Togan and Marena waved them down as they approached the city, and they stopped just out of sight of the main gate. They quickly gave them direction to the each of the stables and left to find the camp. He and Amara entered the city and followed the directions to the different stables. They needed to scout out which would have the horses they required, which had the least security. They exited the final stables and moved into a dark alley.

"Not this one. The owner has paid for extra security here," Amara told him.

"Yeah, I saw one of them in the corner with a crossbow," Malach nodded.

"Not to mention the big guy with the hand and a half sword, I think our best bet would be the second one we went to."

"Agreed, it was close to one of the gates and only had one guard. Togan said they close the gates an hour after sundown. We need to get moving if we are going to make our escape before that happens."

"Fine. I will sneak in and get the horses." Amara left the alley. "You stand guard in case someone comes."

"You can't lead six horses out of the stalls by yourself," Malach took a couple quick steps to catch up to her. "Besides you will have to knock out the guard and I can do that way easier than you can."

"Then who will stand guard?"

"No one will need to if we get in and out quick enough."

"Fine, I'll agree but only because we don't have time to argue about it." Amara stomped her way down another alley. "But I don't think this is a good plan though."

They moved quickly down a side street that paralleled the main street and soon found themselves standing behind the stables they intended to rob. There was a high window and a door barred from the inside.

"Now what, genius?" Amara planted her fists on her hips and scowled at him.

"You will just have to get inside and unbar the door," Malach shrugged as if the answer was simple.

"How do you propose that I get inside?" She poked him in the chest.

Malach bent down and cradled his hands and motioned for her to step on them. "I'll give you a boost."

"I feel like I'm going to regret this," Amara sighed and stepped up into his hands.

Malach lifted her easily. She opened the shudders and peered in. She fiddled with something and it didn't take long for her to open the window. She hoisted herself off of Malach and through the window.

Malach moved to the door and listened intently. He heard a muffled male voice, a scuffle, and then nothing. He was just about to try to beat the door down when he heard the bar slide away and it open. Amara was standing in the doorway smiling smugly at him, the limp form of the guard behind her in the hall between the stalls.

"See? I don't need a man to do my dirty work," Amara turned and crept away from Malach.

He followed, nodding in appreciation.

The guard was still breathing, and they needed to work fast before he woke up. Amara already had the first horse mostly saddled by the time he found a stall housing another horse. It took them a little time but soon they had six horses saddled and ready to leave. Each of them had two horses tied to the horns of their saddles. Malach unbarred the large front doors and gave them a shove, jumping out of the way to let Amara and her three horses run through.

He quickly mounted his horse and kicked it into motion to catch up with Amara. They were almost to the gate when they heard shouting from the direction of the stables. They glanced at each other and pushed the horses to a gallop as they turned on to the main road. It was a straight shot to the gate, and they hadn't yet been seen by the guards, but they were already in the process of closing the heavy doors. If they didn't make it out, it wouldn't be long before they were caught and hung as horse thieves.

More shouting came from behind them. Two guard at the gate moved into their path and those who were closing the doors started pulling harder. Amara didn't show any signs of stopping and Malach wasn't about to slow either. The guards' nerves failed them as they got closer and at the last minute, they jumped out of the way. Amara threaded the needle between the two doors and was out. Malach hunched down lower on his horse as if that would help, and they slide through. Malach was sure that he heard the horses' flanks brush the door as they went through on either side of him.

They were out!

Malach turned to look behind him. The doors shut with a boom and then start to open back up very slowly.

He followed Amara off the main road. They would make a wide circle around the city and then back into the woods where the group would be waiting for them. She slowed allowing him to take the lead. Everything appeared different in the dark, and he was a more skilled woodsman than she. They slowed to a trot and started picking their way through the forest.

He heard distant shouts at first, but they soon faded, and Malach heard no sign of pursuit. Most likely, the city guard would wait until morning and then try to pursue them. They would call off the search long before they got close to finding the stolen horses, and they would have no issues getting away. They arrived at the camp, the other four mounted up without a word, and they all rode into the darkness.

Chapter 16

Daziar walked under one of the main archways at Newaught. His return to the city was not filled with the excitement and adventure his first time had been. No, this time he was apprehensive and nervous.

They had left the refugee camp and traveled to the area where the lieutenant had told them the main group of escaped prisoners had disappeared. They had hoped to find something the Demon Army had missed, but their search came up empty. During the time they had searched the area, Ana had sent a messenger ahead to meet with her contacts in Newaught. They learned she had someone within the Shadows she had worked with in the past and trusted. Daziar wanted to know who it was, but Ana wouldn't give up her source. He had mixed feelings about working with the Shadows, but since the war started again, things seemed to be less black and white for him, and he didn't like it.

Ana's contact had been able to get a few of them forged papers to get them in the city. They didn't know if the escape prisoners would be in Newaught, but it was the closest city to the point where they had disappeared and the direction they had been headed.

Daziar, Ana, and Auron had made it through the city gates without any issues, but the guard warned them there was a new curfew in effect since the demons had taken control of the city. They would have to make their way directly to a tavern and stay there for the night.

Ana had dressed herself in a heavy, thick cloak to hide her wings. Daziar could still see a few lumps that he knew were her wings, but to most, they would appear to be an unsightly growth or possibly some weapon she kept concealed. The guards hadn't stopped them, so he thought they were hidden well enough.

The atmosphere of the city was oppressive as if something was pressing down on them. Normally the hustle and bustle of the city didn't stop until well after dark but with an hour to go before sundown there were few people about. Those who were out in the streets gave them nervous glances and quickly moved away. One person going so far as to almost turn completely around to avoid the three travelers. The buildings grew larger and nicer the farther in they went, but Daziar thought they all looked a little more run-down than he remembered.

They made it to The Bog and Barrel Inn. It was the same tavern Honora, Malach, and Daziar had stayed in when the first arrived at Newaught only a few months ago. The metal sign hanging above the door was crooked and needed a good polish. Ana pushed inside with Daziar and Auron on her heels.

There had been noise and music playing before they entered, but everything abruptly stopped when they opened the door, all heads turning to stare at them. Most of the stares were outright hostile, the rest, wary. After a few long moments, everyone went back to what they had been doing or saying and the music continued. Even the music was different though. The musicians choosing to play something sad and haunting instead of the happy upbeat music Daziar expected.

"You'll find more cheer in a graveyard," Ana commented under her breath to Daziar.

He couldn't help but agree.

The three went up to the counter and a sour faced woman came out from the kitchen.

"What d'you want?" she asked, her voice as sour as her face suggested it would be.

"Two rooms and three meals," Ana replied swiftly.

"Six silvers," the lady growled.

"Six?" Daziar's jaw dropped open. "That's highway robbery."

Ana held up her hand to quiet him and he glanced around. He had drawn the attention of more than a few of the patrons.

"Six silvers is agreeable." Ana nodded and laid the coins on the bar.

The lady snatched them up quickly as if she was afraid Ana was going to take them back and walked into the kitchen without another word.

They found a table in the back corner of the room and all took their seats with their backs to the wall. Daziar didn't trust a soul in this room. Three meals were brought out to them, each consisting of porridge along with a small, hard loaf of bread.

For what we paid for the meal, we should have at least gotten some cheese or meat with it. Daziar picked up his bread and tapped it on the table. It was hard as a rock and he stuck it, end up, in the porridge, hoping it would soak up some of the moisture and become edible once again. He started to eat and almost gagged at the taste. He decided he would rather go to bed hungry and pushed the meal away. Auron studied him over the top of his bowl.

"You're not going to eat that?" He pointed at the bowl.

Daziar raised an eyebrow at him. "You are?"

"I learned to eat a lot of stuff when Prinna and I were first out here in Newaught. If you're not going to eat it, then hand it over."

Ana, who was sitting between the two of them, pushed both Daziar's and her bowl over to Auron.

"You too?" Auron stared at them if they had grown two heads.

"In the short time we have been on this mission, I've seen Daziar eat things I would never, given the choice, let past my lips." She shook her head. "If he won't eat this, I'm not even going to try it. Besides, I don't need the same amount of sustenance as you humans do."

"Huh, I thought you would need more than us." Daziar cocked his head to the side to study her. "I mean even the smallest angel is larger and the largest human. And you have wings and live a very active lifestyle, warring and everything."

"I never thought of it like that," Ana replied. "I guess that's simply not how God made us. Look here comes my contact."

A tall, skinny man dressed in finery had just walked through the front door. He stood out like a sore thumb in the tavern, and all heads seemed to turn toward him as he entered. He went over and talked with the barkeep and most of the patrons went back to their drinks paying little attention to the man. He went and sat at a table not far from where the three sat and didn't once glance there way.

"Are you sure that's him?" Auron asked between bites.

"Yes," Ana crossed her arms and purposely looked away from the contact. "He is wisely waiting for everyone to stop looking at him before making contact. We will wait it out and see if we can connect before the curfew. If not, we will have to try again at a later date."

They waited for what seemed like forever to the impatient and restless Daziar, and he had a hard time sitting still. Finally, once most of the patrons either left to make it home before curfew or passed out at their tables, Ana's contact set down his mug of ale. He looked around at the room one last time and walked over to the three that were in the corner.

"Took you long enough," Daziar mumbled at the man.

"What a blissful life you must live, to have your head filled with cotton, hay, and rags." The man casually took a seat with his back to the room. "But that would be why the guard, which you were briefly a part of, could never catch us."

Daziar ground his teeth, but Ana cut him off before he could retort. "Daziar, Auron, this is Demien. He is here to help, so play nice."

"Right now, *he's* the one not playing nice," Daziar pointed at him.

"Sorry, I distinctly remember watching you arrest one of my pupils to have her hung," Demien scowled at Daziar.

"You were Amara's mentor?" Daziar sat back a little in his chair, his mouth slightly agape.

"I was her handler," Demien corrected. "And she had to leave the Shadows because she chose to save you and your friend. Then you repaid her with betrayal, you barbarous wretch."

Ana held Daziar back from lunging across the table at the spindly man. "Alright, you two, that's enough."

"I'll beat your face in until your brain squirts out your ears." Daziar held up a fist but sat back in his seat. "Then we will see whose brain is filled with cotton."

"I doubt you would be able to lay a hand on me," Demien leaned back in his chair and crossed his arms.

"Wanna bet!" Daziar sat forward again, and again, Ana held him back with one arm.

"I said, that's enough," Ana reiterated. "If I have to say it again, you both will be talking out of the other side of your faces."

Daziar sat back in his chair and fumed while Demien was infuriatingly calm.

Ana sighed, shook her head, and glanced up at the ceiling, mumbling what must have been a prayer for patience. When she lowered her gaze again, she took a deep breath.

"Demien." She looked at him. "We are here seeking information on a certain group of people."

"I'm not sure if I have the information you require; however, I will happily tell you, for a price." He nodded once.

"Wait, after all this, he expects payment?" Daziar thrusted an open hand at the man as he turned to look at Ana incredulously.

Ana raised a hand to calm him. "We have coin to pay you. We have tracked a group of prisoners from the prison camp where they were being held. They vanished somewhere between Lindow and Newaught."

Demien nodded thoughtfully. "Are these prisoners of the Angel or Demon Army?"

"Demon," Ana replied, even toned and stone faced, "and strictly political. They were being used to coerce men into joining the Demon Army. Auron's wife was among them."

Demien nodded a few more times obviously not telling them something.

Ana placed a single gold coin on the table.

One of Demien's eyebrows went up, and Ana slapped another coin down. "That's all I'll pay,"

"We found them wandering through the frozen plains and helped them disappear." Demien pocketed the two coins with a deft motion.

Auron sat up straight in his chair dropping his spoon with a clatter. "Is my wife with them? Prinna Barclay is her name. Please tell me she's alright."

"I don't know that name," Demien holding up his hands as if to defend himself, and quickly added, "but I barely know any of them by name."

"Can we go with you to see them?" Auron pleaded with the man.

"I know how important this is to you," Demien said, and Daziar sensed the *but* coming, "but I have to get permission from the master to let any of you into our lair."

"We understand," Ana nodded. "We will wait here for your response."

Demien stood, "I will bring word of the master's response in the morning."

Demien left. When he opened the door, Daziar could see that the light outside was failing. They wouldn't be able to go anywhere else tonight. He had hoped to find some of his acquaintances in the city guard and ask them for a little more information about the new demon regime.

"Well, that was a big waste of time," Daziar slumped back in his chair, crossing his arms.

"What do you mean?" Auron's brow furrowed. "We found the prisoners. The information Demien brought us was extremely useful."

"But we don't even know if your wife is with them." Daziar didn't want to admit Demien's information had actually been helpful. The man had insulted him the whole time and he didn't like the man. "And he kept us waiting so long that we don't have time for anything else."

"I agree with Auron," Ana said. "Just because he insulted you—rather eloquently, I might add—doesn't mean his information was any less valuable."

"Harrumph!" Daziar slumped down farther in his seat.

"Oh, stop being juvenile." Ana took a drink of the mostly clean water in her cup and twisted her face in disgust at it. "It sounds like Demien's ire is your own fault anyway."

"Harrumph," Daziar replied again. "I was just doing my job. It's not my fault that Amara broke the law."

"Fine, but maybe you should sit out the next meeting with Demien."

"Fine by me. I don't want to see that little weasel anyway."

The three retired to their rooms and tried to sleep. Although, Daziar had a hard time falling asleep on his still empty stomach. Once he finally did, his dreams didn't comfort him any. He dreamt of a feast, only to have it stolen by Demien. Then the dream changed to Auron and Prinna's joy-filled reunion, but they were imprisoned by the demons at Demien's bidding.

He awoke in the morning only to feel more tired than he had the night before. His stomach growled loudly. He threw back his covers and dressed, walking down the stairs into the tavern. Many of the patrons from the night before were still present, passed out in their chairs or on the floor. However, none of them had their coin purses on their belts any longer. Daziar shook his head and walked back to their table from the previous night. Not long after he had sat down, a serving girl came to take his order.

"Can I get some eggs and ham?" He placed a silver coin on the table.

The serving girl scooped up the coin and walked away, laughing mirthlessly.

Puzzled, he wondered if his breakfast would be reminiscent of last night's meal.

Sure enough, a bowl of flavorless gruel was served to him. Although, this time it had chunks of some kind of meat in it, which Daziar didn't think were ham. He tried not to think about it as he ate, swallowing the food as best he could. He didn't think he could stand to miss another meal.

He was just finishing when Ana walked down into the tavern. She took one look at what was left of his meal and shook her head at the serving girl, who was already headed her way with a bowl. The serving girl turn around and walked away without a word. Ana sat down across from Daziar.

"Good morning!" Daziar said cheerfully.

"To you as well," Ana replied politely. "Have you seen Auron this morning?"

"He's not up yet," Daziar shook his head. "When do you think your halfwit of a contact will come back with news?"

"He came to me early this morning,"

"What?" Daziar almost choked on the last bit of food in his mouth. He regained his composure and asked, "what did he say?"

Ana shook her head at him, "I don't want to explain it twice. We will wait for Auron.

No matter how many times he asked, she wouldn't say anything more.

It only took Auron another half hour or so to wake up, but it seemed like hours to Daziar.

Once Auron was finally seated, Ana shared the information. "We are to meet with Demien in the market around midday, and he will lead us to the entrance to the Shadows' lair."

"Really?" Auron all but jumped out of his seat.

Ana put up a hand to calm him down.

Daziar glanced around but no one was looking their direction. "Keep your voice down."

"Sorry," Auron studied the ground.

Ana continued in a quiet voice. "We have been permitted to speak with the master on this matter, and we will be able to find out if you wife is there with them. He warned me that some of the prisoners were recaptured, but the Shadows were able to save the majority of them."

"That's wonderful news." Auron didn't jump or shout this time.

"Can we get out of this tavern? I'm starting to feel boxed in." Daziar stretched his neck, and it popped a few times, releasing the tension he was feeling.

"I don't think that is a good idea," Ana replied. "Daziar, you are wanted for being seen with Malach, and if I was found to be an angel, that would blow the whole mission out of the water. We need to keep a low profile."

Daziar sighed but nodded. He understood.

"We will leave just before midday and minimize our chances of being discovered." Ana stood. "I will be in my room if I'm needed."

They all got up and went to their respective rooms to wait but only an hour later, Daziar found himself at Ana's door. He raised his fist to knock but paused, unsure of what to say or if he should bother her. He lowered his hand and turned to walk away.

The door squeaked open on its rusty hinges.

"Did you need something, Daziar?" Ana was leaning against the doorway. She looked stunning in her silver armor, but she was careful to hide her wings in case anyone happened by.

"Um, I was, um, hoping you might teach me to defend my mind."

"Sure."

"I understand if you don't have time or are too busy."

"I said I would."

"Oh, great!"

"Please, come in, and I will help you." Ana motioned for him to walk through the door.

Ana's room looked identical to his own. There was one bed to the left as he walked in and a small table with one chair to the right. Ana walked in behind him, and he had to move farther into the room so she could close the door behind them.

She motioned for him to sit on the floor, and he did. She sat, crossing her legs and facing him. "Clear your mind and center yourself."

"Huh?"

Ana sighed. "Just clear you mind, and we will go from there."

Daziar closed his eyes and tired not to think of anything. He felt a pressure in his head and his eyes popped open. "Are you trying to access my mind right now?"

"Shhh." Ana didn't open her eyes. "The best way to learn is to do. Defend your mind from me."

Daziar closed his eyes and trying to will her to not enter his mind. He felt the pressure again and a mental image of Ana popped into his head. He tried to think of something else but it was too late.

"You find me attractive!" Ana exclaimed. "That's cute."

Before Daziar could reply he felt the pressure again, and a memory jumped into his mind. Malach and he were sparing in one of their training sessions a few years before they graduated. Malach had soundly defeated him multiple times that day, and this was their last sparring session. His left eye was starting to swell from an over exuberant strike Malach hadn't expected to land, and it was starting to impair his vision.

Malach lunged forward trying to land an early blow on him. He side stepped it and swung hard, frustration fueling him. Malach pulled up his bo staff to block, but Daziar's swing snapped the stick in half and continued into Malach side. He heard a smack and Malach doubled over. A few moments later, he was on the ground gasping for air.

"Malach!" Daziar dropped his staff and fell to his knees next to him. "I'm sorry, I just got frustrated and wasn't thinking."

Malach raised a hand with a thumbs up, still fighting for breath.

Their teacher was there then, rolling Malach onto his back and checking his abdomen. "Hmmmm, at least one broken rib, maybe two." she mumbled. "Not coughing up blood. Good, good. Malach, how well can you breathe?"

"Not...well. Shallow."

"Hmm, Daziar go..."

Daziar gritted his teeth in the present and willed Ana out of his thoughts. The pressure lessened and the memory stopped suddenly.

"You hurt your friend." Ana's voice wasn't in front of him anymore but to his left.

Daziar snapped open his eyes. "I didn't mean to-"

His temporary lapse in concentration cost him. The pressure in his head returned and a new memory sprung into his head. His betrayal of Amara to his captain. The memory didn't last long, but he was unable to push Ana back out of his head.

His reward for all his effort was a splitting headache. As the pressure subsided the pain started. He dropped his head into his hands.

"We are done for the time being," Ana told him.

Daziar relaxed and his headache lessened slightly.

"I didn't pick those memories at random."

Daziar looked up at her. She was sitting in the chair at the table, leaning back in it as if she had made very little effort at all to break through his mental defense. She offered him something in a mug and he took it, guzzling a few swallows before the burn of the strong liquid hit him. He sputtered and coughed as it burned all the way down his throat.

"That will help with your headache."

After he regained his composure, he asked. "What you mean you didn't pick those at random?"

"Memories are like little lights in your mind." She took the mug and threw back the remaining liquid. "If you know what you are looking for, you can bring up the memories that will break their concentration quickly. Once that happens, an angel or demon can delve deeper, breaking through what's left of a person's defense, ripping whatever they want from you. They can't control you, but they can pull memories from you and either suppress, plant, or simply learn them."

"So why those?"

"The first two I could tell were strong memories, but they were more or less random. The third, however, was chosen." She grinned at him. "I wanted to see what you were thinking when you betrayed Malach."

"You mean Amara?" Daziar furrowed his brow. "I betrayed Amara."

"Oh, yes, you did that too, but I can understand your intentions behind that. What I wanted to find out is why you betrayed Malach. When you turned in Amara, you betrayed Malach as completely as Amara. I see now you didn't realize it at the time, and you had only pure intentions, as misguided by your black-and-white sense of morality as it was."

Daziar had to think about her words, but in the end, he was forced to come to the same conclusion as Ana. He had betrayed Malach, in some ways, more than Amara. He would have to talk to his friend about that when he saw him next. Shame made his chest tighten.

"You must think me naive." Daziar didn't look up this time, not wanting to meet her gaze.

Ana took a breath and poured something from a bottle into the mug. "You have done some growing up since you left Brightwood only a few months ago. You can't change mistakes made in the past, only learn from them so you don't repeat them. You need to break out of this errant belief the world is black and white. There is so much grey. Do you fault Malach's parents for settling in Brightwood and starting their family?

"No!" Daziar eye widened at the unexpected question.

"And yet, they betrayed many soldiers and angels when they did. Wouldn't you say that was wrong?"

"No. Well, yes, but they did it for the right reason."

"But it was selfish. Is that really the right reason?"

"Ugh," Daziar held his head again, the headache ramping back up. "No. . . I don't know."

"That's my point," She sipped her mug and handed it to him. "To many people, what they did was wrong, but to others, it was perfectly warranted. You need to find out what you believe and stop living in this world of absolutes you have put yourself in. Sure, there are things which are absolutely right and absolutely wrong, but to look at everything the same way is an error."

Daziar took another long draw from the mug, ready for the burn this time. He sighed and studied the mug, not really seeing it but looking far past it. They sat that way for a long while, passing the mug back and forth while Daziar tried to sort out what he believed.

"I think I get it."

"Took you long enough."

Daziar's head seemed a little fuzzy, and he declined the drink when Ana offered it next.

She shrugged and emptied it. "Now, if you think I let you off with only barring three memories, you are sorely mistaken. I have taken something from you, and you won't get it back until you can best me or break through my defenses."

"What?" Daziar's head snapped up to see if she was telling the truth. "What is it?"

"You won't know until you get it back." She smiled a wicked smile at him.

He thought about his family and friends and breathed a sigh of relief when he found he could still remember all of them. Or could he? Did he just think they were all there and he was missing one of them?

"Don't worry, it's nothing that would hinder you from completing the mission, but it is important to you."

He calmed his mind. His headache was almost gone and steeled himself. "Then let's try this again."

Ana laughed. "Not so fast! It's time to meet Demien in the market."

"Fine, but I'm going to get this and get my memory back from you."

Ana stood, and he followed. The floor seemed a little less steady than when he first walked in, and he stumble slightly before righting himself.

"We'll get you a mug of water first," she laughed. "Then we will go to the market. I don't need you stumbling around and embarrassing me."

Auron was outside the door when Ana opened it. His eyes were wide and his fist suspended in the air where he had been about to knock. He spotted Daziar behind Ana and narrowed his eyes." What were you two doing?"

"Nothing as fun as what you are thinking." Ana chuckled. "Just a little training."

"Uh-huh." Auron gave them a skeptical look. "Either way, it's time to go."

Daziar retrieved his water skin from his room and guzzled down some water. A moment later, he caught back up to the other two, and they exited the tavern. The floor was back to its normal steadiness and his headache was all but gone.

He wondered how they were going to be able to move through the crowded market without someone bumping into Ana's wings and outing her as an angel. His fears were ungrounded, however. The market was not nearly as crowded has it had been before the demon take over. Even some of the vendor stalls were empty.

It didn't take long to find Demien, or more accurately, for Demien to find them. Daziar was pretending to look at something in one of the stalls when he was grabbed from behind and pulled into an alley. He turned swinging a fist as he did. Demien sidestepped and tripped Daziar, and he went sprawling to the dirt.

"Wilted cabbage leaf," Demien mocked him.

Daziar turned over, his face burning with embarrassment and frustration. "Take me in a fair fight, and we will see who the wilted cabbage leaf is."

"Why would I ever do that when I can win by playing dirty?" Demien sneered at him.

"Enough you two," Ana's tone was like a parent who has to constantly stop two bickering children. "You're causing a scene, and we don't want to bring the demons down on us."

Demien nodded placatingly. "Follow me, then."

Ana put out a hand to help Daziar up and he took it. He wouldn't let Demien make a fool of him again. They followed Demien on a winding path through the city. Daziar had never been to this side of the city, but it was clearly the slums. There were a lot of buildings with caved in roofs or crumbling walls. Many of those buildings still had people living in them, and he couldn't imagine how cold they must be.

Demien turned to them. "I need to blindfold you for our safety."

"Oh no," Daziar put up a hand to stop him. "I don't trust you not to do something once I'm blindfolded. Besides, I've already seen the entrance."

"I'm just following orders." Demien shrugged. "If you won't do it, you don't get to come."

"We'll do it," Auron replied, ignoring Daziar. "Anything to find my wife."

"I can deal with that," Ana agreed.

"Well, I guess you're staying here then, Daziar," Demien shrugged, smirking at him.

Daziar fumed. He hoped Ana and Auron would support him in his refusal, but he understood that Auron was desperate and Ana trusted Demien. He would just have to accept it. "Fine, but when this all goes wrong, I'm blaming the both of you." But it didn't mean he had to like it.

Demien blindfolded all three of them and lead them down several different streets. Daziar was pretty sure Demien was making more twists and turns in their path just to confuse them. It worked. Daziar sensed they had walked into a building and he heard Demien and someone else talking. There was a slight whirring noise, then they were moving again. They were instructed to step down a set of stairs, and Daziar heard the whirring noise behind them this time. Their footsteps echo around them as if they were in a cave.

"You can take off your blindfolds now," Demien told them.

Daziar ripped his blindfold off without hesitation.

He had been correct in his assumption. They were in a cave system. Green lights on the wall illuminated the cavern giving it an eerie glow. Daziar didn't see the other person Demien had talked to but he wasn't given much time to look around. They moved down the cave where a cart on a track sat waiting.

Demien motioned for them to get on.

Demien pulled a lever that must have been keeping them in place. The cart moved slowly forward, crawling at first but slowly picking up speed. Ana sat down and Daziar and Auron followed suite. Demien held on to a handle but stayed standing. Daziar almost stood back up just to show he could do it but a moment later he was glad he didn't. The cart all but fell out from under them as it dropped down a steep decline. Even though he was seated, the cart almost slid right out from under him. Then, at the bottom of the drop, the cart leveled out, pulling him down. Then they were out of the cave and into an open cavern. Daziar wondered at the size, and he noticed Auron doing the same.

"All this was just below our feet this whole time?" Auron asked in wonder.

"Yes," Demien replied. "And no one ever knew it."

Daziar glanced down and vertigo hit him. There was nothing below them at all. He sat back quickly before he fell off the cart.

Demien apparently noticed Daziar fall back. "We didn't know what was down there until just recently. Two of our numbers decided to explore those depths and found an underground lake.

Unfortunately, they also found that there is a monster down in those depths. One was able to make it back, but something in his mind broke while he was down there, and he hasn't been the same since.

"What kind of monster?" Ana narrowed her eyes.

"Some kind of serpent," Demien shrugged. "Some are calling it a leviathan of old, but they reported that it had wings."

"What do you think?" Ana pressed.

"I think it's been down there for an unknown number of years, and it can stay down there for the rest of its life."

"It can't make it up here, right?" Auron peered over the edge to try and look for the monster.

"It hasn't yet," Demien shrugged again.

"But it *can't* make it up here, right?" Auron turned to Demien, eyes wide.

"If I tell you what you want to hear, will you shut up?" Demien asked.

Daziar ignored Demien and checked ahead of them.

There was a group of people waiting for them at the end of the tracks. The cart lurched as Demien pulled on the brakes, and Auron noticed they were close. He moved to the edge of the cart, straining forward to see if he could recognize his wife in the crowd.

The cart slide over the tracks onto solid ground again and Auron jumped off before the cart even stopped, yelling his wife's name. No one responded. He called her name a few more times, moving around the crowd. An older man came up to him, grabbing his arm and stopping his movement.

"Son," sadness evident in his eyes, "she's not here."

"Do you know where she is?" Auron grabbed the man by his shoulder and shook him. "Is she farther back in the caves?"

"She was recaptured when we escaped," the man put a hand on Auron's shoulder. "She pushed me ahead of her in the escape, and she was grabbed. It's my fault she's not here. Please, forgive me."

"Sir," Auron collapsed to his knees, "please tell me she is still alive."

"The last I saw of her she was. I'm so sorry."

Auron took a steadying breath, "You have nothing to be sorry about. Prinna saved you. You didn't doom her."

The man knelt and hugged Auron, tears running down both of their faces. Daziar turned to Ana and they shared a skeptical look. If any of the recaptured prisoners were still alive, they would no longer be kept in an easily accessible area. Neither of them said anything, though. Movement caught Daziar's eye, and he turned to see a woman walking toward them the crowd parting to let her through.

Demien bow respectively to her, "Master, this is Ana, Daziar, and over there is Auron. He's just received the bad news his wife is not here but has been recaptured."

"My condolences," The Master bowed her head to Auron respectfully, then turned to Ana. "It's good to meet you in person after all this time."

"It is good to finally meet you," Ana took a step forward and bowed. "Although, I am surprised to find you are a woman."

The Master's laugh was melodic and soft. "Most are. Please, come this way, and we will find you a place to stay for the time being."

Auron thanked and said goodbye to the former prisoners, then followed the master with the rest of the group.

"We have a dozen more people outside of the walls of Newaught," Ana told the master as they walked. "Is there enough room for all of my troops here if we need to stay for a few weeks?"

"We have plenty of room for everyone, and you can resupply if you plan on going after the other prisoners," the Master replied.

"If they have been taken where I suspect they have been taken, I don't believe my superiors would allow us to mount a rescue," Ana replied.

"What?" Auron piped up from behind everyone. "What do you mean we won't be going after them?"

"Auron," Ana stopped and turned to him calmly. "If they are close, then we will go find them, but I believe they would have been taken to the demon compound deep in their territory. I don't think Michael would ever allow it."

"It doesn't matter," Auron threw his hand down in anger as if to dismiss her reasoning. "I won't stop searching or leave my wife to die in a prison cell."

"I understand your frustration. We will wait and decide what to do once we know for sure." Ana put up a hand to calm him.

"There might be other places, like the prison compounds, where she could have been taken. We need to gather more information and find out."

"It doesn't matter where she is, I won't give up," he replied defiantly.

"We can help with information gathering," the Master cut it. "We can move around the streets much easier than any of your group."

"Why?" Daziar asked suddenly.

Everyone stared at him as if they didn't fully comprehend what he was asking.

"We are thieves, and you are Angel Army," the Master started to explain.

"No," Daziar cut her off. "Why would you help us? You are not a part of the Angel Army, and I've never known a thief to do charity work. So why? What do you get out of it?"

Demien started forward to defend his master but she put up a hand to stop him. "It's fine." Then she turned to Daziar. "You're right. We have no allegiance to the angels or the demons, but demon reign has been bad for business. If I help to return the status quo, I benefit from that."

Daziar nodded. "Fine. I'm willing to work with you but know I don't trust you or any of your people."

"Daziar," Ana reprimanded.

"He's bold." The Master smiled. "I would never expect you to trust us, though most wouldn't have the courage to tell me to my face. You are smart for not trusting us. We do what's best for us, just as you do what's best for you. We don't have the same beliefs or convictions, but in this instance, our goals align."

"What happens when they don't?" Daziar crossed his arms. "Will you leave us out in the cold? What happens when your goals align with our enemies? Will we find a knife in our backs? Cold steel on our throats?"

"Never," The Master took a step forward and held up a finger in warning. "I do not go back on my word, and we are not assassins, nor are we soldiers. But I think you know that."

"I know only what I have heard, but what I've heard lines up with what you say." He conceded the point.

"If you are finished insulting our host, may we continue?" Ana replied tersely, starting to walk again.

He was going to get a dressing down from Ana later.

"He is well within his rights to question us," the Master told Ana, to Daziar's surprise. "I would have similar questions if our roles were reversed."

Ana didn't say anything, and they moved on down the caves.

The Master gave them a quick tour, and Daziar was turned around almost instantly. He would have problems finding anything in the maze of caves. They were taken to their rooms after the tour, and Daziar took off his boots for the first time in days. Even at the inn, it had been too cold to take them off. He groaned as he stretched his feet out. The underground cavern stayed about the same temperature year-round, and although he needed a little extra insulation, he didn't need the heavy fur he had on out in the snow.

He flopped down onto the bed and let his thoughts wander. It seemed this would be their base of operations for a while, at least until they found out where the recaptured prisoners went. Then they would decide whether to rescue them or go back to the Angel Army. Personally, he would rather see this mission through to the end. Mostly because he hated to admit defeat, although, he did care about freeing the prisoners too. Leaving the prisoners behind would be admitting they failed, in his mind, and he wasn't about to let it happen. Especially since he had failed Malach by staying behind in Brightwood. He wouldn't fail again.

No.

It didn't matter what the group decided, he would go find the prisoners with Auron and bring them home. He was starting to like Auron again and, whether he liked it or not, he was starting to trust the man. Maybe Ana would come too. She had her duties to perform, and she would have to check in with Michael. He wouldn't ask her to choose between her loyalties.

Daziar sighed.

There was no sense in worrying over it now. For all they knew, the prisoners were within Newaught, and they could have them out and be on their way back to Brightwood tomorrow. He let his muscles relax and closed his eyes.

Chapter 17

Serilda stood at the top of a hill, sun warming her skin. It was pleasantly warm, a slight breeze playing with her red dress. She turned her face up and smiling at the sky. It was so peaceful here. A tear slipped down her face.

It wouldn't last.

Oathbreaker would make sure of it. As if her thought had conjured the blade, which they very well could have, its avatar came up the hill toward her. Once known to Serilda as Fang, her trusted Angel Blade, Oathbreaker chose to appear as a little girl.

Young, happy, and carefree, she skipped up the hill in her bare feet.

Serilda almost smiled at the girl, before remembering what was hiding behind the facade. A monster lived behind the innocent face. She could see it in the girl's eyes. One who had been lying in wait for thousands of years. Now Oathbreaker would play with her until she was broken beyond recognition, until Serilda had given her everything she wanted. Then, and only then, Oathbreaker would kill her. Or more accurately, let her die.

They had already stood on this hill many times in the past few days. This is where Oathbreaker would ask her to do the *right* thing and tell her everything that had happened over the two hundred or so years that they had been apart. As always, Serilda would refuse, launching them into another iteration of torture.

Of course, they were simply in her mind and nothing was real, but by this point, Oathbreaker had control of everything happening. She controlled whether Serilda felt pain or not. She controlled what Serilda saw and felt. She controlled the scenarios and the outcomes that Serilda saw.

So far, they had been through several manners of physical torture, which went well beyond what could have been done to her body. The terrible memories of those started to flood her mind, and she slowly sank to the ground. It didn't stop there, however. Serilda could withstand pain. She had in the past, and she would for as long as she had left to live. The worst part was when Oathbreaker brought her loved ones into the scenarios. That had almost killed her. They tricked her, at first, making her think she was in the real world again, Oathbreaker even taking the form of a demon instead of the child she normally appeared as. They brought Ariel in front of her and tortured him until he no longer breathed.

Then they brought Malach in. Ariel was bad enough but bringing her baby boy into it had all but broken her. She reduced to a sobbing mess. She almost told them everything, if only to save him, but something in her mind had told her it was not real. Some unconscious thought had helped her realize the ruse, and she stood strong until Oathbreaker had taken the vision away. The little girl had rushed at her, enraged when her ploy didn't work, and slaughtered her.

Serilda was on the ground now, too weak to stand, too weak to stop the tears flowing down her face. She was close to her breaking point, and they both knew it. It wouldn't be long before she gave in and told them everything she knew. It wouldn't be enough to satisfy them, and they would kill her or continue to torture her until she was a drooling fool with no mind left.

Why not just tell them? she thought. *Why not just give in and let them have it? No one was coming to save her. No one cared. If they did, they would have already come for her.*

She shook her head. Those thoughts were not truly her own. She snapped her head up to glare at Oathbreaker and spat at the girl's face. She giggled in response, the spittle disappearing before it got anywhere near its intended target.

"Just kill me and get it over with!" Serilda shouted at the girl.

"You would like that wouldn't you?"

The insidious laughter emanating from the child made Serilda's skin crawl. Nothing that evil should come from a child.

"If I killed you, you wouldn't get to greet your husband and son," she clasped her hands behind her back and grinned, cocking her head to one side. "They are on their way here right now. They might even be at the compound by now."

Hope rose in her for only the briefest of moments. Then it all came crashing down again. If Oathbreaker was telling the truth, she would soon see her family tortured and killed, but if she was lying, Serilda would never know and Oathbreaker would be able to trick her again. No, it would have been better not to ever have heard those words.

"Don't worry, you will get to see him again. He comes in the company of not one but two traitors and will no doubt be taken alive. Then he can come play with us."

Serilda was once again filled with despair, the earlier hope draining out of her. If her husband and son didn't know about the traitors among them, they would never stand a chance. If only she could get word to them, but she was a prisoner of her own mind, locked in here by the blade she trusted.

Fang had been a trusted companion and one she confided in. When she had first become a Blade-Bearer, Fang had given her the strength she needed to break out of her old life in the Demon Army. Fang guided her through many missions and adventures. When she started to develop feelings for Ariel, Fang had told her to follow her heart. She listened and their relationship had grown and blossomed. She was devastated when Reckoning and Fang were lost to the demons on one of their final missions. She and Ariel had gone against their orders to rescue the two blades but eventually, admitted defeat when they couldn't be found. She never forgot the blade and the countless hours they spent together. All of that worry and sorrow to find Fang had been Oathbreaker for all those years, manipulating her. When she thought the blade was captured, it was simply returning home to report on the status of the Angel Army.

The thought hit her like a punch to her gut. Reckoning was captured at the same time Fang was. They never found him either. He must have been a traitor too. They manipulated her and Ariel's relationship to make sure they stayed in contact and then manipulated the mission, tipping off the demons who captured them. Reckoning was as much a traitor and Oathbreaker. Anger burned inside of her.

"Good," Oathbreaker purred at her. "You are finally figuring it out. Took you long enough."

"Reckoning is a traitor just like you." She narrowed her eyes.

Serilda leaped up from where she was on the ground, hands extended like claws wanting to tear Oathbreaker to pieces. She never got the chance, of course. Halfway to the little girl, her limbs froze stopping, her mid-leap. She couldn't move anything but her eyes, and they were glued to the monster who stood before her.

"I'll admit, I didn't think it would take you this long to figure it out," Oathbreaker taunted. "But yes, he and I played you and your precious angel like puppets on a string. And now, Angel Reaver, you know him as Reckoning, has been rescued from the clutches of a big, bad demon by none other than your son. He nor Ariel has any clue he isn't who he says he is. Ariel was even kind enough to let Malach keep Reckoning as his own."

All Serilda could do was growl in frustration at Oathbreaker as she hung, suspended, and frozen. She wanted to kill the being in front of her. Rip her limb from limb, gouge out her eyes, do anything to hurt her, but all she could do was make guttural noises. She was totally useless in her current state. Powerless to do anything.

"You should be happy," Oathbreaker told her. "Soon, you will be reunited with your family. Although, you won't even be awake to be with them. Also, I'm going to give you the day off. No torture today. We will have all the answers we need soon enough."

Serilda growled again.

"Oh, don't worry," Oathbreaker cooed, and an evil grin spread across the little girl's face. "I'll still come to play with you every day." The girl started to back away fading like an apparition. "And oh, what fun we will have."

Then she was gone and Serilda was released, and she crashed to the ground, unable to support her own weight. The despair she felt stole her strength. She curled up into a ball on the grass and cried.

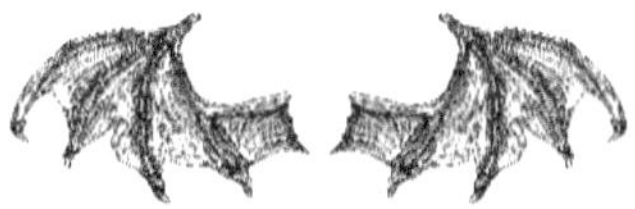

Amara couldn't sleep. They were only a day from the Demon Compound, and she couldn't ignore it any longer. At first, she thought the demon to be a bad, demon-induced dream, but the more she thought about it, the more she knew it hadn't been. The demon would try and make her betray Malach. She didn't know how he was going to do it, but she suspected she wouldn't be able to simply turn him down. But why could it be that he was so confident? She needed to find out before she told Malach. She knew he would help if he could, but if it was a choice between his family and her, she didn't know what he would choose. He had such a black-and-white view of the world, even now. He had all but told her he would turn her and her family of thieves in after the war if he had the chance.

A thought struck her, and she sat straight up in her bed roll. Lawdel. It had to be. The demon must have found her ties to him. He would be the only person, the only thing that would make her turn on Malach.

"Are you alright?" Ariel was studying her quizzically.

"Fine," she whispered, shaking her head. "Bad dream."

She stood up and walked out of the camp, "I'm going to clear my head."

"Don't go too far."

She nodded her understanding and walked out into the woods.

As she walked through the darkness, it seemed like the trees pressed in on her. Like she was trapped. Doomed to fail. She had no idea how to get out of the trouble she was in now. She tried to convince herself that there was no guarantee Lawdel had been taken by the demon, but she just couldn't. Which meant she couldn't run. The demon would either kill Lawdel or track her down and make her come back. But she couldn't betray Malach. He trusted her, and she, for the most part, trusted him. She might even love him. If she betrayed him, he or someone he loved could be hurt or killed, and he would never forgive her for that, no matter what was at stake.

Tears blurred her vision and hopelessness descended upon her. No matter what she chose it was the wrong thing. No matter what she did, someone would be hurt. There was no way out and there was nothing she could do about t.

"Out for a midnight stroll?" The deep gravelly voice of the demon came from behind her.

She wasn't startled this time. It made sense he would have been watching for their arrival and tracking their progress. She wiped the tears from her eyes and turned around to face him. He didn't have the hood over his head like he had the last two times and startled her a little. He was not at all like she had pictured him. Horns stuck up out of his head, but they were so small, she could barely see them from where she stood. She could barely tell he was a demon at all.

"I knew you would be around," she told him. "What do you want?"

"I've already told you what I want. You will bring Malach and company to me and hand them over."

"No." She crossed her arms and set her jaw, wondering what he had up his sleeve and dreading it at the same time.

"Then I will kill your father." The demon's expression never changed from one of boredom.

"I knew you had Lawdel!"

"Who?"

It was the first time Amara had seen the demon's expression change, and a few played across his face within a few heartbeats. Surprise, recognition, and then back to the carefully guarded bored expression he seemed to favor.

"Not the man who pretended to be your father for most of your life. No, I have the one who sired you."

"What? Why do I care about him?" She bluffed, trying to cover her shock. In fact, she cared a great deal about him. He could tell her where she came from, who she really was. She had always wondered who her parents were.

"Haven't you ever wondered about your past?"

It was if the demon had read her mind. Maybe he could.

"He could tell you all about who you truly are."

Amara bit back a retort, which would have given away her bluff. Instead, she replied, "No, I don't really care. Lawdel has been enough family for me."

"Fine," the demon replied, turning to walk away. "I guess I will go dispose of him."

"You would kill him just because I don't care about him?" Amara tried her best to keep a straight face and worked hard to sound more curious than concerned.

"I have no more use for him," The demon with a nonchalant wave of his hand, as if talking about the day's bathwater instead of a man's life. "Unless you really do care about him."

She had been caught. He had called her bluff, and now she either had to let him kill her real father and most likely never learn where she came from or she betrayed her friends to him and allow them to be killed.

"Oh, and if it makes any difference, if you don't betray Malach, I can easily find your precious Lawdel and have him killed as well."

Amara growled and stomped her foot, knowing he most likely could follow through with his threat, "Fine, you spawn of hell, what do you want me to do?"

The demon smiled wickedly and laid out his plans to her. It was simple, and Malach and the group would never see it coming. She knew it would work and hated the demon all the more for it.

More than that, she hated herself. She would prey on their trust like it was a small animal to be killed and tossed aside.

"What is your name?" she asked. "I would like to know who I'm working for."

"My name is Azazel."

Malach, Skie, Ariel, and Elzrod looked down on the empty plain completely dumbfounded. It was deserted. There had clearly been a large army here within the last few days but now there was just an expanse of trampled ground. Not far in the distance was the Demon Compound itself, looming over the landscape. The compound looked like it had been designed for war. There was a large tower jutting over the top of the large stone wall. The tower was attached to the largest building in the compound, but there were a handful of smaller buildings as well. They were too far away for Malach to see any details.

"Well, I guess that takes care of the problem of getting passed the army," Malach stated.

"Yes, but in some ways, it would have been easier," Ariel crossed his arms. "No one would have recognized Amara, Togan, or Marena. They could have snuck through the camp without being noticed."

"Agreed," Elzrod said. "Now we had to find a way to approach the compound without any cover."

"We can get much closer by following the tree line around to the side of the compound," Malach pointed to their left. "Then Amara can scout out a way to enter the compound, and we can make a plan."

Ariel and Elzrod agreed, and they made their way back to the others. By the end of the day, they were as close as they dared to be to the compound. Elzrod didn't think they would send out patrols now the army had left but they camped a safe distance away anyway. That night they escorted Amara to the tree line where they would wait, in case she needed help and she continued out onto the open plain. Malach had to hand it to her. If he hadn't been watching her progress the whole time, he would have never noticed the slight shadow moving toward the compound. Soon she was out of sight around the side of the compound wall, and they sat waiting, listening, and watching.

Time passed slowly for Malach waiting for Amara to get back. Once he was certain he heard her, but it was just Togan joining them. The first light of day started to brighten the sky, and he was getting worried for Amara. He was contemplating trying to go after her, but he would never find her in time. However, if she wasn't back soon, she would surely be seen by the guards in the compound.

He spotted movement. A moment later Skie growled deep and low. Someone was heading toward them. Malach peered closer and recognized Amara. He let out a breath he hadn't realized he was holding and let himself relax. No one was pursuing her, and nothing seemed to be wrong. Why did Skie growl?

She got to them and brushed past him coldly. He didn't understand. She had started to distance herself from him after they left the spider caves, but he didn't know why. Now it was almost like she hated him. The three men followed her, no one daring to speak a word until they were sure their voices wouldn't be carried by the wind.

"There is a sewer line unguarded on the other side of the compound," she told them, a sour expression on her face. "It will get us under the compound and allow us inside. I heard some of the guards talking about the prisoners and they are being held in the large tower. We should be able to get most of the way to it in the sewers and hopefully make it in and out before anyone knows what's happened."

"Great," Ariel replied. "The three of us should go with Amara tomorrow night. Togan is too noticeable, and he and Marena should stand by, in case someone is injured."

"I agree," Elzrod nodded once. "Also, if something should go wrong, they can mount a rescue mission."

"If something goes wrong, they should get back to the Angel Army and forget about us," Ariel corrected.

"I could never agree t' that," Togan shook his head smiling. "Ya know t' much. My duty dictates that I at least kill ya if you're captured."

Ariel gave the man a withering look.

"We just won't get caught," Elzrod replied seriously.

"Agreed," Malach replied.

They walked back to camp and Amara didn't say another word to anyone. Malach thought she might just be tired from the night's escapades and left it at that. She retired directly to her tent and the men informed Marena of what Amara had found and what had been decided before retiring for a few hours of sleep as well.

Malach was restless and uneasy but couldn't put his finger on what was making him that way. He decided he was just excited and anxious over the next night's breakout. He tried to get a little sleep but couldn't, so he got up.

Togan and Marena were not far away but were deep in conversation, so he didn't want to interrupt them. The day passed slowly and Malach decided to go hunting. Skie perked up her head as he strung his bow and started wagging her tail as he sheathed Reckoning as a dagger on his belt. She got up and followed him out of camp.

"Don't go far," Togan warned.

"Only as far as the hunt takes me," Malach promised.

Togan opened his mouth to say something more but shut it without uttering a word.

As Malach left the camp behind, he felt his worry and anxiety slowly fall away. Malach hunted for hours, letting the tracks of a deer and his instincts take him where they will. He made sure to keep in mind which way he had come so he could find his way back.

He finally caught up to the deer he had been tracking, and Skie slowed to let him move ahead of her. He crept forward low and quiet, being careful to stay downwind from it. The doe had a young buck with her, one who only had small spikes for antlers. Following his instincts, he drew his bow with an arrow notched. Just as he released the arrow the slightly smaller buck stepped up beside the doe and took the arrow in its side. The shot was a little high and the buck took off running. Straight at Malach. Malach dove to the side hitting the ground hard as the buck passed him with his head and spikes down. He would have been skewered if he had acted only slightly slower. The buck kept running and Skie took off after it. Malach got up quickly and ran to keep up with the two animals. Skie took the buck down just before Malach would have lost sight of them and he caught up quickly. Skie had killed the buck much cleaner than Malach.

Malach walked up to the buck. "Sorry, little guy, wasn't your day."

Malach hosted the buck onto his back and he and Skie headed back to the camp at a brisk clip. When they got back to the camp, they had time to spare, and Malach cleaned and dressed the buck. Togan put a piece of it on a spit and when night had fallen, risked a small fire to cook the animal.

"We'll make sure to save you some," Marena promised.

"We will?" Togan turned to her feigning surprise.

Marena elbowed him.

"Oomph," Togan grunted but quickly added. "Of course, we will."

Malach, Ariel, Elzrod, and Amara walked out of camp.

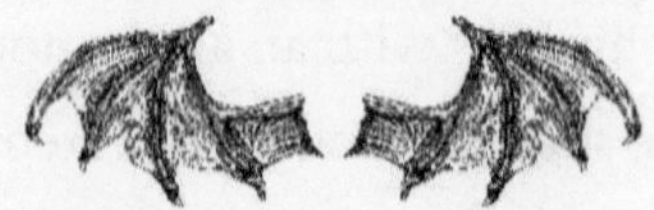

Amara's gut wrenched with every step she took. She hated herself, but she hated Azazel more, and with every step her hate grew. She would kill the monster if it was the last thing she did. She had to make sure her father was safe, both her real father and Lawdel. She hated herself for betraying Malach, but she told herself she would make it right.

She had to.

She had thought about telling Malach all that day, but she knew she couldn't. He would have tried to help her save her father, but Azazel made it clear to her even if he fell, his people would kill Lawdel before she could step foot in Caister. She didn't sleep at all, and she could barely eat anything with her stomach in knots. The time had come, however. The time of her betrayal. She led them out of the trees and onto the plain, heading toward the compound from which some of them would likely never return.

Malach followed Amara out onto the plain. She was moving much faster tonight than she had the night before. He didn't question her, assuming she knew what she was doing and followed her lead.

In the short time he had known her, trusting her had become natural to him, something he didn't question anymore. He would follow her anywhere, even directly off a cliff, and simply trust she had a plan.

He believed that all the way up until he saw the demon standing in the sewers waiting for them. No one said a word, shocked into silence. The demon motioned for Amara to come to him, and she did with little to no hesitation. Before Malach could find his voice, he felt a sharp pain on the back of his head and the world around him went black.

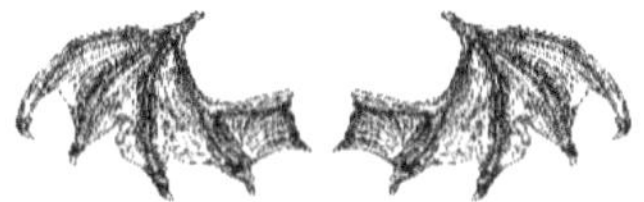

Amara watched, helpless as a soldier clubbed Malach, Ariel, and Elzrod on the back of the head. Malach and Elzrod crumpled to the soggy ground, but Ariel didn't go down so easily. He turned to fight but was overpowered by a dozen soldiers who beat him unconscious.

It pained her to watch, but there wasn't anything she could do about it now. She watched as they carried them out of sight, around a bend in the sewage tunnel. As soon as she found a way to get her father out and protect the ones she loved from this demon, she would break them out. She knew they would probably never forgive her for it and would definitely never trust her again, but she didn't have much of a choice.

She turned to Azazel with a hard light in her eyes, "I did what you want, now call off your goons and lead me to my father?"

"All in due time," he tossed a weighty bag to her.

She caught it by reflex before it hit her in the chest. It was a bag of coins. She looked at him questioningly.

"I told you there would be another thirty pieces of silver to be paid when you delivered." He shrugged. "Originally, I hoped to have you deliver me information, but you delivered something much more valuable."

"I don't want your blood money." Amara ground her teeth together and threw the coins at his head as hard as she could.

He caught it with one hand effortlessly. "Fine, but don't say I didn't try to pay you for your efforts."

"Where is my father?"

"Take the urchin to her father," he commanded the only soldier who had stayed behind.

"I'm taking him from this place."

"Fine," he conceded. "Do what you will with what's left of him."

Amara tried to keep the shock off her face, she didn't expect him to let her go so easily.

"You've both served your purposes," Azazel walked the way the soldiers had taken Malach and the others.

"This way. I will take you to your father." The soldier walked away without waiting to see it Amara would follow.

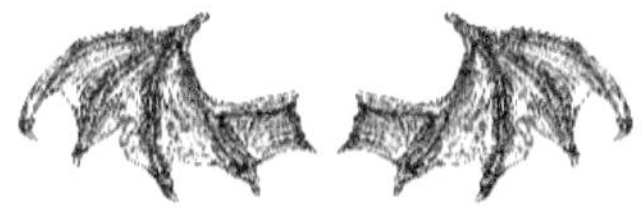

Pain pounded through Malach's head. No matter how much he wanted to stay asleep, his head wouldn't let him. His last memories came back in a rush and rage filled him.

Amara had betrayed them.

She led them like sheep to the slaughter. His eyes snapped open, and he reached for Reckoning. His hand closed on nothing, and he looked down at his hip. Of course, Reckoning wasn't there. They would have taken his weapons. He looked around and saw several other people in his cell, although no one he recognized. There were three older people there two were men and one a woman.

The woman noticed he was awake and tapped one of the men on his shoulder to get his attention. "He's awake."

The man came over to him and gently put a hand on his chest holding him down, "Don't get up. We aren't going to hurt you. You have a nice size lump on the back of your head, and it would do you good to lay back down."

"Where am I?" he asked.

"The tower," the first man replied.

"Get comfortable. You'll be here until you're dead," the second man told him.

"Which hopefully won't be long," the woman said.

"Why do you say that?" Malach asked.

"Because the longer you stay here, the more pain you will experience," the woman told him.

"What are your names?" Malach asked.

"What does it matter?" The second man said gruffly. "You will be dead soon, and they will throw another unfortunate soul in here with us."

Malach arched an eyebrow, "Fine. Obviously, you have lost hope, but I'm not ready to do that, so did you see where my friends were taken?"

"You mean the angel and the old man?" The woman asked. "I assume they were taken to the upper chambers to start their torcher immediately."

"How do I get up there?" Malach asked.

All three heads turned to look at him with incredulous looks.

"How do I get up there?" Malach repeated.

"The stairs at the end of the cells," the woman told him, pointing to the left.

"Good," Malach said, trying to concentrate through the pain in his head and cobble together a plan to escape.

He got up, despite the pain in his head, and walked up to the cell door. He examined the door but couldn't find any weakness in it. He moved to the lock.

If Amara were here she would just pick the lock. He thought before he realized.

Anger coursed through him again, and he remembered the reason she wasn't there. She would pay for this. How long had she been playing them, playing him? From the beginning? From the time they met at Newaught or did the demon get to her somewhere along the way. Maybe Daziar and Honora had been right. Maybe he had trusted her too quickly, been too quick to allow her into his circle of trust. He vowed never to do that again.

Malach sighed. There was no way he could get through the door on his own. He moved back to the back of the cell and sat down to think. He worked through the problem again, trying to think of anything he might have missed.

"Malach?" a voice he didn't recognize called from outside his cell.

"Who's there?" he replied guardedly.

"It's Prinna," the voice replied.

"Where are you?" Malach strained to see through the bars toward where her voice was coming from.

"In the cell next to yours," she told him.

"How long have you been here?"

"A few days, I think. Maybe a week. It's hard to tell since there's no daylight in here. Have you seen Auron?"

"Yes," Malach told her. "We found him in the company of the Demon Army. He was conscripted to fight under threat of your death. We helped him, and he is in Brightwood right now."

Malach heard a sigh of relief, "I'm glad to hear he's alive."

"Did you see where they took my weapon?"

"I saw was one guard take all your weapons down the stairs while your friends were taken up."

So, one way led to their weapons and one way led to his father and Elzrod, possibly even his mother. If he went to get the weapons, he might not be able to get everyone out but if he went to save them first, he wouldn't have a weapon if he got in trouble or had to fight a guard or two. If he got out, he would have a better chance of getting everyone out if he went for the weapons first. He had a plan forming in his head. He needed Prinna's help to pull this off. He would only tell her as much as she needed to know just in case. If it turned out she was working for the demons, then the rest of his plan would still be intact for later.

"Prinna," Malach called.

"What?" she asked, sounding as eager as he felt.

"I have a plan."

The solder left Amara with the keys to an extremely solid-looking wooden door. She could hear talking behind the door, but it seemed like it was the same voice providing both sides of the conversation. She put the key into the keyhole and froze before turning it. Did she really want to do this? Did she want to meet the man who gave her up to freeze on the streets? She had fantasized about the day she would meet her father for years. Now that she was about to live it, she didn't know if she wanted to. Maybe she would be happier living in her fantasies. She realized, however, she would never forgive herself if she didn't open the door. No matter if it shattered her world, she would be torn apart by the unknown if she left now.

Before she could change her mind, she twisted the key and pulled the handle.

The door didn't budge.

She studied it, brow furrowing and pulled harder. It moved slightly. She braced a foot against the wall and grabbed the handle with both hands and pulled. The hinges squealed as the door slowly moved. She had to stop and rest of a minute and the door had only opened a couple of inches.

Malach wouldn't have this issue. He would just pull it open with his superior strength. The thought of Malach made her feel worse.

She turned back to the door and redoubled her effort to open it, trying not to think about Malach. She got the door open just a few more inches and the hinges popped and let go. The door swung wide and she fell hard onto the stone floor. A bare foot pressed down on her chest, pushing her hard into the floor, and she looked up into the face of a dirty bearded man.

"She doesn't look like a demon," the man said, and Amara didn't think he was talking to her.

She peered around him to see if there was another person still back in the room. The sight of the room frightened her. There were drawings and words all over the walls, written and drawn in something that looked an awful lot like dried blood. Most of the drawings overlapped each other. Some overlapped so much it appeared to be a ball of thickly caked gore instead of anything she could make out.

"She has to be a demon," the man muttered again, bringing her attention back to him. "No one comes down here but demons."

"But she doesn't *look* like a demon." The man leaned forward putting more pressure on her chest and providing the other side of the conversation.

"She has to be a demon. She's here to torture us, like every time the door opens."

Amara stared at the man. He had shoulder-length hair and a long beard. His face was scarred and dirty and there were some places on his head and face that were so scarred, hair didn't grow there. He was wearing rags that barely covered the important parts, and he was so emaciated his bones looked like they might burst through his gaunt skin at any moment. She noticed several jagged open wounds on his limbs, and she wondered if he had wounded himself to draw on the walls. The whole time she had been studying him he had been mumbling to himself.

"I'm not a demon," she told him.

"Not a demon?" he mumbled, then started rambling again. "I told you not a demon.

"But only demons come down here."

"She says not a demon. . ."

The pressure on her lessened, and she drew in a breath.

"It's her," the man said almost in awe. "No, it can't be her. She's dead."

He took her foot off his chest and ran back into the room studying the walls as if the answers were written on it.

They might very well be. She thought. Just because she couldn't make sense of it didn't mean it wouldn't make sense to his scrambled mind.

He seemed to find what he was looking for on the left wall close to the floor in the front corner.

He laid down on the ground and started talking to himself again. "She's not dead, see?"

"No, she is dead. I left her out in the cold and the abomination froze."

"No, you couldn't bring yourself to kill her, so you left her on the step of a nobleman."

"You're right! Then you knocked and left. Did you make sure someone found her?"

"No."

"Then she could have still perished."

"Yes, but she could have been found."

"Then this could still be her?"

"The abomination lives, and she's standing outside."

"Do you think she is here to kill us?"

Tears burned Amara's eyes. The abomination he was talking about was her. Her father had tried to kill her but had instead abandoned her, leaving her to her fate. He didn't even wait to make sure she survived. He didn't care about her. The only thing that kept her standing there was the need for answers.

The man ran out and got right in her face. "Are you here to kill us?" he said it almost hopefully, as if he wanted to die, "or are you here to torture us?"

"Neither." She furrowed her brow at him. "I'm here to take you away from this place."

He cocked his head to the side and peered at her as if she had grown two heads. "So you're here to torture us?" He pointed at her and squinted his eyes.

"No." She shook her head, frustrated at his confusion. "I'm your daughter. I'm here to take you away from here."

"You are my seed," he made a disgusted face. "You are not my *daughter*. You're a spawn of that. . . witch."

Even though it pained her to hear her father say she was not his daughter, she didn't run. Tears fell from her eyes, but she was here for answers, and she wouldn't run. She needed to know the truth. She had paid a high price for answers.

"What witch?"

"*The* witch of course."

Before she could ask another question her father launched into another conversation with himself. "She doesn't know! You stole her away as a baby and left her alone."

"How could she not know?"

"Because she wasn't raised to know, you dolt."

"Now don't go insulting me again."

"But you are a dolt. She probably doesn't know anything about her past."

"I don't," Amara interrupted, and her father whipped his head around to look at her as if he didn't believe she could have heard his conversation.

"She can read minds as well," he said, turning back to his alternate self.

"No, you are saying everything you're thinking out loud," she told him.

"Oh."

"Now what about my mother?" She put both hands out, pleading with him.

"Your mother?" he asked.

"The witch!" she almost shouted.

"You do know her then!" He wagged a finger at her triumphantly as if he had caught her in a lie.

"Only that you think she's a witch"

"Hmmm, well, no matter." He frowned at her. "We will tell you everything you want to know but not here. Too many ears."

Amara sighed. "Come on then."

"I can't leave," he told her, shrugging.

"Why not?"

"How will I ever remember anything?" he motioned to the drawings on his cell walls.

"Stay here!" She commanded and stormed out of the cell.

She wanted to scream. He must have been through a lot and his brain must be fragmented from the stress, but he frustrated her to no end. Now he wouldn't give her answers unless she took him out of the compound, which she had intended on in the first place, and he couldn't give her answers unless she found him something to draw his memories on. She hadn't even gotten his name yet.

A guard materialized seemingly from nowhere. "Didn't want him either?"

"No. I mean, yes." She shook her head. "He won't leave without copying the drawings on the walls of his cell."

She didn't know why she was telling him that. Maybe she just needed an outlet. She hadn't expected him to do or say much about it.

She was surprised when he said, "I'll go get you something for him to draw them." And walked away.

He returned a few minutes later with a large, folded piece of paper and some charcoal. She studied him incredulously, not knowing how he had gotten them so quickly or even why.

The guard interpreted her incredulity. "I was an artist before I was a soldier. Not all soldiers are bad people, just like in the Angel Army."

"But why would you help me?"

"To tell you the truth, guarding him every day gives me the creeps, and I heard you were going to take him away. I hope to be reassigned to a new post, and the faster he leaves, the faster I get reassigned. So, if there is anything you need, please let me know."

"A bit of food wouldn't be unwelcome."

"I can do that." He smiled at her. "But I won't bring it down there. There's something not right with him, and I've heard it can spread."

"What's not right with him is that he has been tortured for years on end. It's not contagious."

"All the same, I won't go down there."

"Fine, leave it at the top of the stairs, and I will get it."

She took the paper back to her father. She handed it to him, and he unfolded it and got to work immediately. She sat outside his door on the stairs, so she didn't get in his way and after a while went back up to find two plates of food for them. She brought them back down, but her father was too entranced with what he was doing to pay her any attention. She ate and tried desperately not to think, for inevitably her thoughts turned toward Malach and what she had done to him. She was again disgusted with herself, and it soured her stomach.

"How much longer?" She tossed the piece of bread she was nibbling on back onto the plate sending her fork clattering away from her.

"A day or two," her father said absent mindedly.

"A day?"

"Or two. We have to get everything right or it won't make sense to us."

"Ugh," she half growled and half screamed in frustration, rubbing her face with her hands. "Fine, but at least tell me your name?"

"Our name?" He looked around the room thoughtfully.

"Yes, what do they call you?" she asked thinking they were finally getting somewhere.

"Prisoner." He smiled happily and went back to drawing.

Chapter 18

"Help!" Prinna shouted, panic making her voice shrill. "Help! I don't think he's breathing!"

A guard ran in to see what all the commotion was about.

"Over in the other cell! He hasn't woken up since you brought him in, and the others said he stopped breathing," she explained, tears starting to roll down her face. "Hurry!"

The guard ran over to the door and quickly inserted the key. Before he turned it, however, he shouted, "Everyone against the back wall. I'll gut any of you who make a move toward me."

They did as he asked, and the guard opened the door. He moved toward Malach, never taking his eyes off the three prisoners. He never saw Malach's fist coming until it smashed into the side of his face. The guard fell to the stone floor like a limp rag.

He might have killed the man. He didn't stop to check as he pulled the man's short sword from its scabbard and ran for the door. He pulled the keyring with the cell keys out of the lock where the guard had left it and took a few seconds to hand the keys to Prinna.

"I would stay and help, but I have to go, I will do my best to clear any guards out of your way as I go, but I believe our paths lie in two different directions."

"Thank you, Malach." She grabbed his hand with both of hers. "We have hope because of you! We will find our way out or die trying."

He nodded and pulled his hand back leaving the keys in hers.

He wondered at the change in the woman from the first time they had met. The woman standing before him was stronger and tougher than the one he had met only weeks before. He moved to the door leading to the stair and peeked his head in, looking up and then down the stairs. The stairs had a curve in them, so he couldn't see far in either direction. The commotion hadn't brought any other guards yet, so he went down the stairs to search for Reckoning and the other blades.

He searched through several rooms on the floor below, but they were all abandoned. He moved one floor down and turned the corner on two guards standing in front of a larger wooden door. He reacted quickly, dispatching the guards as quietly as he could. Although, one of them got a somewhat muffled shout off before Malach could finish him.

He moved quickly, searching the guard for the key to the wooden door. He found it and opened the door to find another prison of sorts. But instead of being designed for humans, these cells had been made for Angel Blades. Three Angel Blades stood on pedestals, each in the form of a short sword. Their hilts were suspended by two chains holding them in place and stopping anyone from simply grabbing them and carrying them away.

Reckoning! Storm! Fury! Malach called in his mind.

He didn't receive any reply from any of them, so something must have been blocking their communications. Lines on floor caught his attention. He studied them quickly. They formed symbols around each of the blades. They must be what was blocking his communication. He leveled the short sword at one of the chains securing Reckoning and swung with all his strength. It broke the chain and the blade fell to one side. Malach put a hand on Reckoning's hilt and pulled the blade back up and readied himself for another swing.

Malach, hurry! Reckoning's voice came through loud and clear. Their connection must have been restored when he touched the hilt.

Really? Malach retorted in his mind, pulling the sword back for a second swing. *I thought we might stop for a picnic, then maybe check into the inn for the night. I've heard what their hospitality lacks, their food makes much worse.*

You're hilarious, Reckoning said dryly. *Now drop that mundane sword, and let's free the others.*

Oh, are you jealous that I found myself a new sword? Malach asked but did as he was bidden.

Once the other two blades were freed Malach tucked both into his belt in the form of knives. He charged out of the room and around the corner just in time to see Prinna and the other prisoners pass the doorway leading to the stairs.

Good. They stand a chance at getting out. Malach smiled despite himself.

Prinna is here? Reckoning asked.

Yes, I found her in the prison cells when I woke up there. I staged a prison break. I heard from her that the others are up on one of the upper levels, Malach informed the blades.

I guess they should have put you up with your father, Reckoning chuckled wryly.

"Their mistake," Malach growled audibly and charged up the stairs.

He took the stairs three at a time, not slowing down even as he became more winded. He passed the floor with the prison cells and kept moving. He stuck his head in the door on the next floor, but it was a mirror image of the cells on the floor below with no one in them. They had to be close to the top of the tower by now.

He peeked around the next corner. Four guards stood in front of two cells they were all alert and ready. No doubt having heard his breakneck charge up the stone stairs. Malach didn't hesitate. He pulled Storm and Fury out of his belt, one in each hand, and hurled them at the closest two guards. Both hit their targets and sunk into the men's chests and they slumped forward, hitting the ground almost simultaneously. He took Reckoning in his pole weapon form and sidestep the first attack, then ducked low as the first guard dropped back and the second guard swung horizontally at him. Malach swung and cut one of the man's feet off at the ankle. He fell, holding the stump. The first guard moved forward, only to run into the blade on the other side of the pole. He barely had to stab the man as his momentum carried him onto the blade.

He kicked the man off, who fell back, trying to stay on his feet. His back hit the stone wall and his head snapped back making a wet cracking noise as it hit the wall. His eyes rolled back into his head and he slid down to a sitting position, never to get back up again.

Malach twirled Reckoning bringing one blade to rest under the chin of the guard recently relieved of his foot. "Keys," Malach commanded, and the man wordlessly pointed to one of the two guards he had impaled with the other two Angel Blades. Malach pulled back to strike the man but at the last second twisted Reckoning and hit the man in the side of the head with the flat of the blade. The guard might live, but Malach couldn't have him getting in the way.

He moved to the first cell which held his father. Ariel was suspended upside down, feet toward the ceiling, and pulled out into a V shape by two shackles. His hands were also pulled taut by shackles, so his body was X shaped. Ariel's eyes were closed and Malach wondered if he had passed out from being upside down too long. He got to Ariel and unlocked one of his hands first. As soon as Ariel's hand was loose, his eyes snapped open and his hand shot out to wrap around Malach's throat. It was only a split second but the fear he felt as his father's strong hand wrapped around his throat was crippling.

"Malach?" Ariel let go quickly. "Sorry, I had planned on subduing or killing the first guard that came in."

"Great minds think alike," Malach rubbed his throat. "That's how I escaped. Didn't you hear me kill the guards out there?"

"I must have been deep in meditation." His father frowned.

He means he was asleep, Reckoning put in. *He always could sleep through a war.*

"That's not it at all," Ariel replied. "Let's get Elzrod out before anyone else shows up."

Malach helped Ariel out his chains and handed Fury to him. "You guard the door, I'll get Elzrod out."

"Yes, sir," Ariel replied with a grin on his face.

He moved toward the entrance to watch for any reinforcements, and Malach headed across to the other cell. He got Elzrod down, but the old man didn't recover quite as quickly as Ariel, and it took him several moments to collect himself and get feeling back into his extremities.

Ariel picked him up before he was fully ready to stand, "We need to go now. I will carry him until he can stand."

Malach nodded and took the lead. He headed up the stair once again, hoping to locate his mother and free her as well. He burst through a trap door and up into the large circular room.

The top floor of the tower.

His mother lay on what looked like a stone altar. He almost didn't recognize her malnourished and emaciated form, but as he got closer, he confirmed it was her.

"Mom!" he shouted and ran the rest of the distance to her.

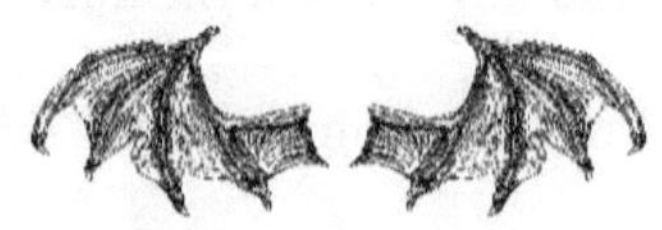

Ariel watched his son as he pushed through the trap door. He followed him and set the now fully conscious Elzrod down on his feet as he heard Malach call out. "Mom!"

"Malach, be careful," Ariel called after him, but everything in him screamed to do the same thing. To run forward and scoop up his beloved wife and carry her from this place. He glanced behind him at Elzrod, who only nodded and turned to guard the stairs.

Ariel moved forward and knelt next to his son. He looked at his wife, pitiful as she was, and could only see the woman she had been; strong, determined, and loving. She was asleep, her chest slowly rising and falling. Ariel was overjoyed to see she was still alive, but they had to go. They would be hard-pressed to get out of the compound alive, and she was in no condition to move on her own.

"Mom, wake up!" Malach called to her, light slapping her face to rouse her. "We have to go! You have to wake up!"

"Malach," Ariel put a hand on his son's shoulder, starting to recognize the symptoms his wife was displaying. "She's in a trance."

"What do you mean?"

"There's something angles and Blade-Bearers can do, but only with the help of their blades," Elzrod explained. "It's a trance-like state we can go into if we are captured, but both the blade and its bearer have to be willing to do it."

They also have to be within proximity, Reckoning added. *At least, initially.*

"Fine, how do we get her out of it?" Malach glanced between Elzrod and Ariel.

"We have to find her blade, Fang," Ariel told him. "The only way I know of to get her out is if the blade and bearer who initiated it end it together."

"I only saw Reckoning, Fury, and Storm in the prison room but there were other places for blades to be held," Malach replied. "Why wouldn't they keep Fang there too?"

Because that's not my name anymore, Fang's unmistakable voice sounded in Ariel's head.

Everyone glanced around for the blade and Ariel realized Fang must not have just spoken to him alone.

"They're coming!" Elzrod shouted from the stairs and shut the trap door behind him.

He slid a metal poker through the handle and metal loop on the floor, but it wouldn't hold very long, especially if a demon was down there. Ariel searched around for another way out of the tower. There was only one small circular window far above his head. They had no way of getting up to it, and he didn't have his wings anymore. He turned to his son.

"I'll boost you up, son, just like we used to," Ariel called memories of the times he and his son had hunted the woods together flooding his mind.

Malach seemed to understand instantly, and Ariel put his hands down, intertwining his fingers to make a stirrup for Malach's foot. He ran toward Ariel. As soon as Malach's foot hit his hands, Ariel heaved, feeling the pressure from his son's weight as he lifted him far into the air. He rammed Reckoning deep into the wood around the window and held on to keep himself from falling back down. He threw the latch and pulled himself up, through the window, and onto the roof. Ariel turned back to the stairs just in time for the trap door to explode inward as a demon pushed through it.

Ariel and Elzrod readied themselves for a fight as a second demon entered the room. This one carried Fang, wreathed in black fire. Soldiers poured in from below as well forming a circle around the two.

"Azazel," Ariel recognizing the demon, then spotted the sword. "Betrayer!"

You may call me Oathbreaker, she replied in her child-like voice.

Bile forced itself up Ariel's throat, but he swallowed it down again. "How could you? After all the years you fought by our side?"

Easy, Oathbreaker replied. *After the years of torment, all I had to do was give in.*

"Drop your weapons," Azazel commanded.

"Dad," Malach shouted from above and Ariel cursed himself mentally for not commanding him to leave earlier.

"Go, son!" Ariel shouted, not taking his eyes off Azazel.

"But-"

"Go! There's nothing you can do here!"

Ariel heard the scraping and scratching of his son sliding down what must have been a steep roof. He had no idea how Malach was going to climb down from that height, but he trusted his son would figure it out. He never took his eyes off the demons as they circled around him and Elzrod. One of the soldiers thought to take advantage of what he assumed was Ariel's blind spot. Ariel ducked the man's sword and swung up with Fury in the form of his battle axe cut a large gash in the man from bottom to top. He once again trained his gaze on the two demons.

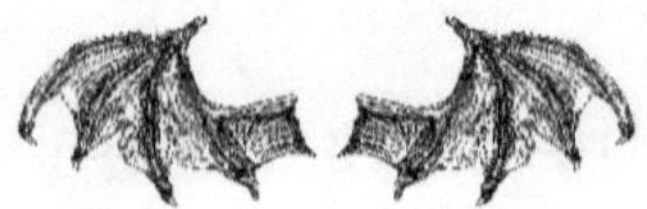

Malach did as his father commanded him, even though everything in him wanted to jump back through the window and fight. He removed Reckoning from the wooden sill and let gravity take him down the roof. Malach watched as the lip of the roof rushed up to meet him and at the last second, he jammed Reckoning deep into the tiles. The sudden resistance almost ripped Reckoning from his hand and he threw his other hand up to grab the hilt. He finally came to a stop, his lower half hanging over empty space.

He sighed in relief.

He pulled himself back up onto the roof and heard the clang of steel against steel, or whatever the Angel Blades were made of, from inside the room.

He almost started making his way back up the roof to help but Reckoning advised against it. *Malach, you can't help them now. You would only be captured again. You need to get away and find the others so you can mount a proper rescue.*

Malach only growled back in frustration, but he was right.

He peeked his head over the edge and almost fell, the feeling of vertigo making his joints go weak. He fell back against the roof and let the world stop spinning before trying again. This time he focused on the wall and not the ground, which seemed to help, and spotted sparse foot and handholds where the rough-cut stone protruded. He could use Reckoning to always have an anchor, but it was not going to be an easy climb. He got a good grip on one of the tiles and then changed Reckoning into a hook he could use to help him climb down. Hooking the edge of the roof, he carefully swung his feet over the side. The tile he was holding onto broke loose, but he managed to hang onto Reckoning and quickly found a foothold to stand on. After his panic subsided, he realized his hand continued to hold onto the tile that had broken loose even though it did him no good. He let go of it and watched it fall.

It was almost dark at this point, or maybe it was just getting light? He hadn't seen the outside world since before he came to in the prison, so it could be either morning or night, only time would tell. He found another handhold, this one much sturdier and used it to reposition Reckoning. He then started his long arduous climb down the tower.

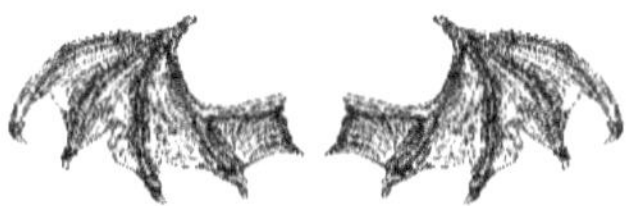

Daziar, Honora, and Anahita watched the compound as the alarm bells rang. Arjun and Auron were back at camp waiting for them to report. It was just five of them now. Michael hadn't authorized the continued rescue attempt and they had decided to go against orders. They had gotten to their position only an hour earlier to scout the compound before their rescue attempt. Daziar had thought they must have been seen but Ana told him to stay put. Sure enough, they spotted a group of people, running from building to building, making their way across the compound. There must have been an escape attempt, but something was off.

Ana kept reporting what was happening, since she could see much better through her spyglass, but Daziar couldn't figure out why none of the soldiers were searching the compound. It seemed like they all kept running into the tower when, by this time, they should have realized the prisoners were not in the tower at all. Ana lost sight of the small band of escapees as they climbed the stairs to the ramparts. The group, here were about a dozen of them, peered over the wall uncertain of how to escape. Then they each started stripping off their clothes and trying them together to make a rope.

They tied it off to something and the first person started down the rope of clothing. The rope didn't make it to the ground, but it made it far enough that there was only a small drop. The first person of the group made it to the end and dropped to the ground. They must have hurt themselves when they fell because they didn't get right back up. Instead, they rolled on the ground for a minute clutching some part of their leg.

"We need to get down there to help," Honora pointed at the man after Ana relayed the last bit.

"I'm all for it, but what if we are spotted?" Daziar tried to be the voice of reason. "We won't get a chance to infiltrate the compound if they knew we are coming."

"We might not have to infiltrate the compound at all if those are the people we are trying to rescue." Honora was already standing up as she spoke

Daziar felt foolish, of course she was right.

"Let's get down there." Ana unfurled her wings

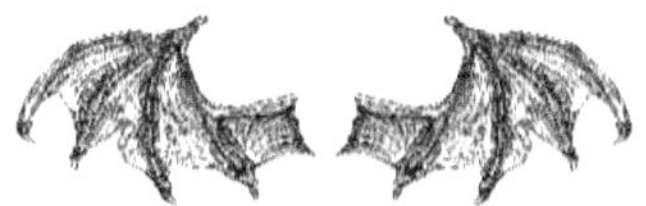

Togan and Marena were sitting at camp trying to brainstorm a way the two of them could rescue Malach, Amara, Elzrod, and Ariel when they heard the alarm bells tolling from the direction of the compound. Togan picked up his war hammer and Marena grabbed her bow. They didn't waste any time talking about what they should do, but instinctively understood what the other was thinking. The pair ran into the woods toward the compound.

Maybe they wouldn't have to mount a rescue at all. Maybe they would just be needed to support the one already in progress. Togan caught a flash out of the corner of his eye and held out a hand to stop Marena. He peered through the trees in the direction of the flash and moved his body from side to side slowly hoping to catch a glimpse of what he had seen again.

He did.

Something was reflecting in the setting sun and it was not something natural to the forest. He crouched quickly and Marena followed suit. They moved forward slowly catching snippets of a conversation on the wind. Togan was close enough to tell three figures were watching the compound from the trees. They must be a patrol. Who else would be this close to the compound?

He could understand a few words they were saying like "escape" and "get down there." He deduced they must be talking about going back to the compound to help stop the escape. He motioned to Marena, explaining they needed to take out this group before continuing, and they moved ahead, readying their weapons.

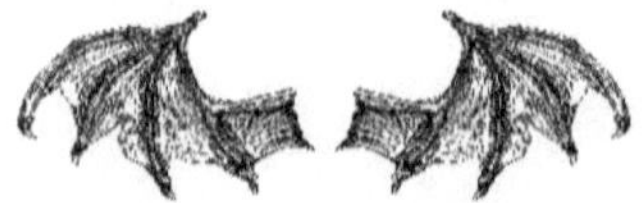

An arrow hit the dirt between Ana and Daziar, and he rolled away from her spreading out to make them harder to hit. A hulk of a man came flying out of the brush with a huge war hammer aim directly at Daziar's head. He pushed himself backward and spread his legs watching the hammer narrowly miss his groin and slam into the ground burying the head in the dirt. Rock shards and dirt flew up and into Daziar's eyes, blinding him.

"Wait!" a female voice called. "It's Daziar and Honora!"

Daziar clawed at his eyes trying to clear them of the debris. He finally managed to open one eye with minimal pain and take in the scene around him. Togan stood as still as a statue in front of him, hammer still in the ground where he had buried it. Ana's sword rested under Togan's chin, which was no doubt what had made him freeze instead of continuing to swing at Daziar. Honora stood frozen eyes wide. But who had shouted?

Marena walked out of the woods her bow and empty hand raised unthreateningly, "It's us, Daziar, Honora,"

Skie followed her out, happily wagging her tail.

"Why are you two attacking us?" Daziar continued to try and clear his eyes now that he didn't have to worry about being killed.

"We can figure that out later," Honora must have broken out of her shock. "Ana, lower your weapon, and let's get down there to help."

"Are you sure?" Ana asked.

"Yes, they are friends," Honora assured her. "Friends who are supposed to be with Malach, but we will have to figure that out later as well."

Daziar was finally able to clear his eyes fully and opened them again

"Alright, we need to get down there and help." Ana sheathed her weapon.

Skie was now walking toward Daziar and licked his face in greeting.

"What's happenin' at the compound?" Togan asked, offering a hand to Daziar.

"Prison break," Daziar took the proffered hand up, pushing Skie's head away from him gently. "We were going to help the prisoners."

"Are Malach, Amara, Elzrod, or Ariel with them?" Marena asked as they started to jog down the slight hill to the compound.

"We don't know," Honora replied, worry crossing her features. "Why would they be with them?

"Long story, but they were captured, and we were hoping they were escaping," Marena replied.

"We couldn't tell you for sure, but about a dozen prisoners are escaping right now," Ana took flight with a burst of wind coming off her powerful wings.

"You have an angel with you?" Marena looked up in awe.

"First, you didn't see her wings?" Daziar asked. "And second, you have been traveling with an angel and two Blade-Bearers for more than a month, and you're surprised *we* are with an angel?"

"Fair points," Marena replied.

Daziar watched as Ana got to the prisoners just in time to catch one as he lost his grip and plummeted toward the ground. She gently set him down and flew up to the few who were left on the wall. The four made it to the wall just as Ana was ferrying the last of the prisoners to the ground.

Several of the former prisoners recoiled at the sight of Skie but quickly recovered as she made no threatening movements. The four picked the prisoners who were the weakest and most injured and helped them to their feet. Togan simply carried the woman who they had first seen fall and hurt herself.

They made it to the tree line without being pursued, and everyone collapsed to the ground in a heap of exhausted limbs and heaving chests. Ana was the only one not winded, and Daziar glared at her with envy. One of the women sat herself up against a tree and he recognized her.

"Prinna!" Daziar exclaimed.

She was much skinnier than the last time he had seen her, but there was no mistaking it was her. They had found her at last.

"Prinna," Daziar addressed her again. "Have you seen Malach?"

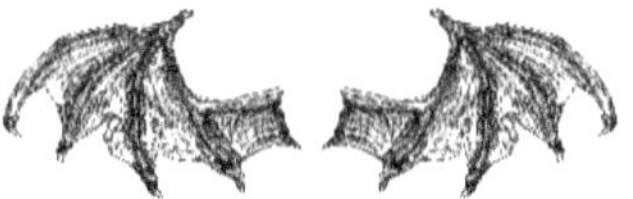

Malach was about halfway down the tower when he spotted movement out on the plains outside the compound. A band of very small looking people ran away from the compound and Malach smiled to himself. Prinna and the other prisoners had made it out and away. At least the prison break hadn't been a complete failure.

His foot slipped and the sudden weight caused the rock he was standing on to crumble away. The only thing that saved him, once again, was Reckoning. He was able to hang on long enough to plant his feet securely. He paused long enough to calm his racing heart, then continued to climb down. His forearms were burning, and his legs were starting to shake uncontrollably. If he didn't make it down soon, he wouldn't make it down alive. Ignoring the pain, he redoubled his efforts.

He tried to think enough about other things it would get his mind off the burning in his muscles, but not so much it would cause him to make a mistake. He wondered why neither the demons nor soldiers had come down from the tower to find him. He was exposed out here to the demons with their bat-like wings. It would only take one strong gust at the wrong time for him to go plummeting to his death. Or one well-placed arrow to end his climb. Even though he kept scanning the skies and watching the ground, he never saw a single enemy.

He was only about twenty feet from the top of the roof of the main building when he fell. He was repositioning Reckoning, but the shift in weight as he swung to place the hook in the wall caused one of the rough stones to shift and his foot slipped off. As he fell, he tried to finish his swing and plant Reckoning into the wall but most of his strength had been lost, and the tip of the hook just gouged a furrow in the stone.

Malach hit the roof and it collapsed under his weight and the impact of his body. Pain ripped through his body, and he fell through into the building, darkness enveloping him.

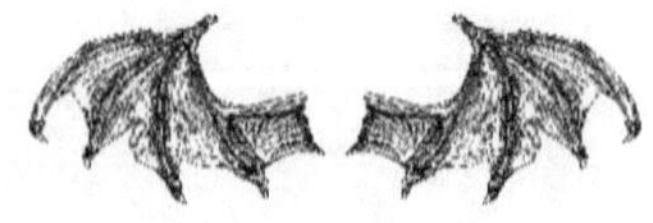

Kragen sat in darkness, the kind of darkness which was almost total. The only light came from under the door to the room he was sitting in but it provided just enough light for him to see what he was doing. He had found this room shortly after he had found the stores of black powder, and he had stolen one of the barrels and carried it here the next night. He then was able to scout the halls of the stronghold to find support pillars, walls close enough to the outside to be blown out, and other targets which would cause major damage.

After that, he had set to work. He made explosives during the day and at night he would set them. No one would find them. He made sure each explosive blended perfectly with its surroundings. That amount of detailed work took time, so he could only plant one or two explosives each night, but he had more than enough time. He had been told to wait until Azazel's master had been freed from the pit and the army was right at the threshold then strike a devastating blow.

He would continue setting explosives until he was sure the stronghold, and maybe the whole mountain, would come down. He didn't expect to survive the aftermath of the explosions, but that didn't bother him. He was told he would be reborn in the new world his master would create. Then, he would rule as a king!

Chapter 19

Daziar petted Skie as they talked about their plan to break into the compound and liberate the others. Most of the prisoners wanted nothing to do with their "plan to get themselves killed," as they put it and decided to try their luck on their own. Four had decided to stay and help. After a good, large meal of venison, provided by Togan and Marena, they tried to insist the travelers be given full packs of provisions. They were denied the request as neither Ana's group nor Togan's had the supplies to spare. Ana's had, at least, planned to have extra people traveling back with them and was able to provide them with some of the things they needed. Togan showed the group on the map where Ragewood City was, and they agree that would be their best chance.

Prinna and Auron decided they would lead the prisoners and make sure they made it to Ragewood City alive. As much as she wanted to help rescue the others, she had an obligation to the prisoners and Auron wouldn't be separated from his wife again.

The group of prisoners left, and they got down to a plan for rescuing Malach and the others. Prinna told them she had overheard the guards say there was only a skeleton crew in the compound.

What she didn't know was how many soldiers were left in the compound. They only numbered ten, not including Skie. The enemy had at least one demon in the compound, and even if they only have enough men to guard the walls, they would be outnumbered five to one. Also, after the breakout, Ana didn't think they would be able to get in without being seen.

Things looked dismal until Togan remembered the remaining explosives in Malach's pack. He ran to get them, and when he returned, he spread the ingredients gingerly in front of the group. Ana had been given a small amount of training on how to combine them, but there wasn't enough to blow even a small hole in the wall, much less one they could fit through.

It was Marena who came up with the obvious idea first. "We can use the explosives as a distraction. If we detonate them on the far side of the compound Ana can get us over the wall on the other side."

"Right and that should give us the time t' sneak into the tower," Togan nodded. "Then, after we free the others, it'll give us a fightin' chance t' get out of the compound."

"And what happens if there are twice as many soldiers as we think there are?" Ana crossed her arms. "Or a second demon? What then?"

"There won't be," Daziar reasoned. "The demons have lost just as many of their ranks as the angels have, and there were less of them to begin with. That means they will have sent all of their power with the army. The fact that there is even one demon here is insane."

"And I'm sure you know this with all the hundreds of years of experience you have?" Ana asked, sarcastically rolling her eyes.

"No, but it makes a lot of sense," Daziar replied.

"But what makes sense and what's reality don't always match," Togan pointed out.

"So, we just sit and wait while Malach and the others are tortured and killed?" Daziar ground his teeth, jumping to his feet.

"That's not what we're saying'." Togan put out a hand palm down to calm him.

"Right," Ana nodded. "I simply think we need to get a better idea of what we're up against. The last thing we want is to get ourselves captured or killed. Then there's no one left to save anyone."

"Ugh, I hate waiting around." Daziar sat down hard and crossed his arms.

"It's settled. We need to know what we're up against before we go in unprepared," Arjun spoke for the first time, settling the matter.

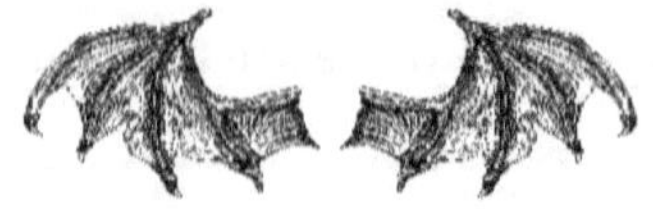

Malach woke up because of pain emanating from his lip. He opened his eye and looked down to see a rat sitting on his chest. He jumped to his feet, which upset and startled the creature. It scurried under a crate and out of sight. Malach lifted a hand to his stinging lip, and it came away with a little bit of blood. The rat must have bitten him. He felt a little disgusted, but it was a blessing in disguise.

He peered up at the open sky and spied the silhouette of a demon circling the tower. It hadn't seen him yet, but it was only a matter of time.

Malach, Reckoning sounded relieved. *I'm glad you're awake. I tried to wake you for some time and couldn't get a response.*

How long have I been out? Malach asked, careful not to ask his question out loud.

Maybe an hour, Reckoning replied. *But you need to get out of here quickly. It won't be long before they spot the hole you made in the roof.*

Malach sat still until the demon passed out of sight, knowing if he moved, he would be much more visible. Finally, after was seemed like an hour, the demon passed from his sight, and he was able to get up and search the room. There were only a few barrels and crates littering the large space, and he had landed next to one, narrowly missing it. He didn't know if God even cared about someone as small as he was in this war, but he sent his thanks to Him anyway.

He pulled a lantern off the wall and lit it with a little piece of flint provided for him on the base of the lantern. He went over to the crate and found it had been hit by some of the debris. The top of it had been broken open and in it were the small cylindrical weapons with the small handle and trigger like a crossbow. The angels had called them firearms. He picked up one of them and turned it over in his hands, studying it.

I should have asked Raphael about these when he was teaching me about the explosives. He mentally kicked himself for the oversight.

He thumbed a metal piece sticking up at the back end of the metal cylinder and it moved. Pulling it back with his thumb it clicked into place and stayed there. He furrowed his brow, and taking aim away from himself, pulled the trigger. The metal latch released and made a clicking noise as it hit the small metal piece it rested on. Nothing else happened.

Malach decided to put two of the firearms in his belt for later and moved to the next crate. In this one, there were hundreds of coin purses. He picked one up, somewhat excitedly, and felt its weight. There must be a small fortune in the crate, but something was off about the coins.

He opened the purse.

It wasn't coins that filled it, it was small metal balls. He pulled one out and, with a little annoyance that it took him so long to figure out, it dawned on him the ball fit perfectly into the firearm. Now he understood. He was missing the last ingredient to make the weapon deadly.

He opened the top of a barrel close by and found it full of black powder. He knew what that did, no puzzling or tests needed. He moved the lantern away from the barrel, not wanting to end his life just yet. He found a few horns that had been hollowed out and capped on both ends. They would provide excellent containers for the black powder, which he supposed were what they had been intended for. He filled two of them and looped them over his shoulders, then went back to the crate with the metal balls and picked up a second sack of those and looped it to his belt. He still didn't know how to use the firearms, but he had what he thought he needed.

You humans are so simple sometimes, Reckoning retorted.

What? Malach asked surprised and a little hurt.

Reckoning communicated a few images of how to load and fire the firearms. Malach unloaded and reloaded both firearms with his help.

How do you know this? Malach asked.

Deduction, Reckoning replied. *The only thing I'm unsure of is the amount of black powder to use.*

If you're wrong, what's the worst that could happen? Malach asked, getting a little worried.

Uh, the firearm explodes, and shrapnel tears you apart, he replied calmly.

Great, Malach rolled his eyes.

I erred on the side of caution, so that is unlikely, Reckoning assured him.

Malach moved to the storeroom door, now armed with his new weapons and opened it a crack to peer out. The hall was dimly lit, and he blew out the lantern. He didn't know whether he should leave and find Togan and Marena first or if he should try another prison break. Either plan didn't have a good chance of succeeding but getting a little backup would probably be a better plan. He opened the door just a little farther and stuck his head out to look the other way. He didn't see anyone down that direction either.

He walked out into the hall and turned left on a whim. He followed the hall to the end. There was a set of stairs leading down, and he cautiously started making his way down. He didn't know how many floors there were, but he had passed three when he noticed a flickering light coming from just around the corner. He retreated up the stairs to the last floor he passed and out into the hall. He glanced behind him to see the light's glow getting brighter. He opened the first door he came to and ducked in, quietly closing the door behind him.

He was swallowed by darkness.

He couldn't even see his hand in front of his face. He heard footsteps heading down the hall and getting closer to the room. He pulled Reckoning off his belt and readied the knife in case he needed to use it. The footsteps came right up to the threshold, the latch started to move, and the door opened.

He recognized Amara as she walked through the door with a lantern in her hand. She closed the door behind her without even a glance back. Malach raised Reckoning, anger swelling inside him. Just as he got close enough to strike, he froze. His mind screamed for him to plunge the dagger into the back of this traitor, but his heart threated to break if he did. He couldn't follow through, no matter how mad he was.

"Why'd you stop?" She asked without turning around.

"I can't kill you," Malach sighed, lowering the blade. "I loved you. I shared more with you than any person I know, and you stabbed me in the back."

"Then why can't you kill me?"

"Argh!" he growled, turning his back on her. "I don't know! I would have just moments before seeing you. You should pay for what you did to us. But I can't do it." He deflated with the realization. "I need to know why you betrayed us?"

"They had my father, my real father, and they were prepared to assassinate Lawdel. I didn't see any other way this could have gone."

"We could have rescued him too," Malach turned back around to look at her, tears starting to well up in his eyes.

"Even if we killed Azazel and saved my father, the demon had people ready to kill Lawdel. He would have been dead before any of us could have helped him."

"We could have tried." Malach grabbed her shoulder and spun her around.

His pain was reflected in her face, the tears forming in his own eyes were already streaming from hers.

"No, the demon knew we were coming since before the spider caves. He had been tracking our progress and visited me before we got to the compound."

"We could have turned their trap around on them." Malach tried again, but even he could see the flaws in any plan he could have come up with. He fell to his knees, defeated.

"Malach, they would have killed both my fathers as soon as they knew their trap didn't work," Amara knelt with him and reached out a hand to comfort him. "I don't expect you to trust me ever again, or even to forgive me. Could you at least understand why I did it?"

Malach pulled away from her touch and stood. He was still mad at her, even if he couldn't hurt her. Turning around, he ran his hands though his hair. He did understand why she did it. He didn't want to admit it, but he did. He might have even done the same thing if their roles were reversed, although he liked to think he wouldn't have.

"I understand," he sighed, turning around to look at her again.

She nodded soberly. "I'm going to take my father back to Caister for him to be taken care of. If you ever want to see me again, you can find me there. If not, I hope you have a good life."

Malach nodded and turned to leave.

"Malach?"

He stopped at the door.

"I loved you too. And I'm sorry. I hope you get your parents out."

Malach didn't reply, feeling his heart shatter inside of him. Physical pain coursed through his chest and threatened to send him to his knees again.

He took a deep breath, the tears flowing freely now, and the pain subsided to a dull throb. He opened the door and left without even checking the hall first. He had a hard time caring about being found or about much of anything.

Malach! Reckoning voice resounded in his mind, snapping him out of his slump. *Pull yourself together!*

He shook his head to clear it.

Reckoning was right. There was no time to feel sorry for himself. He had to get out of the compound and regroup to save his parents. He headed back toward the stairs with renewed purpose and stopped in his tracks as he spotted another light coming up the stairs. He back peddled and ducked back inside Amara's room.

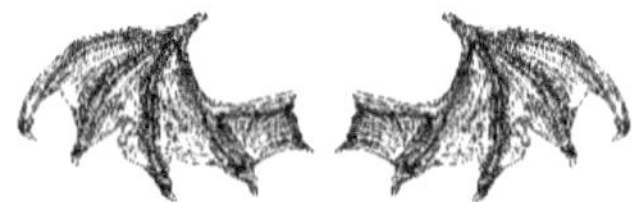

Amara couldn't remember feeling worse in her entire life. Malach hated her. Tears streamed down her face unbidden. The man she had grown so close to so fast probably never wanted to see her again. Which is why when she heard the door open behind her, she was certain it couldn't be him.

She turned and threw a knife at the intruder.

The intruder caught the knife and pulled it away from his face.

Hope swelled in Amara's chest that seemed to mend her broke heart instantly. She couldn't believe Malach had come back so fast, forgiven her so quickly.

"Mal, I–"

He silenced her with a finger to his lips and a glare which shattered her newly mended heart. He motioned there was someone outside in the hall, and she heard the footstep approaching the door. He moved behind the door just as it opened.

A gruff looking soldier with a sour expression stood in the doorway, "Just in case you had any thoughts of aiding the prisoners, I've been sent to guard you. If you need anything, don't ask me."

The soldier nearly slammed the door leaving Malach to stare at her unhappily. Amara cocked an eyebrow at him and shrugged. This was going to be a long night.

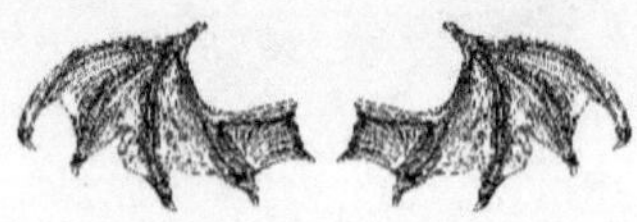

Ana watched them bring out yet another hacked up body and lay it next to the ever-growing row. It was still dark out, so she had a hard time seeing everything, but she could tell none of the bodies were demons. The body being carried out was number thirty-two. Malach, Ariel, and Elzrod had to be responsible for that many deaths. No one else could have slain so many well-trained soldiers with so little help.

The good news was it gave them a much better chance at fighting their way into the compound the next night. The bad news was she had spotted not one, but two demons residing in the compound, and one she recognized as Azazel. He was one of the less powerful lords, but she didn't like their chances of a full-on attack without being able to free either Ariel or Elzrod first. She had been puzzling on it for hours but still had no answer for it. She deduced that half of the soldiers still stationed here had been killed the night before, but she would have to wait for the changing of the guard and full daylight to tell for sure. Hopefully, that would help even the scales.

The door burst in and slammed again the wall. Amara sat straight up in her bed. Soldiers started pouring through the door, and Amara was deafened by an explosion coming from the foot of the bed. The first man's head snapped back, spraying gore all over the man behind him. A second explosion went off before the first man had hit the floor. The next two soldiers, only wearing leather armor, fell back with wounds in their chests. The fourth man turned to run, but Amara had recovered her senses and threw a knife, catching him in the back.

Malach pounced on him and broke his neck before he could recover. He rolled off the man and out into the hall, taking Amara's knife and the soldier's firearm with him. She didn't know why he wasn't using Reckoning but didn't have time to find out.

She hopped out of bed fully clothed and headed after him. Two guards had already fallen to Malach's hand by the time she had made it to the hall, but a demon stood behind the others. It wasn't Azazel, and she realized she had no idea how many demons were still in the compound.

Malach turned to retreat and pushed her roughly back into the room. She tripped over the dead men still laying in the doorway and landed hard on her back. She watched the demon move past the doorway and one of the soldiers stopped to help her up. About the time she was halfway to her feet her knife seemed to materialize out of the man's neck and he collapsed on top of her.

She pushed the soldier off of her and pulled her knife from his neck, sealing his death as blood spurted from the wound. She growled in frustration as she followed a handful of guards in pursuit of the Malach and the demon. Just before she turned around the corner, she heard another firearm go off and black demon gore painted the wall to her left. She peeked around the corner to see the demon slap the firearm from Malach's hand and stab him in the shoulder pinning him to the wall.

Malach shouted in pain.

"I've been meaning to repay you for the wound you gave me back in Brightwood. The day you stole Angel Cleaver from me." The demon growled in Malach's face

Malach's only response was to pull a fourth firearm, no doubt stolen from another soldier. He jammed it up underneath the demon's chin.

And pulled the trigger.

The projectile passed through the demon's head, embedding itself in the ceiling. Gore showered down on Malach and the demon crumpled to the floor like a marionette with its strings cut.

Malach was on his tiptoes, still pinned, unable to pull the sword from the wall behind him. Amara and the soldier stared, dumbfounded, at the scene that had transpired in front of them, too shocked to even move. One of the soldiers broke out of his stupor and started pushing his way forward.

Malach grabbed the hilt of the demon's sword and let out a terrifying shout as he lifted himself and kicked out at the man. His foot caught the soldier in the nose, and he stumbled back. Blood welled up from around the soldier's hands as he clasped his nose. It took two soldiers to catch Malach's flailing limbs and a third to knock him out so they could take him into custody.

Helpless to do anything since she would no doubt be overpowered, Amara watched them take Malach away. As they passed her carrying his limp form something gleamed inside his mouth. What could that gleam be? He had something up his sleeve, and she didn't know what it was. Maybe she could still help him now. Maybe she could do something to aid their escape. But no, Azazel would just have Lawdel killed if not her and her father as well. She hung her head and left for her father's cell. If it was just her life on the line, she would lay it down in a heartbeat to save Malach and the others, but she had to think of her loved ones as well.

She couldn't dwell on it long. She needed to get to her father's cell and get him out. She would head to Ragewood City first and pay for a room for him then come back. Maybe she could still save Malach. She would have to send a message to Lawdel, warning him of the potential danger he was in. Then she would return. The faster she got her father out, the faster she could get back to save them.

She all but ran to her father's cell, taking the stairs two at a time. The sight of the door wide open stopped her in her tracks. She ran to search the room praying her father was still there.

He wasn't.

She ran back up the stairs but the guard who had been so helpful the day before was nowhere to be seen. She ran out toward the front gate and approached the guards.

"Have you seen the crazy prisoner?" She asked in a panic, reasoning most of the guards wouldn't know him as her father.

"Yeah, he left sometime during the night. Took a pack and started walking." The first guard shrugged.

"He'll be lucky to survive the week. He was headed toward the Twisted Desert," The second spoke up and both the guards laughed.

"Ugh, why did you let him go?" She shouted at them, cutting their laugher short.

"We were told the two of you were free to leave whenever you wanted." The second guard shrugged.

"I need and horse and provisions," she commanded.

"Unless you can get permission from lord Azazel, you won't be able to procure a horse," the first soldier told her.

"But provisions are in the main hall and kitchens," the second pointed her to the main building attached to the tower.

"Fine," she fumed and stomped away.

"What a stuck-up woman," she heard one of the guards say before she was out of earshot.

Either the other guard didn't reply or she was too far away to hear him. She needed to gather supplies and go after her father or he would die in the desert. She couldn't believe he left without her, but that's just what he did. He did it when she was a baby, and now he did it again when she was about to get answers from him.

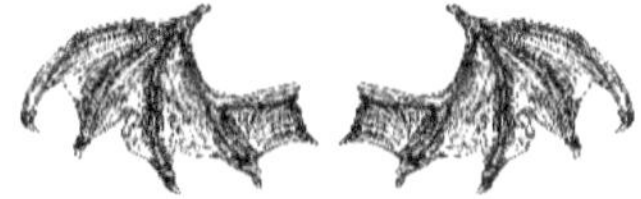

Ana had heard four gunshots ring out over the silent compound just as the sun was peeking over the horizon. The fourth shot was punctuated by the death pulse of either an angel or a demon. She scanned the compound wildly to see what was happening.

The sun was halfway to its pinnacle before she spotted more bodies being brought out. She almost jumped for joy when four soldiers carried the body of a dead demon out of the main building and set it next to the rest. Now they had a chance at success.

She thanked God for their luck and went back to tell the others the good news.

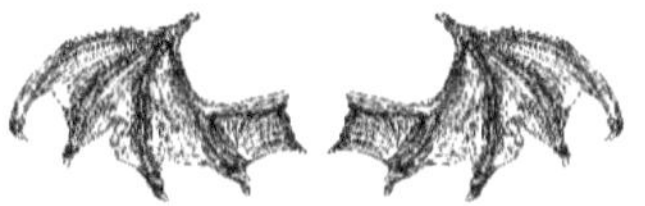

Malach woke up but not in a cell this time. Instead, he was upside down shackled by his feet and hands, spread eagle. His mother was still laying on the stone alter, comatose.

"Good, you're awake," a gravelly voice said.

He turned his head to see a demon. For a moment he thought he somehow hadn't killed the one he shot, but this one was much less demon looking.

Seeing his confused look, the demon said, "Oh no, you definitely killed that brute. Luckily, he wasn't essential to our cause. He always underestimated his enemies. It's a wonder he hadn't been killed before now."

"I'm glad I could accommodate his death," Malach replied sourly.

The demon chuckled. "Always defiant, but I wouldn't expect anything less with who your parents are. Now let's get down to business. I need information on the status and strength of the Angel Army."

Malach thought for a second. "The status is fully ready for war, and strength is much stronger than you could ever hope to defeat."

"Hmmm." The demon walked over to stand in front of Malach. "Since we can't be honest with each other, we will have to resort to more interesting tactics."

He squatted down and sunk his claw into Malach's recently bandaged shoulder. Malach grit his teeth and held back a cry of pain. Just when he didn't think he could take it anymore a soldier came up through the trapdoor and interrupted the demon.

He let go of Malach's shoulder with a growl and Malach felt himself almost swoon.

They talked quietly about something that sounded urgent, but Malach was too busy trying to stay conscious to hear them.

The demon turned back to him. "I'm so sorry, but I have to cut this session short. There is something that requires my attention.

If you wouldn't mind staying put, I will be back soon, and we can continue where we left off."

The demon followed the soldier out of the room and down the stairs. Malach waited for what like seemed an eternity. He listened as best he could over the sound of his blood coursing through his ears.

Reckoning? Malach could still feel the sliver of metal he had transformed Reckoning into and then embedded into his gums.

I'm still here, Reckoning assured him. *It seems that this trick worked once again.*

Yeah, but it's terrible for me, he grimaced. *It hurts every time I even think about moving my mouth. You said my father thought of this?*

Yes, he used it many times when he thought he would be caught.

Remind me to tell him how bad of a good idea this is.

It seems that it might be all for naught, though. I can't help but notice that you have no way or retrieving me as you did in the last cell you were held in.

I noticed. So, what are you thinking?

How do you know I'm thinking anything? Reckoning asked.

Because you always seem to have a plan.

Fine, but it's a long shot, and it's dangerous.

Not like we can do anything else.

So, your mother is in a trance started by Oathbreaker, Reckoning started. *What your father told me not to tell you was we have attempted to retrieve angels and Blade-Bearers in the same trance before but without their blades. We tried to save them and ended up losing both those originally in the trance and those trying to save them when those in the trance succumbed to their wounds or malnutrition. One Blade-Bearer made it back, but his mind was broken and only gave us portions of what he had seen. We were ordered never to try again. But many of us thought, if we found those in the trance earlier, they could have been saved.*

So how does that help us now?

If they were correct, then we could enter your mother's mind and wake her up from the trance. Then, in turn, she could free you, and we could escape.

But if we fail, we die.

Yes, but if you don't, you will have to suffer through a lot of torture. Besides, what do we do that doesn't have a good chance of death?

Good point, Malach replied. *Let's do this.*

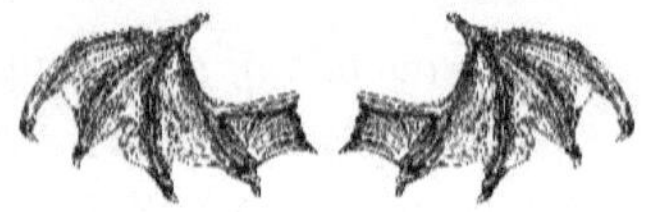

Ana dropped Daziar off at the top of the wall, and he immediately had to defend himself from one of the soldiers. He didn't know why the explosives didn't go off, but they decided not to wait any longer since one the demons had come up dead. Togan was already at the top of the wall, and they automatically gravitated toward each other until their backs were to each other.

"Ana better get here with more people soon!" Daziar shouted.

Five more soldiers climbed the stairs to the top of the wall.

"It only takes her a few minutes. Hold out a little longer!" Togan shouted back.

Daziar found an opening and cut down at the soldier's knee. It struck home and dug into the joint. The man collapsed with a scream, trapping Daziar's sword in the joint. He kicked the man in the face, cutting his scream short, and then put his foot next to his sword and yanked. The sword came free, but Daziar felt the grinding of the bone against the metal, and it made him shudder.

The next soldier stepped up to take the place his comrade and received an arrow to the shoulder for his trouble. The momentum knocked him off the open side of the wall, and Daziar watched him fall to his death. It didn't look like a nice way to go.

Ana set Marena down on the parapet between Daziar and Togan where she started firing arrows slowing the progress of the soldiers. Ana was able to get the rest of the group to the top of the wall and they started moving toward one of the stairs. With her help it didn't take them long to fight their way to the ground floor. Several soldiers lost their will to fight as Ana cut more and more of them down. Daziar heard hoof beats coming from the open courtyard spotted Amara with two horses, galloping from the stables toward the gate.

"Amara!" Daziar shouted, waving to try and get her attention.

She turned her head and they locked eyes for just a moment. She turned away quickly, unable to meet his gaze. She didn't even slow down. As she barreled through the gate, she hit the two guards with knives, dropping them both. They seemed to have been taken by surprise as neither of them even glanced up at her, their gazes focused on the other intruders. He didn't know how they could have been caught off guard with her barreling toward them, but he didn't have time to dwell on those thoughts.

"Demon!" Arjun roared, pointing toward the sky.

All heads turned skyward to see a demon diving toward their group. Ana spread her wings and with a powerful jump, she propelled herself straight at the demon. She hit it mid-flight, trying to deflect him away from the group. Her plan only partially worked, but most of the group had to jump to one side or the other to miss being impacted by the two titans.

Ana and the demon, Daziar assumed this was Azazel, slammed into the ground with Ana on the bottom. They left a furrow in their wake and when they rose to fight part of Ana's left wing was at an odd angle. Daziar ran to help, flanked by Togan and Skie.

"No!" she shouted at them changing her blade into a spear. "Find Malach and the others. I will hold him here."

Togan heeded her words and turned to run back to the main group.

Daziar, however, decided to stay.

He raised his sword and charged for the back of the demon. Azazel must have known he was there, as he tried to take to the sky when Daziar got close. Ana grabbed him by the ankle and, planting her feet, pulled him back down. Slamming him wings first into the ground in front of Daziar. Daziar took his chance and swung down with his sword. Azazel met his sword with his own. The swords met and Azazel's cleaved off Daziar's near the hilt. He fell back and would have lost his head if Skie hadn't clamped her maw onto Azazel's wrist. Daziar landed on his rear, quickly crawling back as Ana came forward to attack. Azazel rolled out of the way, breaking free of

Skie's grip. Daziar heard a couple pops coming from his wings as he rolled.

Azazel continued to roll and used the momentum to get to his feet. Daziar scrambled up as well and regrouped with Ana and Skie. With their backs to the stone wall, he took the time to looked down at his broken sword and ground his teeth in anger. That sword had been in his family for thousands of years and now it was broken.

He sheathed what was left of it and glared at the demon, "You will pay for that."

"Awe," Azazel smirked. "Did I break your favorite toy?"

"That was my great grandfather's sword and it had been in my-"

"Blah, blah, blah." The demon cut him off. "Shut up."

Azazel drew one of his wings around him. Two of the joints where bulging weirdly and he took the first one in both hands, popping it back in place.

The noise made Daziar shudder.

"You three are quite the set," he said. "A cute little angel and her two pets."

"I'm no one's pet!" Daziar shouted.

"Daz, calm down," Ana cautioned. "He's just trying to rile you up and make you do something stupid."

"It's working," Daziar growled.

"Ha, she just loves to tell you what to do doesn't she?" He laughed popping the second joint back into place. "Moreover, you probably love to take orders like the good, little soldier you are."

"Argh!" Daziar pulled his hunting knife and charged.

"No!" Ana shouted, reaching forward to stop him.

Daziar covered the short distance between him and the demon. The demon simply raised his sword and drove it through his chest plate.

"No!" Ana shouted.

Daziar's knife dropped from his numb hand as the demon lifted him off the ground. He kicked him off the blade sending him careening back at Ana. She caught him and set him down on the ground. His chest plate was caved in from the demon's foot, and she couldn't tell how much damage had been done underneath it. Skie jumped forward to attack the demon, but he leaped into the sky and flew away, laughing as he went.

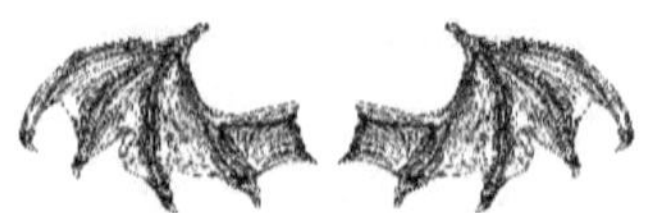

Ariel and Elzrod hung in there cells once again waiting for one of the demons to come back to begin their torture. Elzrod had been injured trying to hold off the enemy. He had a large gash across his chest that was still slowly oozing blood, and he was starting to weaken. If he didn't get help soon, Ariel doubted he would survive. They had heard four small explosions earlier which filled them with the hope of being rescued a second time. Although, after a few hours of waiting they realized either it wasn't what they thought it was or whoever it was had failed. Neither thought comforted them.

When they watched a somewhat emaciated man run into the room, look at the six guards, and run back out, they were quite surprised. The guards glanced at each other for a moment and then sent two of their number after the man. There were sounds of a scuffle and the two guards didn't come back. But the man poked his head in once again, stuck his tongue out at the four remaining guards, and disappeared around the corner.

All four of the remaining guards ran after the man and more sounds of fighting reached Ariel and Elzrod. They turned to each other, hope rising once again.

Togan came into the room next, beaming from ear to ear. "The ol' bait and switch. Never fails."

"Get Elzrod down first. He needs help." Ariel nodded toward the old man.

Togan turned serious and quickly got Elzrod down. Marena started trying to stem the bleeding. Two emaciated men helped Ariel down, although he had to do most of the work. He worked the feeling back into his hands and feet.

"We need to hurry," Marena handed him both Storm and Fury. "Ana and Daz are out fighting a demon right now and it didn't look like it was going well."

"Anahita and Daziar are here?" Ariel asked.

"Yes, and Honora, but she is outside the compound still," Marena told him.

"How did they get here?" Ariel asked.

"Later," Togan replied. "I've stopped the bleedin' for now, but we need t' get him out of here. Where is Malach?"

"You haven't seen him?" Ariel asked but deduced from their faces they hadn't. "He escaped the tower, and we hadn't seen him since. I was hoping he was with you. We will have to find him later. Right now, my wife is at the top of the tower she won't be able to move, but we need to get her out."

"Marena, you and Arjun take Elzrod out of the tower," Togan ordered. "Then find horses and a cart or somethin' t' lay him and anyone else injured in. Ariel and I will go up and get Serilda."

Marena nodded and Arjun came in from where he had been standing guard. They picked up Elzrod carefully and started carrying him down the tower. Ariel and Togan didn't waste any time, taking the stairs two at a time up to the top of the tower. They entered through the trapdoor to find not only Serilda laying where they had left her but Malach trussed up much as Elzrod and Ariel had been. Togan rushed over to him but he had passed out. They got him down and Ariel realized he wasn't passed out but in a trance, just like Serilda.

"Oh no," he said as his heart dropped and despair overtook him.

"What's wrong?" Togan asked still trying to rouse Malach.

Ariel opened Malach's mouth and pulled out Reckoning, in the form of a small pin, from where he had been embedded in Malach's gums. "He has gone into Serilda's mind."

"He's what?"

Ariel quickly explained the trance, "Now Malach and Reckoning must have got into her mind to try and save her."

"Is that a problem?"

"Yes. No one has ever made it back from going into a person's mind who is already trapped in a trance."

"Oh." Togan frowned. "No one is going t' be safe if we don't get out of this compound. We can figure out what t' do about it after everyone's safe."

Ariel nodded and carefully picked up Serilda. They didn't meet any resistance on the way down the tower. Although, they did have to be careful not to trip on a few bodies here and there. They headed out the main door.

Chaos reigned in the courtyard and they immediately had to move to cover to avoid being riddled with arrows. Some of the surviving soldiers had moved up to the top of the wall and were starting to rain down arrows on the people below. Togan and Ariel took shelter behind one of the buildings and started moving toward the stables where they hoped to find the rest of their group.

"Ariel!" Ana called over the noise of battle.

He looked around the corner to see her fighting off several soldiers standing over Daziar's prone form. He caught movement above them and catch sight of Azazel flying overhead, angling toward Ana. He set Serilda on the ground in the relative safety of the building.

"Get Malach to safety, and then come back for Serilda," Ariel ordered Togan.

Togan nodded.

Ariel didn't delay any longer. Drawing both Fury and Storm he charged on an intercept course with the demon. He carefully timed his swing and hacked off one of the demon's wings with Storm as he went by. Azazel roared with pain, spinning just before he hit the ground.

"That's for taking my wings, you degenerate piece of filth," Ariel yelled brandishing both weapons.

He moved forward, kicking Azazel in the face and planted a foot on him, pinning him to the ground. The demon struggled under Ariel's foot but couldn't worm his way out. He did however reach for Oathbreaker. Ariel swatted Oathbreaker away. He drew Fury back but before he could swing, a debilitating screech sounded in his mind. Reflexively he held his hands to his ears to quell the noise. Azazel pushed Ariel off of him and snatched Fury from his grasp. As soon as Fury left his hands, the screeching lessened and became more bearable. But it was too late. Azazel had regained his feet and Fury was already plunging toward Ariel's chest.

Fury struck flesh and the screeching ceased altogether.

Ariel looked down to see Elzrod between him and Azazel, the tip of the traitorous blade sticking out of the back of Elzrod. The demon pulled on Fury, but Elzrod grabbed the crossguard, holding the blade in his body. Ariel swung Storm and lopped off the demon's arm at his elbow. Azazel bellowed one more time and fell back. Ariel caught Elzrod before he fell. Azazel bellowed again retreating toward the tower, leaving only a trail of black sticky blood. Ariel set Elzrod on the ground realizing there was no saving the man.

Elzrod looked up at Ariel, "Goodbye, old friend."

An incoherent wail of anguish sounded in Ariel's mind and Storm mourned the loss of her greatest companion. The death pulse, although faint compared to that of an angel, shook Ariel to his core.

Ariel lifted Elzrod's lifeless body and walked toward the stables. He noticed Marena and a few others had been firing arrows to keep the rest of the soldiers at bay. He moved a little faster and laid Elzrod's body in the cart.

"Time to leave!" Ariel called and everyone loaded up into the cart or on a horse.

Ana ran out and hefted Oathbreaker wincing as she ran back to the wagon where she had already loaded Daziar.

Ariel snapped the reigns of the horses as he climbed onto the cart, and they started moving. They were at a gallop before they were even at the gate. Arjun peeled off to pick up Honora and the supplied with an extra horse as the cart headed out toward the desert.

They got onto the road and rolled along at a brisk pace. Ana and Marena took care of the wounded as best they could while moving, but Daziar needed to rest and heal. Malach wasn't in much better condition; however, he had the benefit of his healing ability to help him. Ana prayed he would make it, but his wounds were serious.

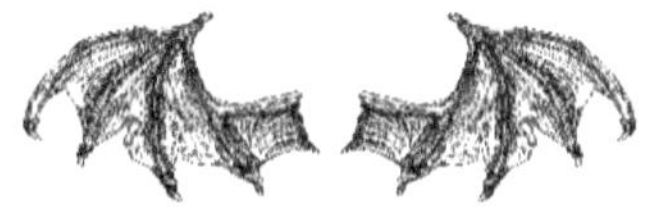

While Ana and Honora took care of Daziar and Malach, the others cared for Serilda and others who have sustained minor injuries. They would have to work around the clock to keep the three alive. Serilda was in much worse condition than Malach; however, Ariel believed if she died, they wouldn't be able to get Malach or Reckoning back at all. They stopped to give the horses a rest, and Ana took the chance to really work on Daziar.

The blade had gone into his right shoulder and stopped. Honora had learned enough to know the demon's blade missed Daziar's lung. If it were punctured, he would already be dead. As she watched, the angel took her blade and, turning it into a needle, used hair from one of the horses to close Daziar's wounds.

Ana caught Honora watching her. "I hope you were paying attention."

Honora dreaded the answer but had to ask, "Why?"

"Because you will have to do this to many soldiers before this war is over."

Honora nodded with grim determination.

She checked Malach's wound, which was similar to Daziar's, but the stitches held fast. Whoever had cared for him was a skilled healer. She replaced the bandages with some of the few they had left and dripped some water into his and Serilda's mouths.

Ariel called for the group to mount back up, and they carefully secured Daziar, Malach, and Serilda as best they could. Arjun took the reins of the cart, and Honora sat next to him now that the injured had been cared for. She watched her father snap the reigns and they started moving, although this time, at a much slower pace. They rolled on through the night, in case they were being followed. As the new day dawned on the group, their hope grew. They had made it. They had a long journey ahead of them, and an army between them and safety. For now, however, they were safe, and the injured had been taken care of as best as they could. They just had to trust Daziar would pull through and Malach and Serilda would find their way back.

Appendix A

Akila: uh – k EE – l uh

Amara: uh - m AH r - uh

Anahita: ah n – uh - h EE – t uh

Anauel: AH n - oo - eh l

Angelcross: AY n - g eh l - cr ah s

Ariel: Ah r - ee - uh l

Arjun: uh r - j UU n

Auron: AW - r ah n

Azazel: uh – z AI – z uh l

Barclay: b AH r - k l AI

Bartholemu: b ah r - th AH L - uh - m oo

Bray: b r AI

Brightwood: b r IY t - w uu d

Caister: c AY - s t eh r

Camael: c AA m - ay eh l

Cathetel: c AA th - eh - t eh l

Celewen: s EH l - eh - w eh n

Daniel: d AA - n ih - y uh l

Darhian: d AH r - ee - eh n

Daziar: d ah - Z EE - ah r

Deadpost: d EH d - p oh st

Demien: d eh m - EE - eh n

Dros: d r AH s

Durvain: d R - v ay n

Dyeling: d IY - l ih n g

Elzrod: EH l - z r - ah d

Emmiline: eh m - ee - l EE n

Enziarel: eh n - z IY - ah r - eh l

Fairdenn: f AY r - d eh n

Fang: f AI ng

Fury: f UU ry

Gabriel: g AA – b r ee – eh l

Honora: h aw - N OH - r ah

Jarsar: j AH r - s AH r

Jecrym: j EH - c r ih m

Jennari: j eh n - ah r - ee

Johm: j AH m

Kargod: k AH r - g ah d

Kath: k AA th

Lanifair: l AA n - ih - f ay r

Lawdel: l AW - d eh l

Lindow: l IH n - d ow

Malach: M AH L - ah k

Marena: m ah - r EE - n uh

Maria: m ah - r EE - uh

Marletta: m AH r - l eh t – uh

Michael: m IY – k uh l

Newaught: n OO - aw t

Oathbreaker: OH th – b r AY - eh r

Pangor: p AY n g - oi r

Prinna: p r EE - n uh

Rafiel: r AH – f iy - eh l

Ragewood: r AY j - w oo d

Ravenbard: r AY - v uh n - b AH r d

Raza: r AH - z AH

Raziel: r AH – z ee – eh l

Reckoning: r EH - k uh - n ih n g

Reybella: r ay - B EH L - uh

Reymold: r AY - m oh ld

Rose: r OH s

Serilda: s eh r - IH l - d aa

Shasta: sh AA - s t uh

Skie: s k IY

Storm: s t OH r m

Tresch: t r EH sh

Togan: T OH - g eh n

Vadis: v AY – d ih s

Viessa: v EE - eh s - uh

Wervine: w R - v IY n

Westbay: W EH - st b ay

Whiteshade: w IY t - sh ay d

Yargate: y AH r - g ay t

Zahra: z AH - r uh

<u>Acknowledgments</u>

First, I would like to thank God, since he has given me the dream and ability to write this trilogy. The idea for this series came to me while I was sitting through a Sunday morning sermon. My pastor mentioned what it might be like if we had to physically fight the spiritual battle that is waged every day. As the idea for this book blossomed in my mind I have to admit I didn't listen to a word he said after that.

I want to thank all the people in my life that have encouraged me through this process. Whether it was just listening to an idea that I was working on or simply an encouraging word. Also, I would like to thank my parents for instilling in me the love for a good story.

There are several people who have really done a lot to help me through the writing, editing, and publishing process. First, I would like to say thank you to my beta readers; Dani, Gabi, Mickie, and Jasyn, and my proofreader, Amanda. The beta readers did a superb job ironing out my plot and making sure the correct feelings were felt throughout the book and were absolutely brutal pointing out my mistakes and I thank them for every comment made. And Amanda my proofreader made sure that everything was pristinely polished after the edits.

Which leads me to the next person I need to thank. My editor, Jonie. She has worked with me through my first book and still was willing to edit my second. Some would say she is a glutton for literary punishment. She has done an excellent job editing and she was so easy to work with.

The final and probably most important person would be my wife. She has done so much for my writing career. She has listened to my endless rantings about ideas for this and many books to come. She has patiently, and sometimes not so patiently, endured me waking her up in the middle of the night as I write down things that have come to me mid-dream. She has encouraged me throughout the process of writing, editing and publishing and many, many more things. I love her more and more each day and I know that she will continue to be there for me as I continue my writing career.

<u>About the Author</u>

H. L. Walsh lives in Kansas City, MO with his wife and their daughter. He has been writing since he was fifteen but only published his first book in 2019. He is a self-employed author and enjoys reading multiple genres including fantasy, science fiction, the classics, etc.

Follow H. L. Walsh on his website at www.hlwalshbooks.com, on Facebook at www.facebook.com/hlwalshbooks, on Twitter @hlwalshauthor, and on Instagram @hlwalshauthor to catch all the updates!